IT STARTED WITH A KISS

Slipping out the door, she strolled to the stone rail of the terrace. Low voices came from the paths below, and lanterns bobbed along the walkways like fairy lights.

Firm steps sounded behind her and she prayed it wasn't Bentley.

"Louisa." Rothwell's deep, smooth voice rolled over her.

She whipped around. "I thought we were trying to stay away from each other."

"I can't . . . I must—" He stopped speaking. "Walk with me. Please."

Taking her arm, he led her to the other end of the terrace where no one could see them.

"Rothwell, what is it?" She tried to search his eyes, but the dark made it impossible.

"God knows I've tried." He groaned and one slightly calloused hand cupped her cheek while the other rested on the balustrade. "Louisa." His tone a reverent whisper. "How I've tried to stay away."

Louisa, he'd called her Louisa. A thrill shot through her as the thought sank into her consciousness just as his lips touched hers. Warm and firm, they moved from the corner of her mouth to the center, nibbling softly. Sighing, she leaned into him, returning his caress. This was what she had always imagined a kiss would be. . . .

Books by Ella Quinn

The Marriage Game
THE SEDUCTION OF LADY PHOEBE
THE SECRET LIFE OF MISS ANNA MARSH
THE TEMPTATION OF LADY SERENA
DESIRING LADY CARO
ENTICING MISS EUGENIE VILLARET
A KISS FOR LADY MARY
LADY BERESFORD'S LOVER
MISS FEATHERTON'S CHRISTMAS PRINCE

The Worthingtons
THREE WEEKS TO WED
WHEN A MARQUIS CHOOSES A BRIDE
IT STARTED WITH A KISS

Novellas
MADELEINE'S CHRISTMAS WISH

Published by Kensington Publishing Corporation

It Started With A KISS

ELLA
QUINN

ZEBRA BOOKS
KENSINGTON PUBLISHING CORP.
http://www.kensingtonbooks.com

ZEBRA BOOKS are published by

Kensington Publishing Corp.
119 West 40th Street
New York, NY 10018

First Printing: April 2017
ISBN-13: 978-1-4201-3959-4
ISBN-10: 1-4201-3959-2

eISBN-13: 978-1-4201-3960-0
eISBN-10: 1-4201-3960-6

10 9 8 7 6 5 4 3 2 1

Printed in the United States of America

Chapter One

Early morning, Hyde Park, May 1815

Dawn had broken only a few minutes before, but a light fog clouded the air making the sun look like a small yellow ball. Gideon, Duke of Rothwell, was certain he was the only rider at this hour of the morning. Needing the calm a hard ride gave him, he thundered down the empty carriage way. Suddenly, from out of nowhere, a dark bay burst through the mist, disturbing his solitude. Yet it was the massive dog, almost the size of a pony, keeping pace with the horse that caught his notice.

What the devil?

Faisu, his black Murgese stallion, pranced nervously as Gideon brought him to a halt. "Easy, boy. We don't need that beast tangling with you. He could sever your hamstrings in an instant."

A moment later, a twist of long, dark hair pulled loose from under the rider's hat, riveted his attention on the woman. By the time she was even with him, he'd taken in the neat figure encased in a dark blue riding habit, and her excellent seat.

She glanced over, slowing her horse for a bare moment as she passed him. Her cheeks were pink from the cool air and a smile graced her lush rose lips. Their gazes collided and held. As if they were the only two people on earth. In that second, when Gideon felt as if he would tumble into the vivid blue of the rider's eyes, they reminded him of lapis.

She cannot be real.

He blinked and she was gone. He might have dreamed her except that a few seconds later, a groom raced by, clearly attempting to catch up with his mistress.

For a moment he was tempted to follow as well, but it wouldn't do him any good. She was obviously a lady, and even if he could obtain an introduction, and their relations proceeded satisfactorily, he was not yet in a position to wed.

It was pure fantasy to think of marriage in conjunction with a woman he'd seen in passing. Still, he would have liked to have been able to dream.

Blast Father! If he were still alive, I'd shake some sense back into him.

But the old duke had been in the ground for over three months when Gideon had returned from Canada. Now all he could do was pick up the pieces his father had left behind.

"Come on, boy." Shaking the blue-eyed image from his mind, he urged Faisu to a trot. "It's time to go back. As long as I am here, I may as well gather information, and settle some accounts."

He should never have left. The waste was his fault. Had he stayed home, none of the damage would have occurred. What was the old saying about reaping what one sowed? Well, it was now his job, his alone, to restore the dukedom's holdings to what they had been only a few years ago, before he'd left for the colonies and played at being a backwoods man. Unfortunately, those experiences would not help him bring back and modernize his holdings.

Fifteen minutes later, as he rode up to the stables in the mews behind his town house, he surveyed the building, searching for any signs that it would soon need to be repaired. When he'd returned from Canada, his first shock was discovering his father had died. A letter had been sent, but it hadn't arrived before he left the colonies. The second shock was the poor condition of the estates. It baffled him that the once prosperous properties could fall into such disrepair in such a short period of time. If only he knew what had occurred to make his father neglect his holdings when he'd prided himself on them in the past. To make it more baffling, no one at Rothwell Abbey could explain, to Gideon's satisfaction, what had occurred to change his father.

If only he had remained at home where he belonged instead of hying off across the ocean. This was a lesson not to allow others to tend to his responsibilities.

He really did not have time for this bolt to Town, but his cousin, Edmond Bentley, had written begging for Gideon's help, and here he was.

"Yr Grace." Barnes, his stable master, strode quickly to Faisu's head, taking hold of the harness. "I've got him now."

"How is the roof?" Gideon asked as he swung off the horse. In the short time he'd been home, he had learned to ask. No one, it seemed, wanted to volunteer information. "I want the truth. It is much easier to fix a small leak than the damage it can do."

"Dry so far, Yr Grace. I'll keep an eye out. The glazing's comin' off from around some of the windows."

If that was the worst of it, Gideon would count himself lucky. It would take time and patience to make the repairs on the buildings that had been neglected, but he'd be damned if he'd allow anything else to fall into disorder. "Make arrangements to have them repaired."

"Yes, Yr Grace. Going to be here long?" the man asked, a hopeful look on his weather-beaten face.

"A few weeks, perhaps less. There is a deal to do at Rothwell and some of the other estates."

"Bad doings all of this." The older man tapped the side of his nose. "I'll make sure the town coach is in good order then. Won't do to have it break down when you need it. Or lookin' shabby."

"If it's the same one I remember, it probably needs to be replaced." Gideon's tone was even grimmer than he felt, which was quite grim enough.

"It's got another couple o' years yet." The stable master started to lead Faisu into his stall and stopped. "Leave it to old Barnes."

"Thank you." Gideon hoped he'd conveyed the gratitude he had for his old retainers. They truly were gems. Without their loyalty and patience, his life and the lives of his family would be much more difficult.

"Now that yer here, what you planning on doing with the new carriages the old duke ordered from Hatchett's?"

"New carriages?" He fought to keep his jaw from dropping. What the deuce had his father been thinking? Although, that bit of unnecessary extravagance went along with the other information he was slowly piecing together about the old duke's recent behavior. Spending that left little with which to maintain the estates.

"Got a landau and a high-perched phaeton—"

"The devil you say." His father wouldn't have seen seventy again. "What was he going to do with a phaeton?"

Barnes flushed. "I think it was fer that high-flyer he took up with."

Gideon's breath stopped. His parents had been the most devoted couple he knew. What could have happened to make his father change so drastically? And why in God's name had no one written to Gideon asking him to return home?

Damn his eyes! It needed only that.

Frustration coursed through him. He raked his fingers through his hair, knocking off his hat in the process. Yet, somehow, this fit the fractured story he'd heard, or rather had not heard, about Father's death. It was probably the reason Mama had been so tight-lipped. No one had or would explain what exactly had happened to make the duke ignore his holdings as he had. Thank God most of the assets were entailed, or Gideon might have found them mortgaged to the hilt at best or sold. "Do you happen to know who this barque of frailty was?"

"Her maid called her Mrs. Rosemund Petrie." Barnes spit as he said the name. "Like she was royalty and should be treated as such. Nothin' more than a whore, if you ask me."

His stable master might not know much about the woman, but Gideon would make sure he found out not only exactly who the female was, but what, if anything, he could recover from her. Then a thought he did not want to consider occurred to him. "I was told he died in Town."

Barnes picked up Gideon's hat where it had fallen, running his hand around the brim for a moment before saying, "Died in bed, he did. With her."

"Here?" He eyed the older man sharply. "At Rothwell House?"

Not looking up, the stable master nodded slowly.

"For the love of Jove! What had Father been thinking?"

"Don't no one know that, Yr Grace," Barnes said quickly, as if he would be blamed for the old duke's indiscretions. "I got her out of there with no one the wiser . . . except'n fer two of the grooms and Mr. Fredericks. Those that works here know which side their bread is buttered on. Won't no one be carrying tales." He made an *X* over his heart. "Strike my name from my Ma's Bible if they do.

Mrs. Boyle even had the mattress changed out. Said it was full of wickedness."

Gideon didn't think that a mattress could have a wicked nature, but he was just as glad for the new one. He would likewise swear that his mother had a good idea where her husband had been when he'd gone to his Maker. "I am sure you did everything necessary."

"Yes, Yer Grace. I'll get them windows fixed. What about that Mrs. Petrie's horses and carriage she's got here?"

He speared Barnes with a hard look. "I would greatly appreciate it if you would tell me everything at one time. How many horses, carriages, and whatnot? Did my father buy them, or were they hers before he became involved with her? Please feel free to add any other information you believe necessary as well."

The stable master rubbed his nose as he thought. Finally, Barnes replied, "The old duke bought her a nice Arabian hack, and two dark bay high-steppers for the phaeton he bought her a couple o' years ago—"

"Matched?" Gideon could barely spit out the word.

The servant looked at him as if he'd gone mad. "Wouldn't have expected anything else from His Grace, would you? Now if I can finish, Yer Grace?"

Clenching his jaw, he gave a curt nod. Not that it mattered how much more there was. It would all be sold as soon as possible. He calculated the costs of the horses alone to be at least three thousand pounds. Father had never stinted on horseflesh. Gideon turned his attention back to Barnes, who was still reciting his father's purchases over the past three years.

"Sell it all."

"I was about to get to the saddles and other tack," the older man said in an aggrieved tone.

"Keep the horses I brought with me and whatever you think best for the town coach. The rest goes."

"What about the curricle? Won't get much fer it, and you might need it."

He could use a sporting carriage. It would certainly save money in hackneys. "Very well. I'll keep it, but contact Tattersalls and whoever else you need to about the carriages and other items." Barnes opened his mouth again. "Keep anything you think I shall require."

"Thank ye, Yer Grace."

Stanwood House, Mayfair

"*Measles?*" Lady Louisa Vivers exclaimed. "All three of them?"

Excited to tell someone about the gentleman she'd seen in the Park, she had gone directly to the parlor she shared with her friend and new sister, Lady Charlotte Carpenter.

Just before the Season began in earnest, Matt Worthington, Louisa's brother, had married Lady Grace Carpenter. Grace had guardianship of her seven brothers and sisters. The marriage had given Louisa a total of ten brothers and sisters, including her own three sisters, not including Grace. Sometime this coming winter, the number of children would increase to twelve with the arrival of Matt and Grace's first child. The girls were ecstatic to be aunts. Even the boys were excited.

However, as Louisa opened her mouth to speak, Charlotte told her of the doctor's diagnosis. Obviously, that news took precedence over Louisa's.

"Yes," Charlotte replied. "Theo, Mary, and Philip. According to Cousin Jane and the information your mama left for Grace, the others, including Grace and Matt, have already had them."

"Will that put off Grace and Matt's trip to Worthington?" The addition of so many family members meant that not only Worthington House but the Worthington main estate as well must undergo extensive renovations in order to accommodate everyone. In fact, the only one of her brothers and sisters not residing at present in the Carpenter town home, Stanwood House, was Charlie, Earl of Stanwood, who was at Eton. Even Louisa's mother and her new husband, Richard, Viscount Wolverton, would stay at Stanwood House for the rest of the Season while Worthington House was being renovated. Well, after they returned from their wedding trip to Richard's estate in Kent, of course. Fortunately, the two houses were directly across Berkeley Square from each other.

"I think they must go," Charlotte said. Sitting at the desk, she tapped the feather end of the quill against her cheek. "Renovations must be started in the schoolroom there if we are all going to reside at your family's estate after the Season."

Louisa and her sister were almost halfway through their first Season. This new development certainly complicated things.

Chewing her bottom lip, she began to mentally adjust her plans to account for the new development. "Hmm, I suppose we should write notes excusing ourselves from the entertainments we had planned to attend." She glanced at the writing table. "What a bother. Why did the children have to choose now to fall ill?"

Charlotte let out a peal of laughter, lightening the mood. "That is almost exactly what Matt said."

Louisa grinned. "What did Grace say?"

"She told him he should ask and see what the children said. Grace is making arrangements for our chaperonage in the event he still wishes to make the trip." Charlotte heaved a sigh. "The poor things. I remember having the measles. The worst part was when I began to feel well again and was still not allowed to leave the sickroom. I wish Charlie was here to help entertain them. I shall, of course, help with nursing."

"As shall I." Louisa picked up her pocketbook from the desk. "We should make a schedule that will allow us to attend our entertainments and help care for the children."

She ducked as Charlotte threw a small embroidered pillow at her. "You and your schedules."

"How else do you plan to accomplish our marriages? By the by, how is it going with Harrington?"

Charlotte's lips formed a moue. "Not as I wish it to. He appears to think he has jumped all his hurdles. Consequently, he has gone off to his estates for a week." She raised a brow. "I can only imagine he thinks me a sure thing."

"That won't do at all." Louisa was not happy about that bit of information. Charlotte deserved to be treated better. "If he ignores you now, imagine what he would be like as a husband."

"My thoughts exactly," Charlotte agreed. "I do like him, yet I shall not be taken for granted. I think I must strike him as a potential husband."

"I cannot say that I blame you." Louisa wandered to the table next to one of the sofas and placed her hand on the cold teapot. "Will you ring for another pot while I change?" Charlotte nodded absently. "I have finally decided what to do about Lord Bentley." Louisa gave her friend a wicked grin. "You must help me find a match for him."

Edmond, Marquis of Bentley, heir to the Duke of Covington, had been one of the first gentlemen Louisa had met this Season, and despite the hints she had dropped, her most persistent suitor. Nothing she had done thus far had convinced him that they were not suited.

Her sister went off into whoops. Several moments later she pulled out her handkerchief and wiped her eyes.

"That is the best idea you have had yet. If he transfers his affections to another lady, you will have managed to rid yourself of him without hurting his feelings."

"Indeed. The only problem is who. She must be intelligent enough to be duchess, managing enough to ensure Bentley performs his duties, and possess a great deal of patience in order to deal with his dithering." Louisa could not help but to grimace. "A virtue I do not possess in abundance."

"More patience than you?" Charlotte's tone was serious, but the corners of her lips twitched. "That does sound like an almost impossible combination. She would have to be a perfect paragon."

Ignoring her sister's facetious comment, Louisa said, "If we are still attending the ball this evening, we can begin searching for her." She paused for a moment, her fingers on the door latch. "It will not be an easy task, yet I am sure we will succeed. I'll see you in a few minutes."

"We are going to the ball," Charlotte called after Louisa. "Will you do me a favor and tell Matt? I was about to change my shoes, but you are already dressed."

Their brother continued to use his study at Worthington House, saying that even with the construction it was quieter than Stanwood House.

"And smelling of the stables. Hold off on the tea, and I shall go straightaway." Making her way down the stairs, Louisa strode out of house and crossed Berkeley Square.

Chapter Two

A few minutes after leaving the stables, Gideon entered the house through the garden door, quickly making his way up the corridor to the hall and the main staircase. A letter on the round heavy oak table caught his eye. It had to be from his cousin Bentley. No one else either knew he was in Town or expected him to be. Gideon should probably thank his cousin. If it had not been for him needing help with an as yet unknown emergency, he'd never have found out about what his father had been up to here.

Drawing off his gloves, he picked up the missive and opened it.

Rothwell,

Seems strange to call you that, but I'll get used to it I suppose. I hope you receive this soon. What I mean is I hope you are already in Town. There is a ball tonight at Lady Sale's and I've arranged for you to receive a card. Not, of course, that you would be denied entry, but I thought it the best thing to do under the circumstances. I shall meet you there.

Yr cousin,
Bentley

Gideon blew out an annoyed breath. How in the name of all that was holy was he supposed to help his cousin when the blasted man still hadn't told him what he needed? Even though he was several years older than Bentley, they had always been close, and Gideon would do what he could to assist. If he ever discovered what that was. He sincerely hoped Bentley either married a woman with sense or managed to develop some before he came into his father's title.

Meanwhile, the ball was hours away and Gideon could use that time to his advantage. Since arriving home, he had done a great deal of research on new methods of farming and increasing crop yields. Yet first, he must have a few words with his secretary. After that, he'd visit a friend.

Less than three quarters of an hour later he knocked on the door of Worthington House. A stately butler opened the door, and Gideon handed him his card.

Stone-faced, the servant bowed. "Follow me, Your Grace."

Gideon stifled a grin. Matt, Earl of Worthington, had always bemoaned the fact that fate had given him a butler who refused to crack a smile or unbend in the least. Why that should bother him, Gideon had no idea. Most butlers were as stiff as boards and haughtier than dukes.

Glancing around, he noticed that the house seemed strangely empty, and there were no carpets on the floor. Then a loud banging started.

A few moments later, the door to Worthington's study opened.

"His Grace, the Duke of Rothwell," the butler said in a somber tone.

"Thank you, Thornton." Worthington rose, coming out from around his desk. "Rothwell, it's good to see you back.

I believe my stepmother wrote our condolences. I am sorry for your loss."

Gideon held out his hand and his friend gripped it. "Thank you. Father's dying was a shock, but what I discovered about the state of the properties and other holdings was even worse. Thankfully, the majority of the estate is entailed."

"These days, it seems as if entails and the daughters of wealthy merchants are all that is saving many families. Have a seat." Worthington waved Gideon to a large chair near an empty fireplace. "Tea will arrive shortly, however, I have wine and brandy if you'd prefer it."

"Thank you, tea is perfect." The one thing he must do was keep his wits about him. "How can you work with so much noise?"

"Believe me, the alternative is worse." Worthington lowered his long frame onto a small sofa facing Gideon. "I hadn't heard you were in Town."

"I arrived late yesterday. One of my family members asked for some assistance. I shan't be here long. There is too much work to do."

"Is this strictly a social call"—Worthington canted his head slightly—"or is there something I can do for you?"

The tea arrived as Gideon decided how much to tell his friend about the problems he faced. If he wanted the best advice he could obtain, there was no point in hiding everything. Yet, he was reluctant to divulge too much information. "Our conversation can go no further. If what I say to you gets out, it will make my predicament much worse."

Worthington lost his smile. "Naturally, you may depend on me."

"I'll be blunt. When it comes to available funds, I'm pretty well rolled up. My father ran through the accounts as if he didn't have a care in the world. Fortunately, my steward was able to husband the resources he had at hand so that we have seed for planting, but it was at the expense of maintenance and improvements over the course of three years."

"Never a good idea to let repairs go," Worthington commented without expression.

Gideon nodded. "I also need to change the way we've been doing things. My steward is a good man, but clings to the older ways. I've done some reading, but I've come for your advice as to which of the new methods are the best." He grinned. "Other than that, I am curious to see how you are adjusting to married life."

His friend's broad smile told him everything he wanted to know.

"If I had known how much fun it would be, I would have wed years ago." Worthington raised a sardonic brow. "Thinking of joining me?"

Gideon's thoughts went back to the lady on the horse he had seen earlier; then he shook his head. "I do wish to marry. It is my desire as well as my duty. Unfortunately, I am unable to offer for a lady until my finances are in better order."

"You could marry an heiress." Worthington tapped a pencil on his desk. "That is a perfectly respectable method of recouping one's fortunes. Particularly as you did not cause the problem in the first place."

"And shackle myself to a woman who cares only about being a duchess." Gideon grimaced. "No, thank you. I want to be beforehand with the world when I take a wife, and I shall economize as much as I am able to make that happen. Fortunately, I have another year or two before my sister's come out." He rubbed the back of his neck before looking Worthington in the eye. "It might be stupid of me, but I don't like the idea of using my wife's money to repair my estates. What a lady brings to a marriage ought to be used for children and her well-being. This is my problem. I'll take care of it."

He refused to leave his wife dependent on the income of certain properties that would most certainly leave her destitute if they were not well managed. Giving himself a shake, he took a sip of tea. Not that he had to worry about marriage. He doubted if any lady would catch his interest. Except perhaps a dark-haired one with a wonderful seat, a body to match, and eyes one could happily drown in. Yet the chances he would meet her were almost nonexistent. Other than the ball this evening, he did not plan to attend any social events.

The moment Louisa approached Worthington House, an eager footman opened the door, and the sound of hammering could be heard echoing from the upper levels of the house where the schoolroom floor was being renovated.

The servant bowed. "His lordship is in his study, my lady."

Which was almost the only reason she could have for being in her own family's house. "Thank you."

On the other hand, she felt more at home in Stanwood House. After all, she had lived there longer. When Mama had brought Louisa and her sisters to Town, they had been in Worthington House for only a few weeks before Matt and Grace married and the family moved to the Carpenters' town home. It was nothing short of a miracle that they all got on so well. Louisa already loved Charlotte and her brothers and sisters like her own.

The carpet runners had been removed during the renovations, and her boots made a hollow clicking sound on the hardwood floor of the corridor. She reached the door, and knocked before opening it. "Matt—"

A tall gentleman, with dark blond hair, and the loveliest gray eyes she had ever seen, stood and stared at her. She fought to keep her mouth from falling open.

It is him!

The same man she had seen not more than an hour earlier. A smile tugged at his well-molded lips, and she answered with a smile of her own.

"Louisa," her brother said as she dragged her gaze away from the other gentleman. "I would like to introduce you to the Duke of Rothwell. Rothwell, my sister, Lady Louisa Vivers."

She stepped farther into the room, and he moved toward her. As she held out her hand, he bowed. "A pleasure, my lady."

"Your Grace." She sank into a deep curtsey. "The pleasure is mine." The moment his warm mouth touched her gloveless fingers, her knees wobbled, and she didn't even care that he should not have actually kissed her hand.

Good heavens! That had never happened before. His molten silver gaze captured hers as it had earlier. "I insist you allow me to be the better pleased, my lady."

For almost the first time in her life, Louisa was speechless. Fortunately, Matt cleared his throat before she could make a complete fool of herself. She gave her hand a tug, and the duke slowly released his fingers, letting it go.

"Matt," she said, sucking in a breath as she tried to still the rapid pace of her heart. It was all she could do to drag her gaze away from the duke's. Yet she finally managed to look at her brother. "I came to tell you we will be going to the ball this evening."

"Yes. I thought we might be," he replied humorlessly. "I had hoped the measles might spare me the rest of the Season, but Grace has other ideas."

"What do measles have to do with a ball?" the duke asked.

"I have acquired not only a wife, but several children as well." Matt explained that before their marriage, Grace had been guardian of her brothers and sisters. A duty he had now taken over. "The three youngest are ill, but not so badly off that we must cancel our engagements."

Louisa glanced back at the duke. "Will you be attending Lady Sale's ball?"

"I shall be there." His eyes turned to silver as he gazed at her. "Would you honor me with a dance, my lady?"

Mentally, she reviewed her dance card. Bentley normally requested the supper dance, but, if her plan to find him another lady were to succeed, she must wean him off her. "I still have the supper dance free."

"Splendid. I shall look forward to seeing you again."

Her brother gave her a look she could not interpret, and said, "Rothwell and I were discussing ways in which he could improve his estates."

For the life of her, she did not know if he was inviting her to join the discussion or suggesting she leave. Still, she really ought to look in on the children. "You came to the right person, Your Grace. Matt is quite knowledgeable about estate matters." She curtseyed again. "It was nice meeting you. I shall look forward to our dance."

"As shall I, my lady." His warm tone washed over her, causing a pleasant shiver to race down her back.

He opened the door for her, and as soon as it was closed, she practically flew back up the corridor to the hall, then across the square. Her heart thudded as it never had before. When she'd seen him this morning, she had almost stopped. Yet as much as she had wanted to throw caution to the wind, she knew she could not. Behavior like that would disappoint not only her mother but Matt and Grace as well. And then, *he* was here with Matt.

That had to be a sign they were meant to at least come to know each other. Louisa couldn't wait to tell Charlotte!

He was a demmed fool, Gideon thought as the door closed behind Lady Louisa. Yet he could no more have ignored her as he could have stopped breathing. When she had asked if he would be at the ball this evening, he could not stop himself from asking her to dance. One dance, that was all. All it could ever be. After that, he would find out what the devil Bentley wanted, help him, and return to Rothwell Abbey.

"Why do I have the feeling you and my sister have met before?" Worthington turned to Gideon, his friend's brows drawn together.

"Not met, precisely," he said slowly, not wanting to anger Worthington. Lady Louisa was not only his sister but his ward as well, and Gideon had just told the man he could not afford a wife. The first time he'd seen her he should have known that she would throw his carefully ordered plans into disarray. Yet as much as he was drawn to her, the fact remained he would still have to wait to marry. He crafted his next sentence carefully. "We passed each other in the Park earlier this morning. She had a great beast with her." He had thought his reaction to her then was strong, as if the time had slowed, and they were the only two people in the world. Yet when he'd taken Lady Louisa's hand, every part of his body had urged him not to let her go.

He hadn't wanted the moment to end. If it had not been for the slight tug of her hand, he might still be touching her. Still, he could not court her. Although, perhaps, he could hold her in his arms for a while.

The sound of someone or something yawning emerged from behind the desk. A long moment later, the very same beast he had seen earlier rose.

Worthington grinned. "This beast?"

"Yes, is it a Great Dane?"

"He is. We have two, but, Daisy, the younger one, can't be trusted to accompany the horses yet."

"Your sister is a very good rider."

"She always has been." Matt gave Gideon a strange look he could not decipher, then said, "Shall we get back to our conversation? I have some books I can lend you if you'd like."

"Yes, of course. Thank you." The vision of Lady Louisa on her horse came back to him. Damn Father. If he had not played fast and loose with the dukedom, Gideon might be able to court her. But he could not. Not while his property was in such bad skin. If for no other reason than he would not betray Worthington in such a fashion.

But, by God, she was beautiful. He looked forward to his dance and supper with her more than he should. Perhaps, if they got on well together, she would wait until . . . No. He could not ask it of her.

Worthington scribbled something on a card. "This is the name and direction of my man of business. He will be able to put you in the way of some safe investments."

"Thank you. That will certainly help." Even if Gideon lost his mind and asked for her hand, Worthington, who knew the state of Gideon's holdings, would never allow it. He had no doubt at all some lucky man would snatch her up before the Season was out.

Hell and damnation! Why couldn't his bloody father have stayed away from ladybirds and the gambling tables?

"What can you tell me about a high-flyer who goes by the name of Mrs. Petrie?"

Again, Worthington leaned back against the seat.

"Nothing from personal experience. I do know your father was 'seen' in her company quite a bit. From what I understand, she is extraordinarily expensive."

"So I have been given to understand."

"Is this about the duke?"

How much should Gideon reveal? He did not wish everyone to know what Father had been up to. Then again, Worthington seemed to know about the connection. Not to mention that Gideon had no one else he could talk to about this particular problem. "Unfortunately. During the inventory, some of the entailed jewelry was found missing. At first I thought they would turn up in my mother's jewelry chest, but she said Father always kept them in the safe. They were not at the abbey, nor are they here. This morning I discovered the existence of Mrs. Petrie. I believe she may have the pieces."

"If they were indeed in her possession, she may have pawned them."

"I thought of that, but they are quite recognizable. It would take a skilled jeweler to break them up."

Worthington took out another card. "Visit Rundell and Bridge's. If they haven't seen them, then the pawnbroker, T. M. Sutton, might be able to help you. Mr. Sutton is known for giving the best value for goods."

"By the by, if you are looking for some good horseflesh, I'll be selling some beasts I have no use for."

"Will you auction them off at Tattersalls?"

"Yes, I need to get as much for them as possible."

"Let me know when they go up for auction and I'll have a look."

"Thank you for everything." Gideon took the card and rose. "I'll let you get back to your business."

His friend stood. "I'm glad to see you again. It's a deuced shame you had to come back to an estate that's in a shambles, but you'll see it through." They shook hands. "Let me know if you require anything else."

"I shall. Thank you again for your assistance."

Worthington held the door open. "I'll have my wife, Grace, send you an invitation to dine with us as soon as we return from a short visit to Worthington Place."

"I do not believe I have ever met her."

A smug smile appeared on his face. "No, I snapped her up as quickly as I could."

When Gideon reached the pavement, he strolled down the street, looking for a hackney coach. A few minutes later he found one letting off another customer. "Hatchett's in Longacre."

"Right then, Gov." The shabby coach lurched forward.

A half hour later, he entered a huge building holding dozens of carriages in various states of repair and assembly. A man he judged to be just a few years older than himself approached.

"I am Mr. Hatchett the younger. May I help you, sir?"

"I'm pleased to meet you. I am Rothwell." The other man bowed. "My late father ordered two carriages from you, one a landau and the other a high-perched phaeton. Unfortunately, I must cancel the orders."

"I remember the commission well, but first, allow me to offer our condolences. We had heard of His Grace's passing. As a matter of fact, it was for that reason we did not start on the landau. The phaeton, however, is about halfway complete." He gave a discreet cough. "The woman who accompanied your father when he gave us the order sent a message asking about it just yesterday."

Rapacious female. "If you will give me her direction, I shall explain the situation to her myself."

Mr. Hatchett gave all the appearance of having a huge burden taken from him. "Yes, indeed, Your Grace. I'll be happy to."

"I also have a phaeton I wish to sell. Do you handle used carriages?"

"We do. I should be pleased to come to you or you may have your coachman bring it here."

Gideon wanted that thing out of his stables as soon as possible, as well as anything else his father's mistress laid claim to that was in his possession. "I shall have it delivered to you."

Hailing another hackney, Gideon gave him the address that was not far from Green Park, then changed his mind, deciding to visit Rundell and Bridge's first. "Ludgate Hill."

"Sure this time?" the jarvey asked.

"Positive," he replied.

Before he informed the woman she would no longer be receiving any more largesse from Rothwell, he wanted to discover if the missing jewels could be found. He also did not wish to let her know he would be investigating whether she had any property that she should not have in her possession. He wondered if the house she lived in was even hers. As enamored as his father appeared to have been, it might very well belong to him. Not only that, but he might as well call on his solicitor while he was out.

An image of Lady Louisa flitted through his mind. If only he could recoup his fortune quickly enough to court her.

Chapter Three

"Charlotte!" Louisa strode as fast as she could, short of running, and burst into their parlor. "I met him."

Her friend set down a pen and turned in the chair. "Met whom?"

"The gentleman I wish to marry." Her heart was crashing around in her chest making her breathless. "At least I think I do."

After studying her for several moments, Charlotte tugged the bellpull. "This is unexpected. Where was he?"

"With Matt. Speaking to him about estate improvements."

Her friend grinned. "I am surprised you did not stay and join them. I know how interested you are in the subject."

Louisa worried her bottom lip. "I would have liked to, but I did not know if I should."

"That's not like you." Charlotte moved to one of the sofas and patted the seat next to her. "I am agog. Tell me about him."

Unable to sit, Louisa paced. "You might think I am mad, but . . . but I saw him for the first time this morning during my ride, and our eyes met. It was almost as if I had known him all my life." She glanced at her sister, who nodded encouragingly. "Then when I found him in Matt's study it was as if it was a sign of some sort. As if fate had planned the whole thing. I could barely stop looking at him, and I think he felt the same." The tea came and Charlotte poured, but when Louisa took her cup, her hands shook. "Dear me. First my knees and now my hands."

Charlotte raised a brow.

"I am acting like a silly widgeon. As I was merely going to see Matt, I did not put my gloves on again, and he, Rothwell, kissed my hand."

"Actually kissed your hand. Wait a moment. You said Rothwell?" Her other brow rose. "As in the Duke of Rothwell?"

"Yes." Louisa nodded. "Have you met him?"

"No, but . . . there was something." Charlotte drew her brows together. "Ah, yes, my aunt mentioned him once. His father died while the current duke was in Canada. No one has seen him since his return. She also commented that during the last two years or so, his father had been acting strangely." She shrugged. "That is all I know. I wonder if he will be at the ball this evening."

Louisa could not stop herself from smiling. "He will be, and I am engaged to stand up with him for the supper dance."

"Excellent!" Charlotte clapped her hands together. "I must say, this all sounds very promising."

"I agree." The sooner Louisa came to know him, the sooner she would know if she was right about him.

"If you have found your future husband, you must definitely settle Bentley."

"Oh, drat. I had almost forgot about him." Blowing out a frustrated breath, she said, "There is nothing for it. I must enact my scheme sooner rather than later."

"Scheme?"

"Yes, yes. The one to help him find a wife."

"I had forgot." Charlotte's eyes began to twinkle. "This does appear to make the matter more pressing. I only wish I knew of someone. Perhaps a thought will occur during morning visits."

Attempting to follow her friend's line of thought, Louisa shook her head. "Morning visits?"

"Yes." Her sister drew the word out. "You remember, normally we go visiting, but today is Grace's at-home." Charlotte cast a brief glance at the ceiling. "You have not been hit on the head have you?"

"No, no. I merely forgot that this afternoon was Grace's at-home." Louisa picked up her teacup again. Thankfully, her hands had stopped shaking. "If only a new lady would come to Town." One suitable for Bentley.

Due to the advice he had obtained from Worthington as well as the number of bills in his father's drawers from Rundell and Bridge's, one of the most expensive jewelers in London, Gideon made the shop his second stop after leaving Worthington's.

A bell above the door jingled as he entered the establishment.

In almost no time at all, a clerk greeted him. "May I be of help, sir?"

"I trust so." Gideon placed the packet of invoices, representing thousands of pounds, on the counter. "I am Rothwell. What do you know of these?"

The clerk looked at the package as if it might bite him. "I believe you will wish to speak with Mr. Rundell."

A few minutes later, Gideon was shown into a small but elegantly appointed office. The walls were painted rather than hung with fabric, but works of art in gilt-trimmed frames hung on the walls. The furniture was all in a rich cherry.

When Gideon was announced, the older man sitting behind the desk rose, coming out from behind it. "Your Grace, I am Mr. Rundell." He bowed. "I assume you are here regarding the former duke's recent purchases."

Gideon gave a curt nod. "I am indeed. There are a great many purchases just before my father's death, and continuing after he'd been buried."

"Please have a seat." Mr. Rundell waved Gideon to a chair near the desk. "Unfortunately, we were not apprised of the date of the duke's passing. I received this from the lady"—he said the word as if it was distasteful as he handed over a sheet of paper—"a carte blanche."

Gideon felt himself pale. This was much worse than he had thought it could be. "May I see that?"

"Certainly, Your Grace."

He glanced at what was little more than a note addressed to the jeweler giving Mrs. Petrie the ability to make any purchases she wished. Surely his father could not have been so lost to his responsibilities. Forcing down his panic, he studied the signature. Something appeared off. Although, it might be that he desperately hoped the carte blanche was false. "Needless to say, this is revoked. However, I believe the signature is not correct. I want my secretary to look at it. He is the one most familiar with my father's hand."

"Naturally, Your Grace, Rundell and Bridge's would not wish to be a party to anyone wishing to perpetrate a fraud. Please take it with you and let me know what you find."

"Thank you." Rising, he was about to leave, when he remembered the missing jewelry. "I am also seeking a parure that is missing from the inventory. The set is quite old, dating to the sixteenth century. The gems consist of rubies and opals."

"I know the pieces, but the last time I saw them was a year or so ago when they were here for cleaning and repair of some loose stones. I shall notify you immediately if it comes my way. If you would like, I shall also provide you a list of all the pieces obtained under the carte blanche."

"Thank you, again," Gideon replied, inclining his head. Allerton had already made up a list of all the jewelry for which they had received invoices, but having confirmation from Rundell and Bridge's couldn't hurt. "I would also ask that you not repeat any of our conversation."

"Naturally, not, Your Grace. We pride ourselves on our discretion."

As soon as he reached the pavement, he turned toward Victoria Street where he would find T. M. Sutton, pawnbroker. Gideon wished to know if Worthington was right about her exchanging the gewgaws for ready funds. Gideon might also be able to discover if some of the jewels she had bought using the carte blanche had been pawned.

The shop was surprisingly clean and well ordered.

"Looking for anything in particular?" a young man standing behind the counter asked.

He handed the lad his card. "I would like to speak with Mr. Sutton."

"I'll get him right away, Your Grace." The man disappeared behind a maroon-colored curtain, reappearing a few moments later with a gentleman who looked to be in his forties. "Your Grace, this is my father, Mr. Sutton."

As expected, the older man made a low bow before quickly appraising Gideon. "How may I be of assistance?"

"I am searching for information on any pieces a Mrs. Petrie may have sold to you."

"Your Grace, you must understand that I cannot divulge that sort of information."

"Is that so?" Gideon asked in a bored drawl. "I had been informed that your business was reputable, and the pieces I am asking about have been stolen." Not, perhaps, quite the truth, but close enough that he did not feel the pinch of guilt. "I have a list."

Mr. Sutton took the paper. As he perused it, his lips thinned. "I recognize some of these."

The total of the list amounted to a small fortune. Enough, if Gideon could prove the note was forged, to significantly help recoup the losses for which his father had been responsible. The question now was what the pawnbroker would do about it. "I shall have my solicitor contact you concerning how to resolve this matter."

"Yes, indeed," Mr. Sutton said, his voice grim. No doubt, this would represent a large loss for his business. Gideon sympathized with the man, but had his own losses to make up. "We are a reputable business. I shall be happy to help you remedy this matter. I assume I may contact you if more pieces are brought to me?"

"I'd appreciate that." This was going much better than he had expected. He said a short prayer that he was right about his father's signature.

Under a half hour later, he alighted in front of Rothwell House and strode straight back to his study. "Allerton."

The secretary glanced up. "Your Grace."

Gideon handed his secretary the paper. "Is this my father's signature? It appears to be like his, but there is something not quite right."

The man took the document, read it, and rubbed the spot between his brows before pulling out a large magnifying glass and studying the note. After a few moments, he raised his head. "No, thank God. It is not. However, it is just one loop that is not correct."

"Rundell and Bridge's said it came with his seal."

"I suspect that under the circumstances that was easily done. In fact, the reason I studied the signature so closely was because that female had the nerve to bring this letter, or one like it, here and ask that His Grace sign it. Instead, he wrote a letter to the shop telling them to give her one piece of jewelry of her choosing."

"She, or an accomplice, must have forged the signature." Gideon sat on the leather chair in front of Allerton's desk. "What do I do now? Raid her house?"

A slight smile appeared on his secretary's face. Lord knew that the man hadn't had much to be happy about lately. "I suggest you have your solicitor wait on you."

"I'll attend to that as soon as I have the list Rundell and Bridge's offered to send."

"That would be wise, Your Grace."

"I wish I had been informed about Mrs. Petrie earlier. As it was, I discovered her existence by sheer chance."

His secretary heaved a sigh. "Her Grace did not want anyone to tell you." Allerton's voice sounded tired. As if he'd had the weight of the world on his shoulders. The older man's light brown hair was starting to gray around his temples. "I believe she wished for you to remember the duke as he was."

"Nevertheless, considering funds were still going to the woman"—Gideon kept his voice calm but firm—"it would have been best for me to have been advised."

"I should have said something earlier, Your Grace. Would you like me to make a list of other items your father bought for her?"

"Yes, that way I can figure out what she procured on her own."

His secretary brought out a stack of invoices. "As you know, some of the purchases have been made recently."

"I assume it is possible that having had success with the letter she gave Rundell and Bridge's, she has done the same at other shops." He took the bills and leafed through them before placing them back on the desk. "Separate them by business and whether the items were bought before or after his death. Arrange them in a packet, and I shall personally visit the shops in the morning."

Allerton seemed to breathe a sigh of relief.

"How much do you believe it all comes to?"

"My best reckoning is close to twenty thousand pounds, Your Grace. Give or take a few pence."

Gideon gave a low whistle, glad his mother was not present to hear him. She'd desist his using such a vulgarity. "That would put us back on our feet again."

"It would be a great relief, Your Grace."

There were still the estates to see to, but this would go a long way. Enough that he might be able to ask Worthington's permission to court Lady Louisa. Although marriage was still out of the question for the nonce.

With a lighter step, he left the office, went to his chambers. "Hobson."

"Your Grace."

His valet had been with him since he'd left Oxford and was elated to be back on English soil. The rough and ready Canadian ways had not appealed to his sense of dignity. Upon Gideon's arrival in London, his valet had insisted that the first place he visit was Weston's to be outfitted with new clothing.

"I am attending Lady Sale's ball this evening."

"Excellent, Your Grace. I shall have everything in order. Will you dine in or out?"

He considered his options. He did not really want the company of his club. On the other hand, it might give him an opportunity to find out more about the woman. "Inquire as to whether Cook is expecting me. If not, I shall dine at my club."

Mostly he wanted to fill the hours between now and when he'd see Lady Louisa again.

Chapter Four

Several hours later, Louisa and Charlotte sat in the front drawing room as Grace presided over morning visits. Unfortunately, there were no new ladies. Young or otherwise.

Louisa really should have taken into consideration that she probably knew everyone who would visit today. Still, there was always the possibility that someone new would stop by.

Watching the hands of the clock move, she was about to lose hope, when their butler announced, "The Duchess of Stillwell, and Miss Blackacre."

Naturally, she had heard of the duchess, but what was she doing here and who was Miss Blackacre? Louisa said another prayer as the two ladies entered the drawing room.

The duchess was a petite lady of an indeterminate age. Her golden hair had a few strands of white, and her skin was largely unlined. Louisa glanced at Charlotte, who sat up straighter. She and Grace bore a distinct resemblance to the duchess. Could they possibly be related?

"Grace"—the duchess glided into the room trailed by Miss Blackacre—"how fortunate you are having your at-home." She turned her cheek for Grace to kiss it. "I do not believe you have met your cousin, Oriana Blackacre."

"I have not," Grace said, smiling at the younger woman. "How happy I am to see you, Aunt Dianna."

"As I am to see you again, my dear, but allow me to finish the introductions or I shall forget about them all together. Oriana," Her Grace continued, "this is Grace, the new Countess of Worthington." The duchess glanced around until her gaze landed on Charlotte, and she smiled warmly. "And here is another cousin, Lady Charlotte Carpenter."

Charlotte, who had risen, along with everyone else in the room, sank into a curtsey. "Aunt Dianna, how lovely to see you."

"Very pretty," her aunt approved.

Grace took the duchess's arm. "Please have a seat. I did not know you were in Town."

The lady sank elegantly onto the love seat next to Grace. "You might have heard that my son-in-law, Oriana's father, died late last year. Naturally, she did not feel as if she would be up to having a Season, but in the end, we decided it was better than her moping about. Naturally, my poor daughter could not come, but I was more than happy to sponsor Oriana." The duchess indicated that Miss Blackacre take the seat next to Charlotte. "Then I remembered you were bringing out Charlotte and Worthington's sister." She raised a brow. "I assume this is Lady Louisa?"

"Yes, Your Grace." Louisa curtseyed, then regained her place on the sofa.

"Perfect. I do hope you and Charlotte will be able to tell Oriana how to go on. Why don't you girls go somewhere and get to know one another?" The duchess's eyes widened as she glanced at Grace. "If you have no objection, my dear?"

Although posed as a question, it was clear that the duchess had no expectation of being denied.

"I have no objection at all," Grace said, giving a rueful

grin. “Charlotte, you and Louisa may take Oriana onto the terrace for tea.”

“I am sure the terrace will be lovely.” The duchess made shooing motions with her hands.

They left the room as Grace reached for the bellpull.

“I’m so glad to finally meet you,” Charlotte said to Oriana as they left the room and turned down the corridor. “My grandfather, Lord Timothy, told us about your side of the family.”

“He told me about your family as well,” Miss Blackacre said in a pleasant, musical voice that appeared to contain no artifice. “I so wished I could have met you before, however, I do know you have had a rather trying time of it lately.” Miss Blackacre’s tone was infused with understanding. “As our family has as well.”

What a sweet lady. Could she be the right woman for Bentley? Louisa wondered. “I am sorry to hear of your loss.”

Miss Blackacre’s eyes took on a moist sheen, and she blinked rapidly a few times. “I miss Papa dreadfully, but I am glad he is no longer in pain.” She smiled mistily. “He was the best father in the world. I only pray I am fortunate enough to marry a gentleman such as he was.”

All Louisa remembered of her papa was him breezing in and out of their lives for short periods of time. Matt had been more of a father to her and her sisters. She most decidedly did not wish to wed a man such as he was.

“Are you truly ready to have your first Season?” Charlotte asked.

“Oh, yes.” Miss Blackacre nodded. “Grandmamma was right. I am much better occupied in Town than I would be at home.”

Louisa wondered if it was fair to attempt to play matchmaker when Miss Blackacre had just lost a father she was so fond of. Still, nothing ventured, nothing gained. And it was possible that she knew him already. "What part of the country do you hail from?"

"The West Midlands. Not far from Wolverhampton."

That was sufficiently far enough away from Bentley's family's estate that Miss Blackacre had probably not met him, or he her. This was good. Very good indeed. A pot of tea arrived accompanied by biscuits, seed cake, and fruit tarts. Charlotte set about serving.

As Miss Blackacre picked up her cup, Louisa caught Charlotte's eye and raised a brow in inquiry. Charlotte gave a noncommittal shrug. Yes, they would need to know much more about Miss Blackacre before they could decide if she was the right lady for Bentley.

"Would you like to accompany us for a stroll in the Park this afternoon?" Louisa asked. The walk would give her an opportunity to get to know Miss Blackacre better.

"How very kind of you." Miss Blackacre's dark brows furrowed slightly. "If it will not put you out, I would love to, my lady. But please, do not feel pressured by Grandmamma. She is a force of her own."

Louisa and Charlotte laughed.

"Believe me," Louisa said, "she is not the only lady we know like that, and please, do call me Louisa. Charlotte and I are something like sisters now, so you must be my cousin as well."

A broad smile lit Miss Blackacre's face. "Thank you very much, and you must call me Oriana. Arriving so late in the Season, I had no expectation of finding friends, much less family. I am happy to be related to you both."

"I quite agree with Louisa. You must call me Charlotte. There is no point in us being so formal."

"Very well." Oriana's smile broadened. "Charlotte and Louisa it is."

Just then the door from the morning room burst open, and the twins with Madeline ran out onto the terrace and stopped.

"Who are you?" Louisa's sister Madeline asked.

"That is rude," Louisa said sternly.

"But we want to know," Charlotte's sister Alice said in a cajoling tone.

Next to her, Eleanor, Alice's twin, nodded. "We do. No one ever tells us anything."

"Very well," Louisa replied. "This is Miss Blackacre. She is a cousin on the Carpenter side."

"We like new cousins," the three girls said in unison.

"And you're pretty." Madeline moved forward staring at Oriana's face. "You have eyes the same color as our blue pansies."

Naturally, that remark made the twins take a closer look at their new cousin.

"Hmm, I think they are more like violets," Eleanor opined.

"Maybe." Alice peered more closely still. "They match that gown you have, Louisa."

"Oh, gowns!" The twins clasped their hands together.

A choking sound erupted from Charlotte. "No matter which plant they resemble more, or which gown, shall we agree Oriana's eyes are quite beautiful and leave it at that?"

Thankfully, the younger girls nodded.

"Good." Charlotte's eyes brimmed with laughter. "Go on now and play before you are called in again."

Oriana giggled. "Are they always so diverting?"

"You have no idea how embarrassing they can be at times," Louisa said, selecting a biscuit. "I hope to be long married and traveling far, far away when they make their come out."

"I take it two of them are twins, and the third is your sister?"

Louisa picked up her cup and took a sip. "Yes, and they are all twelve. It is more like having triplets than twins."

"I can imagine," Oriana responded. "Grandmamma told me all about the marriage. How lucky you are that everyone gets along so well."

"We are," Charlotte agreed. "The only problem is that I now have four more sisters to miss when I marry."

Louisa had just had the same thought. She turned her mind to figuring out how or where to introduce Bentley to Oriana. "Are you going to the Sales' ball this evening?"

"I doubt it. We just arrived yesterday, and Grandmamma hasn't mentioned it."

"You must have a great deal of shopping to do," Charlotte said.

"Not that much." Oriana wrinkled her brow again. "My measurements were sent off to my grandmother's modiste, along with instructions for several gowns. Some of them are due to arrive this afternoon."

"They will still have to be fitted." Charlotte glanced at Louisa. "You are about the same size and coloring. I do not think Grace will mind if you loan Oriana a gown so she will be able to accompany us this evening."

"What a brilliant idea." Louisa smiled approvingly at Charlotte. "Let us finish our tea, then ask Grace and your aunt."

Oriana, Charlotte, and Louisa continued to discuss their families, and the difference between Town and country life, which naturally led to fashion and Town hours.

"What is your home like?" Louisa asked Oriana.

"Our home estate is actually quite small. A manor house, home farm, and a few tenants." She sighed. "I did tell you Papa was a dear?" Charlotte and Louisa nodded. "Well, he was from a large family, and extremely charming. He loved everyone and everyone loved him. Consequently, each time one of his unmarried or childless aunts and uncles died, they left him their property." Giving a slight grimace, Oriana continued, "The only problem is that he was absentminded, and not very decisive. Fortunately, my mother is quite astute, and one of the estates he inherited early on came with an excellent steward. To make a long story short, we were all taught to manage the holdings. I have been in charge, as it were, for the past few years while my two elder brothers were in university, and my mother was taking care of Papa. John, my oldest brother, returned home just before Papa died." Her voice hitched slightly. "He had been staying in Hull with my grandfather Gordon learning newer methods of land management. However, as I said, he is home now, and I was at rather loose ends with him taking over the estate." She smiled ruefully. "Now you probably have heard more about me than you ever wished to know."

"No, no. Not at all," Louisa assured her, wondering exactly how Oriana's father had been indecisive. "I only wish I would have been given the opportunity to learn how an estate operates before now. Grace is teaching me, and I have studied a number of books, but how wonderful it would have been to have practical experience."

"I am glad to have some practical knowledge as well," Charlotte added. "Louisa, I am positive you will be brilliant at managing a house and estate."

Daisy, their female Great Dane, strolled out onto the terrace, coming to them for attention. Oriana giggled as the dog's huge head came up under her hand. "You are a big, beautiful girl." She glanced at Charlotte. "How old is she?"

"She will be two next month, but we still say she is one because she has not yet reached her birthday."

"I sense a story behind that."

"It is to keep the younger children from counting their

years and months." Charlotte grinned. "Philip, our youngest brother, began telling people he was seven years and two months, then seven years and three months. Not to be outdone, the twins began counting the days."

"Oh, dear." Oriana covered her mouth with a serviette. "I can see how they would become irritating."

"Indeed." She lowered her voice as the younger girls came back to the terrace. "That is the reason she is one."

"My ladies, Miss Blackacre." Royston, the Stanwood butler, bowed. "Her ladyship would like to speak with you."

Louisa, Charlotte, and Oriana followed the butler back to the drawing room, where Grace sat with Matt, the duchess having apparently left.

"There you are." She turned to Oriana. "Aunt Dianna wanted you to be able to spend more time with Charlotte and Louisa while she took care of some errands. I have instructions to send you to Madam Lisette's, but I am more comfortable accompanying you." Next to her Matt nodded. "I would send Louisa and Charlotte, but, unfortunately, the three youngest children are ill and have been asking for them." Grace hesitated for a moment. "Do you know if you had the measles?"

"I have had. My brothers never let me forget how full of them I was. Why do you ask?"

"That is what ails our youngest children," Charlotte said. "It appears our planned stroll in the Park must be rescheduled. Grace, we would like Oriana to accompany us this evening."

"I've already spoken to our aunt about the idea. However, she feels that the entertainment tomorrow evening might be better. Oriana has a number of gowns that must be fitted, which is the reason for her trip to Madam Lisette's. Tomorrow, we shall dine at Stillwell House before attending the ball."

"What a wonderful idea!" Oriana grinned happily. She

glanced at Louisa and Charlotte. "I am sorry I will not be able to attend tonight, but I do look forward to the morrow. Thank you for giving me such a warm welcome."

After hugs and pecks on the cheeks were exchanged, Grace rose, signaling for Oriana to accompany her. Matt stood as well and followed them into the hall.

Charlotte and Louisa trailed behind.

"Her birth is excellent," Louisa whispered as they mounted the steps to the nursery.

"Yes, and she is the granddaughter of dukes on both her maternal and paternal sides," Charlotte agreed. "Her dowry is probably more than respectable. One can tell that she is extremely patient, and she knows how to manage an estate."

"And Bentley might be very like her father was. In short, she is perfect for Bentley." Louisa smiled, already feeling the weight of her unwanted gentleman slide from her shoulders.

"As long as she likes him," Charlotte said in a gentle reminder.

"And he likes her." Louisa refused to allow the possibility that Oriana and Bentley would not suit to deter her.

"Should we approach her first?"

"That would be awkward." Charlotte pulled a face. "After we introduce them, I will try to find out what she thinks about Bentley. For all we know she might have her heart set on another gentleman."

"She only arrived in Town last week, and I do not think she has been around much. If only we knew her better."

"Oh, we will." Charlotte went back to her desk, took a seat, and pulled out a piece of pressed paper. "I shall write, inviting her to join us for a stroll during the Promenade tomorrow afternoon."

"What a splendid idea. Why didn't I think of that?"

"Because your preferred method of dealing with a task is to put everyone in place and tell them what to do."

Louisa sighed. She could be a bit ruthless, but only for the good of others. Hopefully, Rothwell would appreciate her way of accomplishing her objectives. It had not occurred to her until now to wonder if he might like a less managing sort of lady. "If only we knew if Bentley had met her yet."

"I doubt it." Charlotte sealed the missive. "As she said, she has not been to any of the evening entertainments."

Louisa sent up a fervent prayer that Oriana and Bentley would fall immediately in love.

Chapter Five

An hour after his conversation with Allerton, Gideon was at Brook's consuming a rare roast beef, when a distinguished older gentleman approached him. "Rothwell, I had heard you were back. It is good to see you again."

Next to him a younger man, Lord Marcus Finley, grinned. Gideon had known Lord Marcus in school and had run across him a few times when he was in Canada. "Welcome home. I was sorry to hear of your loss."

"Marcus, thank you." Gideon stood reaching out to shake the other man's hand. "I heard you married."

"Indeed I did. Unfortunately, I suffered a loss as well. My brother died. I am now the Earl of Evesham. This"—he indicated the older man—"is my uncle-in-law, Lord St. Eth."

"You have my sympathies. Sir," Gideon greeted Lord St. Eth. "I did not recognize you at first. Please have a seat."

Marcus and the Marquis of St. Eth took chairs on either side of Gideon. A waiter brought a bottle of claret.

"I understand that you have received your summons, and I have taken it upon myself to ease your entry into the Lords," St. Eth remarked after taking a sip of wine. "I trust you will remain in Town long enough to take care of that duty."

Gideon had been so distracted by his father's losses and Lady Louisa, although he had only met her once, he had forgotten completely about his seat in the House of Lords. "Thank you, sir. I would appreciate your help."

Marcus and Lord St. Eth ordered beefsteaks as well. Once their meals had been delivered, the men dug into the club's excellent beef. After they had shared a bottle of wine, Gideon asked, "Will you be at Lady Sale's ball this evening?"

"We are attending the theater," Marcus replied. "The only reason my wife is still in Town is to see Kean play this evening. After that, I am whisking her off to the country to await the birth of our first child."

Life was changing so quickly. Soon all of his friends would be married with children on the way. "Congratulations. I could not be happier for you." Gideon raised his glass. "To a healthy mother and child."

"To a healthy mother and child!" the other two gentlemen said in unison.

"If you are attending the ball"—Marcus placed his glass on the table—"I take it you are looking for a wife?"

Gideon chewed on a piece of beef, thinking about how to answer. "There is one lady I am interested in. Unfortunately, I have other matters to settle before I am in a position to court her."

The gentlemen gave him knowing looks, but did not comment. He was learning that his father had not been at all discreet in his affair. What concerned him more was whether the *ton* knew about his financial state. Many families lived for generations perched precariously on the edge of bankruptcy. As peers could not be sent to debtors' prison, they apparently had no reason to change their ways.

Yet the Dukes of Rothwell had always husbanded their resources, and Gideon was not only pinched, but embarrassed about it.

Conversation settled into bringing him up to the present on old friends and other prominent members of Polite Society.

Eventually, he glanced at his pocket watch. "You must excuse me. I have a ball to attend."

St. Eth and Marcus rose. "And we, wives to collect," Marcus said with a smile.

Just as Gideon reached the pavement, Lord Masters, an old acquaintance of his father's, halted Gideon. "A word if you please, Your Grace."

The man had never been a favorite of Gideon's, and still wasn't. His lordship smelled of strong drink, and his cravat sported what looked to be a gravy stain. He felt himself stiffening. "My lord?"

Masters pulled several scraps of paper from his waistcoat pocket. "Heard you were in Town, and I've been hoping to see you. There is a little matter of these debts your father left." He leaned closer and in a loud whisper said, "Debits of honor, you know."

Debts of honor only because one could not bring an action in court to enforce them. Allerton had alluded to Father's gambling debts, but had never given Gideon a total. That his father had lost so much money was in itself strange. The duke rarely played, but when he did, he never lost. To make matters worse, Gideon did not have the funds to cover any of the debts his father had not paid before his death. Not only that, but the more he thought about the horrible position he and his family were now in, the angrier he became. "I find nothing honorable about beggaring one's family, and I shall play no part in it."

"But Your Grace," the man whined, "your father gave his word."

"In that case, I suggest you take it up with him when next you meet."

The older man's already ruddy face grew redder. "Mark my words," his lordship raged. "You will be sorry for your decision."

"So be it." Wondering if his problems could get much more desperate, he watched the older man weave his way down the street. To make matters worse, Marcus and St. Eth were still standing nearby. "I suppose you heard the conversation."

"You will not endear yourself to many," St. Eth replied thoughtfully. "On the other hand, it was clear that your father was not himself. There is nothing honorable in wagering with minors and incompetents."

Gideon shook his head, not understanding. "What do you mean 'incompetent'?"

"It was clear, to me at least," St. Eth said in a dry voice, "that he was suffering from dementia. The few times I saw him, he addressed me by my old courtesy title. I could not have been the only one." St. Eth looked Gideon in the eye. "When he was young, your father was a terrible card player. Eventually, his losses exceeded his allowance and your grandfather reined him in. The next time I saw him in Town, not only had his behavior moderated greatly, but his skill had increased to the point where few would wager against him."

Well, that explained a great deal. More to the point, if St. Eth had figured out that Father was not in his right mind, who else must have known and taken advantage of the fact? A weight lifted from Gideon's shoulders. If Father had not been in his right mind, he wasn't to blame for his behavior. And, as St. Eth alluded to, Gideon could not be blamed for refusing to pay his father's marks of hand. "Thank you for telling me."

"Good luck." Marcus clapped Gideon's back. "If you have need of anything, please do not hesitate to ask."

"I won't." But despite the offer, Gideon knew this was a matter he must handle himself.

The two gentlemen strolled off. Gideon's town coach stood nearby. Barnes had done an excellent job making the older carriage shine. Even the coat of arms looked newly gilded. At least Gideon appeared prosperous, even if he wasn't. He waited while a liveried footman opened the door and let down the steps.

Although he had been the heir his entire life, he would have to get used to the ceremony of being the duke. Perhaps it would have been easier if he had not spent three years in Canada where the formalities received scant attention. Not only that, but if he had been home, rather than running wild on another continent, he would have been able to curtail his father's excesses. Instead of dealing with a randy old duke not in his right mind, Gideon would have taken the matter to court and won guardianship of his father.

Now he would pay the price for indulging himself. A mistake he would not make again. The dukedom, his family, and all his dependents relied upon him, and this time he would not let them down, even if it meant giving up what he wanted.

Leaning back against the soft leather squabs, Gideon contemplated the evening. He would enjoy himself or rather enjoy his waltz with Lady Louisa and supper afterward. But that would have to be the last he saw of her until he was able to get his other affairs in order. If he had his way, he would have waited until just before the supper dance to arrive, but not only would that have been rude, it would single her out, causing the sort of talk he should strive to avoid.

Several minutes later, the coach came to a halt. The large town house was alive with the glitter of candles, music, and voices. After making his way up the stairs, he greeted his host and hostess.

Lady Sale smiled as she dipped into a low curtsey. "Your Grace"—her tone reminded him of a cat with cream—"I am pleased you could join us this evening."

"I was honored to receive your invitation," Gideon replied as he bowed.

Turning to Lord Sale, he held out his hand. "My lord."

"Your Grace," his lordship said as he shook Gideon's hand. "Welcome home."

"I am glad to be back, sir." When the couple turned to accompany him, he realized that they had most likely waited for his arrival before quitting their posts. "Has my cousin, Lord Bentley, arrived?"

"Unfortunately, he sent his regrets." Her ladyship's lips formed a moue.

"That is a shame." In another gentleman, Gideon would have considered the behavior odd. Yet with Bentley, he was surprised he'd remembered to cry off. Gideon would simply have to wait to discover the reason he had been asked to come to Town.

He offered Lady Sale his arm. "Please allow me."

She inclined her head politely. "Thank you, Your Grace. I shall introduce you to some of the young ladies. Although, I am not sure you have arrived early enough to claim many dances."

A fact that pleased him more than he could let her ladyship know. Keeping his comments to himself, Gideon assumed a suitably chastised demeanor. His name was already on the card of the only lady he wished to stand up with.

"I assume you will be looking for a wife." Her ladyship raised a brow waiting for his answer.

"No. Not this Season. I am only in Town for a short while."

"Ah." She nodded. "After being away for so long, you must have a deal to do. Well, I entreat you not to allow that to stop you from a suitable marriage."

His mind harkened back to his discussion with Worthington.

"You could marry an heiress. That is a perfectly respectable method of recouping one's fortunes."

Another reason to keep his financial problems to himself. He did not need to have young ladies thrown at him in hopes of being his duchess. "I shall keep that in mind, my lady."

At that moment he caught sight of Lady Louisa. She was resplendent in a white ball gown trimmed with pink that shimmered each time she moved to the steps of the cotillion. He did not think he had ever seen the dance performed more gracefully.

As if she knew she was being watched, her head turned and he caught her eye, holding her gaze for the merest second, yet it was enough. There was an indescribable electricity, a connection between them he had never felt before. He blinked and she had turned back to her partner.

Next to him, Lady Sale made a murmur of approval. "Shall I escort you to Lord and Lady Worthington?"

"Please." Did the woman miss nothing? Gideon stifled a groan. That had not been well done of him. How many others had noticed? He really did not wish Lady Sale to escort him to anyone, but he was not certain that he could have found his friend without her ladyship's help.

He had forgotten what a crush *ton* balls could be. "This is a far cry from what I've been used to lately."

"I doubt any of the entertainments in the colonies could

match what we have here," she replied in the dismissive manner, typical of those who considered England's colonies somehow less than they should be.

Her ladyship had circumnavigated the ballroom, nodding to her many guests and introducing him to more than one matron who had eligible daughters. Finally, he could see where Worthington stood, on the other side of the room. "Thank you for your escort, my lady. I believe I can find my own way from here."

"It was entirely my pleasure, Your Grace." She curtseyed. "If you require any introductions, you may call on me to provide them."

The set had ended, enabling Gideon to walk across the room and join his friend and soon, Lady Louisa. Or so he thought.

"Rothwell, is that you?"

In front of him he saw an old school chum. "Featherton, how have you been?"

"I am well. I was sorry to hear about your father."

"It was a shock." In more ways than one. He shook his friend's hand.

He took a few more steps, and one of Mama's old friends hailed him. "Your Grace, please give my regards to your mother. I am sorry she could not come to Town this Season." A young lady joined them. "Do you remember my daughter, Lady Jane? She was quite young when last you met."

He bowed to the woman's daughter, unable to place her among all the children who had visited Rothwell Abbey over the years. "You have changed greatly, Lady Jane." Fluttering her lashes, she gave him a flirtatious smile.

He lost no time addressing her mother. "I will tell her you asked about her."

It was amazing how difficult crossing a crowded ballroom could be. A few minutes later, he blew out a breath.

"I thought I'd never find you. Tracking a bear in the woods is easier."

"Welcome back to the *ton*." Worthington laughed. "We followed your progress across the dance floor. Next time stick to the sides."

The golden-haired lady next to him chuckled lightly. By the look Worthington gave her, and the way he had the lady's hand tucked securely in the crook of his arm, she could be no other than his bride. "Ah, my love. Allow me to introduce the Duke of Rothwell. Rothwell, my wife."

Gideon bowed over the lady's hand, while she curtseyed. "A pleasure, my lady. I knew it must have been a rare woman who would finally win Worthington's heart, and I see that I was right."

A rosy blush painted her cheeks. "I am pleased to finally meet you, Your Grace. My husband has told me of your travels. How do you like being home?"

"It has been interesting thus far. Would I could have returned under different circumstance, my lady."

"Yes." Her eyes filled with concern. "It is never easy to lose a parent. But to have arrived back and discover it then must have been devastating. I am sorry to have heard of your loss."

She was the first person since he had returned to have shown such sympathy, and his throat closed painfully with unshed tears. "It has not been easy."

"I am sure that is an understatement. How is your mother holding up?"

"As well as can be expected." Privately, he thought his mother might be relieved that his father had died. Throughout their long marriage, the duke had never before taken a mistress. Even knowing that his father had been ill had probably not mitigated the hurt she must have felt over his betrayal.

"I shall write to her. Many times one receives letters of

condolence after a death, then nothing more. I know that after my father died, my own mother felt it keenly."

"Thank you for your kindness."

Worthington was extremely lucky to have found such a woman. Gideon only hoped he would be as fortunate.

"Worthington said you do not plan to be in Town long. We almost never dine formally"—she grinned—"you are welcome to take your potluck with us."

And be with Lady Louisa. Could he do that knowing he could never do more than be with her in company? "Thank you, my lady."

"Just send word around and I shall have another place set at the table."

"Perhaps I will take you up on your offer." He scanned the room for Lady Louisa, and finally saw her being escorted his way.

He had not paid attention to the time he'd arrived and thus had no idea which set had recently ended. Gideon only hoped the supper dance would come soon.

Chapter Six

Louisa almost missed her part in the dance when her attention was captured by the Duke of Rothwell. His molten silver eyes mesmerized her as nothing had before. It was as if he had willed her to look at him, then captured her with his gaze.

As warm as she was from dancing and the crowded room, a slight shiver ran through her at the sight of the duke.

She had never met a man as commanding as he was. Good heavens! If she was having this type of reaction now, what would she do when she was in his arms during the waltz? Surely he must be The One. She had never had this type of reaction to any other gentleman, and she had only spoken ten words to him, well, maybe twenty. Still, her response was unusual. Mostly, instead of wishing to spend more time with a gentleman she simply wanted whoever it was to leave her alone after the set had finished. She had the feeling that was not what she would want after dancing with Rothwell.

"Lady Louisa." Lord Babcock, her dance partner, broke into her musings. "Are you cold?"

"Not at all." Just the opposite. Yet when she raised her arm, her skin resembled a plucked chicken's.

Shrugging off the strange feeling that something was not quite as it should be, she caught a glimpse of him as Lady Sale led him off, no doubt to introduce him to her other guests.

To the best of Louisa's knowledge, this was the first entertainment he had attended since he returned from the colonies. He would certainly be a feather in her ladyship's cap.

From the day Louisa had come out, she had garnered more than her fair share of attention, but that was nothing compared to the looks Rothwell was receiving from some of the ladies. Goodness, they were practically salivating. The poor man. He must feel like an animal in the Royal Menagerie.

Soon Rothwell was out of sight, and she turned her full attention back to the dance, which seemed to be taking much longer than usual. Finally, the set finished, and her partner escorted her back to Grace and Matt. When she reached them Rothwell was there as well.

She wanted to beam with joy, yet she schooled her countenance into a polite, demure smile and curtseyed. It would not do to let anyone know how interested she was in him. That would only court unwanted speculation about them both. "Your Grace."

"My lady." Taking her gloved hand, he pressed a kiss to her fingers. Heat sizzled where his lips had touched.

Oh, good God! This is worse than this morning!

He looked at her and, although his face was impassive, his eyes danced wickedly. Her breath shortened, and, for a moment, she wasn't sure she would ever be able to breathe again.

Then Grace said something, Matt responded with a chuckle, and Rothwell slowly released her hand. Yet even then his gaze never left hers.

"Louisa," Grace said in a tone of warning. "I believe Lord Babcock is returning with lemonade for you."

"Oh . . . oh, yes. Of course he is." The man believed all ladies should drink lemonade between sets. At first Louisa appreciated the gesture, then realized that he did it not out of kindness, but to give himself what he perceived to be an advantage.

Rothwell straightened, and she glanced toward Lord Babcock as he reached them.

"For you, my lady." With a flourish, he handed the cool drink to her.

"Thank you, my lord. I appreciate it." She did not, but there was no reason, other than malice, to tell him that.

Matt introduced Lord Babcock to Rothwell. Next to the duke and her brother, Lord Babcock seemed even younger than he usually did, and Matt couldn't give Lord Babcock more than four years, if that. Perhaps it was just that his lordship did not appear to be as mature as her brother and Rothwell.

The talk soon turned to the war with Napoleon.

"I am considering touring the Continent as soon as that Corsican devil has been put away," Lord Babcock said. "My grandfather's tales of his Grand Tour have always fascinated me."

"I do not expect Napoleon will be easily defeated," Louisa commented. "He had made his escape from Elba easily enough and appeared to have a great deal of support in his march to Paris."

"I must say, Lady Louisa"—Lord Babcock gave her an indulgent smile, much like he might bestow upon a child—"the bounder was roundly beaten before. There is no reason we cannot do it again."

"I happen to share Lady Louisa's concern," Rothwell said before his lordship could continue.

She was glad to hear they shared the same opinion.

"King Louis managed to anger not only those who did not care for him, but those who supported him. As Lady Louisa said, since his escape, Napoleon's ability to raise troops has been impressive. Add that to the fact that Wellington's most experienced forces were beaten in America, and you have the makings of a bad situation." Rothwell glanced at her. "I am impressed that you are so well informed, my lady."

She gave the duke her most brilliant smile. "It would be hard to remain ignorant in my family, Your Grace. You must know how politically inclined we are."

"Yes, yes." Flushing, Babcock rushed to agree. "If only all young ladies were as astute."

She wanted to roll her eyes. If he thought his sudden change of mind fooled her, he was an idiot. He had a courtesy title, and she wondered if he followed politics at all. Unless they had a family member in the army, many young men did not pay much attention to the government or the war.

Fortunately, the next set was about to start and Rothwell held out his arm. "Shall we, my lady?"

She placed her hand on his arm, preparing herself for the jolt of sensation. Yet she was not ready to feel his heat and the way it warmed her as well. "We shall, Your Grace."

They took their positions for the dance, and the moment his hand held hers and the weight of his palm was on her waist, she knew she was lost. Her heart raced forward, and her breathing became shallow. Her attraction to him really was as the romance novels had described it. Could she be falling in love already? She glanced up at him, and the warmth in his eyes made her want to step closer than was proper.

His fingers on her back tightened. "Oh, dear."

Gideon forced himself not to pull her closer.

"Precisely." His voice sounded rusty, as if he had not spoken for weeks, or months.

"Do you feel—"

"Yes." He bit off the word. "Yes," Gideon said using a softer tone. He did not wish to frighten her away. Although something told him that she would not be easy to alarm.

Standing next to Lady Louisa and not being able to touch her had been bad enough. Holding her was excruciating. There was something to be said for carrying off the lady one wanted. As it was, he felt as if every pair of eyes present was on them. And he had to find something to say that did not involve telling her he wanted to kiss her as well as other far more disreputable but equally pleasant things. He had never had such an immediate and visceral reaction to a lady before.

"Babcock is an idiot." Not precisely the best conversation starter, but for some reason Gideon had been wanting to say it. Perhaps to gauge Lady Louisa's reaction.

"I agree." Her voice sounded breathless, as if she had been running through a forest. "Yet, to be fair, not more so than many other gentlemen."

Gideon didn't want to be fair. Babcock had almost sneered at her understanding, then reversed his position as soon as Gideon had spoken up. "A gentleman should have the confidence of his principles."

Which did not say much for himself at the moment.

"You have been away from the *ton* much too long if you believe that." Her voice was dry as tinder, but the corner of her luscious, rose-colored lips quivered.

"You are a cynic, my lady." Could he make her smile again? For some reason, he wanted, no, needed to see her deep red lips lift and a spark of amusement enter her lapis blue eyes. "Your brother is firm in his beliefs."

"Of course he is, and there are others of his friends who are reasonable, forward-minded men as well." He guided her through the turn, and she tilted her head. "Are you?"

"Sensible and progressive?" He liked that she went

straight to the heart of a matter. "I like to think so. There are many women, including ladies, who have a great deal of power. In Canada, amongst the Indians, women have equal power. In some tribes, it is the women who own the property."

"I would like to hear more about the Indians and Canada."

Somehow she was closer to him than before. Was he making a hash of the dance? Creating a scandal would not help either of them.

He attempted to straighten his arms a bit, but could not manage to do it. "I wish you could see them for yourself."

A wistful look appeared in her face. "That would be wonderful. However, I shall be lucky to visit Europe. Matt has flatly refused to take us to Brussels where much of the *ton* has decamped. Even the Duchess of Richmond is there. Though I do understand his reasoning."

Gideon could imagine Worthington's reaction to the suggestion that he take two young ladies of marriageable age, his pregnant wife, and a multitude of children to a place where a battle was to be fought. The thought of Lady Louisa in danger made Gideon's blood run cold. Then again, she seemed to be equal to anything. "I have noticed that London is much thinner of company than I'd remembered."

"A little." Louisa's brows drew together as she said, "I think Wellington will win, but I am afraid the cost will be high."

"For what reason?" Nevertheless, he did think this battle would be different. Wellington and Napoleon had never gone against each other before.

"I met an officer recently whose orders to Canada were changed to travel to Brussels. He expressed the same concern you did, that many of Wellington's most experienced soldiers were beaten at the Battle of New Orleans in January in America. Not only that, but many of the officers who served under him are away as well."

Gideon had a sudden vision of Lady Louisa presiding over a political dinner. She would be brilliant, amazing and enticing them all with her knowledge and intelligence. She was exactly the type of lady who would make a perfect duchess. *His perfect duchess*. "I suppose we must pray that Wellington is as good a commander as he is reputed to be."

"I feel as if I should contribute in some way." Her brow cleared, and she gave him a rueful smile. "Still, even if Matt agreed to take us, there is most likely nothing *I* could do."

Gideon had the feeling she would have found a way to involve herself. "It will be frustrating waiting for the final result."

Flashing him a smile, she replied, "Yes, it will be. I am often told not to worry myself about it, but I would dearly love to have someone with whom I could discuss my concerns."

"You have me." He blurted out the words before giving them any thought. If he had his way, he would spend the rest of his life listening to and talking with her. If only he had not gone to Canada.

Her bright blue eyes warmed as she gazed up at him. "If you are quite sure, then I accept your offer."

"There is nothing I am more certain of." The set ended, and he brought them to a halt, but could not manage to let her go.

She might not be able to aid the duke in Belgium, but there was another duke who was beginning to think she was exactly what he needed. The sooner he could settle the problems with his estates, the more quickly he could ask Worthington for permission to court Lady Louisa. The difficulty was Gideon did not know when that would be, and he was determined to be beforehand with the world before he courted her. If what they were feeling physically was true, perhaps she would wait.

Once again, Louisa had to force herself to tear her gaze from Rothwell's compelling gray eyes. Goodness, was this how her brother and Grace had felt about each other when they'd met? She had never asked. Mostly because she had not met anyone who made her want to be with him all the time. Now she had.

In no time at all, the set ended.

Rothwell held her hand as she rose from her curtsey, and his breath caressed her ear. "I am extremely pleased that I am taking you to supper."

"I'm delighted you are as well. However, I must warn you, we will be joining my family. Matt will not allow either Charlotte or me to dine alone with a gentleman."

"I would expect no less from him." Rothwell escorted her to where the rest of her party waited for them.

Strolling slowly, they followed the others down to the supper room. "Do you ride again in the morning?"

Had it only been this morning they had first seen each other? Louisa grinned to herself. She had always said that when she found the right gentleman, she would know. "Yes. I inevitably rise earlier than the rest of my family."

"Seven? If it is not too early."

She gave an imperceptible nod. "Seven is perfect. We will not stay much past supper. It did not take long for us to realize that we needed a good night's sleep to keep up with the younger children."

His lips slid into a slow smile. "I cannot imagine having such a crowded house."

If someone had told her ahead of time what would happen, she would have thought the same. Still . . . "I might have agreed with you, but we have been lucky. From the beginning we got on well, and truly think of one another as brothers and sisters."

They joined Matt, Grace, Charlotte, and the Earl of Endicott, who escorted Charlotte, at the table Matt had commanded.

"If you tell me what you like most," Rothwell whispered, causing another shiver to race down her spine, "I shall endeavor to provide it for you."

His hand rested on her waist, and a feeling, as if his fingers had traced her entire spine, skittered up her back. Her cheeks heated. "I adore lobster patties, and ices."

"Your wish is my command, my lady."

She watched him leave with her brother and the earl.

"Louisa."

Grace's voice intruded on Louisa's thoughts. "Yes?"

"Do not stare."

Louisa jerked her head around to face the table. What had she been thinking? She knew better than to make a spectacle of herself. "I'm sorry. I did not mean to—"

"I understand." Grace patted Louisa's hand. "I have heard many good things about Rothwell, and he is extremely handsome."

"Yes, yes, he is, but more importantly, he listens to me, and can carry on an intelligent conversation." She glanced at Charlotte, who seemed to be thinking of something else entirely.

"I noticed that he appears to be interested in what you have to say." Grace glanced in the direction the gentlemen went. "They are returning."

Louisa squeezed Grace's fingers. "I would like to speak with you tomorrow if you have time."

"Very well. After breakfast come to my study."

"Thank you."

The men returned. Rothwell placed a plate piled high with lobster patties in front of Louisa. "Goodness, I'll never be able to eat so many."

"I will be happy to help you." His voice shook as if he was holding back a laugh.

A footman brought several types of ices, and champagne.

Matt scowled. "It's a good thing Rothwell is at our table. Otherwise, the only one to sample the lobster patties would be Louisa."

"Oh, dear." Grace covered her mouth with a serviette. "Do you mean to tell me he was faster than you, my love?"

"Swooped in and outflanked the rest of us. He must have learned the trick from living in the colonies." With a completely bland expression, Matt continued, "Whatever lady decides to take him on will have to re-civilize him."

Once again, Louisa's cheeks warmed, and she bent her head to eat one of the ices. Rothwell was a friend of her brother's. If she and he decided they would suit, would Matt countenance the match? She could ask Grace what she thought in the morning. As well as what all the strange feelings were that Louisa was experiencing around the duke.

Chapter Seven

The following morning, shortly before seven, Gideon rode up to Stanwood House to find Lady Louisa mounting her horse. That was odd. The last time he was in London, ladies generally waited for a gentleman inside the house. "Good morning. I had thought I was early, but I must have been mistaken."

She gave him a startled look. "You had not mentioned coming to the house. I thought we were to meet in the Park."

"I see I shall have to be more precise in my arrangements with you. You are clearly not a lady who is unsure of herself." He could not believe that she was in the habit of meeting gentlemen in the Park. Surely her brother and sister-in-law would not tolerate such behavior. "Does Worthington know we are riding together this morning?"

A faint line appeared between her brows. "Matt and Grace have not yet arrived this morning. I told my maid and the butler." She glanced at a groom who stood not far away. "I shall not need you after all." Once the servant had left, she turned to him. "Shall we be off, Your Grace?"

Lady Louisa did not appear to be sneaking away, and

Gideon's questions had not put her out of countenance, and she had had a groom present. What the deuce was it then that troubled him about her meeting him outside? "Yes. I like the Park better when it is not full of other people."

Her light laughter floated on the air as they trotted down the street, turning the corner onto Carlos Place. Although most of the *ton* was still abed, the rest of London was bustling about and had been for some hours. Carts delivering milk and other items stopped every so often, slowing their progress. Turning onto Mount Street, they kept the horses to a walk until they reached the Park.

Normally, he would have been ready for a good long canter, but Lady Louisa fascinated him, and he wanted to know more about her. There was something about her that was different from any other lady he had met. Yet he could not put his finger on exactly what made her so enticing.

She was strong-minded. If last evening was an example, she had no hesitation in stating her opinions. Her mind was quick and insightful. He had rarely met a lady who was as knowledgeable and aware of the sufferings in the world. Yet she seemed to be inexperienced in flirtation or courting. She did not treat him to fluttering lashes or sly smiles as Lady Jane had done. Lady Louisa was a complete innocent. Obviously, no gentleman had attempted to make love to her. On the other hand, with Worthington as her brother, that was not surprising. He would skewer any man who attempted to trifle with his sister.

"What will you do with your day?" she asked as they turned into the Park.

Speak with my solicitor and go searching a whore's house for the missing jewels. "I have some estate matters to attend to. I came to Town at the request of a family member, but, as it turns out, there is some business concerning my holdings I must deal with as well." She seemed to hesitate, and Gideon wondered if her brother would have told her of his current financial embarrassments. He hoped Worthington would not have betrayed his trust.

If Lady Louisa did not mention it, Gideon decided, neither would he. He did not want her tainted by his father's ill dealings. He cast a lure by saying, "Your brother gave me the name of his man of business. I shall ask him to call on me."

"Does your family not have one?"

Hitchens, their previous man of business, had waited upon Gideon shortly after his return, and spent most of his time wringing his hands. When he had suggested investing in some of the ventures he had seen in Canada, the man had been appalled. "Yes, but he is very set in his ways. I wish to gain more knowledge and find new methods of increasing the estate's income."

"Ah, I understand." She glanced at him, her eyes full of compassion. "It is difficult when a long-time employee cannot embrace more modern ways. Matt had to convince our old steward to retire."

Thank God. She knew nothing. Gideon let out the breath he'd been holding and flashed her a smile. "We must all change with the times."

"Indeed we should." She laughed. It was the most musical sound he had ever heard.

Perhaps he should tell her about his problems. After all, he was extremely attracted to her, and he would not want her to think him a fortune hunter. Then again, Worthington obviously trusted Gideon. Otherwise he would never have introduced him to Lady Louisa or allowed her to dance with him. He need not mention the cause of most of his financial difficulties. No gentleman would discuss women of ill repute with a lady, especially an innocent lady. If he wished to express his desire that they become closer, he would have to give her some reason they could not form a permanent attachment this Season. Possibly not for another year or so. By then he would have recovered, he hoped.

They rode under a grouping of trees that hid them from view, and he halted his horse. "I may be rushing my fences, but I feel a connection with you that I have never felt with another lady."

Lady Louisa had been staring ahead, but now her head swiveled, and she faced him with a slight frown. He wanted to groan. It *had* been too soon, and he had sounded like the worst sort of callow young man. She probably thought he would start spouting poetry soon. Sitting as still as he could, he waited under her scrutiny.

Finally her lips curved up and she met his gaze. "I have felt the same, but I do not know what to do about it. We met only yesterday, and yet it seems as if I have known you forever."

Her hesitancy to dash forward was exactly what he needed. Gideon looked into her eyes. "We should take our time."

Worthington would expect Gideon to have his finances in order before he asked to court her. As he'd told her brother earlier, he refused to have a wife drawn into repairing his estate.

She nodded. "Naturally, we should not rush anything. After all, there is no reason we must."

No reason other than he wanted her to be in his life forever. Wanted to hold her, and kiss her, and . . . her eyes widened as though she could see in his eyes what he wanted. "We would not wish to give rise to gossip."

"I agree. Gossip is not desirable."

Gossip might not be desirable, but by God, she was. Lady Louisa licked her lips as her horse sidled closer to his. The devil take it, she had no idea what she was doing to him. His cock strained against his breeches. Their horses were next to each other, and he reached out, cupping her face, reveling in her soft skin, running his thumb over her rosy lips. Just as he leaned over to kiss her, the damn beasts moved.

Settling her reins, she gave a nervous giggle. "I think we had better go back."

"Yes." Before he lost his mind again and tried to kiss her. *And in the Park for God's sake!* What the devil had he been thinking? Worthington would have his head as well as other parts of his anatomy. If only Gideon were free to speak with his friend now.

They took their time traveling back to Stanwood House. It seemed neither one was ready to give up the other's company.

About a block away from her house, she said, "If there is anything I can do to help you modernize your estates, feel free to tell me. I have been schooled in estate management, though I must confess, I have no practical knowledge."

"Thank you." Her offer was charming, but it was up to him to manage his estates. "I imagine your brother made sure you had the latest information."

Her eyes sparkled as she grinned back. "Grace taught me. She has been running Stanwood's properties for years now."

"Worthington is a lucky man to be surrounded with such intelligent ladies." Would that Gideon were as well. "I look forward to discussing what you have learned. It will be a great deal more enjoyable than reading it in some dry book." A vision of her in bed, naked, her long dark tresses flowing over her shoulders, her lips swollen by kisses, and surrounded by tomes on agriculture struck him, making his body tense with desire.

He tried to hide his yearnings, but her eyes widened. "What are you thinking of?"

"I . . . um . . ." The door to her house opened and two Great Danes ran down the steps, a footman chasing after them, and a groom keeping the smaller one away from the horses. Thank fate for pandemonium.

"Duke, stay," Louisa commanded. The larger dog—the one she'd had with her yesterday—came to a halt.

The groom had the other Dane in hand, stroking her and saying. "Miss Daisy, you behave now."

Gideon swung down from his horse, crossed to Louisa, and lifted her down. "I'd better be going."

She canted her head. "Are you going to answer me?"

Tenacious woman. "Not without embarrassing us both."

He kissed her hand briefly as he was nuzzled out by the dogs. "The supper waltz this evening?"

"Do you know which party we are attending?"

Grinning, he replied, "No, but I am hoping you will tell me."

Her eyes narrowed, but a smile graced her lips. "Lady Pickering's ball." She started toward the door with the Danes, then glanced back over her shoulder. "I shall save you the supper dance."

He knew he was beaming like a idiot, but couldn't stop himself. "I'll see you there."

After the door closed behind her, he mounted his horse. Lord he was a fool. So much for his vow not to engage her affections. He knew the only way he'd be able to stay away from her was to leave Town, and that he could not do. He must still help his cousin, and recover his property from that Petrie woman. Still, this evening was a very long time to wait. Perhaps he could take her for a ride during the Grand Strut, if he had a suitable carriage. He'd have to ask Barnes.

When Gideon returned to his town house, a letter lay on the desk in his study. Recognizing his mother's handwriting, he moved around to his chair and tore it open, praying that it was not bad news.

My dearest Gideon,

I regret that I was unable to speak to you about your father when you were here. However, I have come to realize that you must be told the cause of his debauchery. Several months after you left for the colonies, he began forgetting simple things. I did not think much of it. He was past seventy years, and he had the staff to help him find what he misplaced or had forgotten.

Unfortunately, he quickly worsened. By the time you had been away for a year, he no longer recognized me, or indeed, anyone who had not been in the household since before we married.

When I heard he had taken up with a woman, it broke my heart. Yet, as he had no memory of me, I resigned myself to be happy for him. If I'd had any idea how he was reducing the estate, I believe that I would have written to you to come home.

You might think that I should have taken legal action, and had a guardian appointed. However, I could never have brought myself to do anything of the sort. To me, he will always be the strong, capable man I married. I could not have borne seeing Rothwell reduced to the status of an incompetent.

Forgive me. It appears that both your parents have not done as they should and left you to repair the damage.

Please be assured that I shall take any measures

I am able to reduce my spending and that of the household. Also, you should not be concerned for me. My settlement agreements gave me title to The Roses, a small estate about an hour's ride from Rothwell. Your sisters' dowries are held in a trust by my brother.

With much love,
Mama

Gideon let the letter fall from his fingers and leaned back in his chair. Dementia. St. Eth had been correct. Now that Gideon was faced with the truth, it could only have been that and a very bad case of it as well. No wonder his mother had been unable to discuss it. St. Eth was right about the gambling. No gentleman worth the title would gamble with either an infant or an incompetent. Therefore, no one could blame Gideon for refusing to pay any of his father's gambling debts. If the duke's illness had been that clear to one man, it should have been clear to all who knew him.

He scrubbed his hand over his face. Damn and blast. His mother was correct as well: He was not convinced he could have robbed Father of what dignity he had left. Part of Gideon liked to think he could have curbed some of the worst of his parent's behavior. Yet the duke probably would not have known who he was. No matter how much it would have hurt him to do it, he would have had his father declared incompetent. It would have been his duty. Still, that was water under the bridge. All the wishing and second-guessing in the world would not enable him to travel back to the past.

A decanter of brandy stood on the sideboard, as it had all Gideon's life. He badly wanted a glass. Just for a few hours, he would like to drink enough to forget. Instead, he rang for tea. There was a great deal to accomplish today, and as much as he wished otherwise, brandy would not help.

Reaching for a piece of pressed paper from the stack on his desk, he picked up his pen, dipped it into the ink, and wrote a letter to Worthington's man of business asking the man to attend Gideon at his earliest convenience.

A knock sounded on the door. Fredericks entered. "Your Grace, I understand you requested tea, but have you broken your fast yet?"

At that timely moment, Gideon's stomach grumbled. "Apparently, I have not." No doubt his cook had the sideboard filled from end to end. "I shall be there directly." He picked up the letter. "Have this sent by messenger."

His butler bowed. "Yes, Your Grace."

"And ask Allerton to attend me. I shall be in to eat after I have spoken with him."

"As you wish, Your Grace."

Several moments later, Gideon's secretary knocked and entered the room. "Your Grace?"

"I received a letter from Her Grace, informing me that the duke suffered from dementia." The man started to speak, but he raised his hand. "I do not blame you or anyone on my staff for failing to tell me. It was not your place. I know you did the best you could to protect him." He grinned. "That much was clear from the mountain of unpaid bills you gave me, and your suggestion that I take the list with me to the jeweler's and pawnbroker's."

Allerton nodded.

"I require another list arranged by street of the shops dunning me. I plan to visit them today."

After a moment, Allerton cleared his throat. "If I may make a suggestion, Your Grace. A letter from your solicitor might be more effective than a visit from you."

Well, hell. Allerton was right. For the first time Gideon considered how it would appear if he accosted the shopkeepers. Word of his behavior would spread more quickly than a wildfire.

His secretary's idea was the better one. Not as much fun—he would have to find another way to vent his spleen—but more productive. "You have a point. Please send a message and have Templeton attend me."

"I shall do it immediately."

Gideon rose and made his way to the breakfast room. He'd need sustenance before dealing with the problems that money-grabbing whore had helped to cause.

Chapter Eight

Less than an hour after Louisa had returned from her ride, she dipped a piece of terry cloth into a bowl of water chilled with ice and placed it on her sister Theo's forehead. Charlotte was performing the same task for her youngest sister, Mary, while Grace attended to Philip.

It had broken Louisa's heart when she first saw her brother and sisters. Normally, they were bursting with robust health, and now they seemed so small and fragile. Once she'd heard Theo call out to her, Louisa had forsaken the rest of her breakfast to attend her sister. Fortunately, having nursed her other two sisters when they had come down with the measles, she knew what she was doing. The little ones were blue-deviled now, but as long as their temperatures could be kept down, they would soon be back to themselves.

The older family members had all taken turns with the invalids. Matt had a special way with them that made the children feel better, even when they'd been at their worst. And Charlie, the oldest boy and Earl of Stanwood, who was at Eton, had written every day since he'd been informed of the illness. His letters were always filled with witty, funny anecdotes, and memories of when he and Charlotte had suffered from the measles.

"I don't like being ill," Theo said in a voice that just escaped whiny.

"Charlie said this part doesn't last long," five-year-old Mary replied, glancing at her brother. "Isn't that right, Philip?"

"Yes, then there are ices. Is that true, Grace?" Philip added.

"Absolutely true, sweetheart. It won't be long now if you remain in bed and get the rest you need to recover."

Their fevers had broken last night, but the three children were wan and miserable. Bathing them in cool water helped a bit. Later today, after Grace was sure they were truly on the mend, they would have baths. Fevers, she had explained, were dangerous and must be treated with caution. Her mother had died of one, leaving her to take care of her brothers and sisters just before her twenty-first birthday.

Louisa slipped her arm under Theo's back and fluffed the pillow, before handing her a bowl of gruel. "Try to eat something. Remember, no ices until you can eat on your own."

"I do not understand the reason for that," Theo pouted. "I want ices now."

"They melt so quickly, think what a mess there would be if you had to be fed the ice."

"I suppose so." She took the spoon and ate several bites. "This is better than our old cook's gruel."

Thank heaven for small favors. "That's a good girl." Louisa smiled. "You'll have ices in no time."

Several minutes later, the invalids were asleep, and the nursery maids returned.

"I am going to the music room," Charlotte whispered so as not to wake the children.

The piano was her main solace when she was tired or upset. Louisa hugged her. "I must speak with Grace."

"Rothwell?" Charlotte asked.

Louisa nodded. "Yes. I need advice."

Her sister-in-law must have heard, as she whispered, "I am sorry we were not able to have our discussion earlier. However, we have some time now. Matt is busy, and the children will not need us for a while longer."

Once Louisa and Grace reached her study, she called for tea, which arrived shortly thereafter. "How may I help you?"

Louisa could not keep her brows from furrowing as she stirred sugar and milk into her tea. "I think I may be falling in love, but I am concerned it is too soon."

"Rothwell?" Grace asked as she selected a piece of a sandwich.

"Yes. He is so handsome and charming, but more than that, I have a reaction to him I have never had with any other gentleman."

"Let me guess." She met Louisa's eyes and grinned. "When he kisses your fingers, you can feel it up your arm. When the palm of his hand is on your waist for a waltz, it makes you want to draw closer to him." Raising a brow, she asked, "Shall I continue?"

Heat flooded Louisa's cheeks and neck, and she had the strange desire to fiddle with something. "No, please do not. That is exactly what I mean, but how did you . . ." Grace raised her other brow, giving Louisa a quizzical look. "Oh! How stupid of me. You must have experienced the same with Matt."

"I did and still do. It is my fervent wish that my feelings only become deeper over time."

Louisa had not been quite out yet when Matt and Grace met. In fact, she did not know when they'd met or where, but once the family had arrived in Town, she remembered that Matt had been searching for Grace. Their engagement was not long at all. Barely three weeks. "What happens next?"

"Attraction is only the beginning. For two people to fall in love, it will depend upon how easily they can fully trust each other."

Louisa almost choked on her tea. "Trust?"

"One must be able to open one's heart to the other. The only way to do that is to trust." Grace set her cup down. "If Matt had not convinced me he could be trusted with the children, I could never have married him. Fortunately"—a light blush rose in her cheeks—"he was extremely persuasive."

Louisa barely heard anything after "open one's heart." For some reason her mind had come to a sudden halt. Although Mama would never admit to it, she had trusted Louisa's father and had been miserable. Not that Papa had been unkind precisely. He simply had never allowed her mother into his heart, or his life for that matter. Louisa could understand why Grace found it easy to trust Matt, but other men were a different matter. It was important to Louisa that her husband treat her as a partner as well as a wife. Rothwell appeared to appreciate her intelligence and abilities, but what would he be like after marriage? From the little she had heard, many people showed a different face when courting. Could she trust him as Grace trusted Matt? Louisa wanted to trust Gideon. But how would she know? Perhaps there was a sign she should look for that would tell her. Absent that, she would just need to spend more time with him. Matt did not expect her to marry this Season. Ergo, she could take all the time she wished. But was that what she wanted?

Unable to find the patience to wait for Templeton to come to him, Gideon headed toward Doctors' Common where his solicitor's office was located. Old Templeton would no doubt craft a politely worded statement to the effect that he would have happily waited on Gideon at Rothwell House, but a sense of urgency drove him out the door to the lawyer's office.

He must discover how to deal with Mrs. Petrie's forgery and find out if the house that woman was living in belonged to him. Aside from that, the day was slipping away.

After his stable master had assured Gideon he could have the curricle in prime twig, he had sent a message to Worthington House asking if Lady Louisa would do him the honor of riding with him in the Park this afternoon. Her acceptance was returned several minutes later.

After this morning, Gideon was determined to ensure that everything he did with regard to Lady Louisa was completely proper, particularly since he wanted her to wait for him to be in a position to marry.

Taking the steps two by two, he knocked on the door of Templeton and Templeton. A clerk opened the door, and Gideon handed the young man his card. "I wish to see Mr. Templeton immediately."

"Right away, Your Grace." He motioned to a large room off to the side, with long windows, a massive table, and a fireplace that had been lit. "If you will have a seat, I shall inform Mr. Templeton you are here. Would you like tea or wine?"

"Tea, please."

A few minutes later, a man not much older than Gideon arrived followed by the clerk with a tea tray and a plate of biscuits.

"Your Grace." The man bowed. "I am Mr. John Templeton, the late Mr. Joseph Templeton's son. Allow me to express my condolences on the death of your father." Before Gideon could speak, Templeton continued, "Let me assure you that I, as was my father, am completely conversant with all of the Rothwell holdings. I was about to respond to your request for me to attend you. However, I take it that the matter about which you have come is urgent."

"It is." Gideon poured a cup of tea, adding milk and sugar. "I hope you are able to tell me whether or not a town house on Brick Street is part of my holdings."

"It is, Your Grace. The purchase was made just two years ago. I am pleased to be able to inform you that it was due to my father's long acquaintance with the previous duke that the title to the property is in your name."

Gideon thought he had either misunderstood or Templeton misspoke. "Don't you mean the dukedom's?"

"No, Your Grace. Your name. My father was well aware that the duke, your father, was not himself. That he was, in fact, acting much as he had before he met and married your mother. There was very little Father could do to curb His Grace's excess, but he was able to, by way of a bit of legal beguilement, have the house placed in your name. Since the property was not entailed, it could have been at risk if your father had ceased to pay his legal debts."

Gideon turned over what the lawyer had said as he drained the teacup. "I owe your father my thanks, and you condolences on his death."

"Thank you, Your Grace." Templeton stepped into the other room for a moment, returned, and slid a folder in front of Gideon. "You will note that there is no rent on the Brick Street house nor is there a lease. That was another item we were able to put off."

"How does that help me?" Particularly if he was not receiving any funds for the property.

"The benefit to you is that the woman is staying at the house as a guest. One that can be made to leave on a moment's notice if necessary."

It was the middle of May. With the amount of money

Mrs. Petrie had stolen she should be able to find other arrangements in short order. "I want her out by the end of the month."

Templeton inclined his head. "I shall gladly take care of that for you."

"There is one more thing. Yesterday I discovered that she forged my father's signature on at least one document giving her a carte blanche at Rundell and Bridge's. Based on the number of bills cluttering my secretary's desk, I assume she forged others as well."

"Do you wish to bring a criminal suit against her for forgery? I assume you are aware that the punishment is hanging."

At this point in time, Gideon would happily see the whore hang, but there might be a better way. "Perhaps we can convince her to leave the country."

"I am sure she will appreciate your generosity. I advise that you allow her to remain in the house for a few weeks longer. We will wish to know where she is residing until matters with the woman are resolved."

"Very well." As much as Gideon wanted her out, the solicitor had a point. If only Hitchens had been as assiduous in protecting the dukedom instead of allowing his father to rape the accounts.

"Is there anything else, Your Grace?"

Gideon nodded sharply. "I am in the process of changing my man of business. Please contact Mr. Hitchens and have him send you the files in his possession. I desire a list of all my unentailed property." While he was here he could also set his mind at ease about his family. "I also wish to ensure that my mother's portion is intact as well as my sisters' dowries."

"With pleasure, Your Grace. I am positive we have an inventory here. However, I am sure you would like to see Mr. Hitchens's records in any event."

"I shall have my secretary send you the names of the businesses who might have given Mrs. Petrie"—even her name seemed to taint his tongue—"goods due to the forgery." Gideon rose. "Thank you again for yours and your father's assistance."

"It was Father's pleasure and is mine as well to help in any way we are able," Templeton said, escorting Gideon to the door. "I shall send you a note when I have a complete accounting of your holdings."

As he made his way down the stairs and out to the pavement, he considered his next step. Templeton would not waste any time notifying the shops. Barnes was taking the horses to Tattersalls and the carriages to Longacre today. Soon the woman would realize she had been financially cut off. He would like to confront her immediately about the missing jewels and convince her to relocate her business elsewhere, preferably in a faraway colony, but that might not be the best approach. However, he could try to discover more about her, and there was no time like the present.

Gideon walked back toward Mayfair, finding Brick Street with little difficulty. He glanced at the address again before mounting the shallow steps of a modest, well-kept house. Someone was obviously paying for servants. He just hoped it wasn't him. He raised his hand to knock on the door, when a young woman carrying a velvet bag came up from the steps on the side of the house.

"If you're coming to see Mrs. Petrie she's not here," the female said, looking him up and down as if assessing him.

"Indeed. When do you expect her to return?"

"In time to dress for the evening. If you'd like to leave your card, I'll make sure she gets it."

Leaving his card at the home of his father's mistress was the last thing Gideon would do. "Thank you, but I would rather speak to Mrs. Petrie in person."

"Don't want anyone to know you were here?" The young woman shrugged. "We're all discreet at this house. Won't find your name bandied about, but do as you please. She'll be at the theater tonight."

"Indeed, which play?"

"Don't know, but Mr. Kean is playing in it."

"Does she visit the theater often?" Gideon asked, trying to sound only mildly interested.

The maid nodded. "Loves it she does and now that she's got a box she can use for a while, it don't cost her anything."

A box? Could it possibly be *his* box? He glanced at the bag again, wanting to demand the servant tell him what was in it. Still, if she was going either to the jeweler's or the pawnbroker, he would find out soon enough. "Thank you for the information."

Turning, he strolled off walking a short way down the street before peeking back to see which way the maid was going.

Would she go straight to either Rundell and Bridge's or to the pawnbroker? Turning, he kept a fair amount of distance from her and followed.

Unless she had a new protector, Mrs. Petrie was most likely gathering as much cash as she could to see her through until she cozened another old man. Perhaps he should not be so hard on her. After all, she was doing nothing more than any other bit o' muslin would do. She may have taken advantage of his father, but, as far as he could see, the duke had allowed it. Even his mother had not tried to get rid of the woman. Yet it was the fraud that concerned him, and the feeling he couldn't shake that she had known his father wasn't in his right mind.

He must find those jewels. If only he could figure out a way to gain access to her house and search it. The easiest method, of course, would be to make her his mistress, but the idea of touching intimately the woman his father had been involved with sickened him. Not to mention his growing feelings and plans for Lady Louisa Vivers. Yet would he have to go that far? If only he had the money to hire someone. As the ideas swirled around in his mind, he almost missed the maid handing the sack she was carrying to a young man who, by his dress, appeared to be some sort of clerk.

Before the maid turned back toward him, Gideon crossed the street and followed the young man straight through the door of Hoare's bank. Taking hold of the clerk's arm, in his most ducal tone, he said, "*What* is in that sack?"

The young man's eyes rounded as he glanced wildly around. "S—sir, I—I am not—"

"What is the meaning of this?" an older man, probably some sort of manager, demanded.

Without releasing the clerk, Gideon reached into his waistcoat pocket, removed a card, and handed it to the manager. "I am Rothwell, and I believe the bag your clerk is carrying has property belonging to me."

If the manager was surprised, he hid it well. "Your Grace," he responded, bowing. "I am Mr. Clement, one of the senior clerks. I am sorry to inconvenience you, but the package is meant for a client's safe-deposit box. I am not at liberty to reveal the contents to anyone without the proper legal documents."

Bloody hell! Clenching his jaw, Gideon reined in his impatience. "I understand. However, it will save us both a great deal of time and trouble if you can tell me if it is jewelry. I do not care about anything else. If you are unable to assist me, perhaps I should insist on speaking with Mr. Charles Hoare."

Mr. Clement inclined his head. "I believe I can tell you the nature of the contents. Please follow me." He took possession of the sack and led the way to an office off the main hall. Once Gideon entered the room, the clerk closed the door and opened the bag, peering into it. "It is indeed jewelry. Heavy, old-fashioned jewelry."

Of the sort that had been in a family for generations. "Thank you. I shall hold you personally accountable to ensure it does not go missing between now and when I return with the proper documents."

"Yes, Your Grace. Hoare's in no way wishes to be known as aiding wrongdoing."

This, at least, was progress. Along with the other actions he was taking, finding the gems would make him feel as if he had accomplished something toward reestablishing his family's fortune.

He took out his pocket watch and flipped it open. Almost four o'clock. If he hurried, he could tidy up and still arrive at Stanwood House in time to collect Lady Louisa.

Walking out of the bank, he hailed another hackney for the trip home.

Chapter Nine

Promptly at five of the hour, Gideon drew his curricle to a stop in front of Stanwood House. Based on Lady Louisa's previous behavior, he almost expected to see her walking through the door. However, a footman appeared, quickly taking charge of the horses.

After climbing down from the carriage, Gideon mounted the steps leading to the house. The door opened and a wail from somewhere above echoed through the house.

"*Lou . . . is . . . a!*"

It had to be one of the most pitiful sounds Gideon had ever heard.

Halfway down the stairs, Lady Louisa halted, glanced back up toward the landing, then at him. Pulling her plump lower lip between her teeth, she shook her head. "I am sorry. I cannot leave my sister. She has had a relapse."

"There is no need to apologize." He tried not to let his disappointment show. And, in truth, he admired her decision. "I have younger sisters as well. What has she got?"

Louisa pulled a face. "The measles."

"I remember them well." Feeling as if he'd recovered and not being allowed to go out was his most potent memory. "Is there anything I can do to help?"

A strange, almost shrewd look entered her eyes. "I believe there is." Turning her back on him, she lifted her skirts to climb the stairs. "Follow me if you please."

"I want Char . . . lie," the child cried as they neared the schoolroom.

"Charlie?" Gideon asked in a whisper.

"Grace's brother. He is a wonder with the younger children." Her brows came together and rose. "I am hoping you can take his place for a while. Poor Theo is even more miserable than before because Grace moved Mary and Philip to another room."

"And she has no one to keep her company. I will do my best to help her feel better." If he did not succeed, this visit could be a complete disaster. He'd told the truth about having sisters, but he had never nursed them.

When Louisa and Gideon reached Theo, she was thrashing around in bed unwilling to be calmed by the nursery maid.

"Theo, you must stop. That will only make you feel worse." Louisa dipped a piece of terry cloth into the bowl of cool water before laying it on her sister's head. "There now. I have brought you a new friend." Rothwell stepped forward. "Lady Theodora Vivers, may I introduce you to the Duke of Rothwell. Since Charlie can't be here, Rothwell is here in his stead."

He lifted Theo's warm, limp hand, pressing his lips to it. "A pleasure, my lady."

A small smile trembled on the child's lips. "I don't feel good."

"I am quite sure you do not." He lowered his long frame onto a wooden chair next to the bed. "Perhaps you can tell me what Charlie would do to make you feel better?"

"He'd read to me and tell me funny stories."

With a question in his eyes, Rothwell glanced at Louisa.

"He reads the stories like a play, doing all the voices."

"If you will hand me a book, I shall do my poor best."

It was soon to be seen that his poor best was very good indeed. In no time at all, he had Theo laughing. Then he cajoled her into drinking a nourishing broth and eating the restorative pork jelly the housekeeper, Mrs. Penny, insisted would make Theo better.

Finally, she fell into a deep and, Louisa hoped, healing sleep. Rothwell had been wonderful with her sister. He would probably be an excellent father. Definitely more like Matt than her father.

She took Rothwell's hand and led him out of the room. "Thank you. She is in much better spirits than she has been since she fell ill."

"You're welcome." He gave her a sheepish look. "I must confess that I've never been allowed in a sickroom before."

Well, that was surprising. He appeared to know exactly what to do. "I would never have known. You did very well, especially for your first time. It is probably too late for a carriage ride, but would you like to take a stroll in our garden?"

"I'd enjoy that very much." He smiled and she thought her knees might be made of pork jelly for they seemed to be having trouble holding her up.

Thinking of her desire to find out if she could trust him, Louisa wanted him alone for just a few minutes. "If we go down the back stairs, there is less of a chance we'll be seen by my brothers and sisters."

"By all means. I know that you have a large family."

"It is large and, most of the time, a great deal of fun. I've already told you we are all very close."

"What are their ages?"

For a moment Louisa thought that he must have forgotten what she had told him, but thinking back over their conversations, the actual children had never come up.

Simply the numbers of them. "After Charlotte and me, there is Charlie. You probably already know he is the Earl of Stanwood. Augusta is fifteen and turning into a bluestocking. Then Walter. He is fourteen. Alice and Eleanor, the twins, and Madeline are twelve. Theo and Philip are eight, and the youngest, Mary, is five."

Rothwell's eyes rounded. "Worthington took on . . . I mean to say, not only is there a number of children, but to have such a range of ages complicates things a bit."

She couldn't stop her laughter. "It was quite a decision on both my brother's and Grace's parts. She had guardianship of her brothers and sisters. I am not sure if it would have been better or worse if we were all closer in age. And now Grace is increasing, so we'll be adding one more next winter." She opened the door to the garden, inhaling the sweet scent of roses. "How many brothers and sisters do you have?"

"I have two sisters and one brother, he is the youngest. I had another brother who was two years younger than I, but he died when he was a child."

Which was probably the reason he wasn't allowed in a sickroom. "Are you close?"

He didn't answer for a minute. "I suppose we are, considering the age difference that is. After my brother died, my mother did not have any more children for several years." He grinned at her. "Then there were three in a row. Now that I am back, I want to spend more time with them."

She and Rothwell had reached a rose bower near the back of the garden. Louisa turned to face him. As she was considering marrying the man, he ought to know what she wanted. Gazing into his stormy gray eyes, she said, "I enjoy that my family, including my new brothers and sisters, are close. It is what I want for my future family."

"Yes." He almost breathed the word. "I wish for the same."

His head lowered, and she rose up on her toes. Their lips slowly closed the gap between them as his arm slid around her waist—

"There she is." High, girlish voices came from the other side of the arbor.

Louisa blew out a frustrated breath as Gideon dropped his arm. That had been too close. What would have happened if they had been caught kissing, and when had he started thinking of her as Louisa? Was it the almost kiss? In any event, it would not do. He must keep some sort of distance between them.

"I'm sorry," she muttered.

"As am I."

A bare second later, three girls, two of them twins, burst into the space.

"We came to tell you tea is ready," one of the twins said.

"Thank you," *Lady* Louisa—he must remember they could not become too close—replied in a tone of long suffering. "We would not wish to miss tea."

Three pairs of blue eyes stared at him, and Gideon couldn't help but grin at the girls. Two had golden blond hair and summer blue eyes like Lady Worthington and one had the same color hair and eyes as Louisa's. Damn, he did it again. Lady Louisa. The girls were staring at him. They would be a handful when it was time for them to come out. "It would not do to miss tea."

"Not when Cook has made strawberry tarts," the dark-haired girl said.

He glanced at Lady Louisa. There, that was better. "Strawberry tarts are my favorite."

"Madeline, Alice, and Eleanor." At the sound of Louisa's voice—confound it! This wasn't working—the girls ceased moving. "Now then, allow me to introduce the Duke of Rothwell. Your Grace, Lady Madeline Vivers, Lady Alice, and Lady Eleanor Carpenter."

The girls curtseyed prettily as he bowed. "It is a pleasure to meet you."

A cacophony of high voices answered him.

"You are handsome."

"Do you have high-steppers?"

Those questions were from the twins.

"Ah, thank you, and I do have high-steppers."

He wondered what they would say next, when Madeline tugged his hand. "Are you courting Louisa?"

Suddenly the air stilled, and everyone was quiet. One could have heard a leaf drop, and he couldn't think of a single thing to say other than "yes." Not an answer he could give at the moment.

"Madeline," Louisa said, saving him further humiliation. "A lady does not ask questions such as that. If and when His Grace courts me, you will be informed."

The girl turned her back to them, chastened.

"Run along." She made a shooing motion with her hands. "And don't eat all the strawberry tarts before we get there."

The two Carpenter girls each took one of Madeline's hands, pulling her until she trotted off with them.

Once they were gone, Louisa tucked her hand in the crook of his arm. "Do not feel as if you must say anything. The children can be embarrassing at times."

This was the time to explain why he could not speak now, particularly after he had almost kissed her. Yet they were approaching the terrace where another one of her sisters, he could tell by the hair color, appeared to be speaking with one of the Carpenter lads.

Later. Gideon would explain later. Or never. Still, unless

he could somehow gather all the funds he needed, he would be forced to tell her of his circumstances. But not everything. Not about his father's mistress. And not now.

Tea, as he expected, turned out to be a loud and raucous affair. The room seemed to be swarming with children. Madeline had recovered her spirits and was sitting with the twins. Lady Worthington and Worthington had joined them.

Gideon bowed. "My lady, thank you for allowing me to join you."

After casting a glance around the room, Lady Worthington smiled. "Our pleasure. Theo tells me you read almost as well as my brother Charlie. Thank you for your help."

"It was a joy to be able to make her feel a little more the thing," Rothwell assured her ladyship.

Another girl with the signature Vivers hair entered the room, glanced at him, grinned, and took a seat on the sofa next to Louisa.

"Where are Philip and Mary?" Louisa asked.

There are more? He counted those present. Ah, yes, three more. He could not imagine how much more crowded the parlor would seem then. At least the dogs weren't here.

"They wanted to take tea with Theo when she awoke," Lady Worthington responded, handing out cups of tea to the younger children.

A few moments later, Louisa glanced at him. "Milk and sugar?"

"Both, please." When she handed him his cup of tea and a plate, he was happy to see he'd been given a strawberry tart. He lowered his voice so that only she could hear him. "Thank you. I did not know if there would be any left."

She smiled. "They wouldn't dare eat the rest of them until everyone is served."

The conversation sped around him as higher voices rose to make themselves heard. Occasionally, the elder members of the party stepped in with an admonition to be quieter. He had never experienced a tea quite like this before. It was a bit disconcerting to have children present at what was, he supposed, the normal afternoon tea. His brother and sisters had been relegated to the nursery and still were, as far as he knew.

Next to him, Louisa, who had just finished discussing the relevant merits of adding blond lace to one of Lady Charlotte's gowns, glanced at him. "You haven't said a word. I hope we have not offended you in some way."

"Not at all." For a moment, he was at a loss, but his curiosity won out. "Do you always have tea with the children?"

"Yes." Her chin rose slightly, and he knew he was on thin ice. "Unless Grace and Matt are entertaining formally, we have all our meals together. It is a tradition in Grace's family, and I find it far superior than banishing them to the schoolroom."

Somehow, Gideon knew that if he and Louisa were to wed, their children would join them for meals and tea. Of course, that would be many years from now. Possibly never if he was not able to turn his fortunes around. Although the situation was improving. Still, it was a deuced good thing that he'd not kissed her earlier. Duke or no, Worthington would have flayed him alive.

As if called, Worthington stepped over to them. "The noise can be deafening." There was no way on earth Gideon was going to respond to that statement with Louisa right next to him. Fortunately, his friend continued, "I have some information for you. It is in my study."

"You should go with Matt." Louisa rose. "I'll walk with you to the door."

Gideon said adieu to Lady Worthington and the children before following Louisa out of the room.

Placing her hand on his arm, she led him halfway to the hall before stopping. She raised her bright blue eyes to his, and he fought the urge to kiss her. "Thank you again for helping with Theo. You cannot know how much I appreciate it."

She searched his face, and he made himself grin. "I am happy to be thought almost as good as Charlie."

"A grand compliment indeed." Louisa's lush dark pink lips tipped up. "You should know he is quite a favorite with my sister, so that is high praise."

Lifting Louisa's hand, Gideon pressed his lips to her bare fingers and lost his mind. "I can only hope that I might be a favorite with another member of the household."

Roses stained her cheeks, yet she gazed at him instead of lowering her eyes as another young lady might do. "I think you might be." When Worthington entered the hall, her blush deepened. "Good luck, Your Grace. Perhaps we might be able to take our ride tomorrow."

Still mesmerized by her eyes, he nodded. "I would like nothing more. Will you be at Lady Featherton's ball this evening?"

"I shall."

Taking a deep breath, he said, "May I have two waltzes?"

Without hesitation, she responded, "You may."

Gideon wanted to crow. He had never seen Louisa dance with a gentleman more than once. "Until this evening."

"Until then." She gave him a quick smile before striding back down the corridor.

It wasn't until he was on the steps to Worthington House that Gideon realized she had wished him luck. Did Louisa know about his situation? He couldn't believe her brother would have told her. Yet the only other possibility was that his situation had become known in the *ton*. Something he did not want to happen. Then again, by declaring in a public place he would not honor his father's gambling debts, he might have brought it upon himself. *Devil take it!* Nothing was going as planned. Not only that, he still didn't know what his cousin wanted.

Chapter Ten

Louisa was halfway up the stairs when Charlotte caught up with her. "Are you putting Rothwell through his paces?"

"Rothwell?"

"I cannot imagine I would be referring to anyone else."

At first the idea startled Louisa. Then again, perhaps she was testing him. After being thankful he was able to help calm her sister, her first thought was that Rothwell was not like her father. "I do not know."

Charlotte shrugged. "No one would blame you if you were." She climbed the rest of the stairs. "Marriage is for life. Do you not remember Grace and Matt fluctuating between misery and alt?"

"And Dotty vacillating between finding Merton a bride and wanting him for herself."

Charlotte gave one of her light chuckles. "Or your mother and Richard."

Mama had almost not married the love of her life because he had forgotten which year she came out. By the time he had returned from his biological expedition, she was married to Louisa's father. "They all seem happy now."

"They do, but my point is that one cannot be too careful."

Charlotte paused for a moment. "There is nothing wrong with . . . I don't know . . . putting him to the test. In a way, Dotty did that when she kept asking Merton to take in strays."

"But that was only because she had made a promise to her father," Louisa objected.

"True enough. She did not do it on purpose. Yet when she began to consider Merton, she remembered those kindnesses."

Charlotte and Louisa had reached their parlor and taken seats on the sofa.

Knitting her brow, Louisa asked, "What was Grace's test?"

"All of us." Charlotte laughed. "Fortunately, Matt was more than willing to begin taking over our care."

"And, once Worthington House is completed, Richard has agreed to lease Stanwood House during the Season."

"There you have it," Charlotte said, beaming triumphantly. "All you have to do is look inside yourself, figure out what you want most in a husband and marriage, then test Rothwell to see if he can give it to you."

That did make a great deal of sense. Yet how did one make a test for trust? Or perhaps trust was a combination of little things, such as how much he liked children, or if he believed in a partnership type of marriage such as Matt and Grace had. Surely that would come out in conversation. Though how did one discuss marriage when one was not betrothed? And there was love to consider as well. "How do you think they knew they were in love?"

Charlotte had picked up her embroidery hoop, laying out different colored silk threads over the design. "I do not know, but my mother once told me she knew by Papa's kiss."

"Matt would confine me to Worthington Place if he discovered I was kissing a gentleman before I was engaged."

"There is that," Charlotte said, selecting a thread. "On the other hand, gentlemen want to kiss the lady they love."

Louisa and Rothwell had almost kissed this afternoon. Did that mean he was falling in love with her? And was she falling in love if she wanted him to kiss her?

Gideon entered Worthington's study and was motioned to one of two leather chairs near the fireplace.

"Have a seat."

After Gideon had been offered and refused a glass of wine, Worthington poured a glass for himself, taking the chair opposite Gideon. "I have made inquiries about Mrs. Petrie. It appears that she specializes in older gentlemen. The type who wish to relive their youths."

One of Gideon's hands clenched the wood chair arm. "Those who are losing their minds."

"Not necessarily. Men who feel unappreciated by either their wives or younger women." His friend held his goblet up, seeming to study it for a few moments. "About three years ago Lord Henry Burghley, a bachelor, died, leaving Mrs. Petrie the majority of his estate. Or so *she* claimed."

"Did she have a copy of his will?"

Worthington set his wine down. "She had an original of a will. Unfortunately for her, Burghley was extremely close to one of his nieces who had a copy of another more recent will leaving everything to the niece, just as his family thought he would. It appears he also told a friend, in strictest confidence of course, that his mistress was getting a little greedy, but he had managed to placate her for the time being."

Wishing he'd accepted the glass of wine, Gideon said, "She seems to have changed her tactics, if not her gluttonous nature." He decided not to confide what he had discovered thus far. Although he appreciated Worthington's help, Gideon was now Rothwell and needed to settle the problems himself. "Thank you. I appreciate the information."

"If there is nothing else?" His friend's brow rose along with the question.

"Nothing I can think of at the moment." It was not time to discuss Louisa, assuming there would be a time. He stood. "I had better be going. I still have a great deal to accomplish."

Worthington opened the door. "I take it you plan to attend the Featherton ball this evening."

"Yes. I shall see you there." And Louisa. Mostly Louisa.

A moment later Gideon had collected his hat and gloves from the butler, walked down the stairs, and, having sent his carriage home, turned right out of the square. As he strode toward the Park a voice called out.

"Rothwell."

A pair of showy dark bay horses drew even with him, followed by an extremely fashionable curricle.

"Bentley." Resisting the urge to smile, Gideon raised his quizzing glass, reviving a long-standing joke between him and his cousin. "When are you going to learn to select decent horseflesh?"

"If you really cared," Bentley retorted, "you would have been here to help me, and not off in Canada dressing in bearskins or whatever it is you wore over there."

The carriage came to a stop.

"Harrumph," Gideon scoffed. "While you are here and *obviously* have nothing better to do, I would appreciate a ride to Doctors' Common." He needed to tell Templeton about this latest development. Not waiting for his cousin to answer, Gideon climbed onto the curricle. "You may also tell me what is so urgent I must drop everything and come to Town immediately. As it is, you've left me kicking my heels for two days."

Bentley started the horses, but immediately turned to face Gideon and dropped his ribbons.

"Watch what you're doing!" He grabbed the reins from his cousin's slack fingers.

"Blast. I forgot."

Bentley reached for the ribbons, but Gideon shook his head. "I think I'll keep them until you're finished."

His cousin heaved a sigh worthy of Drury Lane. "I am in love, and I need help convincing her to marry me."

Gideon loved his cousin like a brother, but he had no idea how he could assist in matters of the heart. Then again . . . "Happy to do whatever I can. Who is the lucky woman?"

"Didn't I tell you?" Bentley asked, surprised.

"No," Gideon replied with all the patience he could muster. "I received a letter from you telling me you needed my help, but you failed to give the reason."

"You probably don't know her in any event. She came out just this year."

He raised a brow, hoping to hurry his cousin along.

"Lady Louisa Vivers." Bentley said her name as if she was the sum of all his dreams.

Hell and damnation! Could my luck get any worse?

How the devil was Gideon going to tell one of his closest relatives and best friends that he was not only dancing two waltzes, including the supper dance with Louisa, but was falling in love with her himself? Even if she did not care for Bentley and never would, and no matter how Gideon thought he felt about her, he could not now court her. His cousin would see it as a betrayal of the worst sort. And rightfully so.

By Jove's beard! Perhaps it was a good thing his finances were in a shambles and he was not yet eligible to court her.

And he had almost kissed her this afternoon. Thank the Fates he and Louisa had been interrupted. Worthington would not take kindly to a man kissing his sister and not immediately proposing.

He briefly considered not attending the ball this evening, but he could not simply leave Louisa—no, *Lady* Louisa—without explaining himself. Somehow he would have to tell her about Bentley. Make her understand that he must step aside for his cousin.

Still, after this evening, the best thing he could do was not attend another function where he would see her again. He would concentrate on recouping the money his father had lost and repairing the rest of his holdings. At some point in the future, he might be able to cope with the idea of seeing Lady Louisa married to his cousin. Until then he'd keep his distance.

Rosie Petrie, although she went by Rosemund now—it sounded more genteel, as did the posing as a widow—clapped a double strand of perfectly matched pearls around her neck. Turning her head first to the right and then to the left, she admired the necklace and earbobs. The old duke had been one of her better conquests. Not that Rothwell ever knew that. No, a woman must always make the man think he was the one doing the chasing. She'd found him just in time too. Right after that Burghley incident. Damn the man for crossing her like that. Well, she wouldn't make that mistake again. In the end she had been left with just enough to get by until she could find her next protector.

Luckily, Rothwell was waiting to be plucked. Though she gave good value for money, even if she did say so herself. But after Burghley, she'd been more careful. By the time she had forged the letter giving her carte blanche, he'd been too far gone to notice. With what she had accumulated, she might be set for the rest of her life. She even owned this town house. Maybe she'd go to Paris and let the house out for a year or so. Rosie stared at herself in the mirror. Even at five and thirty, she still had her looks. French gentlemen were said to be passionate. And if she collected a few jewels along the way, she really would never have to worry again. Tomorrow or the next day she would look into ships.

In the looking glass, she saw her maid, Bea, enter the dressing room, the girl's face as white as if she'd seen a ghost. "What is it?"

"I sent Peter around for your town coach as usual, and he just come back. It's not there anymore."

Well, didn't that beat all? Rosie should have expected it. Rothwell's servants hadn't liked her at all. In fact, she suspected it was his valet who convinced him she didn't need a butler. And after she'd gone to all the trouble to find a young, handsome one.

Turning on the padded bench, she pressed her lips together. "Have him go to where it was taken."

"That's just it, ma'am." The maid wrung her hands. "It were sold."

That wasn't possible. The air rushed out of her lungs as if she'd been punched. "Sold?" She almost screamed, but the word came out in a hoarse whisper. "When?"

"From what he told me, the stable master said the new

duke is in Town. He ordered your carriages and horses sold and cancelled the order for your new curricle."

Bloody, bloody hell! The new duke was supposed to be at his estate in mourning. What in blazes was he doing in London? Didn't anyone pay attention to propriety anymore?

Knowing what she did about Rothwell's servants, as soon as the old duke had died, she should have rented a stable and moved her livestock and coaches. But she'd thought they'd be safe for the rest of the Season. Not only that, but she read the society pages in the *Tattler* and there was nothing about the new duke being in Town.

Now she'd have to figure out a way to get her horses and carriage back. She'd also have to find out if Rothwell could legally sell her possessions. Taking a breath, she tried to calm herself. Rosie Petrie had never gone under yet. There was a way to recover her property and she would find it. "Have Peter find me a hackney for tonight."

"Yes, ma'am."

She turned back to the mirror. Her blond hair was free of silver, and her complexion was still good. She could easily pass for a younger woman.

Think, Rosie.

What, if anything, did she know about the new Rothwell? Could he be convinced to pick up where his father had left off? When she was younger, she'd had a father and his son. Her protector had wanted her to teach the young man how to pleasure a woman. Rosie smiled to herself. Those had been some interesting lessons, especially in the beginning when the father remained in the room. After the old man had died, the son simply took over. Until he'd fallen in love and married.

What *was* the *ton* coming to when a gentleman gave up his mistress for his wife? It was all the fault of those romances encouraging love matches. They shouldn't be allowed. Quality ought not to read that rubbish.

Sighing, she picked up her fine silk shawl. At least she would enjoy this evening's play. And she had her house and jewels. Tomorrow was soon enough to make her plans.

Chapter Eleven

Louisa, Charlotte, Matt, and Grace arrived at the Duchess of Stillwell's town house and were immediately shown into a drawing room where the duchess and Miss Blackacre were seated.

"My dear Grace." The duchess rose and embraced Grace. "How beautiful you are." She glanced at Charlotte and Louisa. "You girls are perfectly enchanting. You must be driving Worthington mad with your beaux."

Matt grimaced, but Grace chuckled lightly. "They are indeed. If he had his way, he would pack them up and send them home."

"The only question," Louisa mused, trying not to smile, "is to which home. Worthington Place must be renovated to accommodate our newly enlarged family."

"As you are doing to Worthington House," the duchess commented before turning back to Grace. "I understand from Oriana that you are entertaining a case of the measles as well."

"We are," Grace responded facetiously, "and in fine style as well." She grinned as Matt scowled. "However, despite one of the children having a setback, we hope our unwanted guest will not remain long. Worthington and I must journey to his main estate as soon as possible in order to finalize our renovations. I was in the process of arranging for a chaperone for Louisa and Charlotte when he decided we would remain in Town until the younger children are better. It should only be another week or so."

"Let me know when you will be away," the duchess said, leading Grace to a seat. "I am happy to help."

"Thank you, Aunt Dianna. I truly appreciate your offer."

As Grace and the duchess continued their discussion, Louisa motioned to Charlotte and drew Oriana aside. "Have you filled your dance card?"

"It is practically empty," she moaned. "I shall die of mortification if no one asks me to stand up with him."

"You have no need to worry," Louisa said. There really had not been time for Oriana to meet many eligible gentlemen, but Charlotte and Louisa knew most of them and could easily perform the introductions. "We shall see what we can do. I predict that in no time your card will be full."

A footman arrived with glasses of claret, and soon they were discussing the upcoming entertainments. As soon as the servant left, Louisa slid a quick look at Charlotte, who nodded. It was time to put their scheme into place, and pray Bentley and Oriana would make a match of it.

"There is a gentleman we would like you to meet," Charlotte said to Oriana. "He is extremely nice."

"I think you will like him," Louisa added. "But if you do not, please don't feel as if you must spend time with him because of us."

Oriana canted her head. "Are you matchmaking already?"

"Perhaps a little," Charlotte admitted. "He is Lord Bentley. His father is the Duke of Covington."

"And you did say you wished to marry." Louisa bit down on her bottom lip waiting for her friend to respond.

"Very well." Oriana glanced from Louisa to Charlotte. "I shall look forward to meeting him."

That had been easy, Louisa thought. Hopefully, not too easy. That usually meant the scheme would fail.

Two hours later, their party entered Lady Featherton's ballroom. Mr. Featherton, the lady's eldest son, immediately placed his name on Oriana's dance card.

Following Grace and the duchess, Louisa scanned the room for any sign of the Duke of Rothwell. Not that he had said when he would be here. In fact, now that she thought of it, he had not arrived early last evening. Yet tonight, he had asked for two waltzes.

She started to worry her lip, then stopped as certainty filled her. He would be there for the first waltz if not before. He had been proving himself to be quite dependable, and kind. He had done such a good job with Theo earlier. Still, Louisa wished he would come soon.

"You're scowling." Charlotte nudged Louisa in her arm.

"I am not."

"You are." Charlotte smiled as she greeted a friend and Louisa did the same. "It is the same look you get when something is not going your way. Miss Tully," Charlotte said to the lady who had just joined them. "I would like to introduce you to Miss Blackacre. Miss Blackacre, our friend, Miss Tully. Miss Blackacre has recently come out of mourning. Her grandmother, the Duchess of Stillwell, is sponsoring her." She turned to Oriana. "This is Miss Tully's first Season as well."

Out of the corner of her eye, Louisa saw Lord Bentley approaching. There was nothing like the present to put her plan into place. Touching Charlotte's arm, Louisa whispered, "Bentley has come. Stay with Oriana and make sure he asks her to dance. I am going to play least in sight."

Louisa made her way over to Grace, who was standing nearby. "Will you come with me to the retiring room?"

"Would Charlotte not—"

"Charlotte is introducing Oriana to our friends," Louisa interrupted, watching Bentley's process toward her group.

"Yes, of course." Grace excused herself from the duchess. Once they were in the corridor, she asked, "You are avoiding poor Lord Bentley."

Louisa's eyes flew open. "How did you know?"

"I saw him enter." Her sister-in-law took her arm, strolling to the other side of the room from Bentley. "What is it you are trying to do?"

"He is very nice, and I do not wish to hurt his feelings, but I cannot feel for him as he wants me to."

"I must say, it was clear from the first night that he was not up to your weight. If you had not seen it, I would have attempted to discourage the match. And now there is Rothwell."

"Yes, now there is Rothwell." Grimacing, she glanced at Grace. "Although, I came up with the plan before I met him. Bentley needs a lady who is more patient than I am. I think Oriana might be exactly perfect for him."

Grace laughed. "You are hoping to rid yourself of him by introducing him to another woman?"

"It is the kindest thing I can do." She glanced out over the ballroom to see Bentley being introduced to her friend. "And it might work."

"Hmm." Grace gazed in the direction Louisa had looked. "I wish you luck, but you would be well advised to have another idea in mind if this one doesn't bear fruit."

Her sister-in-law was right, of course. Yet for the life of her, Louisa could not think of another scheme. If only Bentley and Oriana would fall in love at first sight. *That* would settle everything. "In that event, my only other option is perfect honesty. I have already tried hinting to him we would not suit."

"Many men have a difficult time understanding subtleties."

Most likely because they always think they are in the right. Louisa sighed. "Life would be so much simpler if they would just listen to reason."

A slow smile formed on Grace's lips. "They are not *always* wrong."

She must be thinking of when Matt kept after her until she was convinced he loved her and her brothers and sisters. But that was different. Anyone could see from the start how much in love they were and how wonderful they'd be together. Louisa wondered if she and Rothwell looked at each other like that.

In the meantime, she must discover more about the Duke of Rothwell. Such as if they were falling in love, and if she could trust him. She had assumed he was in Town for the Season, but what if he was not?

During their waltzes and supper would be the only opportunities they would have to actually talk for a period of time, assuming no one interrupted them.

When she and Grace reentered the ballroom, Bentley was conversing with Charlotte and Oriana. A group of other unmarried ladies and gentlemen were starting to gather next to her sister. She watched as Oriana smiled at a remark Bentley made. "I think it is going well."

Grace gave one of her *that is wishful thinking* looks. "They just met, and you cannot ignore him all night." Drawing her brows together, she asked, "Do you have any open dances on your card?"

Louisa nodded. "A country dance."

They reached Matt as he was conversing with one of

his friends. Grace smiled and held out her hand. "Lord Huntley, good evening. I did not expect to see you here."

Ah, one of Matt's bachelor-and-not-looking-to-marry friends.

The Earl of Huntley flushed slightly as he took Grace's hand and bowed over it. "My lady, always a pleasure. Lady Featherton is one of my mother's dearest friends and a connection of some sort. I am here to do the pretty."

"Excellent." Grace gave him a rare wicked grin. "You may stand up with Lady Louisa for a country dance."

Well, that was neatly done, Louisa thought.

"Naturally, I would be delighted." He turned to her. "My lady, may I have the honor of a country dance?"

Stifling an urge to giggle, she inclined her head. "You may, my lord."

He wrote his name on her dance card, then sauntered off toward the card room.

"I hope he doesn't forget."

"He wouldn't dare," Matt pronounced. "What was that all about?"

Grace tucked her arm in his. "It is time for Louisa to let Lord Bentley know that she is not interested in him. His infatuation has gone on for weeks now, and it must come to an end."

"Poor fellow," Matt said with feeling. "But I agree. If you don't wish him to court you, it's better not to leave him dangling. There are times when ruthlessness is the only option. Men frequently have trouble giving up the hunt." He tugged Grace closer to him. "Have I ever told you how grateful I am that our courtship was mercifully short?"

She leaned on him so slightly it was hardly noticeable, but the act spoke volumes to Louisa about how deeply in love they were.

"No, but I am glad it was short as well."

Feeling as if she was intruding, Louisa excused herself. "I shall join Charlotte and Oriana now." Louisa looked once more at her brother and sister-in-law. They were proof that one need not know another for a long time before falling in love.

Love was what she wanted for herself and Rothwell. It was what she wanted for Bentley as well, just not with her. She sent a prayer to the Deity that her matchmaking would be successful.

Bentley was in conversation with Oriana when Louisa arrived at their circle. Charlotte shifted slightly so that Louisa could slip in between two other friends instead of next to Bentley.

She knew she was on the right course, but guilt still gnawed at her when, upon seeing her, his face lit and he bowed. He really was a very nice young man. "Lady Louisa. Is there a chance you have left a set open for me?"

She began to assume a soulful demeanor, then stopped. If he thought she was upset that he had not asked for a dance earlier, he would do so for the next entertainment. Thus defeating her purpose.

This was going to be harder than she'd thought. "I do not. Lord Huntley took my last set. However, Miss Blackacre is newly arrived in Town and her card is open."

Bentley grinned at Oriana. "So Lady Charlotte informed me. We are already engaged for a set."

"Excellent." Just as Louisa was about to ask Elizabeth Tully if she would care to stroll with her a buzz rose from the crowded room, and Louisa glanced up.

Rothwell was here. At last.

As he headed toward her, Bentley said to no one in particular, "My favorite cousin has arrived. I do not believe you know him. He has been in the wilds of Canada for a few years and returned not long ago and is a great gun. . . ."

Cousin? Canada? Louisa's heart stopped beating. She glanced from Bentley to Rothwell and back again. There was a resemblance, yet not in their coloring. Where Bentley was fair, had light blond hair with an almost boyish appearance, Rothwell seemed darker. From his darker blond hair to his complexion, which was brown as a nut. The strong planes of his face showed strength and determination. Bentley's eyes were an innocent, pale blue, compared to Rothwell's molten silver that hinted at his experiences.

He met her gaze before turning his attention to his cousin, the corners of his well-defined lips dipped down. Louisa had never seen his visage so grim.

Something had happened between this afternoon and now, but what?

When he reached their small group, he stood next to his cousin and inclined his head. "Good evening. I trust I am not too late."

From Bentley's ready smile, it was clear that the men were close. In fact, he looked at the duke as if Rothwell was his savior.

"Not at all. Welcome. I am glad to see you." Bentley glanced at the ladies present. "Lady Louisa Vivers, Lady Charlotte Carpenter, Miss Tully, and Miss Blackacre, I would like to introduce you to my cousin, the Duke of Rothwell."

Charlotte glanced at Louisa as their friends curtseyed. "Your Grace, Miss Blackacre is a cousin of mine newly come to Town." She turned her smile onto Bentley. "My lord, Lady Louisa and I have already had the pleasure of meeting His Grace. He is a friend of Worthington's."

"Oh!" Bentley said. His mouth dropped open. "I did not know. But I suppose that makes sense. They would be around the same age. Did you attend school with him, Rothwell?"

Rothwell, who had left his cousin's side to greet the others, stopped his peregrinations. "Eton and Oxford."

"Did you see him at the ball last night?" Bentley asked.

"The one you told me to attend?" One of Rothwell's brows lifted, and for a moment, it appeared he might continue, but did not.

"Deuced sorry about that." Bentley looked almost like a child who'd been caught doing something he should not have been. "I meant to be there. Then Roughy, you remember him, don't you?" He waited for Rothwell to nod. "He invited me to dinner with his parents, and I lost track of time."

"Ah, yes. I can see how that could happen." Rothwell had almost reached Louisa. "You need not fear. I was well entertained." Facing her, he bowed and, as she had expected, took her fingers in his large hand. "A pleasure to see you again, my lady."

"You as well, Your Grace." Their gazes met, and the moment stretched. As if they were the only two people in the ballroom. His hand tightened on hers, and myriad emotions appeared to pass through his eyes.

Resignation and sadness.

Something was terribly amiss. Yet what could have occurred between the time he had left her this afternoon and now? There was only one way to find out.

She kept her voice low, for his ears only. "What is wrong?"

His throat moved as if he had trouble swallowing. "There is something I must tell you."

Louisa couldn't imagine what it could be, but her partner for the set was bearing down on them. "Perhaps during our dance."

"We must be alone."

"My lady." Lord Huntley had come to claim his dance.

"My lord." She placed her hand on his arm, allowing him to lead her away.

All the time wishing she did not have to leave Rothwell.

Chapter Twelve

Gideon had to drag his eyes away from Louisa as she strolled away with her dance partner.

Damn Bentley's teeth. Gideon had to tell her he could not see her again.

He almost groaned. He could not tell her what he must on a dance floor. And how could he stand up with her with his cousin watching? Still, he could not fail her. If only he hadn't come to Town. If only Bentley had simply told him at the beginning what he wanted. His heart felt as if it was being torn in two.

"Whatever is bothering you, it will be all right," she had said, squeezing his fingers reassuringly before turning to take the other gentleman's arm.

If only Louisa knew how wrong she was.

He snatched a glass of champagne from a tray one of the numerous footmen carried around. Gideon had spent the hours since meeting his cousin trying to find the words to tell Louisa he could not take her for a carriage ride on the morrow or any other day. His task should not be so difficult. They'd not known each other that long.

Only a few days. A few glorious days.

His eyes strayed to the dance floor, where they immediately sought out Louisa. She skipped back with the movement of the dance, smiling as she joined hands with one of the other men in their square. Her gaze seemed to meet his, and she smiled. Before he could stop himself, Gideon returned her smile. A moment later her back was to him, and his cousin came into view.

Even if he had been free to court Louisa, he could never hurt Bentley. He deserved and needed a lady who had the intelligence and strength to help him manage when he came into his father's title and responsibilities. God knew he couldn't do it on his own.

Forcing himself to look away, he found a matron he remembered from before, the mother of four girls, two of them out, staring at him. He inclined his head and she nodded encouragingly. Apparently, his near poverty either wasn't well known or it didn't matter to some.

Louisa came into view again. She had so much vitality. So much joy. The way she cared for her younger sister had surprised him. Not many young ladies would forgo the opportunity to be seen in the Park with a duke, even one with his financial troubles. Not that she knew about them. He felt like a complete fraud. If only he'd remained at his estate. Yet then he would not have discovered the source of his problems.

A few minutes before the first set ended, his hostess, Lady Featherton, led him inexorably to a young lady who was in need of a partner.

"Oh, Your Grace." The girl blushed and stammered through most of the set.

As soon as the dance ended, he returned her to her mother and made his escape to the card room with the intention of waiting for the first waltz to commence. Never having acquired the taste for gambling, he leaned against a convenient wall as far distant from the tables as possible.

"Your Grace?"

Gideon glanced down to see Lord Manning, one of his father's cronies.

"Sir." Gideon straightened.

"I wish to have a word with you concerning a rumor I heard."

He had known his lordship most of his life and greatly respected the man. If Manning felt strongly enough about something, it behooved Gideon to listen. "Please, continue."

"Not long before your father died, I came across him at the theater." Looking away, Manning paused. Gideon waited, and several moments later the older man continued, "He looked right through me. At first I thought he'd given me the cut direct, then I realized he had not recognized me. I know you have been away, and I thought I should mention the possibility that he was not quite himself."

Gideon breathed a sigh of relief. In fact, he could have danced a jig. Not that his father had been ill, but that more than one of his friends had recognized there was a problem. "My lord, I recently discovered that my father suffered from dementia." He hated saying it. Hated that his father had hurt so many family and friends. If only he'd been here. Despite any doubts he might have had after reading his mother's letter, he would have had his father declared incompetent. It would have been the only way to save the dukedom.

"One of my uncles on my mother's side suffered from the same illness." Manning nodded thoughtfully. "Is that the reason you have refused to pay his gaming debts?"

"It is. If he'd been in his . . . right mind, he never would have accrued them."

"I understand your position. However, your decision will not endear you to many and may harm your position in the Lords. I advise you to find a rich wife and marry."

The Lords? One of the places he wanted to have standing was in the Lords. Gideon stiffened. "Lord St. Eth was present when I made the decision. He is of the opinion that I am in the right. Aside from that, the lady would have to be very wealthy indeed. Even then, I would not use her dowry in that manner. I'll see it through."

"Is he?" Manning seemed to study Gideon. "Was this before or after you told Masters you would not honor the chits?"

"Afterward." Gideon was starting to resent the suggestions that he find a rich wife. Come what may, he would find his footing without relying on a woman's money. Abruptly it occurred to him that even though he did not want the world knowing of his father's condition, it would be to his and his family's benefit if others were aware of his father's illness. "St. Eth said that my father's dementia had been clear to him, and no honorable man would gamble with minors or incompetents."

Manning nodded slowly. "If you have no objection, when next the subject arises, that is what I will say as well."

"Thank you." Gideon wanted to cringe, but he'd made the decision, and something had to be done. Failing to honor his father's gambling debts would reflect on his mother, sisters, and brother as well. St. Eth and now Lord Manning were giving Gideon an honorable way of refusing to further reduce the dukedom's cash reserves. "I have no objection."

"Very well, then." The man tapped a finger against his nose. "I shall be discreet, but leave no doubt about the old duke's condition."

Fortunately, the set was ending, and a prelude for a waltz began. "If you will excuse me, I have an appointment."

"Enjoy your set." Manning's lips curved up. "I remember when I could dance the night away."

Gideon wasted no time collecting Louisa and escorting her to the dance floor.

"What did you need to speak with me about?" she asked as they began to move.

Here was not the place. "We should be alone, where no one can overhear us. After the supper dance."

Her forehead wrinkled in thought, and Gideon wanted nothing more than to smooth the pleats out. Yet he would soon cause new lines on her brow. "That won't work. Matt will expect us to join them for supper. After which we will leave."

Naturally, Worthington would never allow his sisters to go off by themselves. "I must speak with you alone."

She drew her plump lower lip between her teeth and, once again, he wanted to kiss her. "In the morning at seven. We may ride in the Park."

As was becoming their habit. If one could call one chance meeting and one arranged meeting a habit. "It will be my pleasure to escort you."

The smile she gave almost blinded him. God she was beautiful.

He took her in his arms and began leading her down the floor. This would be the last time he'd dance with her. The last time he held her, and he did not think he could bear to leave. But for the sake of his cousin, Gideon must. Still, how could he leave her? How could he stand by and watch her marry his cousin?

Heaven help me. I'm falling in love. And Louisa was wrong. *It* wouldn't be all right. *He* would never again be all right. And he had a feeling *she* was not going to be at all happy. The only one who might be was Bentley.

* * *

Oriana noticed that Louisa had joined her brother and sister-in-law, who were conversing with the Duke of Rothwell a short distance away.

Charlotte leaned closer to Oriana. "I think Louisa is finally falling in love."

"Rothwell?" She studied the couple and there did seem to be something between them.

"Yes." Without expounding further, Charlotte spent the next several minutes pointing out various people and making sure Oriana knew who they were. "Over there in the turban with the purple plumes is Lady Bellamny. She scares a great many people, but I like her."

Oriana had heard her mother speak of Lady Bellamny. "My mama said I must always watch myself around her."

"Oh, pooh." Charlotte waved her hand dismissively. "She is a very high stickler, but she never takes one into dislike for no reason."

A footman brought them glasses of lemonade. "It is much hotter here than in the country."

"Only because there are so many more guests," Charlotte said. "After the next set, we shall ask Grace if we can stand by the windows."

"Is she very strict?" Oriana asked. Quite frankly, she had been amazed that Lord Worthington would take on so many children.

"It is Matt more than Grace. He is terrified something will happen to us. Especially after my friend Dotty, now the Marchioness of Merton, slipped out to warn her future husband of a plot against him."

"A plot?" Oriana couldn't stop her eyes from widening. "London appears to be more exciting or dangerous than I had thought."

"Only with Dotty." Charlotte giggled lightly. "I've known

her since we were in leading strings. Things always seem to happen around her." Taking a sip of lemonade, she glanced around. "Lord Bentley is coming to claim his waltz."

Oriana followed the direction of her friend's gaze. Her new cousins were right, she did like him. He was so handsome, and interesting. They had spent a great deal of time between sets conversing with each other. Yet for a while she had not thought he would ask to stand up with her. "Thank you for introducing us."

"He always seems a bit unsure of what to do next, but once you can get him to his point, he is very nice."

"So, it was not that he did not wish to dance with me?"

"Oh, not at all. Please don't think that. He is merely terribly slow getting anything done."

"Ah, yes. I know what you mean." After all, she had been dealing with that type of male all her life. Lord Bentley bowed as she held out her hand and smiled. "Thank you for being so prompt, my lord."

He seemed to preen under the mild accolade. "My pleasure. Lady Louisa"—he stole a glance at the lady—"is forever telling me I am late."

Oh, dear. Oriana hoped he did not fancy himself in love with Louisa. Even on such a short acquaintance, Oriana knew that would not be a good match. Her friend needed a much more commanding presence than Bentley would ever be. Yet, married to the right lady, one who would encourage him, his lordship could come into his own. At least he did not appear to be an academic. They were the worst sort when it came to making up their minds or getting anything accomplished.

"Lady Louisa does not appear to me to be the type to allow any grass to grow under her feet, as the saying goes. I am sure she does not mean to be unkind."

Lord Bentley looked startled. "I did not mean . . . that is, I would never suggest . . ."

Oriana waited patiently until his sentence faded, then smiled as she placed her hand on his arm. "Of course you did not. She is merely a little brusque and impatient."

"Yes, that's it." He beamed at her. "I'm glad you understand."

When they began to dance, she was pleased to discover that he not only led well, but she felt very comfortable in his arms.

Very comfortable indeed. Which may or may not be a good thing.

She relaxed into the steps of the waltz. Lord Bentley's palm rested securely at her waist as he gracefully led her around the room. He was a good-looking man. Although even with age, he would never achieve the lean, sharply cut features of his cousin or Lord Worthington. Lord Bentley's was a softer, a more open visage with sincere blue eyes that had not, apparently, learnt to mask his feelings. She had immediately felt at ease in his presence. As she did now. The only problem was that the dratted man's attention was not on her.

She peeked in the direction of his gaze. Ah, that explained it. He did fancy himself in love with Louisa. Having brothers, Oriana knew enough of men to understand Bentley's fascination. Louisa was indeed beautiful, but her strength of mind would quickly overwhelm the poor man.

Oriana had seen that type of mismatch before, and it would not do. Her friend had most likely recognized the problem, which would explain why, when Lord Bentley was obviously part of Louisa's circle, she had not saved a dance for him.

Oriana wondered if that was also the rationale behind Charlotte's earlier shuffling around, always making a point of ensuring that Oriana and Lord Bentley had stood next to each other and away from Louisa between sets. During those periods, even though his gaze had occasionally been directed at Louisa, Oriana had discovered that she and his lordship had a great deal in common from horses to love of family and the countryside.

She grinned to herself. When she'd agreed to come to Town, she had been sure her grandmother had a match in mind. Apparently, after meeting her, Louisa and Charlotte had the same idea. It was, after all, Oriana's duty and desire to wed. She had given up her position managing her father's property to her brother, and she missed the responsibilities. But having a husband, her own home, and eventually children to manage was what she desired most of life.

The very least she could do was see if her friends had chosen well. "Are you enjoying the ball, my lord?"

Bentley swung his head to her, flushing. "Yes . . . yes, I am."

"You seemed a bit distracted." A gentle admonition. Nothing more than that would be needed, she was sure.

"Forgive me. I had something on my mind, but I should not have ignored you."

Oriana gave him a bright smile. "Think nothing of it. Instead, you may tell me what of London I should see while I'm here."

He seemed a bit at a loss for a moment, then blew out a breath. "Naturally, you must view the Elgin Marbles."

"An inspired suggestion, my lord. I could not bear to leave Town without having seen them." She left her comment hanging, wondering if he would offer to take her. When a few moments passed and he had not committed himself, she murmured, "I only wish I knew someone who was able to escort me to the museum. I fear my grandmother is not up to it." A lie if ever there was one. The only reason Grandmamma wouldn't go was because she had seen too much of the famous marbles.

A few seconds later, Bentley's countenance brightened. "I would be happy to escort you, if you wouldn't mind, that is."

"Thank you so much for offering." Widening her eyes as if she never would have thought of the scheme on her own, Oriana smiled gratefully. "I would be delighted to accept." His expression of happiness was all she could have asked for, and she waited for him to suggest a day and time, but when he did not, she gave him a nudge. "I am free around eleven tomorrow morning."

For a moment he simply stared at her, then his eyes began to twinkle. Did he know what she was doing? "Thank you. I shall call for you then."

The small amount of tension his intent look had caused her leached out. He was not quite as bad as Papa at having to be led to every decision. Lord Bentley merely required a slight guiding hand and a comforting touch when he realized Louisa was not for him. Which Oriana thought might occur in the very near future by the look her friend was giving Rothwell and that he returned. As her mother always said, it was not important to be a gentleman's first love, but his last. Grandmamma, on the other hand, believed compatibility in a husband was to be most desired, and Oriana thought Lord Bentley and she could be most compatible.

Chapter Thirteen

"You are a very graceful dancer, my lord." Miss Blackacre's low gentle voice knocked him out of his thoughts of Lady Louisa.

"Er, thank you." He thought about what he should say next. "As are you."

Of course, it was the only thing to have said, but she gave him another one of those smiles that made his stomach do a flip of sorts.

At first he thought the feeling had been caused by something he'd eaten, but dinner had been ages ago. Then it came to him. She was as light as a feather and very easy to partner. Much easier than Lady Louisa, who would take over the lead whenever he lost his concentration. He gave himself a swift mental kick. He should not be so disloyal to the woman he loved.

Lady Louisa's intelligence and her ability to take charge were what fascinated him and made him love her. She was a goddess to be worshipped.

Whereas Miss Blackacre was soft and comfortable, or appeared to be. Not that Lady Louisa could not be comfortable. In Town she sparkled like a diamond. He was sure once they were married and living at his estate she would not be so high-strung. It had stung that all her dances had already been spoken for before he arrived. Then again, he was certain Rothwell would be espousing all Bentley's good points.

A few years older than him, Rothwell had always been more like an older brother. If anyone could make Lady Louisa fall in love with Bentley it was his cousin.

Her light laughter seemed to float on the air, but Bentley resisted the urge to turn. He had been discourteous enough as it was to Miss Blackacre, letting his thoughts wander. Yet instead of admonishing him to pay attention as almost everyone else did, she had been kind and patient. And lovely. Her black hair shimmered under the candlelight. He liked the way her nose wrinkled and her eyes brightened when she smiled. He must remember to ask if he might escort her to supper.

"Miss Blackacre, I have a question to ask you."

She raised her deep blue eyes to his, yet did not say a word as he marshaled the words together.

"May I—I mean would you allow me to escort you to supper?"

Her lips curved slowly up. "It would be my pleasure, my lord."

"Thank you." He must be getting better at this. Asking a lady to accompany him had never been so easy.

Early the next morning, Louisa strode down the steps of Stanwood House to find Rothwell had already arrived. "Good morning, Your Grace."

He swung down from his gelding, rounded the animal, and lifted her onto Lancelot, her bay. "Good morning, my lady."

Neep, the Carpenter groom, nodded to one of his protégés, who was mounted on a mare in need of exercise.

Yesterday, Grace had gently reminded her that even when being escorted by a gentleman, Louisa should still take a groom with her on early morning rides.

"Shall we be off?" Louisa lightly tapped her horse's side. Rothwell rode by her side while the groom fell in a little behind her and the duke. After a few minutes of discussing the weather, sunny and amazingly dry for a spring day, and her sister Theo, who was now nicely recovering, she asked, "What did you wish to talk to me about?"

Rothwell's jaw ticked, as if he was grinding his teeth. "You know that I came to Town at the behest of my cousin."

Her hands tightened on the reins, and she made a point of loosening her fingers. "So you said. I assume that cousin is Bentley?"

"Yes." Rothwell bit off the word as if it somehow offended him.

A strange chill crept over her neck. "Go on."

"He—he did not explain in the letter precisely what type of help he required. After I arrived he sent me another missive merely stating that he would meet me at Lady Sale's ball. As you most likely heard, he simply did not attend." He blew out a breath before continuing. "Suffice it to say that it was not until yesterday afternoon that I discovered how he wanted me to help him."

When he stopped speaking. Louisa asked, not sure she wanted to know the answer. "How?"

For several moments Rothwell would not look at her. Then his gray eyes caught hers. The pain in them took her breath away. "He wants me to help him woo you."

Woo her! Never, never had she heard anything so ridiculous. How was that even possible except in a book or a play? Her temper rose, and she wanted to swear long and loud. The only problem was that her vocabulary was sadly lacking in that respect.

Leave it to Bentley to ask for help and not tell the person until *something* had already happened.

She took several deep breaths and counted to at least sixty before she had herself under sufficient control to respond calmly. "À la Cyrano."

Rothwell's shoulders were hunched up to his ears. "I am not precisely sure what he thought I could do."

Nor did she. If Bentley were here she'd box his ears. "What do you intend to do?"

"I have some matters to attend to, after which I shall leave Town. In any event, I should be at the abbey with my family." Rothwell had been staring straight ahead; now he turned to her with a bleak look in his beautiful gray eyes. "Louisa, I cannot hurt him."

What had he called her? She had not given him leave to use her name, but he must have been thinking about her as Louisa. And he looked so sad and solemn. Suddenly her anger faded.

Of course he couldn't hurt Bentley's feelings. No one, especially not she, would expect him to. Still, Rothwell needed to know where she stood. "I will never marry Lord Bentley, nor will I ever allow him to court me."

Rothwell's black brows snapped together and his mouth opened.

She held up her hand. "Allow me to finish. I have known for weeks that he and I would not suit. Before you and I even met, I tried hinting him away. Then I formed a scheme. In fact, I have already put my plan in place."

"But Bentley—" A scowl replaced his surprise. "You do not understand."

"*I* understand perfectly well," she fumed, doing her best to keep her rising temper under control. "For some completely incomprehensible reason *you* seem to believe that because your cousin thinks he has fallen in love with me you should clear the field so that I may fall in love with him. Well. It. Won't. Work. Bentley is a lovely man, but he would drive me mad, and eventually, he would be made extremely unhappy."

"If you believe he is so lovely"—Rothwell made a choking sound—"what makes you think you are incompatible? Technically, he is more eligible than I am. He may not have come into his dukedom yet, and I hope he does not for many years. I have a fondness for my uncle, but—"

"He dithers," Louisa snapped, cutting Rothwell off.

He stared at her as if he couldn't believe what she had done. Well, it was probably not every day a duke was interrupted. "What?"

Closing her eyes for a moment, she responded, enunciating each word clearly. "He dithers." Rothwell continued to stare at her. If it would not have upset her horse, Louisa would have thrown her arms in the air. "He cannot make up his mind. His attention wanders. For the love of all that is holy, when we dance I end up leading. He dithers!"

By this time her voice had risen to the point that some might accuse her of shouting.

The stern, unyielding mask that had become Rothwell's face cracked as the corner of one lip tipped up. "Yes, he does rather." The mask dropped back into place. "Nevertheless, I love him dearly, and if he knew that we"—he clenched his hands on his reins so tightly his horse fidgeted—"if anything was happening . . ."

"You mean if he thought you were paying me attentions."

"Yes. He would feel betrayed."

"I agree, but it could happen that his affections will gravitate to another lady." Hopefully in the very near future.

Rather than the relief she thought Rothwell would feel he scowled again. "And just who do you think could take the place of you?" he asked in a low, almost dangerous tone. "There is no lady in London who is as beautiful, or intelligent, or blasted perfect!" She should feel as if she were walking on clouds. He slammed his hand down on the saddle making his horse jib. In the few moments it took him to calm his gelding, Louisa's heart took flight. Then he bellowed, "Who?"

"Miss Blackacre," Louisa responded, keeping her tone calm so as not to upset him more than he already was.

"And who the dev—is Miss Blackacre?"

Louisa rolled her eyes to the leafy sky.

"You met her last evening." She spoke slowly as if she was addressing a recalcitrant child instead of a duke. He could hardly blame her. He was acting more like an infant. But damn, this situation was intolerable. Gideon signaled with his hand for her to keep talking. "She has black hair and blue eyes."

He remembered now. The lady was on the petite side with a ready smile. She had stood next to Bentley most of the evening and danced with him as well. She always seemed . . . calm. "Who are her people?"

Louisa's smile almost rose to the level of a smirk. "One of her grandmothers is the Dowager Duchess of Stillwell. I do not know who the other one is, but Charlotte, who is related to the duchess in some way, said Miss Blackacre's other grandmother is a duchess as well. She is well dowered and used to managing her father's properties. Her father is a scholar and tends to be a bit absentminded. Therefore she is also used to someone who . . ."

"Dithers," Gideon supplied for her, letting out the breath he'd been holding.

For the first time since yesterday afternoon his spirits rose. Gideon was afraid to even hope that Louisa's scheme would work. Even so, it would most likely take some time for his cousin to transfer his affections from Louisa to Miss

Blackacre. "Have you thought about what will happen in the meantime?"

She speared him with a look as level as any man's. "Grace has already advised me not to stand up with Bentley again." So Lady Worthington agreed that Bentley was not a good match for Louisa. A decision Gideon wholeheartedly agreed with, yet for his own selfish reasons. "Naturally, it would help if I was not always present." She pulled her plump lower lip between her teeth, and he wished it was his teeth touching that enticing lip. "I believe my sisters and brother might require more of my attention than I'd previously thought."

She should have been a general. "Thus leaving the field clear for Miss Blackacre."

"Precisely." Leaning over she covered his hand with her much smaller one. "I truly do not wish to see him hurt in any way. He is a good man and will make some lady a wonderful husband. Just not me."

"Do you have any indication that he could develop feelings for her?"

"Indeed. He is escorting her to the British Museum today. She expressed a wish to see the Elgin Marbles, and he offered to accompany her."

That didn't sound at all like Bentley. "He did this on his own?"

"Well." Louisa raised one shoulder in a shrug. "I assume she nudged him along. That is her way. She is not the type of lady who will tell him he is taking her."

Unlike another lady he knew and wanted to know much more intimately. Gideon grinned to himself. "The question is whether he will take it upon himself to squire her around again."

"I believe the idea is that she will buy a guide book, if necessary."

Good God. The schemes of ladies. He always knew matchmaking mamas were trouble, but it had never occurred to him females were born with the ability to plot. "And we will play least in sight?"

"For the time being I think that would be best."

Gideon was being lured in, managed, but he could not bring himself to care. As long as he could stay away from Louisa in public, he could keep his growing feelings for her hidden from his cousin. Then when Bentley was over Louisa—Gideon prayed she was correct in her thinking—he could begin to court her properly.

If he was successful in recouping the money from the jewels and other items his father's mistress had acquired, it would be enough to have funds for living and putting the estates back in order.

The problem now was that he had to deal with the Petrie woman before he courted Louisa. And from what he had learned about her this morning, if she had the slightest clue about his troubles, she would immediately involve herself. That he could not allow. The problems his father had caused were for him to deal with . . . by himself.

Could his life become any more complicated?

Louisa watched Rothwell as he sorted through everything she'd said. As she saw it, their goals were the same. Both of them wanted Bentley to be happy. She just hoped he agreed with her plan. "I had better be getting back. Breakfast will be served soon."

He frowned. "How long have we been gone?"

"Not above an hour, but we break our fast early." She turned her horse. "You should know, we are very unfashionable. The children have lessons, and, as you are aware, Grace wants us to have our meals together. I also wish to look in on Theo."

He fell in beside her. "How has she been doing?"

"Much better, thank you."

"I'm glad to hear it. Please give her my best wishes."

Louisa thought back to the other courtships she had witnessed. Matt had immediately inserted himself into Grace's life. Dotty had made Merton part of her life as well. Would being invited into Louisa's help her budding romance with Rothwell? "You could join us for breakfast." Louisa gave him a sidelong glance. "There is always room for one more."

His lips pressed together as he thought. "Are you sure it would not be a bother?"

"None at all." She shook her head. It would, though, bring him even more to the notice of her family. "That way you can see Theo for yourself."

"I'd like that." He grinned and she thought she'd never seen him so carefree.

"Excellent." Louisa picked up her pace, and he followed suit.

She would soon discover what it was, aside from Bentley, that bothered Rothwell and help him deal with the difficulty. After all, that is what a partnership was about. And if they did marry, she was determined they would be partners.

Chapter Fourteen

Several minutes later, Louisa and Rothwell arrived at Stanwood House. Before she could slide down from her horse, Rothwell lifted her, lowering her slowly down to the pavement.

Goodness! There were those feelings again. This time her tingles traveled from all up and down her body. Grace was right, Louisa did not want that feeling to ever stop.

Taking his hand, she led him into the hall where the sounds of her family gathering for their morning meal could be heard.

Their butler took their hats and gloves.

"Royston, please have another place setting taken to the breakfast room."

"Of course, my lady."

"This way." She led Rothwell down the corridor, wishing she could hold his hand again. Yet, that would prompt even more questions than his mere presence was like to. "Just follow the noise."

As they entered the room, a footman set a chair, plate, and silver at the table. Her brother's brows rose. "Who is that for?"

"Lady Louisa has brought a guest, my lord."

"Has she?" If anything, Matt's brows climbed even higher.

"No comments from any of you," Grace said, catching all their eyes. She glanced up. "Welcome, Your Grace."

Matt stood, holding out a hand, which Rothwell clasped. "Welcome. I'm glad you could join us."

His chair had been placed at the end of the table next to Theo's vacant one. Louisa took the plate and handed one to Rothwell. "Tea or coffee?"

"Tea, please."

By the time Louisa and he had made their selections from the sideboard, a fresh pot of tea and a plate of toast appeared. She motioned Rothwell to the seat next to hers. "Now then," she said, giving the children what she hoped was a calm look. "All of you except for Mary and Philip have already met His Grace. She glanced at her youngest sister. "Lady Mary, may I introduce His Grace the Duke of Rothwell?"

"Yes, you may," Mary responded promptly. "It is very nice to meet you. Why do you call him His Grace?"

"He is a duke. They are addressed differently," Louisa explained.

"Oh," Mary responded, appearing to tuck that piece of information away until she needed it again. "That's good to know."

Next to Louisa, Rothwell's lips curved up. "A pleasure to meet you as well, Lady Mary."

Her sister smiled, revealing a new gap in her teeth. "Mary," Louisa said. "When did you lose your tooth?"

"This morning." She grinned. "Tonight I shall put it under my pillow and tomorrow I'll have *tand-fé*. Isn't that right, Grace?"

"*Tand-fé*?" Louisa looked at her brother, who shook his head. "I've never heard of it before. Our old nurse used to make us bury them."

"Bury them!" all the Carpenters exclaimed as if she'd blasphemed, and the room erupted as everyone had to have their say.

"But what is it?" Louisa raised her voice to be heard over the clamor.

Rothwell cleared his throat. "It is a payment for a baby tooth. An old Norse tradition, if I'm not mistaken."

"You are correct," Grace said. "It has long been a ritual in my family."

"In mine as well," Rothwell responded.

"I think that is rotten luck that our family didn't do it," Madeline pouted. "Theo is the only one who hasn't lost all her baby teeth."

Rothwell chuckled as Matt dragged a palm down his face. "This is what I'll do. Once Grace gives me an accounting of how much the total amount of money is for baby teeth, I shall pay it to you. Is that fair?" The Vivers sisters nodded. "Good, now that that's over, I have business to attend to." Sliding his chair back, he rose. "Rothwell, enjoy your breakfast."

"Louisa," Philip, the youngest brother, piped up. "You forgot me."

"I would never forget you. We just had to finish the discussion about Mary's tooth first."

She glanced at Rothwell. "Your Grace, may I introduce you to my youngest brother, Mr. Philip Carpenter? Philip, the Duke of Rothwell."

Philip came around the table and bowed. "It's nice to meet you, Your Grace."

"Well done," Louisa whispered, and was rewarded by Philip's smile.

"My pleasure, Mr. Carpenter." Rothwell offered his hand, and her brother shook it.

"Grace," Philip said. "I'm finished with breakfast. May I look in on Theo?"

"Yes, you may. Then it's up to the schoolroom with you."

Philip left as fast as his feet could carry him without running.

Louisa called after him, "Tell her we shall be up in a few minutes."

"I don't think I will," came the reply filtered from the corridor. "She'll be more surprised if she doesn't know."

"What he means," Augusta commented, "is that if she doesn't know, she won't nag him to bring you up."

Rothwell nudged Louisa. "Another strong-willed lady, I see."

"I think it's in the blood." She wondered what his family was like. Obviously nothing like hers. Yet did it matter that much? Matt and Grace had managed to blend their families. Surely Louisa and Rothwell could do the same. If they decided they would suit.

Several hours after leaving Louisa's house, and the liveliest breakfast he had ever experienced, Gideon was reading a report from his new man of business.

A light knock sounded on his study door. "Come."

Fredericks entered carrying a card he held between his thumb and forefinger, as if dirt or some sort of filth was on it. That was strange. Normally, his butler delivered anything he had for Gideon on a silver salver. Leaning back in his chair, he waited.

"Your Grace, a *person* calling himself Mr. Minchinhouse has requested to see you. I have placed him in the small parlor."

Mr. Minchinhouse? Gideon had never heard of the man. One thing was certain, though. By his butler's demeanor, Minchinhouse was not a gentleman. "I do not believe I have ever heard of the man. Did my father know him?"

An infinitesimal shudder seemed to affect Fredericks.

Although it was hard to tell as his posture had stiffened to that of a board. "I would be most surprised if the former duke had any dealings with the man."

Not only not a gentleman, but some sort of unsavory character. Then again, Fredericks was extremely high in the instep. "Did he say what he wanted?"

The butler focused on a spot above Gideon's shoulder. "Something to do with Your Grace's late father."

Surely not a merchant seeking collection on a debt. Gideon had made certain all the trade bills were paid or otherwise resolved. Had his father got involved with the cent-per-centers? "Does he look respectable?"

"Indeed, Your Grace," his butler said in a shocked tone. "If not, I would scarcely allow him to set one foot past the threshold of this house."

This was getting him nowhere. What the hell had his father done this time? "Show him in, Fredericks. I'll find out what he wants and send him on his way."

"Yes, Your Grace. Should I bring tea?"

"Based on your description, I doubt he will be here that long." Before Fredericks shut the door, Gideon said, "Have Allerton attend me."

"As you wish, Your Grace."

Gideon's secretary entered through the door leading between his office and the study shortly before his butler ushered in his unexpected guest. Mr. Minchinhouse, a short, stout man, was dressed conservatively in an old-fashioned, dark brown frock jacket and breeches. After peering around the room for a moment, he bowed deeply.

Gideon debated leaving the man standing, but decided he'd get more information using a little honey. "Have a seat, sir." He motioned to one of two leather chairs standing in front of his desk.

"Thank you, Your Grace." The man took the chair on the right. "Such consideration, as my wife would say."

Gideon placed his arms on his desk, crossing one over the other. "How may I help you?"

"What a nice sentiment, and you not knowing me from Adam. But no, no, Your Grace. It is *I* who am here to help *you*." Minchinhouse mopped his brow with a handkerchief before focusing his muddy brown eyes on Gideon. "It's no secret in my world that your father, God rest his soul, left you at low ebb what with his gambling and other spending."

Who or whatever Mr. Minchinhouse was, Gideon could not imagine the man ran one of the gaming hells his father probably frequented. Unable to keep the incredulity from his voice, he asked, "Are you telling me that my father lost money to you?"

"No, no." Minchinhouse appeared shocked. "Don't hold with games of chance myself. I did, however, buy up many of your father's notes of hand."

"I am afraid you are under a misapprehension," Gideon said in a voice as stiff as his shoulders had become. "I have made clear that I will not pay his gambling debts."

Instead of appearing disconcerted, Minchinhouse nodded genially. "But I doubt you'd want to lose the property and house called The Roses."

Quickly, Gideon reviewed the dukedom's holdings in his mind and could remember no estate called The Roses.

A slight cough sounded off to the side of him where Allerton sat. Gideon glanced at his secretary and was handed a piece of paper.

The duchess's dower property.

He tried to keep his countenance from showing the anger and disappointment surging through him; nevertheless, he had a feeling he'd lost some of his color.

"I see," Minchinhouse said, "that you have placed it."

Gideon had to think quickly, but his mind seemed bogged down in one of the East Anglia marshes. First he must buy time. Then he'd contact his solicitor and find out if his father could have legally conveyed the property. The man was supposed to be finding the information in any event. "Were you given the deed?"

"No, but I believe the paper is sufficient to transfer ownership of the estate," Minchinhouse said in an assured tone.

Unfortunately, Gideon had no idea whether the man was right or not. He studied his unwanted guest for a few tense moments before asking, "What is it you want from me?"

"As I said before, I'm here to *help* you, Your Grace. You've probably never heard of me, no reason you should have, come to think of it, though I'm well known in the City. If you inquire, you'll find I'm a wealthy man. I also have a daughter who is being sponsored by Viscountess Bennington." Gideon knew the lady's husband had a reputation for being perpetually in debt. Minchinhouse had probably bought Bennington's markers and offered him a way of paying them by having his wife sponsor Minchinhouse's daughter. Did the man now think he could buy her a husband? Gideon kept his thoughts to himself and let Minchinhouse make his proposition. "I will pay off all your father's debts, give you the paper for the house, and a tidy sum to put your estates back in order if you will marry my daughter, Margaret." Despite Gideon's attempt to school his countenance, the shock must have shown on his face for Minchinhouse hurried on, "No need to get your back up. I know this must be quite unexpected, and I don't want you to answer me now, Your Grace. Take a few days to think on it." Gideon opened his mouth, but Minchinhouse held up a hand. "I can assure you my Maggie is a sweet girl who is used to managing my houses in Town and in the country. She would make you a good duchess."

He placed his hands on the chair arms, heaving himself up. "I'll be back in touch, and if you're agreeable, we'll plan a small dinner for you and my Maggie to meet. I'll just let myself out."

Unable to respond before the man left, Gideon waited until the door clicked shut behind the other man and until he heard the front door close as well before turning to his secretary. "I want Templeton here within the hour."

He would know if it was possible for Gideon's father to have gambled away his mother's dower property. The estate his mother was planning to remove to at some point. At least he'd been given a few days to discover the lay of the land.

Yet what if Minchinhouse did own The Roses? Gideon did not have the funds to buy it back, even if the man agreed to sell it. If that was the case, the only way to recover the estate would be to marry Miss Minchinhouse. Not only would he be tied to a woman he didn't know, but he would lose Louisa forever. Still, he could not allow Mama's dower property to be lost. Unless he could figure a way out of this mess, he'd be well and truly shackled to the wrong woman.

He never should have gotten out of bed this morning. Better yet, he never should have come to Town.

At quarter past two, a knock came on the door to the parlor Louisa shared with Charlotte. Louisa set down her pen. "Come in."

Royston, Grace's butler, entered, then stood aside. "Miss Blackacre to see you, my lady."

"Wonderful!" Louisa rose, swiftly crossing the room to welcome her guest. "Please tell Lady Charlotte we have company and bring some biscuits, tea and lemonade."

Holding her hands out to Oriana, Louisa exclaimed, "What a delightful surprise."

"I hope I am not interrupting."

"Not at all," she assured her friend. "I was writing a list of things I must do. Some of which I can use to excuse myself from many of the evening entertainments."

Oriana looked at her in surprise. "Why ever would you want to do that?"

"To stay out of Bentley's way."

Oriana's lips pressed firmly together in disapproval. "I see. Well," she said briskly, taking a seat. "I am not sure I agree that you must, but I think you will be pleased with my news. Lord Bentley and I had a perfectly wonderful visit to the British Museum."

"You did?" Louisa cringed a bit at letting her astonishment show. "I mean—"

Oriana waved her hand, stopping Louisa. "We did. He was quite knowledgeable." Oriana gave a satisfied nod. "He even bought a guide book and thought of some other places I should not miss."

"How did you manage to get him to invite you?" This was even better than she could have hoped for.

"It really was not difficult. As you know, I had asked him what I most needed to see while in London. That, apparently, got him thinking of other interesting places. A little hint was all it took for him to ask me to accompany him."

Louisa almost fell onto a chair. "I never would have believed him capable of such planning."

"I know you find him a bit difficult, but I think he is delightful." Oriana smiled widely and seemed to preen a little. "He even took me to Gunter's for an ice afterward, and asked me for a waltz this evening."

"You truly do like him?" Louisa asked, trying to keep the shock from her voice.

"I do, indeed. Thank you so much for introducing us. He"—Oriana's lips formed a moue—"I only hope he has begun to like me as well."

"And therein lies the reason I plan to absent myself from most of the balls and such."

"You should do no such thing," she said firmly. "I know he imagines himself in love with you at the moment, but if he is to decide he could love me . . ."

"It must be despite my presence."

"Exactly. That way he cannot think you could have changed your mind."

"Well, this is a muddle." Louisa tapped her finger against her cheek for a moment. Oriana was right, but she and Rothwell would still be forced to remain apart. Part of the reason she was going to eschew entertainments was so Bentley's feelings would not be hurt.

"What is the matter?"

"Is something amiss?" Charlotte entered the room followed by a footman carrying a tray covered with biscuits, tea, and lemonade.

Once she had taken a seat on the sofa, Louisa replied, "Bentley asked Rothwell to help me fall in love with him."

"Oh, dear." Oriana frowned.

"That does indeed complicate matters." Charlotte poured them each a cup of tea. "I cannot see Rothwell willingly hurting his cousin."

"No." Louisa took a sip of tea. "I do not wish to harm him either. Moreover, if our positions were reversed, I would never hurt either of you."

Oriana nibbled on one of the ginger biscuits. Finally she said, "Let us do nothing for the time being. Something will either come to us or happen for the best. I am sure of it."

"Perhaps you are correct." Louisa nodded. "Although, it goes against the grain for me to do nothing."

"A truer statement you've never spoken." Charlotte laughed. "Yet I believe Oriana has the right of it. Something is bound to occur."

Once again a knock sounded on the door, and a young footman opened it. "Sorry, my lady," he said, looking at her. "There is a note for you and the messenger is waiting for an answer."

She reached out, and the servant handed her a sealed letter. "Give me a moment." The footman retreated into the corridor, closing the door behind him. "It is from Bentley requesting a set this evening." She scribbled her denial and sealed the note before handing it to the servant. Once he'd gone, she blew out a breath. "If you'll excuse me, I must ask Grace if she knows anyone who can help me fill my dance card."

If only Bentley would realize how unsuited they were. She dreaded to think what fate would come up with.

Chapter Fifteen

Later that evening, Gideon watched as Lady Louisa went off on another gentleman's arm. Apparently, she had been unable to remain at home as she had said she would. Not being able to dance with her, hold her in his arms, or even speak with her was unbearable. Yet it was for the best.

He did not know why he'd expected to have a better evening after the devil of a day he'd had. Yet it appeared his situation would not improve anytime soon.

That morning, the running footman who'd been dispatched to the solicitor's returned with the news that the man was not in. However, a message had been sent back informing him that based on the information Gideon had provided concerning the deposit box, it seemed the correct officer to approach was not at all clear, and that Mr. Templeton would do himself the honor of sorting it out and coming to Rothwell House the following afternoon.

Rarely had Gideon been so nonplussed. He had half a mind to go to the whore's house and shake the information he wanted out of her. Who could or would blame him? And what recourse would she really have? He was a duke, after all, and he owned the house she was living in. Yet, if he caused a scandal, he would never hear the end of it from his mother. She had enough of her own problems without him adding to them.

Unable to accomplish anything else, he had visited the theaters where his father, now he, had boxes and left instructions that he was hereby revoking all permissions for anyone to use the boxes for the immediate future. Unless they were paying customers. It was usual for boxes to be let if the patron did not appear.

Then he had arrived at this blasted ball, and had to watch his cousin mooning after Lady Louisa with puppy dog eyes. While she . . . his heart stopped . . . she gazed at him and he could not, did not wish to, do anything but drink in the sight of her.

She always looked lovely, but he was completely unprepared for how absolutely beautiful she appeared this evening. Her dark sable hair was piled on top of her head, with loose tendrils framing her face. Her lips reminded him of ripe raspberries, and he wondered how they would taste. The mounds of her plump breasts could just be seen above the modest neckline trimmed with blond lace. The skirts of the white ball gown covered with silver netting hinted at every curve on her luscious body.

In spite of her planning and his earlier hopefulness, after seeing the look his cousin gave her, Gideon knew she was not for him. Even if he had the wherewithal to court her, he could not betray Bentley. If only she would understand. If only he did not feel as if his life was ending.

Steeling himself to greet her, he bowed and clasped the hand she offered. It was all he could do to refrain from pressing hot kisses on her fingers and up her arm until he reached the top of her glove where his lips could meet her flesh. “A pleasure to see you again, my lady.”

“You as well, Your Grace.” She captured him with deep

lapis eyes that would soon be shooting sparks of anger when he told her of his decision.

Finally, he dragged his gaze from Louisa, remembered his breeding and his loyalty to his cousin, and made his bow to Lady Charlotte, Miss Blackacre, and their friend Lady Elizabeth Tully.

As the others left to join the set that was just starting he grabbed Lady Louisa's arm. "We must speak."

She glanced up at him, a curious look on her face. "Yes, but not now."

Her dance partner arrived, and, once more, Gideon was left standing there not knowing what to do next. Somehow he had to find the will to tell her that no matter how much they were drawn to each other, no matter how much he loved being in her company, and how much he wanted her in his life, he could not see her again.

Ever.

Or at least not until Bentley was betrothed to another woman. Gideon could not betray his cousin. And there was the complication of his mother's dower property. No, duty to his family must come before the stirrings of his heart.

"Rothwell, you look as if you've lost your best friend." Worthington and his wife joined Gideon.

He tried to throw off the feeling that he was not as much in control of his life as he should be. He was a duke, blast it all. Yet what was the point in being a duke if he could not order his life as he wanted it. "I am merely still not used to *ton* events any longer. Canada was much different."

"I can imagine how it must have been," Lady Worthington said as she smiled up at her husband.

A moment later a lady he had not seen in years stood next to him. "Well, Rothwell. It's about time you decided to return. Someone should have written for you sooner. Perhaps you could have done something about your father."

Good God! He'd been right. Everyone did know of his

embarrassments. This was when he should slink away like a dog with his tail between his legs. Instead, he gave himself a shake and summoned up a grin. "Lady Bellamny, I am happy to see some things never change. I wish *you* had written to me. As it is, I have a mess to clean up."

"Running all over Town with that Cyprian at his age. Ought to have known better." None too gently, she tapped her folded fan on his arm. At least she didn't appear to know of his financial worries. "Marry the right woman, and she'll be able to help you. None of those Cit's daughters though. They won't know how to go on. Find a lady of quality."

"Yes, ma'am," he replied contritely. Did she know about Minchinhouse? Probably not, she would have mentioned him if she had. One never had to guess how one stood with Lady Bellamny. "May I have the next dance?"

"Thank you, my boy." She drew her brows together for the slightest moment. "Hmm, I suppose I should call you, Your Grace," she said as if it was a decision she must make to address him as his rank demanded.

Worthington's lips twitched, while Gideon attempted to maintain a serious demeanor. "That would probably be best. I have been given to understand that I should be more aware of my dignity now that I am a duke."

Tilting her head a bit to the right, she studied him for several long moments. Finally she pronounced, "You'll do, Your Grace. Do not take yourself too seriously, but under no circumstances allow anyone to encroach upon you and you shall get along famously." She inclined her head to them. "I see someone with whom I must speak."

He stared after her. "To think I had forgotten her."

"I wish I could at times." Worthington looked as if he wanted to roll his eyes.

"That is not fair," his wife responded severely. "She has been a great deal of help to us."

"The last time she helped us," he retorted scowling, "Merton married Dotty."

"Wait a moment," Gideon interjected. "Merton your cousin?"

"The very same. One of Charlotte's friends, Dorothea Stern, came to us for the Season, and in no time at all she was wed to Merton." The frown lifted from Worthington's mien. "Although it has actually done him a great deal of good. Of course, I was not at all pleased at the time."

"I believe she also helped Evesham and Lady Phoebe marry."

Worthington turned to Gideon. "You'll remember him as Lord Marcus Finley from school. The one who was sent off to the West Indies." Gideon nodded. "He wed Lady Phoebe Stanhope last autumn."

"I think I remember my mother writing to me about that, and I ran into Marcus recently. Did Rutherford not marry as well?"

"Indeed he did," Lady Worthington replied. "To Miss Anna Marsh."

"Harry Marsh's sister? I was sorry to hear he died."

Matt gave a sharp laugh. "He was merely lost for a time. He showed up just before Rutherford's wedding and married a lady from Jamaica."

It appeared that his initial impression that everyone was finding wives was true. "I seem to have missed a lot."

"That is one way to look at it," Lady Worthington replied. "On the other hand, you must have had wonderful experiences in Canada."

"I did." Nevertheless, Gideon could have done without the problems he was facing now. "It is an amazingly rugged but beautiful land. After the American Revolution ended, many of the Indian tribes from New York, along the St. Lawrence River, moved to Canada. It was extraordinary spending time with them and learning about their customs."

"I would love to hear more about it," Worthington said.

"As would I." Lady Louisa appeared next to her sister-in-law. "I have read accounts of Canada, and it sounds wonderful."

Before Gideon could answer, a young man about the same age as his cousin came up carrying a glass of lemonade. "Lady Louisa." The man handed her the glass with a flourish.

"Thank you." She smiled politely, but thankfully showed the man no favoritism.

Not that he could do anything about it if she did. He should probably want her to be attracted to another gentleman. Yet not only did Gideon not want her to show a preference for anyone else, he was within an inch of simply dragging her out of here and making her his.

Damn Bentley.

Louisa had barely finished her drink when another gentleman came to claim her for the next set. She took the arm the man offered and left. The urge Gideon had to go after her was almost too strong to resist.

"Lady Louisa is quite popular." His gaze followed her as she made her way to the dance floor. "Has she settled on anyone?" As if he had not been practically living in her pocket for the past two days. Did Worthington have someone in mind for her? As unpleasant as the thought was, Gideon almost hoped it was so. He snagged a glass of champagne from a passing footman and took a sip.

"Not that I've seen." Worthington was focused on the dance floor as a waltz was forming. He appeared to be counting.

"She does know who does not interest her, other than as a friend," Lady Worthington remarked drily, giving Gideon a look that made him realize he was not fooling her at all. "Which I think is just as important."

"Yes, yes, it is."

He remembered what Louisa had said earlier about her sister-in-law advising her to discourage Bentley. Perhaps her matchmaking scheme would work. He prayed it was so, and that he was not just chasing a dream.

Louisa glanced at her dance card. Only the upcoming set was not spoken for. There was nothing for it. She would simply have to disappear for the half hour the dance took. At least Bentley was still across the room, and she could use the time to make her escape. Thankfully, Grace had promised they could leave before the supper dance.

No matter, Louisa would not have accepted anyone but Rothwell for that dance in any event. It was strange how she missed having him hold her as they twirled around the room. She had never felt such a loss before. Not for a gentleman. The worst part was seeing him and not being able to dance with him at all, touch him, or speak with him except in the presence of others.

If only Oriana was right and something occurred to resolve this predicament. Preferably in the very near future. For Louisa found she was not particularly good at subterfuge. If she had her way, she would simply pull Bentley aside and tell him she was not interested in him as more than a friend and never had been.

She edged her way around the ballroom toward the terrace doors, hoping neither her brother nor Bentley noticed.

Ever since Dotty had ended up betrothed to Louisa's cousin, the Marquis of Merton, by following him into the garden to warn him of a plot, Matt had forbidden either Charlotte or Louisa from entering any garden at night but theirs.

Still, the terrace wasn't a garden. She would remain close to the doors where it was safe. As long as Bentley didn't see her and try to follow, all would be well. Slipping out the door, she strolled to the stone rail of the terrace. Low voices came from the paths below, and lanterns bobbed along the walkways like fairy lights.

Firm steps sounded behind her and she prayed it wasn't Bentley.

"Louisa." Rothwell's deep, smooth voice rolled over her.

She whipped around. "I thought we were trying to stay away from each other."

"I can't . . . I must—" He stopped speaking. "Walk with me. Please."

Taking her arm, he led her to the other end of the terrace where no one could see them.

"Rothwell, what is it?" She tried to search his eyes, but the dark made it impossible.

"God knows I've tried." He groaned and one slightly calloused hand cupped her cheek while the other rested on the balustrade. "Louisa." His tone a reverent whisper. "How I've tried to stay away."

Louisa, he'd called her Louisa. A thrill shot through her as the thought sank into her consciousness just as his lips touched hers. Warm and firm, they moved from the corner of her mouth to the center, nibbling softly. Sighing, she leaned into him, returning his caress. This was what she had always imagined a kiss would be. She opened her lips to copy his movements and his tongue swept in, claiming her. A second later, she touched her tongue to his, moaning at the heat.

Shivers flowing through her, she reached up, wrapping her arms around his neck. Pulling her to him, he held her against his hard body as one palm stroked from the nape of her neck to her waist. Sparks lighted fires as his hands touched her bare skin.

It was as if they could not get close enough to each other, yet not even a thin piece of muslin would fit between them. He slanted his head, deepening the kiss.

Good Lord! This was better than all the books she had read. Better than she could have ever dreamed. Her nipples ached, and she rubbed them against his coat, trying to get relief.

Rothwell growled, as his fingers stroked under her breasts.

Yes, yes, touch me there.

A strange feeling, almost like an itch, started between her legs, and she tried to get even closer to him. She wanted him, wanted him to touch her everywhere. As if he knew what she was thinking, Rothwell placed one hand on her derrière and held her against him.

"Rothwell." Louisa was surprised by how rough her voice was.

He broke the kiss. "Gideon. I want you to call me Gideon."

"Gideon." Louisa pressed her lips to his, never wanting this to end.

Chapter Sixteen

Gideon had asked Louisa to call him by his first name. No one except his old nurse had ever called him Gideon. Not even his mother. But he needed to hear it from Louisa's lips.

"Gideon." Her soft, breathy tone speared through him straight to his groin.

He rubbed his thumb over her nipple again, and she trembled in his arms. He wanted more. He wanted all of her. If only—somewhere in the back of his mind he heard the music stop.

What the hell am I doing?

Practically ravishing her where anyone could come upon them. Worthington would have his head.

What was he doing ravishing her in the first place? He had come out here to tell her he could not see her again. That no matter what they did, his cousin would be hurt. And he'd ended up doing what he had dreamed of almost every night since meeting her. Well, not everything, but too damn much!

There was only one thing to do. He'd return to his estate first thing in the morning. That was the only safe option. He would send her a note telling her the reason. Then later, after Bentley fell in love with another lady, Gideon could return. Perhaps Louisa would still be unattached. Or she might never forgive him for leaving.

Slowly, gently, he broke the kiss. He did not even have to see Louisa to know her lips would be swollen from his attentions. "The music stopped."

"I suppose that means we must go back in." She sounded as disgruntled as he felt.

Placing a light kiss on her forehead, he frowned. If only they could remain here forever. Better yet, sneak out the garden gate and ride to Scotland. That still didn't mean he could actually afford to marry her yet. He probably couldn't afford the journey to Scotland. "Yes. We must."

Tucking her hand in the crook of his arm, she ambled with him back to the doors, halting before they entered. He glanced down and his gut twisted. Her eyes were shining, showing him all the love they had not yet voiced and might never utter. He would tell her now. Try to explain his behavior.

"Well!" A lady with wheat-colored hair stood in front of them. Her gown was in the height of fashion. Her brown eyes sparkled with triumph. There was something familiar about her, but for the life of him he could not remember being introduced to her. "You will not be behaving in that manner once we're wed, Your Grace. I shall expect you to dance attendance on me alone."

"Wed?" He said the word slowly as if it had never been spoken before. Who in perdition was this woman?

Louisa's eyes collided with his for a moment, then she turned to the other lady, her head high. "Miss Minchinhouse," Louisa said, smiling politely. "How nice to see you this evening. However, I believe you are under a slight misapprehension. Rothwell and I are betrothed."

Miss Minchinhouse? Betrothed? For the first time in his life, Gideon couldn't speak. Not a word would exit his mouth, only a grunting sound. Apparently that did not bother Louisa at all. The way she stood next to him, even closer than before, the angle of her chin, told him she was in complete control.

"Are you?" A strange smile formed on Miss Minchinhouse's lips. What the hell was going on? Shouldn't she be angry or, at the very least, upset that her father's plans had gone awry? "In that case, it is my pleasure to wish you happy." Her lips pursed for a moment. "Although, I suggest you keep it to yourselves for a day or so. Yes, that would be best."

On that cryptic note, she left.

"What just happened?" Gideon asked after finally finding his voice.

"I have no idea." Louisa shook her head, seemingly as confused as he was. "She has always been nice to me, to everyone in fact. Yet if asked, she had been quite adamant about *not* marrying into the peerage. I used to think she must already have a man she wished to wed. Yet no . . ." Her words trailed off.

He sucked in a breath of air. Obviously, Minchinhouse had told his daughter of his visit to Gideon, and she wasn't happy about it.

He was trying to think of something to say to Louisa when Bentley pushed through a small group of guests closest to the door. "Rothwell!" Bentley's face mottled red with fury. "Did I hear correctly? You have proposed to Lady Louisa? I trusted you. Why you—you—you scoundrel!"

The next thing Gideon knew, his cousin started swinging, and he was doing all he could to keep either of them from being injured.

"For the love of God!" Louisa grumbled. "It needed only this. Bentley, cease. You are creating a scene."

A moment later, liquid of some sort flew through the air, hitting Bentley square in the face, and he stopped.

"You were supposed to be—be . . ." He dragged a palm down his face, sluicing the fluid off.

Louisa grabbed Bentley by his ear and dragged him out the door. Worthington and his friends, Lord Huntley and Lord Wivenley, blocked any of the other guests from following.

Gideon squeezed through the men in time to hear Louisa's fierce whisper, "You, my lord, have lost your mind if you believe that anyone could convince me to love and or marry a man whom I do not, nor ever will, love. You had no right to ask it of Rothwell. *I* am not a piece of property to be given away, exchanged, or manipulated."

"But—but," Bentley stuttered to no avail.

"Do not even attempt to excuse your behavior. And"—she released his ear to stab her finger at Bentley's chest—"you have no one to blame but yourself. As it was, you took so long getting to the point with Rothwell that we had already met. Now." She jammed her fists onto her hips. "Do you have anything to say for yourself?"

At first Gideon thought his cousin would skulk back into the house, but, to his surprise, Bentley straightened his shoulders. "Yes, as a matter of fact, I do. Thank you, my lady, for showing me that I was mistaken not only in your affections, but in my cousin's as well." He executed a short bow. "Good evening." As he passed Gideon, Bentley paused. "Do not speak to me ever again."

"Would someone," Worthington said in a dangerous tone, "care to tell me what exactly is going on?"

"Rothwell and I are betrothed," Louisa replied promptly, shaking out her skirts as if nothing of significance had occurred.

"Betrothed?" Her brother scowled. "Of course you are. You were in the garden. Who in this family does not return from the garden engaged to be married?"

"We were not in the garden," Louisa objected. "We were on the terrace."

Worthington stared at her as if she had gone mad, then he directed a fierce look at Gideon. "I shall see you at Worthington House no later than nine tomorrow morning."

Gideon was about to object to being so peremptorily ordered about, but it was Worthington's sister, his ward, whom Gideon had come close to ruining. "I will be there."

Turning on his heel, Worthington stalked back through the doors.

When Louisa made to follow, Gideon stopped her. "Louisa," he said with a calm he was in no way feeling. "Why did you tell Miss Minchinhouse that we are betrothed?"

Her eyes widened, and she gave him an odd look. "We kissed," she said as if that explained everything. "Naturally, we are going to be married."

He wanted to groan. Of course, as innocent as she was, that is what she would believe. What young lady wasn't told that kissing led to marriage? And if anyone had seen them, it would have been a foregone conclusion. Not to mention that if she thought that what they had engaged in was merely a kiss, someone needed to protect her.

But now what the devil was he going to do about the Cit, or his father's courtesan, or his damnable finances? What was wrong with him that he couldn't have kept his lips and hands to himself?

Still, the fact remained that he had created this mess, and she must never know that he had planned to tell her he could no longer see her. He had already ruined things with Bentley. Gideon would not do the same with Louisa. "Of course." Gideon forced his lips into a smile. "I had merely thought that I would—"

"Oh!" Louisa's eyes grew even wider as her fingers flew to her lips. "You wanted to propose."

Gazing at her worried, contrite mien, he realized he would not often see that expression. If any lady was meant to be a duchess she was Lady Louisa Vivers. Gideon just hoped he could hide his financial situation from her long enough for him to repair at least some of the damage. He prayed that the plans he had put in place came to fruition, then everything would be fine.

Lifting her hand to his lips, he kissed them. "Yes, that was it."

Louisa gave him her most dazzling smile. "You may still propose if you wish."

"I believe I will take you up on your kind offer." Gideon grinned, making Louisa feel better about having robbed him of his moment.

He placed her hand on his arm and they entered the ballroom. News of their betrothal had quickly spread, and they were stopped along the way by those wishing them happy. Still, she could not get out of her head what Margaret Minchinhouse had said.

Keep it to yourselves for a day or so.

For what reason, and what could Miss Minchinhouse have meant, and why did she think that *she* was to wed Gideon? Louisa gave herself a shake. Well, that horse had left the barn. Nevertheless, when she next saw the lady she would ask.

As for now, she could not be happier. Any doubts she had entertained that her feelings for Gideon were growing too quickly had ended with that kiss. Perhaps she should not have announced their betrothal, but he had appeared so completely shocked by Miss Minchinhouse's unexpected and, quite frankly, astonishing statement that Louisa had to do something to disabuse the lady of her notion that anyone other than she would be marrying Gideon Rothwell.

Naturally, she knew that some gentlemen wed for financial gain. Yet there was no indication that Gideon needed to marry money. And if he did, he would certainly not have kissed her so thoroughly that her knees had turned to marmalade.

She stole a glance at him, so handsome and composed. Then her brother's stern visage came into view. She would have to tell Matt how her betrothal had come about, and soon. Tonight after they returned home would be best. That would give him a chance to calm himself before speaking with Gideon in the morning.

"Matt said you are to meet us in the hall," Charlotte said in a low voice as she fell in next to Louisa. "He has already ordered our coach and His Grace's as well."

Naturally, he had. Just like when Dotty and Merton had become engaged. Although no one, other than Merton and possibly his mother, had been happy about *that* betrothal. There was no feasible reason Matt should be unhappy with Louisa and Gideon. After all, he was Matt's friend, held the right political views, and was perfectly eligible. By all accounts, he should be thrilled with her betrothal. Why wasn't he? Unless it was that Gideon had not approached her brother first. That must be it. There was no other possible reason for her brother's anger.

Less than forty minutes later Louisa sat on a chair in the Stanwood House drawing room with her brother and sister-in-law. Actually, Grace was sitting. Matt was pacing a path on the thick Turkey carpet like the caged lion in the Royal Menagerie. Louisa wished Charlotte had been allowed to remain with her, but she had been summarily dismissed from the room.

When Louisa opened her mouth to speak, Grace shook her head. "Give him a moment."

Finally, Matt glanced at Louisa. The anger gone from his eyes replaced by a sternness she rarely saw. "How did you bring this engagement about?"

"What do you mean?" After all, Gideon had kissed her, not the other way around. Kissed her first in any event.

"Louisa"—he heaved a sigh—"I have known Rothwell since we were children. He would *never* have proposed to you without first asking my leave to address you. I have also known you since your birth. You, my dear sister, are incapable of not acting when you think a matter calls for it. Therefore, I shall ask again, what did you do?"

"Oh." She fought down the warmth infusing her neck and cheeks. "Well, you see"—she clinched her hands in her lap, staring at them as she spoke—"we were on the terrace, and when Miss Minchinhouse saw us coming in she said something very strange about when Gid—Rothwell and she married. But I knew that he could not wish to wed her, so I told her we were betrothed."

"And what exactly"—Matt asked in a low, almost dangerous tone that he had never used with Louisa before—"occurred to make you so certain that Rothwell did not wish to wed Miss Minchinhouse?"

"We—I, er . . . well, we kissed." Louisa finished as close to a whisper as she could and still be heard. She flinched waiting for the explosion she knew would come.

"Kissed?" Matt roared. "That bounder kissed you? I should never have allowed him to leave! I should have—"

"Matt," Grace snapped, stopping his tirade. "It sounds to me as if Rothwell and Louisa have deep feelings for each other. I have noticed the way they watch each other and the looks they have exchanged. I do not think that, under the circumstances, their engagement should have been unexpected."

Jaw clenched, her brother nodded, then said to her, "Sweetheart, there is something you do not know." Matt glanced at Grace. "Neither of you do. Rothwell has suffered some financial reversals."

Louisa's heart dropped like a boulder. Why had he not confided in her? Was he marrying her for her dowry? She had never considered herself an heiress, but others might.

Matt continued in a gentler tone. "His father left him in a bad way, and he told me he was not in a position to marry."

"Miss Minchinhouse?" Louisa croaked, barely able to get the name past her tightening throat.

Her brother nodded. "Someone must have said something to her if she believed she was to wed him."

"Oh Lord." Louisa covered her mouth with her hands. "Oh Lord. What have I done?"

"Under the circumstances," Grace responded drily, "only what you thought he would do. I did hear you say he kissed you, did I not?"

"Yes," Louisa said, wishing now that the kiss, no matter how lovely it had been, had never happened. Still, if she loved him and wanted what was best for him there was only one thing to do. "If he must marry for a fortune, I will release him."

If only Gideon had told her, she would have tried to understand. After all, he was not the one to have caused his problems. "I wish to retire now." She wanted to throw herself down on her bed and cry until she no longer thought of him. "You will tell him in the morning, won't you, Matt?"

His face was as grim as she'd ever seen it. "I will make the offer."

"Thank you." Straightening, she rose and strode quickly out of the room, not stopping until she reached her chamber. Tonight, not even talking to Charlotte would help.

Louisa's maid, Lucy, was waiting. As Louisa was being undressed and helped into her nightgown, she gnawed on her lips until they felt raw. Finally the door closed. An emptiness grew where her heart was, yet the tears she'd sought would not come.

God in heaven help me. Will he ever forgive me?

Chapter Seventeen

Gideon arrived home and poured himself a brandy, which he drank in one long pull. He should have had trouble sleeping. He was a dead man once Worthington discovered, which he would surely do, that Gideon had kissed Louisa without asking to court her. At the very least, he would be on the receiving end of a facer. Being a duke wouldn't help him at all. If Worthington did not punch him, Gideon would receive a bear-garden jaw that would leave his ears burning for a month, possibly a year.

Bentley would probably never forgive Gideon, much less speak to him again, and he still had not heard from his solicitor about his mother's dower property. Absolutely nothing concerning the property the Petrie woman had was settled. All in all, his life was in complete and utter chaos.

Then again, Gideon and Louisa were betrothed. Even if he had not done the asking. That was something in his favor. And instead of tossing and turning, he was asleep within minutes of laying his head on his pillow, dreaming about Louisa and all the ways he could pleasure her once they had wed.

The following morning he woke more aroused than he had ever been in his life. "God, Louisa. What you do to me."

"Did you say something, Your Grace?"

Recognizing his valet's voice, Gideon groaned. "No, Rollins. Nothing at all."

The sooner Gideon was wed, the sooner he could bed her, and that couldn't be soon enough.

As he dressed, he prepared his speech for Worthington. Gideon would assure his friend that none of Louisa's money would go toward repairs or to the estates in any way whatsoever. He would contrive to keep her in the manner to which she was accustomed. She need never know the straits in which his father put him. "I want Mr. Templeton here early this afternoon."

"Yes, Your Grace." Rollins stood with several neck cloths draped over his arm. "Mr. Fredericks asked me to inform you that a *female* came to see you yesterday after you had already left."

A female? None of the ladies of his acquaintance would visit a bachelor residence. "Does this female have a name?"

"A Mrs. Petrie." His valet sniffed. "I have been assured you would not wish her admitted."

Damnation. He couldn't have that woman coming to the house with Louisa here. "Under no circumstances should she be allowed on the property."

"That was what Mr. Fredericks said, Your Grace."

Gideon glanced in the mirror. His cravat was ruined. He whipped the long piece of linen off and took another from his valet. He hadn't been this nervous about an interview since he'd been a much younger man facing his father for punishment. Slowly he lowered his chin, making sure the creases in the neckcloth were just so. There. Perfect. Donning his waistcoat and jacket, he said, "Do not expect me until luncheon."

"Very good, Your Grace."

Taking his cane, hat, and gloves, he went out the door and down the steps. The distance from his house to

Berkeley Square was not that great, and he'd enjoy the walk. It would also serve to calm him down before facing Worthington.

In less time than Gideon had thought it would take, he climbed the steps to Worthington House.

The door opened, and the butler bowed. "Your Grace, I shall take you to his lordship."

In his gloves, his hands began to sweat. "Thank you."

The butler's slow pace down the corridor agitated Gideon even further. At this rate he'd be ready for Bedlam before he even opened his mouth. Or was punched, whichever came first. All he knew for certain was that, come what may, he would leave this house with Lady Louisa Vivers's hand in marriage officially his.

"I can't look!" Louisa moaned as Charlotte stared out the window with a view across the square to Worthington House.

"It doesn't matter at the moment. He is inside, and there is nothing *to* see," Charlotte responded in a voice very like Grace's at her driest.

"Perhaps we should go and stand under the window of Matt's study and listen."

Raising her brows, Charlotte folded her arms across her chest. "We would be caught within minutes."

"How?" Louisa demanded.

"The moment Matt said something to Rothwell that you didn't like you would be unable to remain silent."

Charlotte had a point. Louisa had never been very good at not voicing her opinions. It was something she'd always meant to learn. She just hadn't got around to it yet. "I should have insisted on being there."

"You truly do not wish to be present when your brother

and guardian discuss the propriety of kissing one's sister and ward before one has granted a gentleman permission to court that sister." Grace glided across the room to the window and glanced out. "I take it Rothwell arrived."

"He has and looking very smart as well," Charlotte replied. "He walked."

"Nervous." Grace gave a decisive nod.

"What—what if he agrees to allow me to end the betrothal?" That fear had been praying on Louisa's thoughts all night, and she finally had to give voice to it.

"Somehow," Grace mused, "I do not think he will. After all, if the poor man could not stay away from you after saying he must wait until next year, *and* after Bentley begged him to help you fall in love with him, I doubt anything can make him want to give you up."

Louisa's mouth gaped open. "How did you know about that?"

"Matt overheard what you said to Bentley and what he said to Rothwell. It was not hard to put two and two together." Grace gave a rare smug smile. "However, you might be glad to know that when Bentley left you, he went straight to Oriana Blackacre."

"At least something is going right." Once the man fell in love with Oriana, Louisa was sure that he would forgive Gideon. She might have to ask her friend to nudge Bentley in the right direction. Glancing at the clock she was loath to see that the hands had barely moved at all. "I don't think the footman wound the clock."

"It, as well as all the others, has been tended to." Grace laughed. "It won't do you any good to sit up here and watch the door. Let's go into the garden. Theo is finally well enough to be outside, and I am going to send Hal for ices."

"That sounds like much more fun than sitting up here watching Louisa wear herself to a frazzle." Rising from the chair Charlotte had placed next to the window, she touched Louisa's shoulder. "The time will pass more quickly outside."

"I suppose you're right." The time always went faster when she was busy.

A few minutes later, she sat in one of the chairs her sister-in-law had placed on the terrace so they could enjoy the warmer weather. Theo, Mary, and Philip played with Duke and Daisy while one of the nursery maids kept watch nearby. The tea tray arrived, and Grace poured.

"How long do you think it's been?" Louisa twisted her cup around in the saucer, wishing she'd worn her pin watch.

"Not as long as it feels," Grace responded kindly.

This was going to take forever. Louisa should have gone shopping or something equally diverting, but there was no way she could have absented herself from the house when Gideon was due to arrive. If only she had had the forethought to have insisted that it all be resolved last night, like Merton and Dotty had done, instead of waiting until this morning.

What *could* be taking them so long?

"Louisa said what?" Gideon was so shocked he'd forgotten to use her title. By Worthington's expression, it was clear he had noticed that slight lapse. When Gideon had entered the study and noted his friend's angry countenance, he decided to speak to Worthington as a friend and not as one of Louisa's suitors. Gideon might be a duke, but Worthington had held his title much longer and, more importantly, was Louisa's guardian. Unless Gideon wanted to run off to Gretna Green with her, provided of course that he could convince her to do such a thing, it behooved him to honor his friend's position.

"After I told her of your problems, she realized why Miss Minchinhouse said what she did." Worthington's mien became even more forbidding than it was earlier. "She is willing to step aside if you need to marry for money."

For a moment he felt as if he'd been stabbed in the gut. Gideon did not know anyone who was more selfless than Louisa was proving to be. "No. Especially after last night, I cannot allow her to make such a"—Damn. He'd almost said *sacrifice*. As if he were the most eligible gentleman in England—"No." He would not give her up. He may not have wanted to court her due to his not being quite beforehand with the world, but now that she was his, that is how she would remain. "No. I have no intention of tying myself to Miss Minchinhouse or any other lady who will wed me only for a title."

"Is there a reason you did not tell her about the difficulties you are having?" The question was posed in a matter-of-fact tone, but he could tell Worthington was concerned that Gideon had not been honest with Louisa.

He dragged a hand over his face and wished he was holding a glass of brandy instead of a cup of tea. "I had planned to put off courting her until my dibs were in tune. Last evening I'd meant to tell her that I was going back to my estate until Bentley fell in love with Miss Blackacre or another lady."

Worthington set his cup down with a snap. "Miss Blackacre? What does she have to do with this?"

"Quite a bit, actually." Gideon took a sip of tea. "Louisa had them introduced. She believes that Miss Blackacre would be perfect for my cousin."

"And what does Miss Blackacre think of all of this?"

"I have not spoken to her, of course, but she did go to the museum with Bentley," Gideon said optimistically. "And he is planning some other excursions."

"But then you *kissed* Louisa?"

Naturally, it came down to that. "Yes. I could not help myself." He glanced at Worthington and saw what Gideon hoped was understanding in his friend's eyes. "I know I'm not the most eligible man in Town at the moment, but I will come about. I have already tracked down where most of the money went and have taken steps to get as much of it back as I can. As you know, I am refusing to pay my father's markers of hand. I should have at least enough to put the estates in order again and make some small investments." He twisted the teacup around in the saucer. "I promise you. Louisa will never suffer. No matter what I have to do, she will be provided for."

"Why would Miss Minchinhouse think you and she were to wed?"

Gideon stifled a groan. And here he'd thought Worthington had forgotten about the woman. "Her father came to see me. He had bought up some of my father's gambling debts, to include my mother's dower property." Worthington's lips formed a thin line. "As far as I know, my father was not the trustee for the property. I mean, he was not the trustee for my sisters' portions. Ergo, I do not think he would have been made trustee over anything my mother brought to the marriage. From what I learned recently, before he met and married my mother, he was fairly wild." Gideon drained what little was in the teacup. "In any event, Minchinhouse proposed a match with his daughter and told me to think on it for a few days. I was waiting for my solicitor to inform me as to whether the paper transferring the estate is valid. But it doesn't matter any longer. Minchinhouse must have said something to his daughter." Gideon thought back to the lady's reaction last evening. "The strange thing is that I don't think she wanted to marry me."

His friend, who had been leaning back in his chair, sat up. "What makes you say that?"

"She seemed almost angry when she first saw Louisa and me. Then when Louisa announced we were betrothed, she gave us a curious look and said to wait a day or two. I suppose that is not going to happen, but . . ." He shrugged.

"Minchinhouse is very wealthy and a powerful figure in the City, but he does not run in our circles." Leaning forward with his elbows on the desk, Worthington tapped the tips of his fingers together. "He would have to rely on someone else for his information."

That was interesting. "Such as his daughter or the lady sponsoring her."

"Indeed. I would suggest you take her advice and wait a few days before sending the announcement to the paper."

As consumed by his worries as he was, Gideon almost missed what Worthington had said. Suddenly, several tons of stone and bricks dropped from Gideon's shoulders. "You mean Louisa and I may marry?"

"I don't see how I can stop you." Worthington grimaced. "I have developed a well-honed sense of self-preservation. Knowing my sister, I would have no peace until I agree. Not to mention her recruiting every female in the family to help her. There are quite a few of them."

"She is rather formidable." Gideon grinned. Exactly the type of lady he needed as his wife and duchess.

"A word to the wise," Worthington said, obviously not finished yet. "She has been trained to manage an estate and will expect to be a partner in all you do. And, in case you have not noticed, she also has a tendency to take the bit between her teeth given the opportunity."

Gideon couldn't help but grin. He was perfectly ready to share some of the duties of his dukedom with her. He would, naturally, be in control and determine what she would and would not do. His mother had not been interested in that sort of thing, but his grandmother had . . .

Grandmamma. She and Louisa were like two peas in a pod. He sucked in a breath.

God's teeth! Not only must he get rid of Mrs. Petrie before Louisa found out about her and decided to deal with the woman herself, but he also would have to make clear what her responsibilities were and were not. Otherwise his life would be pandemonium.

The ices came, were consumed, and the children sent up to the nursery to rest. Louisa could sit no longer. Standing, she began to pace. "What is keeping them?"

"Look at it this way," Grace said mildly. "If Matt had decided to send Rothwell packing, he would have been back by now."

"He wouldn't." Louisa would not allow it. She would force her brother to allow her to marry Gideon. However, if Gideon had decided to marry elsewhere . . . then Matt would have returned. Unless he had decided to fight Gideon. Louisa covered her face with her hands and groaned.

"My dear, Matt is not a stupid man." Grace infused her voice with meaning. "He will, however, ensure that Rothwell is able to support you and treat you well."

"Of course." If only she could bring herself to believe what Grace said was true. Still, it must be true. Matt would never allow her or any of her sisters to marry a gentleman unless he was satisfied the man was worthy. Even a duke.

Still, now that she knew what Gideon's father had done, she was determined to help him rebuild his fortune and ease his burdens. Perhaps she would ask Lady Evesham for advice. After Grace had been abducted from in front of Worthington House, Lady Evesham had given Louisa, Charlotte, and Augusta lessons on defending themselves using not only their hands but daggers as well, and Matt had not only taught them how to shoot several different types of guns, but had purchased pistols made especially for them. Such a formidable lady might know of other things she could do to help her future husband.

Drat them for taking so long.

The sound of footsteps coming to the back of the house reached Louisa. "I think it's them."

"I believe you are correct." Grace signaled to a footman standing several feet away. "Please have tea and some biscuits and sandwiches brought."

"Wine as well," Matt said as he walked through the French windows followed by Gideon. "It's early yet, but some champagne would not go amiss."

Louisa's heart lodged in her throat.

"Champagne," she whispered to herself.

Gideon reached her and bowed before taking her hand. "My lady, it occurred to me that, in fact, neither of us has proposed to the other. That being the case, I would like, most humbly, to ask that you do me the great honor of being my wife."

The lump in her throat grew larger and, for a moment, she could not speak.

"Louisa?" he asked, as his thumb drew circles on the inside of her wrist.

"Yes. I would be happy to be your wife." She had never thought, never believed that she could fall in love so easily and quickly as she had with Gideon. Although she regretted that he had so many problems at present, she looked forward to helping him, working with him to resolve all the difficulties.

"The only thing to decide is the wedding date." He gazed into her eyes as if he was willing her to make it soon.

At all the weddings she had attended lately, actually, the only ones she had attended, just family and a few friends had been invited. The wedding breakfasts that had been put together in a matter of a day or two had been huge. Louisa did not see why she could not do the same. "What would you like?"

"The day after tomorrow? I can procure the special license"

Looking up at his clear gray eyes, she chuckled. "Two weeks. My mother must be informed and have time to travel back to London."

"As you will, my lady." Smiling, he kissed her lightly on the lips.

Happy, happy, happy. Louisa wanted to dance. She had never been happier. Her life was going to be perfect.

Chapter Eighteen

Edmond, Marquis of Bentley, heir to a dukedom for God's sake, gingerly touched his left ear. It still hurt where Lady Louisa had pinched it last night as she'd dragged him onto the terrace. The last time anyone had done that, he'd been five years old and his nurse had punished the maid.

Well, he couldn't very well punish Lady Louisa. Nor did he wish to. He had seen her true nature and was miraculously cured of his infatuation. For it must have been nothing more than a passing obsession. He could never actually be in love with a woman who . . . was . . . well . . . hard-hearted. No, that wasn't it. She showed compassion to almost everyone. Except him. Whatever it was, he now knew she was not the sort of lady he wished to marry.

Unfortunately, the lady Bentley decided he did want to wed had refused him. Well, not refused exactly. After his altercation with his cousin and Lady Louisa last evening, he had gone directly to Miss Blackacre and proposed. She'd peeped up from beneath her thick dark lashes, her blue eyes wide, and told him, very kindly, that she did not believe now was the right time for her to accept his lovely proposal. Yet, and this was very important, if he would like to woo her properly for the next two weeks, her answer could very well change.

Right then and there, he knew that was what he would do. Court Miss Blackacre. For two weeks. Then he would propose again.

Not only would he send Miss Blackacre dozens of bouquets of flowers, and take her riding in the Park, and sightseeing, he also had written a letter to be sent to Mama asking that she come to Town so that he could introduce her to the charming Miss Blackacre and invite her and her grandmother to dine with him.

He would ask her for two waltzes each evening. Hmm, perhaps he had better write that down so he didn't forget to request the sets. On the other hand, he seemed able to remember many more things he had planned to do when he was with Miss Blackacre. Well, he would write it down in any event. It wouldn't do to forget.

"Turkel," Bentley called to his valet, indicating with a very slight movement of his head the letter on his desk. "Please see that this is sent to my mother immediately." He finished tying his cravat. "I also want flowers sent to Miss Blackacre at Stillwell House."

"Very good, my lord. What type of flowers would you like for the lady?"

What kind? How was he supposed to know what kind? He thought of Miss Blackacre's deep pink lips and lovely blue eyes. He should select blooms to complement her face. "Pink and blue."

Turkel bowed. "I shall see to it immediately, my lord."

"And I am to drive with Miss Blackacre this afternoon at five o'clock."

"I shall have your carriage sent round at half past four."

The valet gave Bentley his watch fob and quizzing glass.

"After the duchess arrives, I believe I shall give up these rooms."

"A very wise decision, my lord."

After all, he would most likely be married soon. He touched his ear again. And to a much nicer lady than Lady Louisa had turned out to be. Two weeks Miss Blackacre had said. "What is the date two weeks hence?"

"The twentieth, my lord."

"Thank you." He should write that down. It would not do for him to forget to propose to her again.

Immediately after their celebration drink, Louisa was about to suggest they bring the children down and tell them of her betrothal to Gideon, when Matt said, "I believe it is time to discuss the settlement agreements. Louisa, Rothwell, if you will come with me we can finish them in short order."

"Grace?" Louisa glanced at her sister-in-law. "Will you join us?"

Grace's forehead wrinkled a bit as she thought. "I believe I shall. The children will not be down to luncheon for another hour."

"As you will, my love." Matt tucked her hand securely in the crook of his arm.

Louisa took Gideon's arm as they left the terrace, making their way through the morning room, up the corridor, to the hall. Earlier, Charlotte had excused herself to go to the music room, and the haunting melody she played flowed through the house. Louisa gave herself a shake. Just because her sister played a morose song did not mean anything was going to go wrong. Charlotte was most likely just feeling a little left out. After all, Dotty and now Louisa had found their loves, and Charlotte had not yet met the love of her life. That was all it was. Still, the tune stayed with Louisa as she strolled with Gideon across the square, and she had no idea why.

Minutes later she and Gideon were seated on the large sofa in Matt's study. Grace sat next to him at his desk. Apparently, he had been giving Louisa's settlements a great deal of thought, as he merely handed Gideon a sheaf of papers.

"Take a look at that. I believe it will accomplish both our purposes."

Slightly miffed that her brother had not handed them to her first, she said, "And what purpose is that?"

"To ensure that you keep your funds," Matt answered absently.

She was about to agree to his goal—after all, she had heard horror stories about ladies being left with little to nothing of their dowry—when Gideon said firmly, "I do not wish any of your money to be used for the dukedom."

"I beg your pardon?" Louisa asked, taken aback. Was this not going to be her home as well? Did she not have the right, in actuality a duty, to help where help was needed?

"I will handle," Gideon said in a high-handed tone, "the financial problems the dukedom is currently having without resorting to my wife's funds."

The pain started in her back teeth as they ground together. "What if I wish to be of aid?"

"Louisa, *I* do not want to be taken for a fortune hunter. My dear," he softened his tenor, "let us not argue about this. I am sure you will find much you wish to do, but until you've seen the estate you cannot know what should be done in any event."

She was about to argue when he pressed his lips to the backs of her fingers, causing those delightful shivers to warm her arm. She understood his desire not to be perceived as marrying her for her dowry. Perhaps there was no need to have this discussion at present. He was correct. She did not know what was required. However, despite what he seemed to think, she would do as she saw fit. They were her funds after all.

When Matt suggested the amount she should receive for pin money, Gideon countered with a much higher figure.

"Are you quite sure?" Matt asked.

"It is not much more than my mother received." Gideon's jaw barely moved. "Louisa will be a duchess, and I will not have my father's dealings adversely affect her."

It was then she realized she was being treated to a fine display of male pride. *Dukish*, if that was even a word, *dukish male pride* might describe it even better. Arguing would get them nowhere. It would be much better to let him have his way now and approach the issue later. When his sense of self-esteem was not so much at stake. After all, he *was* trying to take care of her, and she could not object to his intentions even though she did object to his methods.

They next discussed where she would live in the event she became a widow with either a grown son or if Gideon's brother became the duke. After that, she let her mind wander as the discussion delved into how the trusts were to be set up.

"Would you like to inspect Rothwell House tomorrow?" Gideon asked, bringing her attention back to him.

"When tomorrow? I believe I am engaged for a Venetian breakfast in the afternoon."

Gideon squeezed her hand. "You could start early and finish the next day."

She dearly wanted to begin and see how she would get on with the servants. Meeting with the housekeeper and forging a working relationship with her before her marriage would be the best way to start. That is what Grace had done. "Yes, I'd be happy to."

"Grace, my love," Matt said as he stared at Gideon, "wouldn't you like to accompany Louisa?"

Her sister-in-law's eyes lit with laughter. "No. I believe I would be decidedly *de trop*. Louisa must learn to get on with Rothwell's housekeeper on her own." For some reason, Matt's answering scowl made Grace laugh. "They will be wed soon enough. I heard Louisa and Rothwell mention two weeks. That is just enough time for Patience and Richard to be notified and travel to Town."

"Very well. If you see nothing wrong with the plan," Matt said dubiously.

Goodness. What did he think would happen during a house tour? The most exciting thing Louisa would be doing was taking account of linen and such. Well, perhaps seeing where she and Gideon would sleep might be a bit thrilling.

"None at all, my love." Grace rose, shaking out her skirts. "Rothwell, as you are to join the family, I invite you to take luncheon with us. That will be the best place to tell the children the news."

Gideon gave Lady Worthington a polite smile. "I would be delighted, my lady."

She would not be so sanguine if she knew what he had planned for Louisa, and meeting his housekeeper was not part of it. However, introducing her to where she would sleep was. The hours between this afternoon and tomorrow morning would be some of the longest in his life.

"Please, call me Grace."

"Thank you."

She inclined her head. "I shall go across the square and make sure an extra plate is set. Louisa, you may bring Rothwell."

Louisa smiled for the first time that afternoon. She had

taken the discussions seriously and, for a while, Gideon thought she was going to argue with him about his pronouncement that she not spend her funds for the house or estate. Yet she had seen reason and not pursued the matter. All in all, the meeting had gone very well indeed.

Shortly after Grace had departed, Louisa took his arm. "I hope you like cats."

"Barn cats?" Gideon asked, a little confused. "I used to play with them as a child."

"No, house cats." Louisa had a smug look on her face.

"I do not think we have ever had a cat in the house. Well"—now that he thought about it—"I may have seen one in the kitchen."

"Mine does love visiting the kitchen. Our cook is very fond of her for she is a great mouser and loves almost everything he makes."

That he did not believe at all. Meat and some morsels of cheese perhaps, but everything? "Such as?"

"Garlic, melons, croissants." She gave an airy wave of her hand. "I must admit she is not fond of onions."

They had crossed the square and were climbing the steps to Stanwood House. "I have never heard of a cat who likes garlic."

"Well, she is French. Jacques, our cook, dotes on her."

Gideon was beginning to think Louisa was making a May game of him. "I look forward to meeting this paragon of a cat. What have you named her?"

"Chloe."

"That is quite grand."

"She is a very special breed of cat." She led the way to the main staircase. "I shall introduce you."

He followed her up the stairs into a sunny parlor.

"Chloe, *allez ma petite*."

Two kittens, one with a red ribbon around her neck and the other with a pink ribbon, peeped out from under the sofa. "Ah, there you are." Louisa bent down, giving him an excellent view down her bodice. "*Allez*, my Chloe."

The kitten with the red ribbon scampered to Louisa. Sitting at her feet, the kitten looked up with large yellow eyes and raised a paw, tapping at Louisa's skirt. "Such a perfect girl." She grinned. "The one with the pink ribbon is Charlotte's. Her name is Collette."

Louisa picked the creature up, cuddling it close to her bosom. Still the cat had not made a sound. He'd never seen a cat that didn't meow. "Is there something wrong with it?"

Her brows came together. "What do you mean?"

"Most cats make sounds." Surely he did not need to mimic a cat.

"Oh!" She chuckled. "The Chartreux is a silent cat. Even when they speak, it is not a meow such as other cats make. It is more like a chirp."

He reached out, touching the soft fur, but the animal huddled closer to Louisa. That was strange. Most cats liked him. "She isn't very friendly."

"They do not like strangers. I believe it became bred into the breed when they were hunted in the Middle Ages. Give her some time, and she will allow you to stroke her."

"How did you come by her?"

"My friend Dotty, the Marchioness of Merton, rescued them. Her mother-in-law, the dowager marchioness, knew the breed and told us about them. What do you think of her?" Louisa's bright blue gaze collided with his.

He doubted she was asking for permission to bring the cat with her when they married. She would do it as a matter of course. "I think she is"—how to describe a kitten?—"beautiful."

Louisa's smile was all he could wish for. "I'm glad you like her."

A loud sound rumbled through the house, almost like a herd of elephants.

"There are the children," she said, placing the cat on the floor. "We should go down to luncheon."

All—he counted to himself—eight of them. Lady Charlotte could not be counted among the number stampeding down the stairs. He had managed to make it through his interview with Worthington this morning without being bloodied, and Gideon had already been introduced to all of Louisa's brothers and sisters. Why then was he nervous about telling them he was going to wed their sister?

Taking his hand, Louisa led him to the same room they had dined in before. This time a place had already been set for him on Grace's right. Louisa took the chair on the other side of him. Sliding him quick looks, the children quickly took their places around the table.

"We have an announcement," Louisa said, smiling at the children. "Rothwell and I have decided to marry."

The room was silent as he lifted her hand to his lips, then pandemonium broke out.

"Aren't you going to kiss her properly?" one of the twins asked.

Apparently, he looked confused as the second one added, "On the mouth. Like Matt and Grace kiss."

"He's probably afraid Matt will plant him a facer," Walter replied sagely.

"Not if they are going to marry!" one of Louisa's sisters, Madeline, chimed in. "Isn't that so, Matt?"

Rather than replying, Worthington sat back with a smirk on his face. Taking Louisa's chin between his thumb and forefinger, Gideon brushed a soft kiss against her lips.

"Ugh!" the youngest boy exclaimed.

"If you have all had your say . . ." Louisa began.

"I haven't been able to say a word yet," the smallest dark-haired girl pouted.

"Neither have I," the one with two missing front teeth—Mary, that was it—commented.

Louisa smiled at the two youngest girls. “Theo, you go first, then Mary.”

“Welcome to our family,” Theo said. “We can always use more brothers.”

“I want to wish you are happy.” Mary glanced at Grace. “Did I say that properly?”

“You did fine, sweetheart.”

Gideon hoped they would be happy as well. It amazed him that he had known Louisa for only a week. If anyone had told him he would have fallen deeply in love with a woman in that amount of time, he would have thought them mad. Yet he had. And although he knew Louisa cared deeply for him, he was not sure she loved him. It was a damnable position for a man to be in. He did not dare ask her, and he did not want to leave himself open to be the first one to express his feelings. What the devil was he to do?

Chapter Nineteen

Later that day, Matt sat with Grace in her study enjoying a brief respite while the children were either with their tutors or, in the case of Charlotte and Louisa, visiting the modiste and some other shops.

"I'm not sure about this," he said, tucking Grace closer to him. He nuzzled her hair, enjoying the feel of her soft body next to his and breathing in her light, spicy scent.

Grace lifted her head from his shoulder. "Not sure about what?"

"Louisa and Rothwell. I think they are moving too quickly."

"This from the man who wanted to propose less than a day after he met me," Grace scoffed. "That, my lord, is the pot calling the kettle black."

He settled her head back on his shoulder. "Be that as it may, you were older, and we agreed on almost everything."

"Would it help you to know that Louisa came to me with her concerns that her feelings might be growing too quickly?"

"Did she?" That surprised Matt. His sister always seemed so self-assured.

"I told her to trust herself. She is extremely levelheaded."

"Yes, but I had the feeling this morning that Rothwell will seek to control her."

"And she will seek to manage him and everything else around her." Grace laughed lightly. "Did you know that she paired Bentley with Miss Blackacre?"

"I had no idea. It would be a good match, though."

"And so will Rothwell and Louisa's. They are both proud and strong-willed and will no doubt butt heads, yet I believe they will be able to work out their differences."

"And if they cannot?" Matt would not leave his sister in a situation where she was deeply unhappy or mistreated.

"If he does something we consider to be beyond the pale, then she will always have a home with us." Grace placed a finger on the side of his jaw, turning his head toward her. "You have known him for quite some time. Do you think he will mistreat Louisa?"

He took a breath and let it out. "No. I think any problems they have will be the result of his pride and not being able to share his burdens with her. I am positive there are details about his situation that he has not told her."

Grace shrugged. "As you attempted to hide from me the fact that the men who abducted me were planning to take me to a brothel?"

"I wondered if you had put that together," he said ruefully. "You never said anything."

"I remembered the name Miss Betsy's. When Dotty and Merton needed help it all fell into place."

"Rothwell is having a problem with his father's former mistress."

"I see where this is going." She snuggled back down again. "I just hope that when Louisa discovers what is happening, he is honest with her."

"The fool should tell her now." Yet he had not told

Grace. Perhaps it was a failing of his sex, trying to protect the women they loved.

She was quiet for several moments before saying, "Did they ever find Miss Betsy?"

"No." If the woman was smart, she'd have left England by now. Loud footsteps pounded down the stairs, doors opened, and the sound of children spilling out into the garden reached him. "It will soon be time to take the children to the Park."

"Poor Daisy," Grace said softly. "I know she is missing her walks."

"She might be, but I do not miss having half the dogs in London following behind her," Matt responded drily.

Daisy had come into heat a few days ago. According to Grace it was the second time. He'd considered breeding her to Duke, but the idea of having a litter of puppies born when they were in Town was enough to make him change his mind. Perhaps in autumn, but not now.

"Including Duke," Grace retorted in the same tone Matt had used.

"Unfortunately." They had had to build a special pen for Daisy. The few times he'd allowed Duke to accompany him to Stanwood House, Matt would swear that the Danes were trying to figure out a way to release Daisy from her confinement. It had been a week already. Another two weeks should see them clear.

Suddenly, shouting and screaming erupted from the garden. "What the devil?"

Matt, followed by Grace, jumped up and ran to the windows just as Mary and Theo reached the French window to Grace's study.

"Grace, Matt," Theo cried. "Duke is climbing on Daisy."

"Oh God," Grace moaned, covering her eyes with one hand. "Just what we needed."

Matt glanced out the window to find the two dogs joined together, Duke wagging his tail as Daisy seemed to smile.

"What are they doing?" Mary asked.

"Right, then." Grace took Theo and Mary by their hands. "I shall talk to the girls and you may speak with the boys."

"But Grace," Mary objected. "You didn't answer my question."

"They are making puppies. Or trying to." Grace motioned to him as she gathered the rest of the girls.

"Puppies!" Mary and Theo jumped up and down with joy, firing questions at Grace too quickly for her to answer.

"Once I have everyone together, I'll explain."

Bloody hell! Patience, his stepmother, was going to kill him. She had always been so careful that none of his sisters were around when any of the animals were breeding. "Philip, Walter, come with me."

At least explaining to the boys what was going on would be easier than telling the girls. But he was damn sure going to have the dogs back in the country before Daisy gave birth. Ten to twelve puppies running around a town house would be a disaster.

The thought reminded him of Louisa inspecting Rothwell's house on the morrow, and Matt groaned. When Grace had inspected his house, the only thing on his mind was getting her into his bed.

Surely, Rothwell wouldn't . . . "Grace," Matt bellowed. "We may need to reconsider Louisa's visit to Rothwell House."

"You are quite sure that you wish your breeches, Your Grace?" Rollins's tone conveyed his pique at being overruled in the matter of what Gideon was wearing that day.

"Quite sure." He had plans for Louisa and having to

take off boots would only get in the way. "I may change after luncheon, but this morning I shall wear breeches."

"As you wish, Your Grace." His valet sighed.

If it wasn't for the fact that the vast majority of his clothing required specialized care, he'd make due himself. After all, he hadn't had a valet in Canada. But there had been women who had done his laundry when it needed it, and his clothes were not nearly as fine. "Thank you." He finished tying his cravat and was headed out the door when he almost bumped into his butler. "What is it, Fredericks?"

"That Minchinhouse person insists on seeing you immediately, Your Grace."

The man probably wanted a decision about Gideon marrying his daughter. "Have Mr. Allerton attend me." Gideon had not looked at the post at all yesterday. After luncheon, he'd escorted Louisa and her sister around Bond and Bruton Streets, returning home just in time to change for dinner and escort Louisa to a rout.

He hoped Templeton had sent the information concerning his mother's dower property. If not, Gideon did not know what he'd do. Marrying the man's daughter was not an option, for which he was extremely grateful. Yet he needed to save his mother's property. "Give me a few minutes, then show my visitor into my study."

"Very good, Your Grace."

Then again, this would not be a pleasant interview. It would be easier to get the man out of the house from the front parlor. "Better yet, leave him where he is. I'll see him in the parlor."

He strode down the stairs and into his secretary's office where Allerton was hard at work. "Have I received anything from Templeton recently?"

"Yes, Your Grace." From a stack on the corner of Allerton's desk he removed a letter, handing it to Gideon.

He quickly popped the seal and perused the letter.

My Lord Duke,

It appears that I do not have a complete copy of your mother's settlement agreement. I have contacted the other law firm requesting a full copy of the trust documents. This leads me to believe that your father was not the trustee, and therefore could in no way sell or convey the property. In actuality, as trustee he would have had a fiduciary . . . I will contact you as soon as I receive the other documents.

As to other developments, I have been in contact with most of the establishments doing business with your late father and Mrs. Petrie. I also provided them with a copy of the suit for criminal conversion that will be filed with the court. I am pleased to be able to inform you that you will not be held responsible for those debts arising from the fraudulent letter authorizing purchases for Mrs. Petrie. If you could provide me with a list of invoices that were paid, I shall set about having those funds returned.

Yr Servant,
J. Templeton

Gideon breathed a sigh of relief. "Did you pay for any of the things Mrs. Petrie bought using the letter?"

"Unfortunately, I was forced to do so," Allerton replied.

"Send the list with the items and amounts to Templeton."

"I'll see to it immediately."

"Oh, and Allerton?" Gideon smiled as the man glanced up. "You may be the first to wish me happy. I am betrothed to Lady Louisa Vivers. The announcement must be sent to the *Morning Post* today for publication tomorrow."

The grim look on his secretary's face cleared, replaced

by a broad grin. "Congratulations, Your Grace. I know of the family. They are well thought of."

"Thank you." He strolled out of the room in a much better mood than he'd been in for a very long time. "Now to face down Minchinhouse."

Gideon entered the small parlor near the front door. "Good morning, Mr. Minchinhouse."

The man had been gazing out a window, facing the street. A heavy frown on his face. Had he found out about Gideon's betrothal?

"Your Grace." Minchinhouse bowed wearily. "I'm so sorry. I don't know what that girl was thinking."

Was he talking about Louisa? Gideon was at a loss for words, but that didn't seem to matter as Minchinhouse continued, "She is generally so levelheaded. Just like her mother. God rest her soul. I thought, I believed, that she wanted the same thing for herself that I wanted."

Ah, he was talking about his daughter. Miss Minchinhouse's words came back to Gideon.

"I suggest you keep it to yourselves for a day or so."

The man stood up straighter. "Well, there is no need to beat around the bush. She's up and married. Told me I hadn't been listening to her."

"Gretna Green?" Gideon asked, trying not to let his astonishment show.

"Oh no, Your Grace," Minchinhouse said, equally shocked. "She would never do anything like that. She attained her majority yesterday. She and the man married with a special license that morning. They told his father and me after the deed was done." Minchinhouse pulled out a handkerchief and mopped his forehead. "It's not what I wanted for her, but it's a good match. Even if he isn't a duke." Minchinhouse's look pleaded with Gideon. "I hope you can forgive me for raising your hopes."

Gideon sent a prayer to the Deity that Miss Minchinhouse

had the determination to wed whom she wanted, thus saving him from another uncomfortable interview. Actually, he felt like dancing a jig. However, he maintained a sober countenance. "I understand. It is much better for your daughter to marry a man who has attached her affections."

"Yes, yes, so she said." He paced the room for a few moments. "The thing is that I still have your father's notes and the conveyance for the estate. It's not that I want to do you any harm, Your Grace, but they are no good to me now that . . ."

It appeared to Gideon that the older man was at a loss as to what to do with them, or, perhaps, to tell him what was planned. He cleared his throat. "As to the notes of hand—"

"Unless you want to buy them back?" Minchinhouse appeared more hopeful than he had since Gideon had entered the room.

"I am not honoring any of them," Gideon said before the man could go on.

Minchinhouse's jaw dropped. "But they are debts of honor. I can't tell you how many times I have heard that those debts must be paid first."

"In general, you are correct. However, a gentleman does not play with either minors or incompetents." He wondered when telling others that his father had been ill would become easier. "My father had dementia and was, therefore, not competent when he accrued the debts. He was also not the owner of the estate he gambled away."

"Not the owner?" Minchinhouse gaped.

"It is my mother's dower property, and he had nothing to do with it." Since his father did not even remember his mother, he could only surmise that Father had seen a report on the property and had thought it was part of the estate.

Minchinhouse stared intently at Gideon before saying, "Did many people know that you refused to pay his gaming debts?"

"Anyone who has approached me and asked me to honor the notes would know. As to who else would be aware of the circumstances, I truly don't know." Although by this time the entire *ton* knew.

"I see, I see. And the estate?"

"I don't think anyone, other than the lawyers, would know about that. Why should they?"

"Thank you, Your Grace." Minchinhouse bowed. "I have learned an expensive but valuable lesson. As the papers are now worthless, I will send the notes and conveyance to you when I return to my office."

"Thank you." Gideon wondered briefly who had sold the notes to Minchinhouse, but it really did not matter. At least now he knew why Miss Minchinhouse wanted Gideon and Louisa to wait before announcing their engagement. And he was relieved he would not have to try to buy his mother's dower property back. He smiled to himself. Louisa would enjoy knowing about this turn of events as well. They might even send the lady a wedding present.

"Fredericks, you may give yourself and the rest of the servants the morning off in celebration of my betrothal to Lady Louisa. Please have Cook leave something for luncheon."

If Gideon had expected his butler to actually show any surprise, he would have been disappointed. Fortunately, unlike Worthington, who lived in perpetual hope that his butler would crack a smile, Gideon knew better.

"May I wish you happy on behalf of the entire staff, Your Grace? If you will tell me when her ladyship wishes to meet with Mrs. Boyle, I will notify her."

Congratulating himself on his forethought, he replied, "Tomorrow morning will do."

"Very good, Your Grace. I shall inform Mrs. Boyle of the meeting and Cook of your wishes for today."

"I shall also need one of the grooms to carry a letter to Her Grace."

Fredericks bowed as Gideon strode down the corridor to his study. It was past time he wrote his mother not only about his impending marriage but the progress he had made in recouping at least some of their funds.

After that, he'd break his fast, collect Louisa, and introduce her to her new home. Or one part of it.

Chapter Twenty

Louisa had seen many town houses since she'd come to Town for her Season. Most of them elegant, some ostentatious, but Rothwell House had to be the most beautiful house she had ever imagined. The hall was paved with pink marble, as were the three niches, two of which held statues and the other a bust.

Standing behind her, Gideon pressed his lips close to her ear, and a shiver ran down her neck. "That gentleman came over with William the Conqueror."

"How interesting." Even more interesting was the feather-light touch of Gideon's tongue as he traced her outer ear, pausing at a spot just above her jaw. His large body pressed into her, and she resisted the urge to lean back. They would never finish looking at all the rooms if he kept this up. "You said I needed to inspect the house. Is your housekeeper waiting on me?"

"Eventually." A wicked gleam came into his eyes.

His hands held her waist, burning through her light muslin gown, causing flames to leap in her stomach. Other than the lone footman left to guard the door, she hadn't seen any servants since they entered the house. Was his situation so desperate that he had let almost all of his servants go? "Gideon, if you do not have a housekeeper—"

"My circumstances are not that bad. I thought to escort you around while we are alone and show you the most important room first. She is not necessary at the moment."

She wondered what Gideon had planned. "And that would be?"

"Come with me." He grabbed her hand, leading her up the curved staircase. Thick carpeting muffled their footsteps. "The carpet was made in Turkey to fit the stairs."

"How was that possible if the staircase was here?"

"It wasn't. It was made in Italy and transported to England."

"It's beautiful."

"I'll show you something even more beautiful." His voice, as smooth and warm as velvet, covered her like a cloak.

They climbed the next set of stairs and strolled down the corridor to the right. When they reached a massive set of carved oak doors, he threw them open. "This is what I want you to see."

She stepped into a large bedchamber. Light streamed from the windows along two walls, and a huge bed anchored the third wall. A door, probably leading to a dressing room, was on the fourth, nestled amid bookshelves.

"You must like to read," she said, tamping down nerves that suddenly screamed for attention. She had never before been alone with a man like this. Though why she was anxious she didn't know. After all, Gideon would soon be her husband, and her family knew she was here, although not that she was alone with him.

"It is a family trait," he said in a low, seductive murmur.

Releasing her hand, he stepped back and closed the

door. The latch clicked shut. Her chest tightened, making it hard to draw a deep breath. "I enjoy reading as well."

"I have some books we shall read together." He prowled toward her, like a lion stalking his prey.

In seconds he had her up against a wall. "Gideon"—her heart pounded so hard she could barely hear herself—"what are you doing?"

"You don't know." His lips curved up, giving him a roguish look. His gray eyes darkened like storm clouds as he trailed one finger from her ear, along her jaw, down to the space between her breasts. "Do you?"

Breathless, Louisa replied, "Kiss me?"

"Ravish you," he growled as his lips descended to hers. "Just as I've wanted to do since I first saw you."

He caught her bottom lip between his teeth, tugging gently. "The servants."

"Won't be back for another two hours."

She was sure her brother would never approve, and was about to say something to that effect, when Gideon claimed her mouth, and she no longer cared. His tongue slid between her lips, caressing her tongue. She struggled to match him stroke for stroke. Sliding her arms up around his neck, she rose on her tiptoes.

Her bodice sagged. "Gideon?"

"I want to see you, Louisa." He kissed her neck, pausing at her pulse. Then his tongue dipped into the spot between her breasts, where his finger had rested earlier. "Please."

Her body was on fire, her nipples hard. His palms covered her breasts, lightly rubbing. That was what she needed. They were going to marry. What did it matter if she allowed him to . . . "Yes."

That was all Gideon needed to hear. He'd had many women, but none who inflamed him the way Louisa did.

Her creamy skin was flushed, and she pressed her breasts into his hands, wanting him as much as he wanted her. Quickly he pushed her bodice down, freeing her arms, then her petticoats, and finally he was able to unlace her stays. Thank God they were the short ones. Untying her chemise, he loosened the fine linen, allowing it to fall on its own. Then her breasts were free, and he almost froze. How had a bit of fabric and boning hidden such treasures? Cupping them, he lifted the heavy mounds. Her dusky pink nipples had hardened into tight buds, begging him to taste. Louisa moaned as he dragged his tongue over one of the buds, taking it into his mouth.

Her fingers moved from the back of his neck to his cravat. Seconds later the long piece of starched linen hung loose. He shoved her gown and petticoats over her hips, taking time to caress her bottom as he did. Her hips pushed forward, making his cock even harder than before.

Soon he'd have her naked.

Bed. Now.

Toeing off his shoes, he started walking her back to the bed.

"Gideon, this jacket needs to come off." Her voice was so frustrated he almost laughed.

"It will. I promise." He shrugged off the offending garment, as she unbuttoned his waistcoat.

His shirt went next, she gasped, and for several moments he was afraid she would balk.

Louisa's lovely, deep blue eyes were wide as she stared at his chest. "You are beautiful." Placing her hand over his heart, she asked, "May I?"

Yes, yes. He had no idea what she wanted to do, but it didn't matter as long as her hands were on him. "Do whatever you wish."

Her tongue darted out, and she licked one nipple then the other. "They get hard like mine do."

He groaned as her fingers splayed over his chest, tangling with the hair. "Sweetheart."

"Yes?"

"Bed." Without waiting he picked her up, carried her a few steps, placing her gently in the middle of the soft feather mattress. "God, you are exquisite."

Her lips curved into a slow smile. "No more than you. But I think I'd like to see the rest of you . . . now."

Gideon had planned to leave his breeches on for a while longer, but if his cock was going to frighten her, they may as well get it over with. Giving her a wicked grin, he released one button, then the other, watching her eyes widen and her breathing come faster. He'd never imagined an innocent would be so . . . fascinated, or unafraid, but this was Louisa Vivers.

Unfastening the last button, he pushed his breeches down and climbed onto the bed. "Well?"

"Magnificent." Louisa traced a path from the top of his chest to his stomach, stopping just before the brown curls around his member.

Her body had cooled a bit when Gideon put her on the bed, but now . . . just looking at him, her breasts began to ache again. Then he kissed her, stroking her and rubbing his hot body against hers. A fire began to burn at the apex of her thighs. Then his fingers were there, caressing the place that hurt. No, not hurt, but something she had no words for. She stiffened, and her toes curled.

"Let it come, sweetheart."

Gideon pressed one finger into her and wave upon wave of pleasure coursed through her. But there was more. He rubbed his shaft against her, nudging at her core. She squirmed, wanting something she did not have words for. "I want all of you."

"You'll have me, sweetheart, but we need to take this part slower." His face was set in hard lines, as if he was in pain.

He eased into her, slowly stretching her to accommodate him. Just as she was about to tell him to hurry, he surged forward.

Louisa bit her lip against the sharp pain.

"Are you all right?" His voice was filled with concern.

"There is a burn still."

Brushing his lips across hers, he frowned. "I did not want to hurt you."

"I don't think you had a choice." Louisa smiled, reveling in the hot, heavy feel of him inside of her. "It's almost gone now."

He drew back and thrust forward again. Oh . . . Lord . . . yes. This was what she, her body, had wanted. The tension tightened as they found their rhythm. She wrapped her legs around his waist, and soon the waves of pleasure washed over her. "Oh, Gideon."

"Louisa, sweetheart. God." He trembled as he shouted her name, then collapsed.

For a few moments, they lay together, heart to beating heart. Then he rolled off her, pulling her next to him, feathering kisses on her shoulders and neck. "I don't want to wait to marry you."

She didn't want to wait either, especially not after experiencing how wonderful being with him could be.

He nuzzled her hair. Louisa had never felt as close to anyone before. Yet there was something missing. He had still not told her he loved her, and she could not bring herself to say the words until he did.

Grace had said they must trust each other. Did Louisa's

inability to tell Gideon her feelings, her love, mean that she did not trust the man who would be her husband? The man who would have more control over her than even her brother did?

"Are you all right?" he asked.

"Never better," she lied.

Beneath Gideon's hands Louisa's body tensed. He knew she was not being truthful with him. It was his own fault. He had rushed her. She was, had been, an innocent, and he had wanted her too badly to wait until they were wed. In reality, he had wished to ensure that she could not cry off. If only he knew she loved him as much as he loved her. But what if he told her what was in his heart and for some reason she could not say the same words. What if she was confusing lust with love? It was not as if she had any experience of knowing the difference between the two emotions.

God! I'm the worst kind of fool! I may as well just tell her. Louisa and I are getting married and she deserves to know how I feel about her.

"Louisa, I lo—"

A crash sounded from below.

"I tell you His Grace is not here," the young footman yelled.

"What the dev—deuce is going on?" Gideon jumped out of bed.

"You give him this card and tell him no one bilks King Sullivan."

The door slammed shut. "I must find out who that person was."

Louisa scrambled out of the bed. "You'll have to help me get dressed first."

She grabbed her chemise, but he took it from her hand, reveling in her soft, lush curves and waist-length hair that formed curls around her breasts and stomach. "Just"—he swallowed, his mouth suddenly dry, forgetting the confrontation below—"let me look at you."

A blush rose from her breasts, painting her cheeks pink. Then her eyes were drawn to a spot below his waist, and her color deepened. "Gideon, I—I should put something on."

Spearing his hands through her deep chestnut tresses he lowered his lips to hers. "Yes. But. Not. Quite. Yet." He'd punctuated each word with a kiss. "Lord, Louisa, I love you."

A slow smile curved her lips, and her eyes sparkled as if the sun, moon, and all the stars shone in them. "I love you, too."

"Gideon?" A voice sounded from the corridor.

He groaned. There was no way his letter about his betrothal had reached Rothwell so soon. "Mama?"

"Yes, dear. I could no longer leave you to settle this mess yourself. Are you dressed?"

In his arms Louisa moaned.

He had to get rid of her. "Give me a few minutes and I shall meet you in the morning room."

"Where are all the servants, dear?" Mama asked in a worried voice. "Did you have to let them go?"

"Umm, no. I merely gave them a half day off." If he'd known his mother was coming, he'd have made sure his butler was here.

"Very well, I shall see you soon."

Thank God. Now to deal with Louisa.

Louisa wrested from his arm, yanking her shift out of his hands. "I must go."

"No. You have to meet her sometime."

"Are you mad?" She stared at him as if he indeed belonged

in Bedlam. "I will never get my hair back up properly, and—and she will *know* what we were doing!"

It was a good thing Louisa hadn't looked in the mirror and seen her swollen lips. He helped her don her chemise, taking time to run his hands down her body. "I cannot sneak you out the back as the morning room overlooks the garden. As to your hair, surely we can manage a simple knot. I just need to find your hairpins." He scanned the floor, hoping he could locate enough of them. "As soon as we are properly dressed, I will take you down to meet my mother."

Louisa placed her hands on her hips, stretching the fine linen of her chemise across her ample chest. "And what exactly are you going to tell her we were doing with the door shut in your bedchamber?" She glared at him. "You told her you were not dressed."

Raking his fingers through his hair he tried to think. "No. I might have given her that impression." From the look on his beloved's face, he might just as well have proclaimed himself naked. "But I distinctly remember saying I would meet her downstairs."

She moaned again.

"Sweetheart." He took her in his arms. "She will not think less of you. I was born less than nine months after my parents' wedding."

"An early baby."

"Indeed." He chuckled.

"Oh." She had heard the saying that many firstborn children were early, but the subsequent ones were not. "I see."

He helped her slip her arms through her stays, then laced them up. Several minutes later they were dressed.

For a moment she'd thought of putting her bonnet back on, but that would indicate, as the only servant present appeared to be the footman, that she had come to the house alone with Gideon. There was nothing for it. She would simply keep her chin up and pray. "I suppose we may as well go down."

Gideon grinned. "You are not facing a firing squad." He kissed her again. "It will be fine. My mother and you will get on exceptionally well. And if it helps, you will shortly outrank her."

Only a man would think that important.

However, when they entered the morning room, the duchess was not there, but several covered plates were set on a table. "What is this?"

"Our luncheon. The meal I ordered be left for us." A wicked look appeared in his eyes. "I thought we might be hungry."

"You were right." She was famished. "Should we wait for your mother?"

"No. I think we should eat before she sees it."

A footman knocked on the door. "Your Grace. Her Grace said to tell you she is rather fatigued and will see you after she has rested from her journey."

"Thank you, Jacobs." Gideon uncovered the dishes. He glanced at Louisa and grinned. "You escaped."

Louisa had the impression that the duchess had discovered she was here and decided not to embarrass anyone. One good turn deserved another. "Do you think your mother would like to join my family for dinner?"

"I don't see why not, as long as I am invited as well." He placed a plate with cold chicken, salad, bread, and fruit in front of her.

"Of course you are invited," Louisa said, exasperated. He grinned boyishly, and she realized he was funning her. None of her other suitors had been at all playful, and she rather liked that Gideon was. "Tell me about your home."

"It's beautiful. You probably already know it was built on the site of an old monastery. My cousins and I played in the ruins."

They had the remains of the original castle at Worthington, but none of them had been allowed near it. The structure was too unstable. "That sounds dangerous."

"No. It is well preserved." A shadow crossed his eyes. "I will have to see what the condition is now."

"How much work needs to be done?" she ventured, picking up a leg bone.

"Louisa, my love." He covered her hand with his. "It is my responsibility and mine alone to bring the property back to the condition it should be in."

She stifled a sigh. "If you insist."

"I do."

Somehow she would find a way to help Gideon refurbish their home. No matter what he thought, he need no longer face all his difficulties alone. He would simply have to come around to her way of thinking.

Chapter Twenty-One

Dressed in her most flattering walking gown, Rosie approached Rothwell House. She would have rather driven up as she used to, but she had not been able to replace the phaeton that had been sold, and her new high-perched phaeton was not complete. At least that was what the carriage maker had written.

As she was about to cross the street a large traveling coach pulled up to the house. One of the outriders dismounted, sprinted to the door, and plied the brass knocker. Moments later, the carriage steps were let down and an elegant lady dressed in gray was assisted from the coach.

Bloody hell! It must be the duchess. What was she doing here?

So much for seeing the duke today. Rosie would have to find another way to meet Rothwell and convince him to be her new protector. The problem was how. Staring at the house, she thought of options. A young man like him must go somewhere for fun. But where? She'd just have to attend her friend Aimée's next drawing room this afternoon. All the young bucks attended Aimée's parties. Someone there was sure to know Rothwell's haunts. If the son was anything like the father, he would not be too hard to persuade.

Several hours later, Rosie was being kissed on the cheeks by Aimée, who wore what seemed to be layers of transparent silk fashioned in the style of a Greek gown. "I have not seen you in such a long time." Despite having fled France several years ago, Aimée's accent was still pronounced, and she used it to entice her protectors. "I am sorry to hear your duke departed us. I sent you a note. Did you receive it?"

"I did." Rosie drew off her gloves, handing them to a young, handsome footman. "Thank you."

"You are looking for a new protector, *oui?*" Aimée escorted Rosie into a large room at the back of the house.

Already the parlor was filling with gentlemen of all ages and other courtesans as well as artists, authors, and poets. She pasted a small but provocative smile on her face. "I am. I do have a man in mind."

They had reached a small group of men who ogled Aimée. No doubt wondering if the gold clasps on her shoulders released her gown and how soon they could convince her to allow them to be the one shown the prize.

"Is he here?" Aimée asked as she glanced around the room.

If only Rothwell were in attendance, but he was not. "No."

"Who is this man who entices you? Do I know him?"

"The new Duke of Rothwell," she announced confidently. After all, she had never met a man yet who could resist her.

"You think the son will be as good to you as the father? Is he in Town? Why have I not met him?" Aimée asked to the room in general as if someone would provide an answer.

One of the gentlemen suddenly spit the wine from his mouth back into the goblet. "Rothwell you say?"

"*Mais oui*." Aimée turned her golden gaze on a rather stout gentleman of indeterminate age. "Do you know him? Why does he not attend me?"

"Because he just got himself engaged," a handsome man with dark features and a hard mouth answered brutally as he raised his quizzing glass to Rosie. "And I happen to know that if he plays his betrothed false, her brother will have his stones."

Betrothed? A sharp pain started in Rosie's chest and spread. She hadn't realized how much she had wanted Rothwell. Still, she was no silly miss to pine over a gentleman. It must be what he represented. The respect she would have earned in continuing to be Rothwell's mistress, and the wealth. Definitely the wealth.

"I'd leave him alone if I were you. Even before he went to the colonies, he wasn't much for the muslin company," the gentleman with the wine glass added. "Heard it was a love match."

Not so much like his father then. If only she had known that before she had come here.

"Is she a young lady?" Aimée asked, slipping her arm around a handsome, dark-haired gentleman.

"Just out." The man passively stroked Aimée's bottom. "Not to my taste, as you know."

"*Oui, mon ami*." Her lips curved in a wicked smile. "I know very well what you like, and it is not what an innocent can give you." She turned back to Rosie. "*Mais*, my dear Rosemund," Aimée said soulfully. "I am afraid Rothwell will not do. The young ones are frightfully *vulgaire* when their beloved strays. Is that not correct, Kenilworth?"

"Definitely vulgar," the marquis agreed. "And indiscreet when their perceived lover strays."

"*Non*." Aimée shook her head. "For the time being you must decide on a different gentleman."

Rosie gazed languidly around the room. She was by far

the oldest woman present. Was she too old? Perhaps she would be better off selling what she had and moving to somewhere warm. After all, she had the jewels and the house. Then again, enticing Rothwell away from his new bride would be quite a coup.

"We shall see. I am in no hurry." Or so she wanted the gentlemen to believe. It was time to pawn more of her jewelry.

After arranging to take Louisa riding in the Park, a meeting with his solicitor, telling the man that everything to do with Mrs. Petrie must be stayed until after the wedding, and a consultation with his new man of business, Gideon was finally able to visit with his mother.

He had just taken a sip of the fine Assam tea his mother preferred when she said, "I hear you are betrothed. I hope that was who was in your bedchamber this morning?"

Quickly pulling out his handkerchief, he covered his mouth to keep the tea from spewing over himself, the table, and possibly his mother.

"Mother," he said in the most repressive tone he could manage. "Is that the reason you came to Town?"

She widened her eyes and smiled. Actually, it may have been more of a smirk. "Of course not, my dear. I could not possibly have managed to travel from Bedfordshire to London this morning."

He rubbed his cheek and considered how to answer her. "When did you hear about the betrothal?"

"It is very disconcerting the habit you have developed of answering a question with a question." Setting her cup down, she smoothed her skirts. "I may have heard a rumor that you were interested in a young lady. However, it was not until I was on my way here that our neighbor, Mrs. Potter, saw me and said she had received a letter from her cousin Lady Danfourth that you had got betrothed at a ball."

The damn women must use homing pigeons. "I wrote to you, but the letter must not have arrived before you departed."

"Well?"

"Well what?"

"Really, Rothwell!" By this time his mother looked ready to do murder. "Answer the question."

"That is what you get for asking who was in my bedroom," he replied smugly. "Which is none of your business. I became formally betrothed yesterday to Lady Louisa Vivers."

"And?" his mother asked expectantly.

"And you will meet her this evening." He grinned. "We are to dine with her family."

"That is all very well and good." Mama cast her eyes at the ceiling. A sure sign she was frustrated. "What I want to know is if you love her."

She was so much fun to tease, he thought about continuing the game, but decided to take pity on her. "Yes, I love her. So much so that even for Bentley's sake I could not stay away from her."

"Oh, good." She clapped her hands together twice. "I was so afraid you would decide to marry for money." She picked up her cup and took a sip. "Now you must tell me the whole story."

If that was all Mama wanted, Gideon was happy to comply. "You know that Bentley wrote to me asking for my help, but he did not tell me what it was he wanted?"

Gideon could have sworn Mama rolled her eyes. "Well, someone has to help the poor boy. He's as pigeon-brained as his mother." She took another sip of tea. "Although, nicer people you will not find anywhere. I just wish they had more sense."

He thought back to the day his betrothed found out what Bentley had wanted from Gideon. "Louisa says he dithers."

"I think that describes him quite well." Mama nodded. "I would like a glass of wine." She tugged the bellpull. Fortunately, Gideon's butler had returned, promising to bring a decanter immediately.

"By the time Bentley told me he wanted help making Louisa fall in love with him, I had already begun to fall in love with her myself. Though I felt I should not court her due to our money situation."

"Ridiculous. We are not in the poorhouse yet, and no lady worth her salt would turn down the man she loved due to our situation. Not to mention that you are a duke." Mama frowned. "She does love you, does she not?"

"She does, and could not care less about my rank." Gideon was not going to tell his mother about Louisa's insistence that she use her funds to aid the dukedom. Mama would probably think he was being foolish to forbid Louisa from helping him. "She had also already decided Bentley was not for her and selected a young woman she thought would suit him."

"I am starting to admire your young lady." His mother took a sip of her wine. "Go on."

And so he did. Mama's brows came together when he told her about Minchinhouse, she laughed when he related how Louisa had announced she and Gideon were betrothed, and her confrontation with Bentley, as well as how she had chosen Miss Blackacre.

"Goodness. I do not think anyone has ever spoken to poor Bentley in that manner." Then a gleam entered his mother's eyes. "Did he go running off to this Miss Blackacre?"

Gideon shrugged. "I don't know. Why?"

"I received a message from his mother that she was preparing to come to Town and asking if I had any commissions for her."

That couldn't have been more than two days ago. "What I want to know is how word travels around the country so quickly."

"My dear son, that is what messengers are for. They must earn their wages, you know."

"I doubt Mrs. Potter can afford to have horses posted all over the country."

"No." His mother tapped her cheek. "I believe they use pigeons."

Gideon closed his eyes. "Pigeons?"

"Yes, do you not remember Mr. Potter's fascination with the Persian method of using birds to deliver messages?"

"No." The blasted woman *had* used homing pigeons.

"You might have been too young to remember the conversation he had with your father. It was quite interesting," she mused. "Nevertheless, if Lady Louisa did not frighten Bentley to death, it probably did him a world of good."

"It did, actually. For the first time in his life he actually became truly angry." Although Gideon had lost one of his best friends. "He is not speaking to me at the moment."

His mother fluttered her hand. "He will come around once he realizes that Miss Blackacre is a much better choice." A thought must have occurred to Mama because she grinned. "Your Lady Louisa would have terrified my sister-in-law."

Gideon considered his flighty aunt Camilla and nodded. "I hadn't thought about that."

"If she brings up Lady Louisa, I must make a point of mentioning it to her." Mama glanced at the clock. "Oh, my. It is almost five o'clock. Where has the day gone? Tell me what I may expect this evening and then you must go."

"We will dine informally." He rose, strode to the door, and gave his parting shot. "With eight children under the age of eighteen. And dinner is in an hour."

"I beg your pardon?" his mother shrieked as he strode out of the room. "Gideon Rothwell, you come back here right now."

"I'll have the coach ready for you, Mama."

"You rogue," his mother called after him as a last parting shot.

Chuckling, he hastened down the corridor, reaching the front door as his curricle was brought around.

Louisa was his, and his fortunes had begun to turn. Gideon hadn't felt so lighthearted in months. Finally, the Fates were with him.

A slight pang struck as he climbed into his curricle. He should have waited until his mother was ready to depart, but a small voice told him he would need to support Louisa when his mother arrived.

Chapter Twenty-Two

Although Gideon had assured Louisa his mother was not at all high in the instep and had a wonderful sense of humor, she flitted around nervously over the preparations for dinner.

As Gideon had only given his mother one hour to dress, an action that had caused Charlotte, Grace, and Louisa to roundly abuse him, dinner was set back. After all, what lady could be ready to dine in less than an hour? Particularly after she had just arrived in Town.

Louisa's younger sisters were excited to meet Gideon's mother, but her brothers did not seem to care. They were more interested in having another gentleman to speak with. Especially after Matt said her brothers and Gideon would remain behind in the dining room for a little while after the ladies left. That was fair. In this house, the females greatly outnumbered the males. They deserved some time alone.

"Louisa," Grace said. "Go dress for dinner. The staff is well able to take care of the rest."

Giving one last look at the flower arrangements on the table, Louisa nodded. "I know they can. I am just a little nervous."

"I understand." Grace hugged her. "Although there is no need to worry. All will be well."

When Louisa reached her bedchamber, Lucy had her new cerulean blue gown hanging over the wardrobe door, and a tub stood near the fireplace.

"Let's get you cleaned up, my lady. You didn't leave me a lot of time to dress your hair."

Perhaps Louisa would be better occupied by having herself dressed than worrying so much about the table arrangements. It was important she make a good impression on Gideon's mother. Particularly as the lady probably knew who had been in his bedchamber this morning. Just thinking about hearing the duchess out in the corridor made her cheeks heat.

When Gideon had brought her home and Grace had asked about the house, Louisa was sure her sister-in-law had known what she'd been doing.

Sinking into the copper tub, she had twinges in muscles she hadn't known existed before. If Lucy hadn't been in the room, Louisa would have touched the places Gideon had touched her. It was as if she could still feel his slightly rough hands on her breasts. The bathwater lapped lightly over her nipples and she moaned.

"Did you say something, my lady?"

"Nothing. The water is wonderful." If only she could be in the bath with Gideon.

An ache started at the juncture of her thighs. Now that she knew what caused the feeling and what relieved it the throbbing was harder to ignore. Even worse, with his mother in Town there would be no repeat of this morning. Not until their wedding night.

"My lady." Lucy shoved a soapy cloth at Louisa. "There is not much time."

"I'll hurry." Her maid harrumphed as she made quick

work of scrubbing the cloth over her body. "There, I'm ready to be rinsed."

Half an hour later, Louisa was in the drawing room with Gideon when his mother was announced. By now, Louisa had met at least three duchesses. Yet none of them was like the Duchess of Rothwell.

She stepped in the room and smiled at Louisa, blue eyes sparkling with laughter. "You must be Lady Louisa. I can tell by the way Rothwell looks at you."

"Mother," Gideon said repressively.

"Do not mind him." When Louisa began to sink into a deep curtsey, the duchess stayed her. "He is afraid I'll embarrass him, which I will do if he doesn't behave. Especially after the way in which he absented himself, leaving me to travel to you on my own."

It was impossible not to laugh at that remark. "I am very pleased to meet you, Your Grace."

"As I am to meet you, my dear. Rothwell told me how you met and about the rift with Bentley." Flustered, Louisa opened her mouth but couldn't think of anything to say. The duchess held up her hand. "Whatever you do, do not apologize. Bentley needed someone to give him a push, and I think you might have done it."

"I do hope so, Your Grace. I know that he has begun to court Miss Blackacre." She turned toward Matt and Grace. "Allow me to introduce my family."

Once Louisa had introduced Matt and Grace, and the duchess had been given a glass of sherry, she greeted all the children one by one, asking their names and ages. When Mary smiled, the duchess said, "Have you received *tand-fé* for those teeth?"

Mirthfully, Mary nodded. "I got a whole shilling."

"A shilling!" Gideon exclaimed. "I only received a six-pence."

"Apparently, even the price of teeth has increased," the

duchess said, shaking her head. "I am extremely happy that Rothwell is marrying into such a delightful family."

During dinner the conversation was lively with the duchess as willing to talk across the table as the children were.

"I shall never teach them proper table manners at this rate," Grace said in a dismayed tone. Yet as this was related in a voice loud enough to reach the other end of the table everyone laughed.

"I think they are doing very well. Refinement can come later. At least they are all eating with the proper silver," the duchess called back down the table.

Never in her life had Louisa expected such unaffected behavior from a duchess. She liked that her future mother-in-law was lighthearted and playful.

Although she knew she would soon be a duchess, she had not truly given the matter much thought. After all, it was Gideon she loved, not his rank. Her gaze strayed to him. He was the only one of them who had not said a word. Would he want her to pretend to be someone she was not when they were in public? She was not sure she could do that without feeling like a fraud.

Next to her Theo tapped Louisa's arm. "Aren't you having fun?"

There was no point in making trouble for herself and Gideon. "Of course I am. I was just thinking about something."

"Making lists." Theo nodded.

"Yes, making lists." Of all the problems she might confront once she wed. Or was that borrowing trouble? She glanced down the table at him.

Gideon caught himself scowling at the same time everyone else at the table was laughing at his mother's retort. He was happy that Mama had finally shed the sadness she had worn like a mantle since his father's death and probably long before that. Still, for his own purely selfish reasons, he couldn't help but wish she had given him some notice of her arrival or, better yet, not come at all. The thought of not having Louisa in his arms and in his bed was enough to drive him mad. And when he had agreed to wait two weeks to wed her, he had assumed he would be able to spend the time introducing his beloved to the more carnal delights of marriage.

Was there some law that decreed a man could not have everything go well at the same time?

He glanced at Louisa and found her looking at him. She probably wondered why he wasn't joining in the merriment. Knowing her, he would be asked to explain himself. It had taken him a while, after his conversations with Grace and the children sitting near him at the table, but he had finally come to the conclusion that Louisa was not the typical managing female he was used to. She was the type of person who was driven to find a solution to any problem presented to her or anyone else. Whether the other person wished for her help or not.

That posed a problem Gideon did not even want to consider. Already he disliked having to put off finalizing the actions with regard to his father's former mistress until after he and Louisa were married. But with Louisa in and out of his house, as she was sure to be with his mother in residence, he could not take the chance she would find out what he was doing and decide to help. No, much better to marry her, take her home, then return to Town for a few days while the legal actions against Mrs. Petrie were finished. He had also discovered from Jacobs, the footman who'd been left to guard the door this morning, that Mrs. Petrie had been in the street not far from Rothwell House when Mama arrived. When Fredericks returned, Gideon had given orders that if the woman even attempted to approach the door she was to be sent swiftly away.

No wonder he was scowling. Still, he would have to come up with two good reasons for his mood. One for Louisa and one for his mother.

"Are you in trouble?" The high, childish voice belonging to Lady Mary Carpenter interrupted his thoughts.

He smiled. "No, why do you ask?"

"You were scowling."

Gideon looked into the girl's innocent blue eyes. Well then, three reasons. For he had no doubt that this female was as dangerous in her own way as her older sister. "I am merely, er"—he'd better think of something quick—"wondering if I should bring my brother and sisters to Town for the wedding."

Screwing her face up, Mary tilted her head first one way then the other as if trying to decide if he was telling the truth. Finally she responded, "I think you should. We liked Grace and Matt's wedding, and Jane's wedding, she is our cousin, but she used to live with us. And Louisa's mother's wedding. And I'm sure we'll have fun at your wedding, so your brother and sisters should be allowed to have fun too."

Well, that settled that. "I shall speak to my mother about it. We would have to take my brother out of school."

"If he is at Eton, he can come with our brother Charlie," she proclaimed cheerfully. "That way they may keep each other company."

"How old did you say you were?" Surely he was talking to a midget instead of a child.

"I am almost six," she said firmly.

He'd been right. Lady Mary would be a right terror disguised in golden blond hair and summer sky blue eyes when she finally came out. Taking a gulp of wine, he thanked the Deity that he was not responsible for firing off the girl. Nevertheless, he might have to ensure he was around for the pure joy of watching her run circles around all the gentlemen trying to court her.

"Ladies." Grace stood as did everyone at the table. "It is time we left the gentlemen to their port and brandy." She glanced at Worthington. "Do not keep them long. The younger children must go to bed soon."

As soon as the door closed on the ladies, the men—Gideon used that term loosely as two of the males were fourteen and eight—moved to Worthington's end of the table. Lemonade was brought for the boys. Worthington poured a glass of brandy, and Gideon accepted a goblet of port. The ensuing conversation centered around boxing and horses.

"I would like to go to Gentleman Jackson's salon," Walter said wistfully.

"Me too," Philip added.

"Perhaps next year." Worthington sipped his brandy. "Give Grace some time to get used to the changes. We should plan our visit when Charlie can accompany us."

"I suppose that's fair." Watching his brother-in-law, Walter copied the way Worthington held his glass and other mannerisms.

Gideon wondered if his son would act in the same way with him.

"Will you attend Eton in the autumn?" Gideon asked the older lad.

"Yes. I think I should have gone this year, but this is Charlie's first year there, so I had to wait."

"Trust me when I say that having an older brother already in residence will stand you in good stead." Gideon had always wished for an elder brother to show him the way.

"That and boxing lessons." Walter nodded solemnly. "Matt is teaching me."

"Indeed." Gideon remembered when his father had taught him how to fight. For some reason, being the heir to a dukedom seemed to attract troublemakers. "You should also make a close group of friends."

"Like you and Matt?" Philip asked.

"Indeed." Although Gideon's relations with Louisa might test that friendship for the nonce.

Worthington glanced at the clock. "It is time Rothwell and I joined the ladies, and you two made your way to bed."

Surprisingly, Walter and Philip rose without argument. "Good night," they said in unison before heading out the door.

"They seem like good boys," Gideon said as he followed Worthington out of the door.

"I am lucky to have a hand in raising them. Philip is going to be the only lad left at home next year. With all the females in residence, I'm not looking forward to that. He will require much more attention."

"Eight is old enough to start school. Why not send him?" Gideon had been sent away at nine years of age.

"Grace won't hear of it, and it is not important enough to have the argument. Besides"—he grinned—"I still have a great deal to teach him. Have you told Louisa about Mrs. Petrie?"

"No, and I do not intend to sully her ears with the story of a prostitute."

One of Worthington's brows rose. "In my opinion, you are making a mistake, but it is yours to make. I will not become involved unless I am forced to."

"By the time Louisa even gets a hint of Mrs. Petrie, if she does at all, the woman will be far away from England."

"I hope for your sake you are right," Worthington said with a large measure of doubt coloring his tone.

Gideon hoped he was right as well. He had no clue how he would explain what had occurred to an innocent, or mostly innocent, lady.

Entering the drawing room he found Louisa sitting in a window seat with Lady Charlotte.

"I think I see Grace signaling me." Charlotte hopped down from the seat, leaving him and Louisa alone.

"Is she always so accommodating?" Gideon asked, taking a place next to his love. He might not be able to pull her into his arms, but at least their bodies were touching.

"She is the sweetest person in nature." Louisa leaned slightly against him, increasing the heat coursing through his body. "What was bothering you at dinner?"

"I had intended to spend much more time alone with you during the next two weeks."

"Ah." Her voice was soft, sultry as the word came out on a breath. "I like your mother a great deal."

"So do I." He took her much smaller hand in his. "Most of the time. I simply wish she'd give me some notice."

"Now, with that I agree." Louisa's cheeks colored lightly. "I am fortunate she did not mention this morning."

"She would never purposely embarrass you. It is not her way."

"I am glad to hear that."

"My love, you must remember, she wants me to marry." Although having his mother around effectively curtailed his amorous plans for Louisa.

Chapter Twenty-Three

"She wants me to marry," Gideon had said. Louisa could only be glad for that circumstance, and that she was getting on well with the duchess.

"Gideon?" After this morning, Louisa had hoped to be able to spend more time alone with him as well. Yet with his mother in residence and a full house here, that was going to be difficult. "Would you like to take a stroll in the garden?"

"The arbor?" The corners of his lips twitched.

"Yes, if you do not think it is too forward of me." She used a teasing tone to make herself feel better about not having waited for him to ask for an amble to the back of the garden.

He raised her hand to his lips. The shivers started the moment his breath touched her fingers. Fire licked her skin when he kissed them.

"I would be delighted, and I do not think it is forward of you at all. You will soon be my wife and must become used to telling me what you want." His tone was laden with meaning she was just now learning.

They slipped out the door and onto the terrace. Louisa

took them on a meandering path to the arbor. Finally they reached the rose covered structure. "Gideon."

"My love." His fingers stroked her cheeks as his lips brushed her mouth before settling firmly on her lips.

She opened for him, seeking out his tongue with her own, caressing him as he caressed her. God, was it only this morning that they had lain together naked? "I want you."

"As I want you. This next two weeks are going to be hell."

His member hardened and her body responded with a dull throbbing between her legs. Pressing against him, she rubbed. "There must be a way."

Releasing one of her breasts from her bodice, he licked her already tight nipple. "I love the sounds you make when I pleasure you. It's as if you have written and performed an entire concert for me alone."

A symphony consisting of her grunts, moans, and screams, which he had managed to quiet with his kisses. Yet she loved how he, in turn, growled, and the way his arms held her so tightly, possessively. As if he would never let her go. "How do we join?" Her cheeks grew hot. She was turning into a wanton. "I mean, you have experience."

"The things you say." Gideon chuckled lightly. "Hmm, the trick will be not to get you too mussed. Kissing will be accepted. I'm not so sanguine about anything else. I might find myself barred from your presence if anyone found us out."

Louisa raised one leg, caressing his calf. "I think whatever you have in mind, we had best do soon. Someone might come looking for us."

"Very true. We dare not be gone too long." Especially with her brother and the rest of her family a short distance away.

If they were interrupted, it would not be the children. Although all that could be done would be to bring up their marriage date. She would be more than happy with that occurrence. A cool breeze wafted up her leg and his fingers found the apex of her thighs. The heat of desire flooded her as he rubbed lightly. "Yes. Oh, yes."

She unbuttoned the falls of his breeches and his member jutted out, hard and ready, and she stroked him. If only she had taken off her gloves as Gideon had.

"Love, that feels good." He groaned as he tucked her skirts up and lifted her. "Put your legs around me and let me do the rest."

He kissed her again. She wished she could curl up next to him and never leave.

"Louisa?" Charlotte's voice came from the other side of the arbor.

"What the deuce?" Gideon's whisper was rough.

Drat, drat, drat! "It's Charlotte. You have to let me down."

"Despite how it appears, this is *not* a good trysting place," he complained, and Louisa could not blame him.

"No." Louisa felt the ground under her feet, and called, "We are here."

"So I imagined." Her sister chuckled quietly. "You had better come in before Matt notices how long you've been gone. So far, Grace and your mother have been keeping him occupied."

Louisa straightened her bodice, and Gideon smoothed her hair. "We shall walk back with you."

Before they left the shelter he took her in a hard kiss. "If only we'd had more time."

She held him tightly for a moment, wishing they could have been together longer. "Soon."

"I will, naturally," Charlotte said, "love playing gooseberry. Shall I swear that you and Rothwell were sitting innocently on the bench holding hands?"

Taking his arm, Louisa rounded the corner of the rosebushes. "Do you think Matt would believe you?"

The moon was full and the garden lit with hanging lights. Charlotte's brows rose as she studied Louisa and Gideon. "Nooo," she mused. "I do not think I shall attempt what would be an obvious lie. You look a great deal like Grace did every time Matt visited. In disarray."

Louisa wished she could have been present. "I don't suppose you would like to mention that fact?"

Her sister tapped her cheek, appearing to consider the request. "In your case, I doubt that what is sauce for the gander is sauce for the goose." Charlotte began to straighten Louisa's bodice and hair. "That is better. You should attend to Rothwell's cravat and hair."

For the first time since they'd come into the light, she took a good look at him. His neck cloth was crushed, much like her brother's whenever he left his wife's study. His hair was also in a state from where she had speared her fingers through it. "Indeed. You cannot go back in like that." Reaching up, she rearranged his cravat into something resembling a style she'd seen and smoothed his hair. "Let us go."

He tucked her close to him as they strolled to the terrace. His mother glanced up when they entered. Fortunately, Matt, sitting next to Grace on the small sofa, did not appear to notice. Or had he decided that whatever time she spent with Gideon was all right as they were betrothed?

"Rothwell, dear." Her Grace rose. "I believe we must take our leave. We all have a great deal to do in the next two weeks."

His coach was called and arrived much too soon. Louisa snoozled with Gideon to the front door. More than anything she wanted to go with him. "Will you be home when I arrive tomorrow?"

"I would not miss seeing you." His warm breath caressed her ear. "We will contrive, my love."

Gideon was right. Two weeks was going to be an eternity.

Later that evening, as Grace snuggled next to Matt in their bed, she glanced up at him. "I was very proud of you for *not* saying anything to Louisa and Rothwell when they returned from the garden."

"I'm proud of me as well," Matt murmured against Grace's hair. "I suppose it is because Rothwell is clearly in love with her and she with him. And I am not such a hypocrite. I would be more worried if they were not sneaking off by themselves."

She rose, propping herself on her elbow, and scowled at him. "You are being almost scandalously large-minded."

"Sweetheart, the Viverses have always been a randy bunch." Closing the short distance between their lips, he covered her mouth, silencing her for a moment. "You should know that by now." He leered at her, making her blood heat. "I would think the Carpenters are not prudes."

If her grandparents, parents, and she were examples, they'd been pretty lustful as well. Yet she had to bring this conversation back to the point she was trying to make. "What do you think Patience would say?"

"Nothing good." He kissed Grace again. "It's an excellent occurrence that she's not here yet. She wouldn't understand."

"She was young once too, and she is in love with Richard," Grace pointed out. "She might—"

"Not when it comes to her daughter." Matt rolled her under him. "I must trust that Rothwell is experienced enough not to be caught with Louisa."

"Mattheus Worthington! Of all the things to say." Grace laughed.

"I shall have a word with him. After all, I know what it's like to have to wait."

"You never had to wait." She'd meant to sound forceful, but her voice was much too breathy.

"I did it to get you into my bed every night. I'm so glad I found you."

"As am I." Grace sighed as he stroked her breasts. "I hope Patience is not too upset that Louisa found her love while she and Richard were out of Town."

"Trust her to know everything about Rothwell's father," Matt said in a grim tone. "She is always au courant concerning the latest *on dits*."

"Well, that would not be helpful." Grace recalled the objections her stepmother-in-law had to her and Matt's quick wedding and resolved to do what she could to help Louisa if her mother tried to interfere.

Having sent his curricle home, Gideon was ensconced on the back-facing seat of his town coach while his mother occupied the front-facing bench. Normally, he did not care to watch the world from that angle, but for the first time, he did not mind. Now he could look at Louisa much longer as she watched him drive off. If only she were with him, everything would be perfect.

All evening, he had tried to find a way to marry her sooner, yet her mother had still not arrived in Town. Surely the woman had to have been notified by now. Worthington had sent the messenger as soon as Gideon had verified he wanted to wed Louisa. Kent wasn't that far, unless she was near the sea. In that event, the journey would be more than could be made in a day.

Perhaps he and Louisa could hold the ceremony the day after her mother arrived. Unless the lady wanted to hold a ball. Fortunately, Mama was still in half mourning and could not hold or attend any large entertainments. Louisa vanished from sight into the house, and he missed her already. He wished he knew more about the former Lady Worthington.

"Rothwell," his mother said. "You must be careful with Louisa's reputation."

He stared at his mother, but her face was only partially lit by the carriage lights, and he was not sure what she meant. "What do you mean?"

"You may have fooled Lord and Lady Worthington. Although I doubt it," she mumbled. "Nevertheless, you did not fool me. I know what you two were doing in the garden."

"Kissing?" he ventured. That was true. Yet if it had not been for Charlotte, there would have been much more.

"Harrumph." His mother's chin lifted. "Remember, I know who was in your bedchamber this morning." He grimaced. How could he have forgotten that? "If you are caught even kissing her at any of the entertainments, her reputation could be damaged."

"I am her betrothed," he retorted using his haughtiest tone. "I dare anyone to speak badly about Louisa."

"You"—his mother stabbed her finger at him—"are a young man with one thing on his mind." He opened his mouth and shut it again. He could tell she wasn't finished. "I suggest that after she has met with the housekeeper, you show her the household accounts. She will need to familiarize herself with them at any rate. You may use my old study as I no longer require the space."

Household accounts? There would be plenty of time for that after they were wed. Why the devil would he want to—

Ah. There was a daybed in his mother's study. "Where we won't be disturbed."

Still, he thought it was exceedingly odd that his mother would help him bed his betrothed. Then again, he was not going to ask.

"Exactly." Mama folded her hands in her lap. "I plan to be busy reacquainting myself with my friends and relatives."

"Including Aunt Camilla?" Even if he did not regret his engagement to Louisa, he did wonder how his cousin was doing. That was a fence that must be mended.

"The children were lovely and very well-behaved," his mother said. "I trust I shall have a grandchild soon."

Gideon blinked. Somehow he had missed something. Grandchildren? "The children?"

"Yes, dear. You really must pay more attention. Louisa's brothers and sisters. They are all well-behaved."

"They are," he answered slowly. "But I could have sworn you said something about grandchildren."

"Of course I did. That is what a woman my age lives for. What good is having children if they do not in turn give one grandchildren? I should like one as soon as you can manage it."

Stunned. And speechless. For the second time this week he tried to think of a response. One thing was certain, he was not going to discuss the getting of children with his mother. "You still have my younger sisters and brother at home."

"Not precisely at home, dear. Lucinda comes out next year and Anthony is almost ready to attend university. You are correct that Matilda has another year or two before she is ready to come out, but I am quite sure she will be delighted to be an aunt. All girls are, you know."

Devil a bit. Were they that old already? Where had the

time gone? Gideon had still been thinking of them as they were when he'd left for Canada. He drew in a breath, then let it out.

"It would be much better"—Mama continued as if this was any sort of normal conversation—"if Louisa could manage to give birth in time to attend the Season next spring. It is important that you attend. You do share guardianship with me."

Gideon couldn't believe his mother was discussing this now. Before everything was settled with their finances and before he and Louisa had wed. "Mother, at this point I don't even know if I can afford a Season for Lucinda next year."

"There is no need to worry about that, my dear." Mama's hand fluttered dismissively. "I have it all well in hand. Your father's estate manager is not the only one with an eye to keeping the family intact. Not only that"—he might not be able to see her eyes, but he could feel the intensity of her gaze across the coach—"but Lucinda has already had her Season put off by her father's behavior. She would have been a little young, but she was dearly looking forward to coming to Town last spring."

Gideon stifled a groan. He had never before realized how determined his mother was. How was Louisa going to take this news that his mother was attempting to coordinate her possible pregnancy for his mother's own purposes? On the other hand, a pregnancy would happen when it occurred. There was no predicting when that would be. And there was no reason he could not take his mother up on her offer of giving the accounts to Louisa. She did want to be involved in the estate, and it would give them time alone. As long as his mother did not mention her outrageous ideas to Louisa, all would be well.

Then again, he did not wish to find out what would

happen with the two of them in the same house. He'd have to send a letter to this steward having him ensure that the dower house was made immediately habitable. Otherwise, he would have no peace at all. He would simply have to keep them from having private conversation before then.

Chapter Twenty-Four

The next morning, Louisa had just finished tying the ribbon of her bonnet when a footman knocked on the door. "My lady, the Duke of Rothwell is waiting for you."

"Thank you, Hall."

When she reached the top of the stairs, Gideon smiled up at her. "Good morning, my love."

Her heart fluttered, and butterflies took up residence in her stomach. How wonderful he was, and how handsome he looked. "Good morning to you. I had hoped you would join us for breakfast."

She reached the bottom step, and he took her hand, pressing her fingers to his lips. "I would have loved to, but my mother commanded my attention."

"Perhaps dinner before the ball this evening." It wasn't perfect. They would not be alone, but they would be together.

"There is nothing I'd like better." He placed her hand on his arm, escorted her outside, and lifted her into his curricle.

A few moments later they turned the wrong way on

Carlos Place. "I thought I was to meet with the housekeeper today?"

"I have decided your duties will begin all too soon, and that we deserve a day to ourselves. I am abducting you for a picnic in Richmond."

"How wonderful!" She clapped her hands together. "Matt was to have taken us, but it never came about."

"Then I am glad to be the first." Gideon smiled smugly. "Richmond is beautiful this time of year. You'll love it."

She would love being alone with him. "I am sure I shall."

About a half hour later, they reached the park, driving through the gate. Louisa was greeted by the gently rolling landscape. Meadows mixed with thickets of trees, and farther ahead there was a wood. "It is hard to believe such a lovely place is so close to London."

"Would you like to see the Thames? It is much different here from Town."

She had long wished to view the famous river, but Matt absolutely refused to take them to the docks. "Very much."

"Then you shall." Gideon lifted her down from the carriage, allowing her body to slide against his as he lowered her feet to the ground. Shivers of anticipation coursed through her and her breath caught. A slow smile spread over his face. "Are you ready, my lady?"

The rogue. He knew exactly the effect he was having on her. She only hoped that he felt the same. One should not suffer alone.

"Absolutely." She smiled back. Two could play at this game. She might not be the more experienced, but she was a quick learner. She moved her hands from his shoulders down over his chest and stomach, hiding her delight as his body tightened beneath her fingers. "Lead on, Your Grace."

He brushed his lips across hers. "Minx."

Once he had unhitched the horses and hobbled them under a copse of trees, they strolled through the woods to a path leading along the river. There was a man standing up in a boat using a long stick instead of rowing. "Look at him." She pointed in the direction of the flat boat. "What is he doing?"

"Punting. He moves the boat by sticking the pole in the water and pushing it along the bottom. The boat is flatter to enable it to be in the shallower water without running aground."

"I've never seen anyone punt before. We have a lake at Worthington, but it is only used for rowing and swimming."

"Look at the ships over there." He drew her attention to a few huge sailing vessels farther out in the river. "They are East Indiamen."

"I have heard it takes half a year to reach India." She wondered if she would ever be able to travel overseas. Maybe not all the way to India, but France or Italy would be nice.

"Yes, and that is only if they have no problems. Someday steamboats will cut the journey in half."

"Steamboats?" She shook her head. "I have never heard of ships that run on steam."

Gideon turned her back along the path. "They have engines that use coal. Ireland and America are already using them. I met a man looking for investors for a ship that can cross the ocean. They expect it to be built in the next few years."

He seemed so excited about the idea. She would have to learn more about it. "Did you invest in the venture?"

"I did. No more than I could afford to lose." His gaze strayed to the river again, and his face became wistful. "It would be nice to see a return."

"I am sure it will be successful." Louisa had almost forgotten about his financial problems. During the short time she was in Rothwell House, she had noticed it was beginning to wear around the edges. When Grace had bought the new fabrics for Worthington House, she'd explained to Charlotte and Louisa how quickly materials can show their age. Grace also told them how to make curtains and bed hangings last longer.

At the time, Louisa had been a little taken aback at how quickly her sister-in-law had assumed control of Worthington House, but Mama had explained that was the way of the world. When a peer married, his wife became the mistress of his properties. Louisa hoped Gideon's mother was as amenable to the idea as her mother had been.

"Someday," Gideon said, "we shall travel to the Continent if you'd like."

"I would enjoy visiting all the countries and cities I've only read about." So much was changing in her life. It was as if her life had been a bud that was just opening its petals. Showing her a new world.

"As would I. My father talked a great deal about his Grand Tour."

Gideon glanced down at Louisa as she looked up at him. Bending down, he had just touched his lips to hers when a small boy ran past them, pushing a ball along with a stick.

An older woman, who reminded him of his elderly nurse, hurried after the child. "Master William. We must turn back immediately."

The child just laughed and continued to run.

"Wait here," Gideon said to Louisa. "I believe that young man needs to learn a lesson."

"I shall help his nurse." She released his arm and made straight for the older woman.

Within a few moments, Gideon had caught up with the child. "Halt right there, young fellow."

The lad turned, glanced at him, and looked nervously around for his nurse. "Who are you?"

"Someone who means you no harm. Luckily for you." He took the boy's hand in his. "I am going to escort you back to your nurse." They had arrived where Louisa was fanning the older woman. "You had better hope she doesn't tell your father about this."

The child, who had appeared chastened a moment ago, shrugged. "He is never home to care."

Suddenly, a deep sadness crossed Louisa's eyes. A moment later it was as if she had pulled a mask over her normally expressive face.

"Master William," the woman spoke in a stern tone. "You know very well the captain is at sea and will return soon." The servant glanced at Louisa then Gideon. "It has been hard on the boy, but this is his last voyage. Captain Harrow has decided his family is more important. A good thing it is, if you ask me." The woman nodded. "It wasn't as if he had to go in the first place. But he begged his father until his lordship let him have his way."

During the course of the nurse's explanation, Louisa's mask faded away. "Were you William's father's nurse as well?"

"Dear me, yes." The woman looked fondly on the lad and lowered her voice. "I'm afraid he'll be my last one though. Once the captain returns my niece will take my place and I'll retire. I'm getting too old to chase after little boys." The servant motioned for William to head toward one of the paths through the woods, then bobbed a curtsey. "Thank you for your help, my lady, Your Grace. I need to get this one home."

As the pair strolled away, the boy going much slower

this time than previously, Gideon glanced at Louisa. He needed to discover why she had reacted so strongly to what the nurse had said. "Louisa, you never speak of your parents."

"Oh!" She appeared startled for a moment before glancing away. "There is not much to tell. My father died several years ago, shortly after Theo was born. My mother recently remarried and"—she paused for a moment as if considering what to say—"she is very happy. You will meet her before the wedding."

That meant Louisa was about ten years of age when her father had died. Old enough to have known him. Yet her tone was dismissive, and she obviously wasn't ready to tell him what was wrong. "I look forward to it."

They ambled in companionable silence back to the main part of the park. When they had first arrived, there were not many people around, but by the time they returned to the carriage, the park had begun to fill and the sun had risen higher in the sky. He fingered his pocket watch. "I think it must be around noon."

"I think you must be correct." She tilted her head, regarding him quizzically. "If you truly want to know you could look at your watch."

"I could," he said slowly, wondering if she would think him silly for what he was about to say. "But I like to be able to tell the time without relying on my watch. It was something I learned to do in Canada."

"How nice." She turned away and tugged at his arm. "However, at the moment, I am more concerned about my stomach than the time."

He stood still, not allowing her to move him. "Yet I do want to know if I'm right."

Narrowing her eyes, she gave an exasperated huff. "In that case, look at your watch."

"What if I'm wrong?"

"Then you're wrong." She shrugged lightly. "I am extremely peckish."

When he still didn't move, she closed her eyes for a moment and her lips moved. Was she counting? Gideon was tempted to laugh. His cousin would have been no match for her at all.

"I do not like to be wrong," he teased, wondering what she'd do next.

Her hand moved to an elegant brooch pinned on her pelisse, and she flicked it open. "I am pleased to be able to inform you that it is five minutes past twelve, Your Grace. You were correct. Now may we eat?"

Despite the number of people milling around, he pulled her into his arms. "I wondered how long it would be before you took charge."

Unsurprisingly, she did not appear at all embarrassed. "When I am hungry, no time at all."

He tucked her hand into the crook of his arm. "If you will take the blanket, I shall carry the basket. I believe my cook made enough to feed a small army."

They found a place under a nearby tree. He was impressed by the way she quickly placed the dishes out in an orderly manner. This was the fashion in which she would approach any task, and it pleased him. She soon filled their plates with cold roasted chicken, buttered bread, stuffed eggs, cheese, and fruit. He poured the chilled white wine.

"This is excellent. My compliments to your cook."

"Like yours, he is French and takes pride in what he creates."

"Will he return with us to your estate or remain in Town?"

That was a very good question. Their regular cook used to travel with them, but when his father became ill and moved to Town permanently, the cook decided to remain with Mama. "I don't know. I really have not given it much thought." He frowned for a moment, then a thought occurred to him. "I believe that will be your decision, my love."

She gave him an exasperated look. "Very well. I shall consult with your mother and make a decision."

He leaned back on his elbows. "I knew you would make a wonderful duchess."

"Is that the reason you kissed me?" she asked, tilting her head to one side.

"That and I could not resist your lips." Gideon enjoyed watching the pink blush paint her cheeks. If only he could take her in his arms here, but there were too many people and someone was sure to see them. "Would you like to visit the theater?"

"Indeed I would." Louisa's joy was contagious, and Gideon found himself grinning. Something he had been doing much more often since he'd met her.

"I shall make the arrangements. Would you rather see a comedy or a tragedy?"

"You choose. I have not seen either." They repacked the basket and put it into the curricle, and then he handed Louisa up.

"Very well. I'll find out what is playing and tell you at dinner this evening."

He was glad he'd told the theater managers that Mrs. Petrie was not allowed to use any of his boxes. It would not do to have her around when he was with Louisa. In fact, he would be best served to take her immediately to the abbey after the wedding. Then he could return to Town and finish with the woman once and for all.

"You will have to make up a party," Louisa said as she took in the scenery. It always amazed her how different trees, houses, and fields looked when traveling a different direction. It was as if one had never passed them before. "Gideon, did you hear me?"

"Yes. I was merely wondering why I needed to make up a party."

She glanced at him. Although she could only see his face in profile, he did look perplexed. "For the theater. I am almost positive that, even though we are betrothed, we will not be allowed to attend alone."

"Hmm." He appeared to consider her assertion. "I think you are correct. Who would you like to have accompany us?"

"Matt and Grace, Charlotte, she will enjoy it immensely, and your mother. What do you think?"

"Definitely enough people to chaperone us."

Louisa chuckled. "More than enough. We may attend alone after we are married."

"I had thought," Gideon said slowly, "that we could travel to the abbey immediately after the wedding. I want to introduce you to your new home. If you wouldn't mind, that is."

This was unexpected. "I thought you said you planned to take your seat in the Lords."

He slid her a quick look. "Yes, but I doubt that will take more than a day or so. I can make a bolt to Town and return almost immediately."

She had enjoyed the balls and other events, but being at his estate would give her an opportunity to make a list of what needed to be done at Rothwell Abbey and begin making the changes without having to argue with him about using her funds. Sometimes it was easier to obtain forgiveness rather than permission. "I would enjoy seeing the abbey and getting to know the servants and tenants."

He seemed to breathe a sigh of relief. She hoped he

did not think she was averse to the country. If he did, she would have plenty of time to rectify any misperceptions he may have.

"The market town as well is part of my holdings. I think you will love it there. I do. I enjoy Town for a while, but I'm always glad to be home."

"I feel the same." She was also ready to begin her new life. With Matt and Grace's marriage and her mother's it was not really as if she had an old one to go back to. Louisa would miss Charlotte and the children, but something told Louisa her sister would soon wed as well. "Will your mother return with us?"

A look of consternation appeared on Gideon's face. "I had not thought to ask her."

"If you would like, I shall discuss it with her when we speak about the cook."

"Excellent." The corner of his mouth kicked up.

Before she could respond, the wind blew up and she clapped a hand on her bonnet. She hoped they were not about to get wet, but a quick glance at the sky reassured her that the weather was holding, at least for the time being. "How far from Town are we?"

"The outskirts are just ahead of us." He slid another look at her and grinned. "Would you like to go to your current home or your future home?"

"My future home. There is no time to do more than meet your housekeeper, but I feel as if I owe her that."

"I am sure Mrs. Boyle, as well as the rest of the household, knows I took you on a picnic today. Nevertheless, I agree. You should meet her."

Visiting Rothwell House—Louisa still had trouble thinking of it as home—would give her an opportunity to speak with the duchess as well. Something had obviously happened between his parents, and, not that she wished to pry, but she should discover what it was. It might affect her and Gideon. If so, she must be prepared to deal with any potential problems that might arise. After all, her betrothed had not been exactly forthcoming about the financial problems he was having or how he planned to resolve them.

Chapter Twenty-Five

Gideon glanced at Louisa. For a moment he thought she was scowling, but her brow cleared so quickly it could have been a shadow. Still, she had such an active mind. He would need to keep her well occupied until the wedding when he could take her home. She was much less likely to discover the full extent of the havoc his father had wrought in the country than in Town. He would also ensure he was present when she spoke with his mother.

By the time he drove up to Rothwell House, he had a list of items that would keep his beloved engaged. Everything from dealing with the French cook to the household accounts, which had not been kept in at least two years. That and the wedding preparations should give her no time to put her lovely nose where he did not want it.

By the time he'd placed his foot on the first step his butler had the door open.

"Good afternoon, Fredericks. Is Her Grace in?"

"Yes, Your Grace. She is in the drawing room awaiting your return." He turned to Louisa and bowed. "Welcome, my lady. We are glad you are here."

"As am I, Fredericks."

"Does she have visitors?" Gideon asked. That was the

only reason he could think of as to why his mother would not be in either her parlor or the morning room.

"A few ladies did come to visit, Your Grace. However, they departed not long ago."

"We shall join her." His butler gave him an odd look, as if something had occurred, but he was hesitant to speak of it with Louisa present. "Come, my love. Let's see what Mama wants."

He escorted Louisa to the drawing room, excusing himself to speak with Fredericks and praying his mother would not mention grandchildren while he was gone. Striding up the corridor, he regained the hall where his butler waited. "I have the feeling you wished to tell me something."

"Your Grace, a rough-looking fellow left this for you." He handed Gideon a folded note.

The missive was short and to the point, telling him to bring fifty thousand guineas to the Golden Palace this evening or other means would be used to obtain the money from him. It was signed *King Sullivan*.

King Sullivan? The man obviously thought highly of himself.

Gideon could only assume that the Golden Palace was a gambling hell and Sullivan its proprietor, and that Gideon's father was responsible for the debt and the correspondence. "He mentions a second notice."

"Yes, Your Grace. The footman who was on duty when you gave the staff an extra half day received a verbal message from the same place. However, with Her Grace's arrival, he forgot to tell me about it. I discovered the oversight today."

Ah, yes. Gideon strode down the corridor, crushing the missive in his hand. He'd be damned if he would respond to a gaming hell owner. He would like to toss the note in the fire, but perhaps he would be better off consulting his secretary as to how to handle the matter. Fifty thousand bloody guineas. Had his father had any wits left at all?

He strode into Allerton's office wishing he could go straight to Jackson's afterward.

"Look at this," Gideon said, throwing the missive on his secretary's desk.

Impatient, he paced while Allerton spread the paper out and read it. "Well?"

He took off his spectacles, wiping them with a handkerchief. "Naturally, the debt cannot be enforced. However, I do not believe we can allow this to stand. People such as this can be dangerous."

Gideon could not believe that the man would attack a duke. Then again there was the letter. He also had Louisa's and his mother's safety to consider. "What do you suggest?"

"With your permission, I'll send it immediately to Mr. Templeton. I am sure he will know how to deal with this sort of person."

"I agree. Please take care of it immediately."

Less than a half hour later, he entered the drawing room to hear his mother and Louisa laughing. The sound gladdened his heart. "May I know what the joke is?"

"Not a joke," Louisa said, wiping her eyes. "Your mother visited Bentley's mother this morning, but I shall let her tell the story."

Gideon sat next to Louisa, who poured him a cup of tea.

"The more I thought about Bentley's hurt feelings," his mother began, "the clearer it became to me that I was the only one who could repair the rift. As bad a match as it would have been, in a strictly personal sense, he did think he was in love with her. So I visited your aunt Camilla this morning."

"Your mother is ruthlessly brilliant," Louisa interpolated.

Mama beamed, and Gideon had the feeling she had not had so much fun in a long time.

"As I was saying, she came at Bentley's behest, for he has decided to court Miss Blackacre and wants to be able to do it properly. Although for the life of me, I do not know why one needs one's mother present to have a proper courtship. Nevertheless, Camilla was quite put out with you, my dear Rothwell, for snatching what she considered to be a much better match for her son right out from under his nose. Principally, as he had requested your presence to help him with Louisa."

Mama took a sip of tea before continuing. "You are aware that it is the custom in their family for everyone to live together." She shook her head in disgust. "Which I believe just creates more problems than it solves. As much as I loved your grandmother, I could never have resided in the same house with her. Be that as it may, I let drop that Louisa has already begun making changes in anticipation of the marriage. And that I was absolutely delighted that I no longer needed to be responsible for anything as she had it all well in hand, being the strong-minded young lady she is."

Imagining his aunt's reaction to having another lady try to take control, Gideon grinned.

"Then I congratulated her on Bentley's choice of a lady who was not only the granddaughter of dukes on both sides of her family, but had a generous dowry as well. And who had a reputation of being a very easygoing woman. Suffice it to say, that by the time I rose to take my leave, your aunt was hugging me and begging me to thank you for saving her from Lady Louisa."

Louisa had a broad grin on her face. "The best part is that your aunt is now going to do what she can to promote Miss Blackacre and make Bentley see what a close call he had. They are joining you for dinner tomorrow evening when your mother will make a passing remark about me rearranging the portraits of your ancestors."

Gideon couldn't help laughing as well. "I'm looking forward to seeing her expression. It will probably be one of horror. I don't think the Covington gallery has been changed in over two hundred years."

"It hasn't," Mama assured him drily. "The newer paintings are just put under or over the original ones. It is a complete hodgepodge. I do hope that when Miss Blackacre becomes the duchess she will take things in hand."

"I believe I am correct in saying that you may count on it," Louisa said. She picked up her cup and took a sip. "Mrs. Boyle should be ready for me now."

His mother glanced at the gilt clock on the mantel. "Indeed she should. If you do not mind, I will leave you to it. After all, this will be your house in the very near future. I have already expressed to my maid how pleased I am that you will be my daughter-in-law. Which means the senior staff will be well aware of my sentiments."

"Thus relieving you of the necessity of having to view every room in the house along with Louisa," Gideon retorted. Brilliant indeed. "Will you remain at the abbey after we are wed?"

"No, dear. I meant what I said to you earlier. A house cannot have two mistresses. The staff must never believe that Louisa's orders could be countermanded. After your father's death, I had the dower house put to rights. Not that there was much to do. I also plan to visit The Roses. I understand it has been let, and I wish to see if it is in good repair."

A light tapping sounded on the door, and the housekeeper entered. "Your Graces." She curtseyed. "My lady, are you ready for me?"

Louisa smiled and nodded. "I am indeed, Mrs. Boyle."

The housekeeper was a slender-looking woman in her mid-fifties. She took out her notebook when she and Louisa entered the hall. "I thought we could start with the schoolroom and make our way down."

Remembering Grace saying that a new mistress should inspect all areas of a house, Louisa said, "I shall wish to see the servants' quarters as well."

"As you wish, my lady."

It was soon apparent that, other than the cleaning, which was perfect, nothing had been done in some time. "I am surprised that the duchess has not ordered most of the hangings and curtains replaced."

"She has been in the country, my lady," the housekeeper replied, keeping her eyes averted.

There was more there than met the eye. The duchess had told her she loved London. "When was the last time Her Grace was in Town?"

"Must be about three years now."

Before her husband's death? "Why is that?"

They had reached the schoolroom, and the housekeeper smiled. "I had just become housekeeper when His Grace was born. Such a beautiful baby . . ."

She spent the next three hours with Mrs. Boyle, who told Louisa a great deal about the family and Gideon when he was a child. However, whenever she ventured a question concerning the previous duke, the servant changed the subject.

When she and the housekeeper had finished, she was

escorted to the morning room where the duchess and Gideon were waiting.

"I hope you had a pleasant time." Gideon rose to greet her.

"Indeed. Mrs. Boyle is extremely knowledgeable." Louisa decided to take the bull by the horns. "Did you know that most of the soft furnishings must be replaced soon?"

Gideon glanced at his mother.

"I know you must think I was a neglectful housewife." The duchess waved a hand. "However, you would not believe how busy the Season becomes. Then one is back in the country and has forgotten to do what needed to be done."

Why was the duchess trying to make Louisa believe she had been in Town when the housekeeper said the duchess had remained in the country? "I can understand how that might happen," Louisa said slowly. This would take further investigation. She glanced at the clock on the mantel. "Gideon, I must return home."

"Of course, I'll call for the carriage."

The moment the door closed behind him, she looked at her future mother-in-law. "Is there something you are not telling me?"

The duchess's lips pressed together. Several moments later, she sighed. "It has nothing to do with you, my dear, or Rothwell. Nonetheless, it is a subject that gives me great pain, and I do not wish to discuss it."

Well, that put Louisa in her place. "I understand. Forgive me."

"There is nothing to forgive. You could not have known." Her Grace smiled. "I understand your mother will be in Town soon. I look forward to meeting her again."

"She is Lady Wolverton now. She and her husband will be traveling up from Kent. I do not know exactly when she will arrive. Soon, I hope." Louisa would play this game now, but eventually, she would discover what had happened to make the subject of Gideon's father so unwelcome.

The next day, at Gideon's suggestion, Louisa started to work on the household accounts. Those too had been neglected. She hoped she could find the date certain that the duchess stopped working on the books.

Shuffling through the receipts, she was again grateful that her sister-in-law had made her put the Worthington House accounts in order. Louisa's mother had left a much larger mess than Rothwell's simply because Mama had never been able to make the books balance, nor could she bring herself to tell Matt.

As Louisa sorted the bills she put them in order by date, then began to enter them neatly into categories as she'd been taught. It would take more than a few days to catch them up, but having a well-ordered set of books gave her a sense of satisfaction. A pattern of spending started to take shape. The amounts for actual food items and other household goods decreased while the bill for wine and liquors rose dramatically. It almost seemed as if only the servants were eating.

Stuck between two bills for brandy was one for a pair of diamond earrings. But the date was not a year ago, as the other invoices were, but three months ago. Had he even returned from Canada?

If Gideon was having money problems, what was he doing spending a small fortune on earrings? Perhaps Mr. Allerton would know. He had offered to help her in any way possible.

Standing, she took the invoice, walked to the door connecting the secretary's office to her study, and knocked before entering. "I found a bill from Rundell and Bridge's."

"Rundell and Bridge's?" he asked, the color fading from his cheeks. "Please give it to me." He reached out his hand. "It should not have been in the household invoices. I must have overlooked it."

"Who were they for?" Louisa asked, letting the invoice go.

"I am not at liberty to say, my lady." He swallowed nervously. "I would appreciate it if you did not mention the matter again."

Something else no one wanted her to know about.

There was definitely some secret or another. But what? Not that it could be something that would interfere with the wedding. After making love with Gideon, that could not happen in any event. Still, she did not like being kept in the dark. Somehow she would discover what it was and decide for herself whether it was worth worrying about.

Chapter Twenty-Six

Gideon had no sooner returned from taking Louisa home when his mother pounced on him.

"Rothwell, you must be honest with Louisa." Mama paced the room with rare agitation. "She will be extremely upset when she discovers you have been less than straightforward with her. Any woman would be. After all, it is not as if *you* were the one engaged in scandalous behavior."

"It is not something I intend to discuss with a gently bred lady." Ever since yesterday when he had told her about Sullivan's threats, Mama had been after him to tell Louisa everything his father had done.

"Rubbish." She stopped in front of him. "She will find out and when she does you will have a great deal of explaining to do."

"Mama," he said gently, taking her hands. "Please understand. If I thought I could tell her and have her leave everything to me, as it should be, I would do so. However, I am concerned she will want to help me. She has no fear, and would not hesitate to confront the man." Or, in the case of Mrs. Petrie, the woman.

"What I understand," his mother snapped, "is that you are treating her like a stupid young girl, and she is anything but. She is a grown woman who will soon be your duchess. She has a right to know."

He'd had this conversation with Worthington. He did not need to hear it from his mother as well. A tic began in his jaw. "It is my problem. I will deal with it in my own way, without her help."

"Let me tell you something," his mother practically growled. "Your life and the management of the dukedom will go much more easily if you stop trying to do everything yourself. However, as you will not listen to reason, you must excuse me."

Gideon watched as Mama swept out of the room. He had never seen her in such a taking. He was sure that his course was the correct one, yet a small feeling nagged at him. What if she was right? What would Louisa do if she discovered he was hiding his father's behavior from her?

Allerton knocked on the open door. "Your Grace, I have heard from Mr. Templeton regarding the Sullivan matter."

"Go on."

"As the debt is not enforceable in court, he agrees it is a definite threat to you. Mr. Templeton respectfully requests that you consider hiring some men to provide additional protection."

Bodyguards? Sullivan would be an idiot to attack Gideon when he had the man's threat in writing. "I shall carry on as I have been."

"Yes, Your Grace." A troubled look appeared on his secretary's face. "There is one other matter. When Lady Louisa was working on the household accounts earlier, she found a bill for a pair of diamond earrings. I must have missed it when I sorted the invoices."

"The devil you say." He raked his fingers through his hair. "What was the date on the bill?"

"Three months ago. It was obviously one of the pieces that woman bought using the fraudulent authorization."

There was nothing he could do about it now. "Send it to Mr. Templeton. He will have to add the baubles to the list."

"Right away, Your Grace." Allerton hurried from the room.

It was probably Gideon's fault Louisa had found that bill. If he had followed his instincts, he would have been making love to her rather than seeing to estate business. Then she would never have found the bill. The memory of her in his bed, her silky dark hair curling wildly on the snowy pillow, made him groan. Why hadn't he been with her? Ah, yes. Allerton. With him working in the next room, Gideon had not wanted to take the chance of being found in an embarrassing position.

Who was he trying to fool? Stuck among the other invoices, she was bound to see it eventually. More to the point, if she found one invoice, there might be another his secretary had overlooked. Blast it all. He'd have to find another way to distract her, but the next time he and Louisa were in Town, he would find the keys and keep them in the doors ready to turn.

Bloody hell! Perhaps he should settle the Petrie problem before he wed, but then there was a greater chance Louisa would discover what his father had done. No. Staying the course was best. All he needed to do was keep her occupied until the wedding.

He glanced at the ornate mantel clock his great-grandfather had brought back from Switzerland. The gilt alone must be worth a fortune. If he was not able to recoup a sufficient amount from Mrs. Petrie, the clock would be one of the first items he sold. Perhaps he should have Allerton contact an appraiser. Gideon would have to speak with his new man of business before the wedding.

If only he could be with her this evening. They wouldn't be able to make love, but at least he could hold her. Yet tonight Bentley and his mother were dining with Gideon and Mama. He hoped it would serve to mend the rift with his cousin.

He would send Louisa a note and flowers. Perhaps that would make her forget the earrings.

Three hours later, Gideon was in the drawing room when Bentley and his mother were announced. While his mother was being smothered in an embrace which, for some reason, contained a great deal of dyed feathers, Gideon strode to a sideboard holding an array of decanters and crystal containers containing everything from brandy to lemonade. He knew his cousin would probably enjoy a glass of claret.

When he turned, hoping that his mother had survived the attack of the feathers and to ask what his aunt was drinking these days, Bentley stood before him.

"Rothwell." He cleared his throat. "I must ask your forgiveness." His cousin's throat worked for a moment or two. "I was wrong to blame either you or Lady Louisa. It is not possible, I realize now, to command one's heart."

Gideon was stunned. In all the years he'd known Bentley, the man had never been so . . . articulate. "There is nothing to forgive. Lady Louisa and I did all we could not to hurt you, but as you said, one cannot command one's heart." Or, apparently, one's kisses. "We did not plan for any of this to happen."

"I realize that. Miss Blackacre pointed out to me how you and Lady Louisa could barely keep your eyes from each other. I suppose I should have seen it as well, but Oria—Miss Blackacre said that men usually do not, and I was not to blame myself."

Louisa had been right. Miss Blackacre seemed to be perfect for Bentley. Gideon was also glad the lady and Bentley were on a first-name basis. Things must be progressing well if that was the case. "I have been given to believe that Miss Blackacre is a lady of exceptional understanding."

Bentley's smile could have lit the room. "Yes, she is. I hope to ask for her hand"—he screwed up his face in thought as he had since childhood—"again. But she is making me wait at least two weeks." His brow lightened. "That is the reason I asked Mama to come to Town."

Finally, Gideon was going to discover why his cousin, or any man for that matter, required his mother to court a lady. "What do you want her to do?"

"Help me entertain Miss Blackacre and her grandmother. I cannot very well do that without a hostess. I have invited them to dine with us and there is the theater, and Vauxhall. Do you know Miss Blackacre has never seen fireworks?"

"I did not," Gideon replied, wondering if Louisa had ever seen them. That might be better than flowers.

Louisa had dressed early for dinner and was in the Young Ladies' Parlor making a list of her concerns about Gideon. If she was to trust him, he must trust her as well. That was obviously not occurring.

"You're scowling again." Charlotte sunk gracefully onto the wooden chair next to the desk. "It must be Rothwell."

"He is hiding something from me, and I am attempting to sort out what it could be. This is the list of the things that do not make sense."

"Well." Charlotte turned the paper Louisa had been writing on, perusing it. Then her mouth dropped open. "You found an invoice for diamond earrings?"

"Yes. The odd part about it is it was dated only three months ago." That more than anything else confused her. Matt had said the dukedom was in poor financial condition. Why then would Gideon buy diamond earrings and for whom? Unless his mother had bought them, but somehow that did not make sense either.

"Let us set that aside for the moment," Charlotte said, "and look at what we know. First, the old duke caused the problems while Rothwell was in Canada."

"Second, he does not want my help in repairing the damage." Louisa pulled a face. That he did not want her help gnawed at her each time she thought of it.

"That is probably simple male pride speaking," Charlotte said firmly. "I truly believe that the reason Grace had so many problems with my uncles was due to their sense of pride."

Louisa still could not get the earrings out of her mind. "Yet what if it is something else? Rothwell wasn't even in Town three months ago. He had just returned from the colonies."

Charlotte tapped her fingers on the desk as she thought. "And his mother was in the country in mourning. So who bought the jewelry?"

"I wish I knew. I believe if I discover the answer to that question, I shall be able to solve the mystery." Louisa was certain she was on the right path. The only question was how to proceed.

"I agree. Although I must say, jewelers are very protective of their clients. I doubt if you could obtain any information from them."

She mused over what her sister had said. "I suppose you're right. Perhaps the best thing I can do is wait and see what else I can discover."

"It is not what you want." Charlotte grimaced. "But your wedding is less than two weeks away, and you really must pay some attention to that."

"Indeed." Louisa tried to shake off her trepidation. "Thank you for helping me."

"I do not know how much of a help I was, but I do hope

you are feeling better." Charlotte rose and shook out her skirts. "We should go to the drawing room or we'll be the last ones down."

"I feel as if I have not been here for days. Have you heard anything from Harrington?"

"Matt received a letter from him asking if he could wait on him when he returned." Charlotte didn't sound any happier than Louisa was about her problems.

"And?"

"I do not know." Her sister shrugged. "I have not met anyone else who interests me, but I will not settle. Even though you and Dotty found your husbands this Season, I do not believe I shall. And, as Grace keeps reminding me, there is no hurry."

"It is more important to wed the right gentleman than to marry just anyone."

"That is exactly what I think. I just don't know if Harrington is the one. I have a feeling someone else may come along."

They opened the door as a footman had raised his hand to knock. "My ladies, Miss Blackacre to see you."

Louisa glanced at her sister and grinned. As soon as she had discovered Gideon would be dining with his cousin this evening, she had asked Grace to send a note around inviting Oriana and her grandmother to dine at Stanwood House. "I am so glad to see you." She hugged Oriana and waited for Charlotte to hug their guest as well. "I heard that Bentley brought his mother to Town so that he could court you properly."

Oriana rolled her eyes to the ceiling, but a smile tugged at her lips. "He did and almost overturned himself."

"Oooh, I must hear all about it," Charlotte said, pulling their friend into the parlor. "As absolutely no one is courting me, I am living vicariously through you and Louisa."

"If no one is paying you attentions, it is because you show no interest," Louisa retorted.

"Or all the gentlemen believe that Harrington has stolen the march on them," Charlotte said as she sat on the sofa, drawing Oriana down with her. "From the beginning, please. We ladies who are without stories must be entertained."

"I was not surprised in the least when Bentley's mother showed up," Oriana said. "He had told me he'd asked her to come to Town. But"—a slight frown marred her smooth brow—"I was taken aback by her cool welcome when she met me. Although, I must say"—she grinned at Charlotte and Louisa—"her attitude made him all the more determined to make her like me. It must have worked because when Grandmamma and I visited today, the duchess could not have been nicer or more accepting. Which was quite fortunate as Grandmamma had been prepared to offer Bentley's mother a sharp set down."

From what Gideon had told Louisa of his aunt, she had no doubt the redoubtable dowager would have had the woman in palpitations. "You have Rothwell's mother to thank for her quick turnaround. She visited her sister-in-law earlier and spoke of me in glowing but terrifying terms. So that she would be more than happy he had not engaged himself to me. She also praised you, your connections, and your dowry."

Oriana blew out a breath. "I am glad to know it was not merely whim on the part of the duchess. I have only met her three times, but she seems a bit featherbrained, and you know how changeable people like that are. If I have any future doubts, I shall apply to you."

"Please do." Louisa laughed. "I have the feeling that Rothwell's mother is more than willing to keep her sister-in-law on the right path when it comes to your courtship. In fact, they are all having dinner together this evening."

"Indeed?" Oriana's eyes widened. "I would love to be able to listen in on that conversation. You do not happen to know of any secret passages in Rothwell House, do you?"

"Sadly, no." Louisa shook her head. "Yet I am certain to hear about it in the morning when Rothwell and I ride."

"Oriana," Charlotte said. "Do you love Bentley?"

Oriana was quiet for a few moments, then replied, "I am coming to love him as I think he is starting to love me. Before I accept his next proposal, I must be certain of both, but"—she smiled gently—"he is always attentive, and I do not think that will wane with time. He is also the kindest gentleman I know." She glanced at Louisa. "He has missed Rothwell's friendship greatly. I do hope they make up."

"As do I," Louisa agreed. "They were very close." And they would be again.

Despite her worries about Rothwell, Louisa knew she loved Gideon and would never want another man as her husband. The only question was how could she convince him to trust her as she trusted him?

The Golden Palace, Covent Garden, London

"Bloody eyes! What kind of gull does he take me for?" Patrick "King" Sullivan crumpled up the letter his accountant, legal adviser, long-time friend, and partner, Michael Hammond, had handed him a few moments ago. "Won't pay his da's debt because the old man was mad. He never looked mad to me. Who bloody hell does he think he is?"

"I believe he thinks he is a duke," Michael replied primly. "And I told you he was refusing to pay any of his father's gaming debts. The old man was mad."

"What the hell kind of gentleman is he?" Nothing like this had ever happened to Patrick before. Oh, there had been some who tried to run out on their losses, but no one had just said they weren't going to pay. "Bloody duke or not, no one bubbles King Sullivan."

The door to his office swung open. "Somat the matter?" his other partner, Robert, asked. "I heared yer bellowing all the way down the stairs."

"Nothin'. Don't you have somewheres else to be?"

"That's right." Robert laughed and closed the door.

"I seem to remember advising you not to send that letter." Hammond's calm tone irritated Patrick even more than he already was. Michael was the only one of them who'd gone to more than a couple of years of school. He also had a knack for talking like a toff. "If anything happens to Rothwell, the authorities will know exactly where to look."

"I'll get my balsam," Patrick grumbled.

"And just how do you plan to do that?" Michael asked patiently.

"I'll send Sean and Liam." Patrick's two meanest bullies. "Once they're done with him, duke or not, he'll pay up."

One of Michael's reddish brows shot up. "You're going to send them to Mayfair?"

"I ain't stupid. I'll get him when he comes down around here."

"In that case, you are going to have a long wait. I did some research and the man doesn't come down here. He doesn't gamble. He is not in the petticoat line."

"The what?"

"Whores, he doesn't visit the brothels."

Patrick didn't know how his friend knew so much about the swells, but his information was never wrong. "Got to have some vice. A mistress?"

"No." Michael shook his head. "He has just become engaged to a young lady."

"We can snatch her. He'll pay to get her back." Or he could sell her to someone who would pay for her.

He narrowed his eyes at Patrick. "I know what that look means. Do not even think of trying to threaten her. Her brother is the man who took down Miss Betsy's and that flash ken using the kids. You would then have two peers after you." He blew out a breath. "You are not in St. Giles any longer, Patrick. Let this one go or we could lose everything."

Patrick grunted. Miss Betsy and that baud she had work'n for her were just plain stupid. Think'n they could get away with taking those gentry morts when their old men were overseas.

The problem with not collecting what was owed him was that word would get out. Then he'd have even more problems. Sending his bullies to Mayfair wasn't something he wanted to do. The bloody watch was everywhere. He eyed his friend. He'd just have to tell his men to go canny, and not let Michael know what he was doing.

Chapter Twenty-Seven

Gideon arrived at seven in the morning to go riding with Louisa, but, for the first time, he was made to wait. The butler attempted to put him in a parlor, but he refused. He had never known Louisa to be late, and he resolved he would be right where she could see him when she came down the stairs.

His gut feeling, as his Canadian friends would say, was justified when she appeared at the top of the stairs. The minute she saw him, her shoulders, which had been up around her ears, dropped, and she smiled.

She met him as he made his way up the steps. "Forgive me for keeping you waiting. We received a note from my mother this morning. She is at the Pulteney and is joining us for breakfast. I almost had to cry off, but if we depart immediately we will be able to have a nice gallop."

Gideon tried not to groan as visions of ladies surrounding Louisa wherever she went attacked his mind. He lifted Louisa onto her horse, all the time wondering if he could escape with her now. Yet that would cause more problems. "Will I be able to see you at all before the wedding?"

Her palm cupped his cheek. "Of course. She will be in alt about our marriage and will probably want to take me shopping a great deal. However, I shall explain that I am putting the ledgers in order." She grinned at him. "And I have other duties I must begin attending to. Once her new husband arrives, she will not give me another thought."

"I am glad you do not think she will interrupt us too much."

"Indeed," Louisa said sweetly. "She will have him to distract her. Unlike your mama, who has never interrupted a thing."

Blast it all. She had him there. "Perhaps I should find my mother a cicisbeo."

"She is still in mourning," Louisa pointed out as she took the reins in her hands. "Shall we be off?"

Once they reached the Park, they gave their horses their heads. The morning was crisp and clear. Yet their ride was too short. Then again, the time he was able to spend with Louisa was always too short. He wanted her with him. In his home. In his bed. Next to him every day and night. On the other hand, perhaps her mother arriving was for the best. She would be too busy to discover what he didn't want her to know.

He was invited to break his fast with the rest of her family. There would be no opportunity to change his clothes, but that did not seem to matter when breakfast was consumed with twelve other people, most of them under the age of fifteen. He still had to blink to make sure he wasn't seeing double. Although in the case of the twins, he was.

He and Louisa entered the breakfast room. She immediately moved toward a petite woman with blond hair and light blue eyes he had never seen before, and he followed along behind her.

"Mama," Louisa said. "When did you arrive?"

Lady Wolverton hugged Louisa. "Just a few minutes ago. You know I stayed at the Pulteney last night. With everything going on, I did not wish to put Grace out. My trunks will be sent over this morning, and Richard will arrive later today."

Louisa returned her mother's embrace. "I am happy you are here." She took his hand. "Mama, I would like to introduce you to the Duke of Rothwell. Rothwell, my mother, Lady Wolverton."

"My lady, I am delighted to finally meet Louisa's mother." He bowed, expecting her to hold out her hand, but she did not. In fact, she looked none too happy to see him.

"Your Grace." She curtseyed politely. "Delighted." Yet her voice was cold enough to chill champagne.

His beloved led him to the opposite side of the table from where her mother had taken a seat. He held out Louisa's chair and then held out one for Theo. At least he was flanked by ladies who did like him.

What in perdition could he have done to get in Lady Wolverton's black books? He had never met the lady before.

He ended up being directly across the table from her and her penetrating stare. As he suspected, she did not look at him as one might imagine, to preen over the fact that her daughter had caught a duke, but to assess him as proper husband material for the lady's daughter.

Although she did not direct any questions to him, he was acutely aware of her sharp gaze burning a hole into his face as she assessed his suitability. He had never felt so uncomfortable in his life. It was as if she could see his lust for her daughter. Knew that if he ever got Louisa alone again she would be in his arms. Even Red Indians weren't as alarming as the viscountess was turning out to be. Not only that, but his shoulders were hunching up as if to shelter him from an attack.

Trying to relax, Gideon held on to the knowledge that no one could take his love away from him. He tried to ignore the woman as he conversed with Louisa and Theo, making them both laugh with a story of his time in Canada.

"I wish we could have sleigh races on the river here," Theo said, a wistful look in her big deep blue eyes.

"Someday you'll be able to," Walter, who sat on Theo's left, opined. "I heard that the Thames froze a few years ago."

Finally, after the footmen had brought around dishes, then set them on the table, Lady Wolverton ceased staring at Gideon and addressed herself to one of the twins sitting next to her.

"I do not think your mother likes me," he whispered to Louisa.

"No doubt she merely wishes she had been here when I met you." She spread apricot jam on her toast and took a bite, chewed, and swallowed. "I'm sure she was surprised to discover we are engaged. She almost didn't marry because of us, but we convinced her to follow her heart."

"I understand." Not that he really did. Sometimes women were a mystery to him. Yet it seemed the right thing to say.

Theo tugged on his sleeve. "She'll be fine once she comes to know you. I shall tell her you read stories to me when I was ill."

"I think Theo is right. There is no reason I can think of that she would not like you." Louisa gave Gideon a smile before tucking into her baked eggs.

Gideon was not the only one surprised by Mama's greeting and subsequent appraisal of him, and Louisa did not like it one bit. Mama, who prided herself on her manners, had been barely civil to the man who would be her first son-in-law. Not only that, but he was a duke. More than a few parents would have done just about anything to have their daughter marry so high, even if he did have some financial troubles.

Louisa suppressed a sigh. No doubt she would discover what her mother was about after breakfast. If Mama did not address the matter, Louisa would.

Almost an hour later, Louisa walked Gideon to the door. He raised her fingers to his lips and the warmth that his touch caused seemed to intensify. "I shall send the town coach if you think you will be able to come to Rothwell House later."

She turned her hands around, exposing his palm and kissed it. "I doubt I'll be able to visit today. Mama will wish to spend time with me, and Charlotte reminded me that I must attend to the wedding details."

"I suppose I should have expected that at some point." He held her eyes with his. "My love, every moment you're not with me I miss you. Waiting another week is torture."

She breathed in his scent, wanting to melt against him, feel his strong hands on her body as he brought her to heights she had never dreamed of before. "I miss you as well. I miss being with you."

He glanced quickly around the hall, then pulled her into his arms. "Kiss me."

Sliding her arms up over his shoulders, Louisa clung for dear life as his hard, warm lips touched hers, playing softly before claiming her. Tilting her head, she opened her mouth, inviting his tongue to dance with hers. His hands swept up from her waist, cupping her breast, and she groaned. She had no idea how long they stood there, locked in each other's arms. It could have been hours, days, and it would not have been enough.

A loud knock echoed from the servants' door, and they broke apart.

Gideon rested his chin on her head. "I suppose I should be grateful we were given these few moments."

That was probably due to either Matt or Grace. "As am I. If only I could come with you now."

Leaning back, he gazed at her and grinned. "My lady, if I were to take you with me now, I would not bring you back."

"Not even for our wedding?" she teased.

"The service would be conducted at Rothwell House no later than tomorrow morning." His tongue traced her ear. "Although I would be hard pressed to let you out of bed."

"I never knew you were such a wicked man, Your Grace." If heavy feet had not pounded on the steps leading to the lower level, she would have pulled him back into a kiss.

"Only for you."

The green baize door opened, and Royston entered the hall. "My lady, you are wanted in your chamber." He opened the front door. "Your Grace, I am to tell you that you are invited to dinner tomorrow evening. Lady Worthington is sending an invitation."

Well, Louisa thought, that was efficiently and very well done. "I'll see you tomorrow evening if not before."

"Perhaps we may ride together in the morning," he said in a low murmur.

"I shall do my best to get away." She ascended the steps, then rushed to the parlor overlooking the street and watched as Gideon mounted his horse. Yes, she would do her absolute best to be with him come morning.

Now to speak to Mama about her very poor behavior, but before Louisa did that, she must bathe.

"I am not at all happy about this betrothal of Louisa's." Patience Wolverton paced her stepdaughter-in-law's study as she heaved a sigh. Worthington had better get here soon. He had a great deal of explaining to do. Such as how Louisa had met Rothwell in the first place.

As if Worthington knew Patience wished to speak with him, he entered the room. "What is going on?" he asked, his tone not at all conciliatory. "I would have thought you'd be happy that Louisa is marrying a man she loves and who loves her. Yet you greeted him as if he were some sort of here-and-therian."

Patience stopped pacing and turned. All her fears that her daughter would be forced to suffer as she had in her first marriage flooded her. "How do I know he will treat her well?" she demanded. "His father spent his last years making a spectacle of himself. Wolverton heard that the dukedom is not in good shape. What if Rothwell is marrying Louisa because of her dowry? How would we even know? Any man can be charming for a few weeks. I think the wedding should be put off until sometime this summer. That would give her time to find out his faults."

She should have done that before she had wed the old Lord Worthington. She had been a little younger than Louisa and he had been charming. But once they had married, he had taken her to Worthington Place, made sure she was breeding, and decamped to Town or Bath or somewhere in the shires hunting. Matt had been more of a papa to his sisters than his father had ever been.

"I know he loves her because of the look in his face when he watches her," Matt said. "I know he is not after her money because he insisted it all be put in a trust for her use. He has even attempted to forbid Louisa from spending her money on his estates. Though, I'd like to see him try enforcing that bit of foolishness."

This was even worse than Patience had imagined. Louisa did not deserve a life of poverty. Oh, why could she not have fallen in love with someone more suitable? Lord Bentley, for example. "Then how will they live if the estate is bankrupt? He will not even be allowed to take his seat in the Lords."

"Patience," Matt said gently. "He is not bankrupt. He does not have much ready cash, but he is taking steps to address that issue. I predict he will come about much sooner than even he thinks he will be able to." She was about to make another objection when Matt held up his hand. "You are allowing your marriage to my father make you judge Rothwell too harshly. Not only that, but you of all people cannot blame the son for the faults of the father."

She did not like it, but he was right. Irritated that no one agreed with her, she threw her hands in the air. "Why could she not have married someone more suitable?"

Her stepson's brows rose. "Such as?"

"Lord Bentley. He is in love with her, and his father would ensure they had sufficient funds to live on, and—"

Grace choked.

Matt barked a laugh. "And we might just as well put a ring through poor Bentley's nose like we do to the bulls to make it easier for Louisa to lead him around."

Somehow the image of Lord Bentley with a large iron ring in his nose did not seem so strange. Unfortunately, it also made Patience want to laugh. "That is not fair. I am quite sure my daughter would have made him an excellent wife."

"The only one of your daughters Bentley might actually survive is Augusta, and she is not yet out." Matt raked a hand through his hair. "Thank God."

Patience felt like a sail luffing for lack of a breeze. She was not even sure about Augusta. She might not appear to be as strong a personality because of Louisa. Who knew what would happen when she married.

Matt was right. None of her daughters were biddable. "Well," Patience said, trying to save face. "I am willing to be persuaded that he is the right gentleman for Louisa."

"You shall have an opportunity tomorrow evening," Grace said, rising. "I have invited him and his mother to dine with us." She opened the door. "If this is now settled,

I have work to accomplish before we all go to the modiste to see what can be done about a gown for Louisa's wedding."

"Patience." Matt tucked her hand in his arm as they went into the corridor. "Does any of this have to do with the fact that you have not been here?"

"I do not know." As much as Patience loved her husband, Richard, she was not fully reconciled with not being in Town for her eldest daughter's first Season. "It might."

"Give Rothwell a chance. I think it is an excellent match. She will stand toe-to-toe with him, which is what I believe he needs, and she will never have to worry about having something to occupy her. You must admit, she is more than able to help him run his estates and support any political ambitions he may have."

"She is just so young." Patience wanted to wail.

Matt chuckled. "May I remind you, that you were the one who insisted she be brought out this year? I would have happily waited." He glanced up, tapping his chin with his index finger. "In fact, I believe your words were something to the effect of 'she knows her mind much better than I did at her age.'"

"When I was her age, she was already a year old," Patience retorted.

His mien sobered. "Despite what you always claimed, I know you were not happy married to my father."

"No, I was not." During the years of her last marriage and after her husband's death she kept telling herself that she had had a good marriage. Now wed to Richard, she could admit she had been lying to herself. She blinked back the tears in her eyes and straightened her shoulders. "Nevertheless, he gave me four lovely daughters, and a wonderful stepson." Reaching up she bussed his cheek. "I shall be happy about that."

"You'll be pleased with Rothwell, too."

"I hope so." Although, now with her initial fears calmed, she trusted she could give him a chance to prove himself. She should probably tell Louisa as well. Her daughter would be furious with her behavior at breakfast. "Do you know where Louisa could be?"

Matt's eyes lit wickedly. "Looking for you, I imagine."

Chapter Twenty-Eight

With Louisa busy with her mother, and his mother busy with friends, Gideon had made plans to dine with a friend. He strode down the street and across the square to the house Marcus Evesham used when he and his wife were in Town.

People, mostly servants, running footmen being sent with messages, and merchants were out and about while the *ton* prepared themselves for whatever evening entertainment they were attending. There were some nurses taking a last stroll with their charges before dark. A young lad leaned against the iron gate of the square, possibly hoping to earn money doing a service for one of the many visitors to the area. The gaslights were being lit, Mayfair being one of the few areas of London that possessed such a luxury. In the house he was passing, a footman held a small torch to a bunch of candles.

All perfectly normal, except for the strange tingle on the back of his neck. A warning sign he had not felt since he'd been in the colonies. Pretending to search for something in his waistcoat, he glanced around. No one seemed to be paying any more attention to him than they were anyone else. He scanned the square and stopped. The boy was staring at him. Someone was having him watched, but who?

Gideon continued on his way to Dunwood House in the middle of the street. As he approached, a young footman knocked on the door, which opened. Marcus made his way down the steps.

"We must stop by St. Eth's house before going to Brook's."

"Is he coming with us?"

"No. He and his wife left for Yorkshire this morning. One of Phoebe's sisters is about ready to give birth, and Lady St. Eth always attends her nieces' lying-ins. However, there is an important vote coming up, he is giving my father his proxy."

A few minutes later, Gideon and Marcus had just about reached Piccadilly when they passed an alley, and the feeling of being observed became stronger. Listening intently as Gideon had been taught by one of the Canadian trackers he had gotten to know, he sensed that they had been joined by at least two men behind them.

"Are you armed?" he asked Marcus in a hushed voice.

Marcus flashed a smile. "Always. A habit I learned while I was in the West Indies, and never gave up. The two behind us?"

Gideon did not even bother to ask how his friend knew. "Yes. A lad was watching me earlier."

"I take it you are armed as well." A statement, not a question.

"My cane is a sword stick." A present his father had given him when he'd left Oxford.

"Excellent. In that case, I propose we introduce ourselves. I am a firm believer in taking the offensive."

"Shall we?"

As one, they turned and faced the thugs.

The men were dressed much like middling shopkeepers,

probably so that they didn't attract undue attention. But scars marked their faces. The two had probably seen their share of combat, either in the military or on the streets of St. Giles. One of the men had a barrel chest. His chin stuck out pugnaciously, as if he not only expected a fight but wanted one. The other ruffian was taller and would have been good-looking if not for the nasty scar slanting from his forehead across his thin nose and down his cheek.

Who the devil were these men? Well, there was only one way to find out. Gideon raised a brow. "Is there something you want?"

"You got a lesson comin' to you, dook," the shorter one said.

"I imagine I have many lessons to learn," he said, using a dismissive drawl. "However, I doubt there is anything you could teach me."

"Enough talking," the taller one said. "We come to make sure you paid the king."

Sullivan. Gideon honestly had not thought the man would attempt to physically threaten him. Next to him Marcus tensed, shifting his weight to the balls of his feet. "It is not my debt to pay. I suggest you carry that message back to *Mr.* Sullivan."

"Your da, your debt." The shorter man attacked, but Marcus was faster, slicing the man across his side.

Gideon unsheathed his sword as the taller thug lunged at him aiming his fist at Gideon's head. Bringing his sword up, he slashed the man's arm, cutting through his wool coat. The ruffian's scream rent the night, and someone called for the watch.

"Don't let them get away," he called to Marcus.

Grabbing the barrel-chested thug's arm, Marcus twisted it back and up. "He's not going anywhere."

Gideon backed up the taller man to a building, holding the point of his blade at the ruffian's neck.

The sound of shoes pounded down the pavement. "What's going on here?"

Inclining his head, Gideon said, "I am the Duke of Rothwell. These two men attacked me and Lord Evesham. I believe their employer to be a man by the name of Sullivan."

"Yer Grace." The watchman bowed. "If you give me a few minutes, I'll get a coach to take them to the magistrate."

"We are in no hurry," Marcus said, grimacing at his blood-spattered jacket. He looked at Gideon. "Although we would make quite a spectacle continuing on to dinner like this, I propose we change."

Gideon, though, was in no mood for humor. His blood was boiling. Only his overwhelming desire to see Sullivan brought to justice was keeping his anger under control. What if the blackguard had attacked him when he'd been with Louisa or his mother? The man had to be stopped. "I want Sullivan arrested."

The watchman glanced at Gideon. "Think you'll have to talk to Bow Street about that, Yer Grace."

Marcus shook his head. "It never ceases to amaze me that islands in the West Indies have established police forces and London does not."

The thug Gideon was guarding began to slide down the wall. "He's losing too much blood. I'll have to bind his wound."

"Don't touch me," the thug growled. "No point in savin' me for Jack Ketch."

"Jack Ketch?" Gideon mouthed, glancing at Marcus.

"The hangman," Marcus replied.

"Sean's right," the barrel-chested man said. "If he doesn't hang, Sullivan will kill him. Same with me."

"Holy hell!" Marcus swore. "I didn't think I'd cut him that deep, but he had been running toward me."

Gideon looked around, unsure of what he was looking for until he didn't find it. "Where's the boy?"

Sean's laugh was weak. That of a dying man. "Gone back to report. You'll never get the king now."

"Curse it. Where's that watchman?"

"Right here, Yer Grace." A wagon drew up next to them. "I'll take this rubbish to the magistrate."

"I doubt they'll make it there alive," Gideon remarked.

"Just saves us a trial, then." The watchman had them bound and loaded into the wagon.

Gideon hailed a hackney. "I'm going to Bow Street."

"I'll go with you." Marcus climbed into the faded black coach. "With luck, we'll be able to roust them into trying to arrest this Sullivan tonight." Marcus pulled a face. "I had no idea you knew so many criminal elements."

"*I* do not." Gideon scowled. "It was my father." He was thankful the street was relatively thin of others during the fight. He did not want either Louisa or his mother knowing about the attack. He would have to make sure that the servants obeyed him when he gave orders that no one was to mention the blood on his clothing.

"*Are you out of your bloody mind.*" Michael's hands clenched involuntarily into fists. More than anything, he wanted to wrap them around Patrick's throat.

A few minutes earlier, Jack, the lad they used for running errands, had burst into the office. Michael had had to make the boy sit and catch his breath before he could make sense of what Jack was trying to say. Liam and Sean arrested and possibly dying. That was bad enough, but they had both, according to the lad, mentioned Patrick when they'd talked to the Duke of Rothwell, some other lord, and the watch. Idiots!

Sending Jack to the kitchen, Michael rounded on Patrick.

"I told you to leave it alone, but you just couldn't do it, could you?"

"How was I supposed to know the nobs knew how to fight?" Patrick had been in a murderous sulk since Jack had returned with the news. "I'm going to slice that duke up just like he did Sean and Liam."

Michael's jaw throbbed from gnashing his teeth. Why in the name of Mother Mary couldn't his old friend see reason? "What you're going to have is Bow Street coming after you."

Patrick shrugged. "I'll pay 'em off."

"You don't understand, do you? This. Was. A. Duke. You went after. Have you any idea how pleased their chief at Bow Street will be to see you hanged?"

Michael dragged a hand down his face. When the three of them had begun this venture, Patrick had been picked as the public face because of his intimidating, swaggering stature. Easygoing and jovial, Robert dealt with their guests, and Michael ran the business. Now Patrick had ruined everything. If they didn't all get taken into custody and the Palace didn't get shut down, it would be a miracle.

The problem was what to do with Patrick. Somehow he had to disappear. The Palace couldn't survive the scandal. There was also the possibility the militia would be called out.

And Michael did not trust the English. They hated the Irish and the Irish hated them. The memory of a sunny day in Dublin turning into hell as his mother was dragged into the street. His last image of her slammed into him. His beautiful mother being beaten by English soldiers searching for rebels. Even his father, an Irish peer with a seat in the House of Lords, couldn't help her. She had screamed at Michael to hide, and he did. Later, his father found him cowering in a neighbor's cupboard and sent him to school in England. Not Eton or Rugby of course. He wasn't born on the right side of the blanket for that, but a good, decent school. Later he attended university in Edinburgh.

Patrick and Robert had made their way to England as well. But instead of going to school, they'd been learning to survive on the streets. After learning the two were here, it had taken Michael months to find them and build the life they now had.

He strode out the door and into his own office before he could actually murder Patrick. Pouring himself a glass of good Irish whiskey from his own stash, he tossed it back, then poured another and sat in his large leather chair. What the hell were they going to do?

The door opened and Robert rushed in scowling. His hair standing on end as if he'd been tugging at it. "Is it true?"

"What?"

"Did that fool actually try to have a duke killed?"

"He had him attacked."

"Bloody hell." He dropped onto a chair before looking up at Michael, his eyes bleak. "I got Rebecca and the boys to think about."

And Michael had his father to consider. If anyone discovered the connection, which quite frankly would not be all that difficult, that would be another scandal. "He must go away, and we will have to convince the authorities that he acted without our permission or approval."

"How do you plan to get rid of him?"

That was the problem. Neither of them were murderers. "I don't know. Give me time to think. Maybe there is a boat we could put him on or turn him over to the runners ourselves—"

He hadn't finished his thought when the door bounced off the wall as Patrick crashed into the room waving a large coaching gun around. His eyes had the feral look of a rabid dog. "I go down, we all go down."

The last time Michael had seen that look was eight years ago, right after his friend's mother had been murdered. He rose slowly, sliding the right top drawer open as he did. Wrapping his fingers around the bone handle of the pistol he kept loaded, he eased it out of the drawer.

Robert stood facing Patrick, his hands loose, unthreatening, a lopsided smile on his face. "Are you going ta kill us then, Patrick? Like you tried ta with that duke?"

"I had a right to try to get our money from him," Patrick snarled, swinging the weapon around so that it was pointed at Robert.

"No, you didn't. And you know it"—Robert motioned to Michael—"You've been told before not to use the bullies. We're not in St. Giles anymore. Messing with toffs brings nothing but trouble. You had no right to put us all in danger."

The room fell silent. Then the click of Patrick pulling back the hammer on his gun broke the stillness.

Michael's stomach lurched. *Good Lord! He's gone mad.* "Robert, down!"

Robert hit the floor as Michael shot. He'd aimed for Patrick's hand, but at the last moment the man turned, and the ball hit him in the side.

Patrick's mouth fell open as if in shock. Blood seeped down his jacket and breeches. For a moment it appeared as if he'd remain standing, but he fell. First to his knees, then to the floor.

"Ye shot me," he gasped.

"You didn't leave me much choice," Michael said as he placed the pistol on his desk. He tried to harden his heart against his childhood friend, but his throat tightened with tears. All these years together. How had it come to this? The sad part was, he would probably never know.

Robert, lying on the floor, seemed too stunned to move.

The sound of boots pounding on the wooden stairs and

down the corridor brought Michael out of his stupor. No one should be here. The club wasn't open yet. Before he could think of who might be in the building two men he had never seen before rushed into the room, guns drawn, followed by two gentlemen with blood on their clothing.

"Sullivan?" one of the gentlemen asked staring down at Patrick's body.

"Yes." Michael nodded, desperately wanting another glass of whiskey. "He was going to kill my partner. I shot first."

The nob who'd spoken strode to his desk and took the full glass of whiskey, pressing it into Michael's hand. "I am Rothwell."

"Michael Hammond." He took the hand Rothwell held out. "This never should have happened. We told him to leave you alone."

Gideon stared down at the man who'd wanted him beaten up. "Was he the owner of this place?"

"The three of us"—Hammond motioned to the man who had picked himself up from the floor—"had a partnership. Decisions were to be agreed upon. Mr. Sullivan acted on his own in this matter, after we ordered him not to bother you."

There was something about Hammond that made Gideon believe him. Or perhaps he just wanted this to be finished. "I'm glad it's over."

"Yr Grace," one of the other men who must be Bow Street runners, said. "We should take these two to the magistrate."

"That will not be necessary. I believe Mr. Hammond when he says he had nothing to do with the attack on me." The runners appeared unconvinced. "Look at the evidence. Sullivan was about to shoot one of his own partners." Gideon glanced at Hammond. "What do you want done with the body?"

Gideon waited while Hammond gathered his thoughts. "I know it might appear odd," he said. "But I will take care of it. We have been friends for a long time. I just wish I knew what had gotten into him lately. He was always brash, but never out of control."

Taking in the body on the floor and the tears in the eyes of the man who was almost shot by his partner, Gideon nodded. "I understand."

Would he have been able to stop the carnage if he'd paid the debt? Then again, even if he had managed to scrounge up that amount of money, hundreds of his tenants would suffer for it. Still, a sense of guilt descended on him. If only he could be with Louisa, holding her. Perhaps that would help.

He speared the runners with a sharp look. "This goes no further. The gossip would not help anyone."

"Thank you," Mr. Hammond said quietly.

"You're welcome. It is the least I can do." For everyone concerned.

Gideon walked through the door and out into the corridor, then toward the stairs.

When he'd reached the side door they'd used to enter the building, Marcus's hand landed on Gideon's shoulder. "Do not blame yourself."

"How did you—"

"It's written all over your face." Marcus opened the door and stood aside. "You cannot know what was going on in Sullivan's head. He, apparently, defied his partners and was willing to murder them."

"You have a point." And at least it was over and the man could never again threaten Gideon or his family.

"It's still early. After we change, we'll meet again for dinner."

Gideon had lost all sense of time. That almost never happened. He pulled out his pocket watch, flipping open the cover. God's teeth, it was only a little past eight. If he couldn't be with Louisa . . . Her mother had wanted to spend the evening with her. The woman was probably trying to talk Louisa out of throwing herself away on an impoverished duke. "That sounds like an excellent idea. Will you be able to change without your wife knowing?"

"She is at my father's estate in Kent. I'll join them tomorrow." Marcus grinned. "Aside from that, she would probably wish she'd been here. Except that I am sure her advanced state of pregnancy would have slowed her down a bit."

Gideon remembered what his betrothed had said. "She gave Worthington's sisters lessons on shooting and knives, did she not?"

"Indeed. Not all of his sisters, naturally. Just the eldest three and his wife."

"I trust they will never have need of the skills." Despite what he had just been told, Gideon did not truly believe that English ladies would take that kind of thing seriously. And Louisa would *neve*r have a need to defend herself. Her protection was his duty and pleasure, as was her support. No matter how much she brought to their marriage in terms of wealth, he would provide for her. Thank God she had finally agreed with him.

Chapter Twenty-Nine

The next morning, Louisa dressed before sitting on the window seat of the Young Ladies' Parlor. Soon there would be only one young lady left. As happy as she was to be marrying Gideon, she wondered how Charlotte would get on by herself. It would be lonely. At least that was how Louisa felt before Matt and Grace wed. Yet it was most likely a problem with which Louisa would not be able to help.

Chloe tapped Louisa's skirt, and she picked the kitten up. "We're going to have a new home soon. I know you'll miss your sister just as I shall miss all of mine. But we shall have a new family. What do you think of that?"

The kitten purred as Louisa stroked her soft fur.

Her discussion with her mother had been short and productive. By the time Louisa had found Mama and forcefully enumerated all Gideon's good points, she had agreed to stop staring daggers at him and give him an opportunity to prove what a good husband he would be. Louisa's wedding was only a week away, and she could not wait to begin her new life as Gideon's wife, helpmate, and duchess.

Glancing at the mantel clock, Louisa rose. He would arrive soon, and she detested being late.

After much thought, she decided that she'd ask him about the earrings. After all, it was possible the invoice had been sent to him by mistake. It was clear by the state of the books that his secretary had not kept them. Apparently, after his mother retired to the country no one did. No wonder his finances were in such disarray. All sorts of bills could have been sent to the old duke with no one the wiser. *How* that could have been allowed she had no clue, but as long as she was in charge of the accounts it would not occur again. She wished that she could continue putting the books in order, yet she had other appointments to attend to this morning and later this afternoon.

Louisa arrived in the hall as a footman opened the door and Gideon strolled in.

"Good morning," she said, pulling on her gloves.

"Good morning to you." He took her hands as he usually did, and Louisa wished that she had not been so quick to don her gloves. "That is an unusual hat." He tilted his head from one side to the other as if trying to get a look at it. "It is a hat?"

"It is a bonnet." Although even that was stretching the description of the small velvet disk decorated with one feather that fell down alongside her cheek. "Do you like it?"

"A great deal. I have never seen anything like it before."

Smiling, she shook her head. "We should be going. I have a great deal to accomplish today."

She tucked her hand in the crook of his arm as they descended the outside steps. There horses stood, grooms at their heads.

Gideon placed his hands on her waist, and as he lifted her up, his thumbs caressed the underside of her breast. Heat, fierce and penetrating, shot through her. Lord how she missed his touch. By the time she was sitting on her mare, she was practically panting.

"I have an idea," he murmured.

Louisa licked her suddenly dry lips before answering, "What is it?"

"Let's go to my house."

"Your mother . . ."

"Will not be up for hours. We'll go in through the mews." His tone was soft, seductive, and irresistible. "My study has a door to the garden. No one will see us." Oooh, what he proposed was almost wicked. Very well, it was wicked. Yet if they could get away with it, she would not deny him, or herself, the pleasure of being together. Before she could respond, his hand crept under her skirt, caressed her leg. "Louisa, I need you."

She was not proof against his plea, and if they were discovered . . . Well, they'd be married in a week in any event. "I need you as well."

Dodging carts and other delivery vehicles, they quickly made their way to the mews behind Gideon's house.

Dismounting, he tossed his reins to an old man, helped her down, and gave her horse's reins to the man as well. "Barnes, see that they are exercised, I'll need them back in an hour."

"Yes, Your Grace."

Gideon took her hand, but rather then leading them away he said, "My love, this is my stable master, Barnes. He has been with the family as long as I can remember. Barnes, make your bow to my betrothed, Lady Louisa Vivers."

The servant did bow, and grin. "Glad to finally meet you, my lady, and may I wish you much happiness."

"Thank you, Barnes. It is a pleasure to make your acquaintance."

Still grinning, the old servant winked as Gideon opened the gate, and Louisa's cheeks flooded with heat.

"That was very clever of you to think of exercising the

horses," she said to Gideon. "Now my family's stable master will have no idea I have not been out riding."

"I occasionally have a good idea." They strode across the garden to a wall of windows on the right side of the house. "I left the door unlocked when I left. All the way to your house I prayed you would return with me."

How could she not love this man? He was everything she had dreamed of. Intelligent, strong, handsome, passionate . . . what more could any lady want in a husband? "I'm glad you did."

They entered the room, and Gideon twirled Louisa into his arms. Finally, he was alone with her. "Now"—he studied the hat—"how do I get that thing off your head without ruining it?"

Reaching up, Louisa slid out a long, wicked-looking pin from her bonnet. The way her breasts pushed against her tight habit had Gideon hardening. The sooner he could get her out of her clothing, the better he'd like it. An hour was not nearly long enough, but it was all they had.

Taking the piece of velvet from her head, he placed it on his desk. One by one, the gold-threaded frogs holding her jacket fastened opened to his questing fingers.

She untied the silk belcher handkerchief he'd worn in anticipation of having her here. Much less of a bother than a cravat. After shrugging off his jacket, he pulled the sleeves of hers until the garment fell to the floor. His waistcoat was next to go.

Cupping her face, he took her lips, commanding her to meet him, to taste as he tasted her. Her tongue slipped into his mouth, challenging him to return her caresses.

"Gideon." Louisa's voice was breathy and sultry all at once. "The windows."

In moments he'd closed the curtains, plunging them into near darkness. "I'll light the candles."

More time taken away from them. He drew her back

into a heated kiss, walking her back until they reached the daybed. The only pieces of clothing left to dispose of were her stays, chemise, and stockings.

Hmm, the stockings can remain.

Finally, her lush rose-tipped breasts were free. He brushed them with his fingers, enjoying how they furled into tight buds under his touch. Before he could bend his head to taste them, Louisa licked his nipples. He sucked in a harsh breath.

"Do you like that?" She grinned.

He groaned. "More than you can imagine, my love."

"I can imagine quite a lot, I think." Her hands traveled over his chest, down to his stomach, to his cock. "Show me how to touch you there."

Skimming his fingers down her body as she'd done to him, he caressed her silken skin, luminous as a pearl's. Her dark chestnut curls covered the embroidered pillows he had placed under her head. Louisa's eyes fluttered open, and his breath hitched at the desire lurking in their lapis depths. His palms skimmed her sides, from her ivory mounds to her small waist and the swell of her hips, finally reaching the small nub hiding in her dark curls.

Gideon was ecstatic to find she was as ready as he. "As I touch you?"

She shuddered, pressing into his fingers. "Yes. I want you to feel what I do." Her arms slid around his neck.

This wasn't the time to show her how easy it was to make love in a variety of different positions. That would come later after they were married. Not a moment passed that he didn't want her. If he were not so concerned about her reputation and his, he would plan a rendezvous at the next ball. "Excellent idea." He propped himself up with his arm, glad that the daybed was just wide enough for the both of them. "Tell me what you want, sweetheart."

"If only we had more time." She turned to face him. "I want you to make me feel like you did last time."

They had had hours then, but she deserved all the pleasure he could give her. "I shall do my poor best." She sighed as he fluttered light kisses down her breast and stomach. "Do you trust me?"

"Always."

Sliding down, he nestled his head between her legs, and supped. Her moans and sighs filled his ears as she lifted her hips to his mouth. Small tremors coursed through her as he sheathed himself into molten heat. Her legs hugged his waist, then wrapped around him. The silk of the stocking rubbing against his sides added a new feeling. He would spend the rest of his life loving the feel of her as she convulsed around him. The rest of his life loving her.

Louisa thrust up as her love buried himself deep inside her. This time there was no pain, only the fire they created with their bodies. She reached her peak, tumbling over it much sooner than she had before. Soon after she came, she felt the warmth of his seed, and he collapsed to her side, holding her tightly against him as he kissed her hair as he'd done before.

She had never before felt this close to another person. If only they could remain here forever.

"You are quiet," Gideon said.

"I was thinking about how I love being next to you like this." And the children they might have. Even now she could be carrying his child.

He kissed her tenderly. A brush across her mouth. He chuckled as her lips followed, wanting more, wanting him again. "Sweetheart, we must dress. Your mother will send the Bow Street runners after us if we are gone much longer."

"You're probably right." A notion came to her and she

had to ask, "Is it like this with every couple who are to marry?"

He seemed to consider her question for several moments, then shook his head. "I doubt it." She wiggled around to look at him. His eyes were the color of storm clouds. "Too many marry without love. Or perhaps only one person loves and the other does not."

She thought of her mother and father. They had probably not experienced the joy she now had. Although it seemed as if Mama and Richard were in love. Was she afraid Louisa would end up in a marriage where one loved more than the other? Perhaps she should speak with her mother about it. Yet if she did that, Mama would know what Gideon and Louisa had done. And that would cause a much larger problem. She was better off letting her mother simply come to know her betrothed.

Still, there was the little matter of the earrings. "My love." She liked the way the words rolled off her tongue.

"Hmm?"

"Did Mr. Allerton tell you I found an invoice for diamond earrings dated about three months ago?"

For a moment it seemed as if Gideon tensed. "I think he may have mentioned it. Neither of us was in Town then."

She nodded, knowing her guess had been correct. "I believe you will discover that the bill was sent to you by mistake."

His brow creased. "I think you might be right."

"If I had the time, I would go back through all the receipts and match them up with the items. After all, that might not have been the first error."

"That is a good idea." Gathering her into his arms, he kissed her. "I shall have him do that."

Louisa nestled against his shoulder. "He was quite upset that I'd found the receipt. I am positive he will wish to ensure no others are present."

"No doubt you are correct."

She cuddled closer to him for the few minutes they had left to each other. Silence enveloped the room until the clock struck the hour. "We must dress."

Without responding, Gideon helped her off the daybed, and a few minutes later, they were dressed. Their time together had passed too quickly. No wonder all those she knew who had recently wed had not waited long. If only she and Gideon could marry sooner. But then, her younger sisters would not have special dresses, and they were so thrilled to have new gowns, especially the twins and Madeline.

One week was not so much longer to wait to become Gideon's wife and be able to make love with him anytime they wished. "Will you break your fast with me?"

He shook his head. "I think not. In fact, you might wish to bathe as soon as you return."

She drew in a large breath. The scent of their lovemaking was stronger than she had imagined. "I shall. Fortunately, I normally wash after riding."

And no one would know what she had been doing or where she had been. Heavens, how Louisa detested sneaking around. The love she shared with Gideon should be in the open.

She buttoned the last of the frogs on her jacket, and he pulled her into his arms one last time. "I love you with all my heart."

"I love you with my body, mind, and heart. Nothing will ever separate us."

Chapter Thirty

Twenty minutes later, Gideon bid Louisa farewell, pressing kisses into her palms before closing her fingers around his token. "I shall see you this evening."

"Indeed. Dinner then the theater." She smiled broadly. "I will not even pretend that attending my first play is anything other than wonderful!"

She was the only lady he had ever met who never bothered to hide behind a mask of ennui. He would find more joy in watching her see her first play than in the performance itself. "It is one of the many things I love about you. Do you care to know which play we are seeing?"

"Yes, of course." She waited expectantly.

"*Romeo and Juliet*. I have been told that the lead actor is quite good."

"Is that Mr. Kean?" Gideon nodded, adoring her happiness. "Lady Evesham says he is the best actor of our age."

"I can hardly wait until tonight."

Louisa climbed the steps, stopping to blow him a kiss before entering the house.

His heart swelled. If only he could have come to her with his estates intact and no secrets from her. He had almost cringed when she mentioned the earrings, and had sent up a prayer to the Deity when she said nothing would separate them. Louisa was so very truthful. What would she do if she ever found out what he was keeping from her?

Climbing back on his horse, he remembered that he'd not spoken to his mother about a betrothal ring for Louisa. Not that everyone did so, but his family had three or four rings that were normally used. He would have to see if any of them were at Rothwell House. If not, he might take a bolt to the abbey. He dearly wished to see his ring on Louisa's finger.

An hour later as he was digging into a plate filled with rare beef, gammon, kippers, eggs, and toast, his mother entered the breakfast room. "Goodness, Gideon. Are you truly going to eat all of that?"

He glanced down at his plate. He *was* hungrier than usual this morning. It was probably from making love to Louisa.

"Your father used to have that exact look when he had a large breakfast," she said casually, as if nothing had been or was amiss.

"Mother." He'd wanted to warn her not to continue this vein of conversation, but his tone was much too high for that. "I really do not wish to discuss Father."

She took a seat on Gideon's left and signaled for a fresh pot of tea. "My dear, your father and I were married for well over thirty years, and for most of that time we were very much in love." She paused for a moment, blinking rapidly. "I am angry that his madness robbed us of our last years together. I wish that he had never taken up with a person who has helped to put us in such a horrible financial state." A lone tear slid down her still smooth cheek. "I am sorry you have been left to pick up the pieces. Nevertheless, I will always love him. I will not allow you to pretend he did not exist solely because he was not in his right mind for the past few years. Had it been left to him, I am sure he would not have chosen to fall victim to dementia." Fredericks arrived with her tea, and she stopped speaking as she poured, adding sugar and milk to the cup. "I pray you do not become ill. I have done some research and discovered that the disease most likely is in your grandmother Rothwell's mother's side of the family. I decided to tell you only because you are not at all like her."

"Thank you for telling me." Before Mama mentioned it, Gideon hadn't given the disease much thought at all. None of his grandparents had suffered from it. He might want to make provisions in the event he did begin exhibiting symptoms. Fortunately, that would be years from now.

A few moments later after finishing her cup of tea, she rose. "I seem to remember that you have not given Louisa one of the Rothwell rings. I brought them with me." She eyed his plate again. "You may attend me after you have broken your fast." She strolled to the door and turned, facing him. "I am still praying for a grandchild."

Vixen! He'd forgotten all about that conversation. Thank God Fredericks was the only one who served the family at breakfast. Yet even having him hear Mama was embarrassing. Gideon was beginning to feel as if he had not really known his parents. Perhaps children were not supposed to know certain things about their elders until they were adults as well. He would never humiliate his children like that. "Thank you very much, Mother."

"Oh, dear. Now you are vexed with me." She wiggled her fingers at him. "Never mind. Come see me when you've finished."

Chuckling, she whisked out of the room.

Gideon took his time eating, even calling for a fresh pot of tea. Mama could deuced well wait his pleasure after making a game of him. He would give the ring to Louisa this evening before they attended the play.

About twenty minutes later, Gideon took himself to his mother's new apartments. After knocking on the door, he waited until her lady's maid opened it and let him in. Mama already had five rings set on a cream-colored velvet cloth.

They ranged from an ancient gold ring set with an emerald the size of a quail's egg to a much more modern setting with an array of small stones.

The one that stood out was an intricately crafted band of gold set with a deep blue stone that was almost opaque and reminded him strongly of the color of Louisa's eyes. Lighter lines radiated from the center. He had never seen anything like it before. "What kind of stone is that?"

"It is a star sapphire," his mother responded. "If you look closely, you will see that the lines resemble a star. It was brought back from India by the fifth duke and given to his betrothed."

"Did they have a good marriage?" For some reason that was important. He would not give Louisa a ring from a bad union.

"Yes. The match was arranged, but they had known each other for many years and were deeply in love."

"That is the one I shall give to Louisa."

His mother smiled. "I think it will be perfect for her."

Gideon agreed. Now if he could leave his mother's room without a reminder of grandchildren his day would be perfect.

Not that he did not want a child. He ached to hold a baby in the image of Louisa in his arms. He simply did not wish to discuss it with his mother.

Yet . . . he and Louisa had made love twice now. There was every possibility that she was carrying his child. Even more reason for him to take her to the abbey as soon as possible.

* * *

Louisa knew she should not have blown a kiss to Gideon. She knew it was vulgar, but few of her neighbors were awake at this time of morning, and she had wanted to do it. At least she had not done what she wished to do even more, which was to hold him in her arms and kiss him on his lips. No matter how many people were not around. Someone would have seen that!

As she had ascended the stairs, she'd felt lighter than she had ever felt before, as if her feet were touching air or fluffy white clouds instead of stone. She could not stop herself from sharing her love for him and the joy of the life they would have together.

And this evening they would attend her first play together. Pausing, she listened for sounds of her family in the breakfast room but could hear nothing.

She ran lightly up the stairs. When she reached her bedchamber, Lucy was laying out a day dress. "I must bathe."

Louisa was in the act of removing her bonnet when her maid sniffed the air and wrinkled her freckled nose. "The tub will be ready in a moment, my lady."

Surely she could not smell that bad! Then she gave thanks to the Deity that Lucy would not recognize the scent of Louisa and Gideon making love. Fortunately, she had put up her own hair this morning, so no one would know the difference. "Good. I do not wish to be late for breakfast."

Not that her brother, sister-in-law, or the children would mind, but with Mama in the house, Louisa must be more careful.

Her maid helped her out of her clothing, handed her a wrapper, and stepped into her dressing room. "Your bath is ready."

"Thank you." As she slipped into the warm water, it occurred to her that ever since she and Gideon had announced their intent to wed, Matt had not been concerned about the amount of time she spent with Gideon, nor had Grace commented.

In fact, Louisa had been given a great deal more freedom than before. She wondered what her mother would think of her new independence, and decided Mama would not be happy with it.

"My lady?" Lucy asked as she handed Louisa a cloth and scented soap.

"Yes?"

"Is Rothwell House as big as this one?"

At first the question took Louisa aback, but naturally Lucy would accompany Louisa after she married. "A bit larger. I do not know much about Rothwell Abbey, but there is a guide book in the library you could look at."

"It will be a big change for me, being lady's maid to a duchess," Lucy said as she scrubbed Louisa's back. "I should probably speak with your mother's maid as well as Lady Worthington's maid about how to go on when I get there."

"That is an excellent idea." Lucy had been with Louisa for the past year now, but they had never visited anywhere but London, and Lucy had always taken her lead from Mama's dresser, who had spent time not only in Town, but at grand house parties.

She stood to be rinsed and a half hour later entered the breakfast room just before the sound of her younger brothers and sisters could be heard on the stairs. Grace and Matt were engaged in a quiet conversation at one end of the table, and Charlotte was at the other end. Most likely to give them some privacy.

Patting the seat next to her, she smiled. "How was your ride?"

"Very nice," Louisa said, trying to stop the heat crawling up her neck as she thought of Gideon's broad chest and the way he tasted. Oh, my. She must learn to control that reaction. "Not as long as I would have liked." Dear Lord. Everything she said seemed to be taking on double meanings. Pouring a cup of tea, she tried to hide her face as she took a sip. Yuck!

Charlotte laughed quietly and murmured, "You forgot the milk and sugar."

Unfortunately, Louisa's face flamed at the precise moment her mother and Richard entered the room.

"Cough," Charlotte whispered harshly as she slipped a piece of toast she'd taken a bite from onto Louisa's plate and slapped her back. "There, that is much better."

The children poured into the room, filling the remaining seats at the table. At the same time footmen began carrying around plates of food.

"Thank you," Louisa muttered gratefully.

"You are very welcome." Charlotte sighed. "Someday I will know what causes blushes like yours."

"I would tell you, but it defies explanation."

Her eyes widened. "That good?"

"Indeed," Louisa replied, fighting to keep another blush from her face. "Will you join us shopping today?"

"I shall, but I'll warn you that your mother insists we attend morning visits afterward."

"It seems an age since we've done that. Not since the children fell ill."

"Well"—Charlotte lifted her eyes to the ceiling—"our reprieve is at an end. Not that I mind them for the most part. However, there is always someone who must spread nasty rumors." The corner of her lips tipped up. "When you are the new Duchess of Rothwell I shall expect you to quash that sort of behavior."

Louisa let her sister's statement sink in. As a duchess there were a great many things she could do to help others. Yet was she any more prepared to take on that role than

Lucy was her new position? A shiver of nerves ran down her back. "It is a great deal of responsibility."

Setting down her cup, Charlotte speared Louisa with a look. "One you are well trained to perform. Manners and how to go on have been drummed into both of us. You know how to manage a house, estates, and servants. You already are well read and hold strong opinions. Most importantly, you know right from wrong. You shall make an excellent duchess."

"Yes." All of that was true.

Her sister took another sip of tea. "What caused you to doubt yourself?"

"My maid said she would ask Grace's maid and my mother's maid what else she needs to learn. That made me think about my new role."

"Well, she will probably find she has already learned most of the knowledge she needs simply by watching them. I know my May has made a point of increasing her understanding of how to go on in a great house." Charlotte gave Louisa a rueful look. "Although, now that I think about it, I believe Dawson, Grace's maid, may have had something to do with it. This Season has taught us all a great deal."

That was a true statement. "Thank you. I'll miss you."

Her sister patted Louisa's hand. "I shall miss you as well. Perhaps when I finally marry, we will be close to each other."

Rosie Petrie's hand shook with rage as she held the letter from her modiste roundly informing her that if she wanted to keep the gowns she'd ordered, she'd have to pay for them herself as the Duke of Rothwell had not paid the bills she'd sent him. "That scheming, odious bounder! How could he do something like this to me? After all I did to make the old duke's last days happier."

It wasn't enough that he'd taken her horses and carriages. She never should have agreed to let the old duke take care of them for her, but he had said that she should not have to support his gifts to her. Now the devil was going after her clothes.

"I ain't got much better news from the pawnbroker." Her maid stood holding the bag of gems she was to have sold. The sack looked empty.

Rosie narrowed her eyes. "Did he try to bamboozle you on the price?" Unlike some other two to one shops, Mr. Sutton had never tried to cheat her before.

The maid shook her head. "Said he was told they was all stolen and kept them."

"Stolen!" she shouted. "They was—were all gifts from His Grace!" Most of them were at least. She thought through the list again, realizing that some of the jewelry had been bought using that letter she'd had forged. But the others the duke had given to her during his last days. What the devil was she going to do now?

Rosie heaved a sigh. She'd have to go to someone who would give her less. If worst came to worst, she could have that old set the duke had given her broken up and sold for the stones.

Looking up, she saw the maid shaking like blancmange. "It's not your fault," she said gently. "How were you to know he'd turn on us like that? After you dress me, take some time and see if you can find me another broker."

"Thank you, ma'am." The girl nodded before rushing up the stairs.

Rosie tied her silk wrapper tighter. No matter what happened, she would not go to debtors' prison. That meant she would have to return some of the gowns she'd bought over the past several months. But somehow, some way she would see the new Duke of Rothwell paid for robbing her.

Taking a large breath, Rosie tried to calm herself with

thoughts of the play she was going to see this evening. She had seen it before, but Kean was so fabulous that she had to attend another performance. That would do a great deal to calm her nerves.

Then a thought occurred to her. If Rothwell was not paying her debts, what other debts was he refusing to pay? And who else might wish to aid her in a little revenge against the new duke?

Chapter Thirty-One

Gideon had sent a note around to Louisa asking her to meet him in the drawing room of Stanwood House several minutes earlier than the appointed time. Only to find himself disappointed that she was not waiting in the drawing room. Most likely because he had become so used to her being in the hall for their morning rides.

"I shall be happy to pour Your Grace a glass of wine or sherry while Lady Louisa is informed you have arrived," the butler said.

"Sherry, please," Gideon replied, flicking open his pocket watch. He really could not complain. It took him longer to dress for the evening than it did for riding.

Several minutes later, the door opened and Louisa entered the room. A smile appeared on her deep rose lips that matched the tiny roses embroidered on the sheer overdress of her gown. The small puffed sleeves were layered in a fashion he had not seen previously. He did not even want to know how much the gown had cost. He was not sure he could keep her in the type of fashion she was used to.

"Gideon." She glided toward him, casually tossing her long kid gloves on a table. "What is it?"

When she reached him, he kissed her lightly on her lips. "I want you to have"—her deep blue eyes met his and, for a moment, he could not speak. What had he done to deserve this beautiful, clever woman? Fumbling in his waistcoat pocket, he took out the small satin sack—"I wanted you to wear a betrothal ring. It is a tradition in my family."

Her eyes seemed to mist. "Oh, my love. I would be pleased, no, proud to wear your ring."

Turning the sack over, he shook it, dropping the ring onto the palm of his hand. "I chose this one because it matches your eyes."

He slipped the ring onto her hand. It was too large, almost dangling on her slim finger.

"I shall wear it on my index finger." She smiled, her hand caressing his cheek.

"Wear it tonight." How had he not thought to make certain of her ring finger size? "Tomorrow we shall visit the jeweler and have it altered to fit."

"It is beautiful. I have never seen a stone such as this before. What is it?"

"It is called a star sapphire because of the lines in it."

Louisa seemed to study it for a few moments before saying, "Did you know that a blue sapphire signifies love, commitment, and fidelity?"

"No." He drew her into his arms. "But I'm glad. I want us to have all those things."

"As do I." Tears misted in her eyes. "All we have to do is love and trust each other."

"Louisa, my love. Are you going to cry?" The possibility frightened him more than he'd imagined it would.

"No, no," she chuckled wetly. "These are tears of joy. Truly, they are nothing to worry about."

"I'm happy you like it. I had never seen it before today. It is over three hundred years old." By Jupiter, he sounded like a callow schoolboy.

"Sweetheart." Her thumb brushed his bottom lip, and he caught it in his teeth, watching as her eyes warmed. "I love it. You could not have chosen a more perfect ring."

He was about to kiss her when the door opened. They stepped back from each other, but only enough to put a small space between them. She tucked her hand into the crook of his arm.

Her mother entered with a man Gideon presumed to be Lord Wolverton.

"Mama, Richard." Louisa pulled him forward. "Rothwell, you have already met my mother. This is her new husband"—her lips turned down for a moment—"my stepfather, Lord Wolverton. Richard, my betrothed, Rothwell. It is still strange to have a new father," she said to no one in particular.

Gideon held out his hand. "A pleasure to meet another new arrival to the family."

Wolverton snorted. "It appears you have passed all the tests, such as they are. Theo, Mary, and Philip have sung your praises."

"I was happy to be able to help make Lady Theo feel better. I hear you are from Kent?"

The man strolled over to the sideboard, motioning Gideon to follow. Glancing at Louisa, he noticed her mother seemed to want to speak with her, and he joined Wolverton. "How long have you been married?"

"Not quite a month." He held up the sherry bottle.

Searching for his lost glass, Gideon shook his head. He spied it on the far corner of the sideboard. "I have one, thank you."

Wolverton took a long drink and said, "I am afraid I did you a disservice."

How so, Gideon wondered. He had never met the other gentleman before. Although it might explain the reason his wife had been so rude when she had first met him. "I do not understand."

"I know how much my lady loves her children, and when I heard you were courting Lady Louisa, I requested information from a few of my colleagues." Wolverton took another drink. "They are not young. In fact, one could say that they are elderly. Though, I would never say that to their faces. A couple of them knew your father."

Ah, the light was beginning to dawn in Gideon's mind. "And they knew him during the past few years."

"Actually, no." Wolverton rubbed his cheek. "They knew him when they were all young. It was not until a year ago that they saw him again."

In that event, the men would have known Gideon's father only in his wild youth and when he was reliving his youth. Still, there was a question he had to ask. "Did my father recognize any of them?"

Wolverton appeared startled. "Yes. He greeted them as old friends."

"That makes sense." Gideon pressed his lips together, as if his secret would escape if he didn't lock it in. He debated leaving the conversation at that, or telling his future stepfather-in-law the truth about his father. After a few moments, he decided enough other people knew that it would not make much of a difference. And he was going to be related to the man. "My father had dementia. It is not widely known, and I would like to keep it that way."

"Have you told Louisa?"

"Not yet. There are some matters I wish to attend to before discussing it with her. Worthington knows."

Wolverton rubbed his cheek again. "I do not agree that you should keep this from Louisa, but if her brother has decided to let you handle it in your own manner, who am I to say nay?"

"Thank you." Gideon would have to tell her soon, but

not until they were at the abbey, where he would have an opportunity to explain, and no one would interrupt them. And if he were honest, when he would be convinced she would not leave him.

"You look beautiful, my dear," Mama said to Louisa, pulling her away from Gideon.

Goodness, what did Mama think would happen in a room full of people, or was she concerned that Louisa and Gideon had been together alone? They were betrothed. "Thank you." She held up her hand. "Rothwell wanted to give me this before everyone else came down. It is a star sapphire."

"I have heard of them, but I have never seen one before." Mama sounded impressed. "It looks quite old."

"Yes. One of his ancestors brought it back from his travels." Louisa showed the ring to Charlotte, who had joined them.

"Lovely," she said. "He must have been thinking of your eyes when he chose it."

Louisa laughed lightly. "That was exactly what he thought of."

Gideon's mother arrived and shortly afterward dinner was announced. As the children had already eaten, Grace decided dinner would be served in the small dining room. Although the table could still seat sixteen with all the leaves in, this evening, it had been reduced to accommodate their smaller number.

Louisa was happy to find Gideon placed on Grace's right while Richard was on her left. Mama and the duchess were seated next to Matt. Charlotte and Louisa were in the middle, but she was next to Gideon. The table was narrow enough to allow conversation across it.

Normally, the footmen would serve each person, then

put the serving platters in a prearranged pattern on the table. However, this evening, due to the size of the table, they were set on a sideboard. Dinner began with a clear soup Jacque had named "essence of celery."

"I've never had anything like this," Gideon said after eating the soup.

"The very reason I would like your French cook in our kitchens both in Town and at the estate."

"I see your point. Perhaps he could travel with us."

That was an idea she had not considered. "We must discuss it further."

The soup was removed for a salad consisting of various greens, as well as sole sautéed in brown butter and served with slivers of almonds, collops of lamb, thin green beans, and stuffed quail. By the time dessert was served, Louisa was sure that he was convinced his chef was necessary as well.

She dabbed her serviette against her lips. "How did you like it?"

"Marvelous." His mouth turned down at the corners. "The last time I dined with you, the food was excellent as well, but I do not remember it being such a treat."

"That is because we ate with the children and Grace insists that simpler fare is better for them."

"I now understand why you want my cook to remain." He paused for a moment, selecting a small dish of potted white cheese with fruit. "What did my mother say?"

Louisa fluttered her fingers airily. "Only that your cook at Rothwell had been with you for years, and that she will be moving to the dower house."

His frown deepened. "I do not remember her nursery fare being nearly as tasty as your cook's."

"Shall we settle the matter then?" During her house tour, Louisa had already spoken with Gideon's chef, Anton, and determined that he would be happy to remain with them. "I think your old cook should remain with your mother. That will save the duchess from having to hire a new one."

Gideon took a bite of the cheese and swallowed. "Do as you wish, my love. If I could eat even what the children do here, I would be a happy man."

Smiling to herself, she selected a small lemon curd tart. "Thank you. I am so pleased we are in agreement."

Suddenly his hand stroked her thigh, and flames licked the place between her legs. "That is not the only thing we agree upon."

No, it was not. In fact, the only thing they appeared to disagree about was her using her own money for the estate. That, she decided, would come as well.

An hour and a half later, Gideon led their party—he already thought of Louisa as his wife and partner in life—to his box at the Theatre Royal or, as it was more commonly known, Drury Lane.

When they entered the theater, the manager met them. "Your Grace. There has been a slight delay in preparing your box." The man paused for a moment. "Not because it was the last to be done. I assure you that is not at all the case. However, when I inspected it, it was not to my liking. I do hope you understand. I have also included another bottle of champagne by way of an apology."

"Of course."

Seconds later, Gideon's party ascended the stairs to the lavish space that belonged to the Dukes of Rothwell.

An open bottle of champagne was nestled in a bucket with ice. Lemonade and wine were also on the table as well as the appropriate glasses.

"Champagne, my love?" he asked Louisa.

"Please. Where shall we sit?"

Fortunately, the Rothwell box was quite large, allowing up to six persons to sit along the front. One of their party would have to sit in the second row, but it would not be Louisa's sister or any of the other ladies.

"I'll sit behind my wife," Worthington said quietly.

"Thank you." Gideon was grateful for the offer. Now he could sit next to Louisa.

While he spoke with his friend and soon-to-be brother, Louisa and Lady Charlotte exclaimed over the theater.

Gilt trimmed all the boxes and much of the plaster. Huge crystal chandeliers hung from the ceiling, and dozens of candles lit the space.

"I have never seen anything so opulent," Lady Charlotte said.

"Only because you have not been to Brighton," Worthington responded drily. Her eyes rounded, and he quickly continued, "It is a place I would not wish you to visit. I am afraid the theater will have to do."

"Do not forget that the opera house is even more lavish," Lady Wolverton added.

"Yes, indeed." Lady Worthington handed her husband a glass of champagne. "I have a box there. If you would like we may attend next week before the wedding."

"Rothwell"—Louisa squeezed his arm—"why are those people staring at us?"

At first his eyes were drawn to the pit, where young gentlemen mixed with others not so gently bred. "They make a sport of attempting to attract a lady's attention."

"No, I refer to the box across from us."

He followed her gaze to a party of one man and two women. One woman was wearing a pair of diamond earrings he could see from here. She wiggled her fingers at him before he could turn away. *She's as bold as brass*. "I do not know them. Nor do I wish to."

Still, he had a good idea of who the female with the

earrings was. Could that have been the reason they were delayed? Had that light-skirt actually attempted to use his box?

"The gentleman is Kenilworth," Worthington remarked. "I did not think he planned to come to Town this Season."

"Who?" Louisa asked.

"The Marquis of Kenilworth. An old school friend of mine. Do not concern yourself with the women with him. None of you shall be introduced to them."

Lady Worthington drew her sisters' attention elsewhere as Worthington took Gideon's arm.

"The female with the large earrings is Mrs. Petrie," Worthington said, a hard edge to his voice. "The other I understand to be this year's reigning courtesan and Kenilworth's current mistress. Unless he is in his cups, he will not bring them over here."

"I shall send for one of my footmen to stand outside the box," Gideon said, thus ensuring the marquis did not attempt anything foolish. The only fortunate part of this situation was that Gideon now knew what the whore looked like.

Louisa was at his side again. "Why would she have waved to us?"

"I am not sure I wish to know."

"Despite Kenilworth's contributions to the Lords," Worthington said in a bored drawl, "he keeps low company. One would not wish to know what that woman thought she was doing."

Pulling her full bottom lip between her teeth, Louisa nodded. "I understand. She is one of those women ladies do not recognize."

"Precisely, my dear." Gideon's mother took Louisa's arm. "Come and taste the biscuits. I believe I detect a hint of lavender."

Did Mama know his father's former mistress? If so, how?

"Well, I think his lordship is rude for staring so boldly," Lady Charlotte pronounced. Her nose was slightly pinched as if there was an odor she did not like.

"You need not be so hard on Kenilworth," Worthington said. "He is the only boy and all his sisters are older and married with families of their own. They rarely come to Town. His mother has never attempted to control him, and his father has been dead for years. In most respects, he is responsible, but he has no reason to bow to Polite Society." He grinned. "At least not until he seeks a wife, which, according to him, will be many years from now."

"It does not matter." Lady Charlotte's nose was now in the air. "One should always display good manners."

"I agree with you." Grace led her sister to a seat. "As we will now do by paying attention to the performance."

Gideon glanced at Worthington and rolled his eyes. As Lady Charlotte was glowering at the box across the way, her brother was surreptitiously raising his glass in response to Kenilworth. He must know that having two ladybirds in tow would stop any attempts by matchmaking mamas to approach. Still, for a man, that was no reason to cut a connection. Particularly one that was politically valuable and an old friend.

Taking the open seat next to Louisa, Gideon wrapped his fingers around her hand. "This is turning into an interesting evening, and the play has not even begun."

"It is." She looked at her sister. "Charlotte has certainly taken a dislike to his lordship."

"That is just as well as, according to your brother, he is not in the market for a wife."

"I suppose you are right." Louisa sighed. "I have simply never seen her do anything like that before. She is generally the most generous of souls."

The play began, obviating the need for him to respond. Her eyes lit as the actors came onto the stage, and for the rest of the time until intermission, she seemed to be lost in the performance.

Gideon's mind wandered back to the diamond earrings. Could they be the ones on the invoice? He would have to read the description again and inform his solicitor. As much as he had gone on about confronting the woman himself, it would not be wise. He now had a wife, soon to be in any event, and possibly a child to consider. They were more important than any whore.

Chapter Thirty-Two

"My lord, would you be so kind as to escort me to Rothwell's box during the intermission?" Rosie used her sweetest voice. The one that almost always got her what she wanted. She had learned the hard way not to make demands. Gentlemen didn't like being told what to do.

"You want me to do what?" The look on Lord Kenilworth's face was full of disdain. Making her wish she'd had more sense than to voice the request. Of course, he would not insult a member of the *ton*. Not unless he had a very good reason.

Aimée laughed lightly, breaking the tension. "And what will you do? Introduce yourself as his father's mistress? Unless I am mistaken, the duchess is present as well." She tapped Rosie's arm with her fan. "You are upset that you may no longer use the box. That was to be expected. You may not cause a scene over it, and my poor Kenilworth will not sacrifice his good will." She turned to him. "Is that not correct, *mon ami?* It is not at all *comme il faut*."

"Completely correct, no gentleman would introduce a courtesan to a lady. Not only is Rothwell present, but Worthington as well. Were I to even attempt to slight either of them in that fashion, Worthington would cut me. And I would not blame him."

Before Rosie could open her mouth to argue, Aimée exclaimed, "*Oui, oui!* You see *j'ai droit*. This thought oversets him so much that his lips did not even move during that little speech." She cut a sharp look at Rosie. "You see, *moi*, I 'ave learned the English ways very well. To be in this profession, to be the most sought after courtesan, one must not be *maladroite*. No matter the provocation." She pouted prettily for a moment, then her lips curved up as if she had found the solution to everything. "If you wish to always have a box again, you must find another protector. With this, I can help. You are still *très belle*. It will be no problem at all."

Yet that was the problem. Rosie did not want just a box part of the time. She wanted one all the time. But most of all, she wanted Rothwell to pay for taking her belongings. They had been given to her by his father. He had no right to steal them from her. If she didn't do something soon, she would either have to take Aimée up on her offer to find another protector, or sell her house and move to a small village in the country. Some women might like a quiet life, but Rosie loved London. It had everything she wanted; parks, the theater, shopping, and all her friends were here.

She stared at Rothwell's box again. He was glaring at her as if he would like to wrap his hands around her neck and squeeze until she was dead or run her through with a sword. The young lady next to him was so occupied by the play she did not seem to notice the tension radiating off him. Then she glanced over, narrowed her eyes, and went back to watching the performance.

Perhaps if she could get to that lady or if Rothwell thought she could, he would give Rosie her possessions back. Even better, if she could convince the other woman that he was having an affair with her, she would jilt him.

Rosie knew that Lady Louisa was an heiress. It was probably the real reason he'd wanted the match in the first place. Causing him to lose his betrothed would go a long way to revenging herself on Rothwell. It might even make up for having to go back to work again.

Louisa slid a look to Gideon, found him scowling at Kenilworth's box, and wished she knew the reason. He had said he did not know the two women or, it appeared, Kenilworth, and she believed him. Then Matt had whispered something to Gideon. She wondered what her brother had said and if she could find out. Perhaps he did not approve of prostitution in any form. If so, she wholeheartedly agreed with him.

No matter how much a woman appeared to like it—and she had to admit that the younger lady sitting next to his lordship seemed to be enjoying herself as she tapped her fan on the other woman's arm—no female ought to be forced to sell her body in order to live.

That was most likely the reason Charlotte was so upset. How could she not be after they had heard about the poor women who had been abducted, taken to Miss Betsy's, drugged, and forced to be prostitutes. Now to see a gentleman, a peer, here with two ladybirds must infuriate Charlotte as much as it did Louisa. Now that she would be able to help in a much greater way, she must speak to Dotty Merton, who had set up a charity for women in trouble.

Charlotte's mouth was still set in a thin line, and Louisa turned her attention back to the play. She had read Shakespeare and at Christmas acted some of the parts, but they had never performed *Romeo and Juliet*. Many people called it a love story, but a love story should have a happy ending. And no matter what one thought, both lovers dying was not *happy*! One would think that someone could have helped them run away together. After all, they had married. At some point their families would have been forced to acknowledge it. Then again, she had recently heard of a couple who were disowned by their families for not agreeing to the matches their parents had made. That, she knew, would never happen to any of her brothers and sisters, no matter how angry Matt or Grace became. There was always a better way. Another course of action. And they would never stop one of their brothers or sisters from marrying for love.

A flash of light caught the corner of Louisa's eye and she saw the older woman in Kenilworth's box shaking her head, causing the earring to catch the light of a candle. During the intermission, Louisa decided to try to get a better look at those earrings. They seemed to be very like the description of the ones on the invoice she had found. If they were, then Gideon would be able to discover to whom to send the bill.

The act ended, and the curtain closed. It seemed as if the whole theater began speaking at once.

"I do not even have to ask how you are enjoying the performance," Gideon said to Louisa. "You never took your eyes off the stage."

"No, I didn't," Louisa responded. "Lady Evesham was right. Kean is remarkable."

"I agree." Gideon kept Louisa close to him during the intermission, but, as Worthington had said, Kenilworth knew better than to visit with two high-flyers.

Although everyone else in Town stopped by, even Bentley, who was squiring Miss Blackacre.

"Rothwell," his cousin said, "I believe you have been introduced to Miss Blackacre?"

He bowed. "I have, indeed, had the pleasure. I trust you are enjoying the play?"

Before replying, she curtseyed gracefully. "I am having a great deal of fun, Your Grace." Puckering her brow, she looked around as if sorting through the crowd. "I thought I saw Ladies Louisa and Charlotte."

"Here we are." Louisa appeared with her sister. "Isn't this magnificent?"

"It is. I was just telling His Grace how much I like being here." Miss Blackacre tugged Bentley's arm. "Lord Bentley could not be a more perfect host."

Bentley appeared to be in shock. Silence fell and stretched for what seemed like hours, but it could not have been more than a moment or two before Louisa curtseyed. "My lord, how happy you look."

"Yes, yes, I am." He smiled at Miss Blackacre as if she were the only person present. "I should thank you."

Louisa smiled as well, and Gideon had the feeling that all was forgiven.

Aunt Camilla accompanied by the Duchess of Stillwell, Miss Blackacre's grandmother, made their greetings as well.

"I would say this Season is coming along most satisfactorily," the duchess said, addressing his aunt. "Would you not agree, Duchess?"

"Most definitely, Duchess," Aunt Camilla responded as they took themselves off to greet Gideon's mother.

"I am so happy everything seems to be working out between Miss Blackacre and Bentley," Louisa murmured. "And we have been forgiven."

Gideon tucked her a bit closer to him. "As am I. Our families will continue to be close."

Soon the signal for the play to resume was given, and their guests began filtering out of their box. "Louisa, my love?"

Her brilliant deep blue eyes gazed up at him. "Yes?"

"Was it my imagination, or is Miss Blackacre managing Bentley?"

"She is definitely managing him, but in a very subtle way."

Gideon was pleased that someone had finally taken Bentley in hand. "Then all is well."

She grinned. "You heard the duchesses. It is a very satisfactory Season."

"I would have to agree." Bending down so that his lips touched her ear, he said, "And even more so when we are alone."

"Perhaps we may"—she cut a look at her mother—"ride again on the morrow."

"I cannot think of a more pleasant way to start the day. And I'll show you a different way of riding."

She unfurled her fan, holding it so that only her eyes, gleaming wickedly, were visible. "I do so enjoy learning new things."

Yet their meeting was not to be. The following morning, as Louisa and Gideon were about to leave Stanwood House for their ride, her mother caught up with them.

"Louisa, you shall be married in less than a week. There is too much to do for you to continue your rides." Her mother's tone sounded as exasperated as Louisa felt. "Rothwell," Mama said, "if you wish to remain for breakfast, you are welcome. If not, you will see Louisa this evening. However, she must now make herself ready for the day."

His jaw ticked, but he bowed, saying, "I shall be delighted to join the family for breakfast."

The next time she saw him, she was dressed for the day as well. "I had not counted on this."

"Neither had I." Louisa passed him more toast.

The next week flew by. Louisa had little time to herself and none at all for Gideon, except in the company of others. Nights were spent dreaming of him, and more than one morning had found her hugging her pillow wishing it was him. Whatever he had planned to show her would have to wait until they were married. They had managed to sneak off into the rose arbor a few times, only to be called back in after a few stolen kisses.

"This is going to be the death of me," he grumbled more than once.

"May I remind Your Grace that you are not the only one suffering," Louisa had replied tartly.

"Forgive me, my love. I know this is not easy on you either. I'm just lonely for you."

"Forgive me as well," she would respond. "I miss you every moment of the day."

Louisa did not know if it would have been easier to be a bit lonely or, as she was being, dragged from modiste, to milliner, to glove makers and shoemakers. It appeared that her family was making sure she would not need another item of clothing until next year, if then.

The rest of the days were spent making and receiving morning visits. For some reason, she had never thought of how one actually has her own at home day. However, this week, she watched carefully how her mother and Grace handled their visitors, and was pleased that something must have sunk in as they did not respond differently than Louisa thought they should.

Evenings, Gideon escorted her to their entertainments, making sure she saved all the waltzes for him. Whenever they were at the same entertainment, she made sure that Bentley and Oriana joined them at supper.

The afternoon before her wedding, Oriana joined Louisa and Charlotte for morning visits.

"Thank you for including me," Oriana said as they climbed into the landau.

"How is your courtship going?" Louisa asked.

"Very well." Oriana sighed. "Better than that. Wonderful. Bentley and I are in love. He proposed last night. The wedding will be in six weeks at his parents' estate. His mother said that is where they all marry."

Louisa and Charlotte exchanged pleased glances before wishing their friend happy.

"I do hope you and Charlotte will be able to attend." Oriana blushed slightly. "I would like you to stand up with me. If it had not been for you, I do not think Bentley and I would be together."

"The tradition is for a single lady to be the maid of honor," Louisa reminded her friend. "Charlotte would be the better choice."

"I want both of you. Married or not. If you do not mind, that is."

"Definitely not," Charlotte declared, glancing at Louisa.

"I would be honored. Thank you for asking." She was relieved that Rothwell Abbey was not too far from the Covington estate.

They arrived at Lady Jersey's home, and Oriana said, "Now, let us put any leftover gossip to rest. Everyone will know that our families will be as close as they always were."

Louisa widened her eyes. "Gossip? I thought that had been laid to rest long ago. I am not even sure what caused it in the first place."

"Bentley," Charlotte said. "He was in a high dudgeon after you finished ringing a peal over his head."

"I dare say no one would wish to anger you by saying anything in your presence." Oriana took the footman's hand as she stepped down from the carriage. “However, there are still some spiteful cats wagging their tongues.”

“Then by all means, we should correct any mistaken impressions they might have.” At this rate, Louisa was very glad she was leaving Town right after the wedding.

Chapter Thirty-Three

Finally, the morning of Louisa and Gideon's wedding arrived. She didn't know how she managed to sleep a wink, but she awoke rested, and alert.

"My lady," Lucy said from behind a screen set up in front of the fireplace, "your bath will be ready in just a moment, and I'll ring for breakfast. Lady Worthington said you would probably not be too hungry this morning, but I took the liberty of ordering some ham for you in addition to the baked egg and toast."

Louisa rose up on her elbows. "Thank you, Lucy. I am hungry."

Her maid nodded. "If you want me to add some kippers to that, I'll get them."

"Thank you, but no."

A knock came on the door, and Lucy opened it. "Pour four of those buckets in the tub and leave one next to the fireplace."

"Yes, Miss Cottonwood."

Once the door closed, Louisa swung her legs off the bed and padded to the screen. "Miss Cottonwood?"

"Bolton, Lady Worthington's maid, said I needed to be treated with more respect," Lucy explained, as she removed Louisa's nightgown. "Last week she started making everyone call me Miss Cottonwood."

Sinking into the warm water, Louisa replied, "We're in for a great many changes."

"Yes, my lady. I believe we are, but first we must get you dressed."

Louisa not only finished her breakfast, but had Lucy call for the kippers as well. "I wonder why Grace thought I would not be hungry."

"Nervous stomach. That's what Bolton said."

Was it a good or bad thing that Louisa was not at all anxious about her marriage to Gideon? Actually, she was looking forward to it and hoped he was as well.

Lucy slipped Louisa's gown of Saxon blue over her head, then covered it with a wrapper. "I didn't want to make the same mistake as before and get your hair done before you had your gown on."

Soon her hair was pulled up in a knot, with tendrils framing her face. When her maid handed her the mirror to view the back, the knot, rather than being a simple twisted thing, was a beautiful mass of curls and thin braids. "Lucy, or should I say, Cottonwood, I have never seen a more lovely arrangement."

The young woman colored up. "Thank you, my lady. I must let their ladyships know you are almost ready."

Before Louisa knew it, her room was awash with her female relatives. The younger girls clutched a posy of yellow flowers tied with a bright blue ribbon. "We wanted to each give you one," Mary said. "But Grace wouldn't let us."

"One is perfect. Thank you so much." She kissed Mary and Theo. "You must visit me often."

The twins and Madeline gave Louisa three hand-embroidered handkerchiefs with Rothwell's crest. "These are very prettily done. You have been practicing your white work."

"We have been. Grace told us you would like them," Alice said as the other two nodded.

"And I do, indeed."

Augusta handed her a pair of velvet slippers also embroidered, but in bold flowers and vines. "I thought an abbey might be cold."

Tears started in Louisa's eyes. After Charlotte, Augusta would be the next of them to come out. "You are probably right. You must visit to find out."

Charlotte sniffed. "Do not make either of us start crying. I am lending you my butterfly brooch for the service."

"Thank you. You'll be next you know."

"We'll see. I'm in no rush."

Mama and Grace exchanged a glance, and Mama stepped forward. "I have thought of this moment since you were a little girl. You would have thought I'd have got used to the idea." Moving behind Louisa, her mother clasped a necklace of pearls interspaced with round sapphires. Using her finger, she wiped her eyes. "I promised myself I would not cry."

Louisa took her mother's hand and squeezed it. "As long as they are happy tears, Mama."

"Yes, my love. They are. I have come to believe Rothwell is perfect for you."

"Last, but not least, I hope." Grace handed Louisa a pair of earrings. The tops consisted of small sapphires mixed with diamonds from which hung a single pearl. "I think we have covered old, new, borrowed, and blue." Her sister-in-law hugged her gently. "Don your new finery and we shall depart. Matt has already left with the children. Rothwell will meet us at the church." She reached into her pocket. "Before I forget, this came for you from Rothwell."

Grace opened the black satin pouch, drawing out a pearl and sapphire bracelet that matched perfectly the necklace her mother had given her and the earrings as well. Louisa was relieved that the clerk at Rundell and Bridge's had convinced her to buy Gideon a simple tiepin in the same stone.

She took one look around the room she would never sleep in again. Most of her clothing and other possessions were already at Rothwell House in trunks that would be sent to the abbey. "I am ready to leave now. Cottonwood?" she addressed her maid.

"I will have everything prepared as you said, my lady."

Louisa might not be experienced in seduction like her soon-to-be husband was but, with some suggestions from Grace and Dotty, she had learned to set a scene that her husband would appreciate.

Rollins had just released Gideon to go downstairs and wait for the coach, when he decided to look in on Allerton. The man rose as he entered. "Today is the day, Your Grace."

"It is, and I could not be happier. Are you ready to leave for the abbey tomorrow?"

"I am, however, this came for you this morning." His secretary's tone was somber. "You will want to read it before leaving."

Gideon spread the letter out on Allerton's desk.

The Duke of Rothwell
Governor Square
Mayfair

I am sorry to inform you that my former partner, Mr. Sullivan, did not die from his wound. He came to my place of business demanding to be allowed entrance. Instead, my other partner and I paid him the price of his third.

Unfortunately, that did not appear to mollify him. I greatly fear he still seeks to do you harm.

Yr Servant,
M. Hammond

Perdition! Bloody, bloody hell! Of all the days to receive a letter like this it had to be on his wedding day!

He must ensure Louisa and his mother were safe before he could do anything about the cur.

Gideon started to rake his fingers through his hair when he remembered the pains Rollins had taken this morning.

"I will notify Bow Street if you wish, Your Grace."

"Notify Templeton instead. We leave for Rothwell today." He tugged hard on the bellpull. A moment later his butler appeared.

"Your Grace, the coach is waiting for you."

"I will leave for Rothwell Abbey after the wedding breakfast instead of in the morning. Please make the arrangements. Tell Rollins I would like him to find a hotel suitable for my wedding night. I want everyone out of here as quickly as you can manage it."

"Yes, Your Grace. Shall I tell the coachman you will be a while?"

"No. I'll come now." He shoved the letter across the desk to his secretary. "You know what to do with this."

"Yes, Your Grace. I shall see you at the abbey."

Nothing would make him late for his marriage to Lady Louisa Vivers. He just hoped that blackguard Sullivan didn't have anyone watching the house.

Gideon had been headed to the front of the house when he changed direction and went to the stables. "Barnes."

"I sent the coach round front, Yer Grace," the man said with a disgruntled look.

"I know. What I want you to do is send some of the grooms around to the square and see if anyone is watching the house."

"If there is?"

Gideon thought for a moment. "Keep them busy until the rest of the staff has left from the mews. Only my mother may depart from the front of the house. Send the traveling coach to Stanwood House."

Drat, he'd have to tell his mother it was not safe to remain in Town. Fortunately, he had not brought his brother, who was studying for his entrance into Oxford, and his sisters.

"Yes, Yer Grace." Barnes went off with a jaunty step.

The man probably hadn't had to do anything like this in his life. Thank God, Gideon had received the letter while he could still make plans.

He lost no time getting back to the house and into his town coach. Soon, he would be the happiest man on earth.

A half hour later, he glanced for the fourteenth time, if not the hundredth, toward the side door that Worthington had said Louisa would enter through.

"She is late. She is never late."

"She's not late. It is not ten o'clock," Worthington said. "Even the children aren't wiggling around yet. And there is probably some female ritual she will have to go through before leaving the house."

A rush of fresh air heralded the side door opening. Grace entered followed by Lady Wolverton, Charlotte, and finally, Louisa. In one fell swoop, all the air in his body left, and he grabbed onto the pew.

"Do you feel like Jackson just punched you in the stomach?" Rutherford, a friend who had agreed to stand up with Gideon when he and his cousin were not speaking asked, his voice shaking with mirth.

"Exactly like that." God she was exquisite.

"You'll do then. Although, I was pretty sure you would. Anna is never wrong about this sort of thing."

Louisa was dressed in a deep blue gown that seemed to sparkle when she moved, no, floated toward him.

The young cleric, who had been running back and forth, now stood in front of the altar waiting patiently.

Worthington walked toward Louisa, took her arm, and led her to Gideon. "I think we are ready to begin."

The vicar opened his prayer book, but it was clear he had no need of it. "We are gathered today in the sight of God . . ."

Louisa raised her beautiful blue gaze to Gideon and, again, he was lost as he stared at her. His friend poked him in the side when it was time to say his vows. Yet the only ones he really remembered were to love and cherish her, to keep her all to himself, and worship her with his body. If that was all he had to do, they would have a long and happy marriage.

When she spoke her voice was strong and firm, as if she were making her vows not only before God but the entire world. Lord he loved her. Loved her beauty and her strength.

Then the vicar pronounced them man and wife, and she was his. Forever.

"We're married," Gideon said somewhat giddily.

"I know." Louisa smiled, and smiled some more until her cheeks hurt, and still she smiled. Gideon's wife, she was finally, absolutely, and irrevocably Gideon's wife.

"Your Grace." The cleric stood in front of her, and it took her a moment to realize he was speaking to her.

“That was a wonderful service.”

“Thank you, Your Grace, but you must now sign the register.”

“Of course.” She tugged on Gideon’s hand, stopping his mad dash to the door. “We have to sign the register.”

Rutherford laughed. “I almost forgot that part myself.”

Just a few minutes later, Louisa and her husband—she loved how that sounded—were in Grace’s landau making their way to Stanwood House.

Gideon brushed his lips against hers. “My wife.” He sounded as proud and happy as she was. “Do you mind leaving for Rothwell Abbey after the wedding breakfast?”

“Not at all, but why?”

“I feel the need to return. I have been in Town much longer than I had planned, and I want you to meet my brother and sisters.”

“Then let us go. I want to meet them as well, and I know Grace will not mind if we leave early.” Louisa couldn’t keep the blush from her cheeks. “I think it might be required.”

“I put my valet in charge of finding a good coaching inn for us tonight. We shall only be on the road for two or so hours. The rest of the journey can be made tomorrow.”

“Will your mother come as well?”

“I haven’t asked her, but I believe she will.”

They pulled up in front of the Carpenter family’s house, and Royston himself let down the steps. “Your Graces.” The butler bowed deeply. “Everything is in readiness.”

Louisa and Gideon had less than an hour before their guests would begin to arrive. Thankfully, her mother, Grace, and her mother-in-law had done most of the planning. If it had been left to Louisa, she would not have bothered.

A few minutes later those three ladies arrived. Gideon took his mother aside for a moment, and Louisa saw the lady nod. It was all settled. She would see her new home tomorrow.

All she needed to do was tell her mother and sister-in-law. "Grace, Mama," Louisa said as Matt opened a bottle of champagne. "Rothwell and I have decided to begin our travel to Rothwell Abbey today. Do you mind?"

"Not at all," Grace replied. "I know you will be anxious to start making the changes you want."

Mama, however, gnawed on her bottom lip. "Are you sure about this, Louisa?"

"Absolutely. I do not wish to remain in Town, particularly when there is so much to do on the estate." There was also the small hope that she would be expecting a baby. For the first time, her courses were late.

"If that is what you wish . . ." Her mother looked none too happy.

Louisa wondered if Mama's reaction had something to do with her former marriage. "It is."

Gideon pressed a glass of champagne into Louisa's hand as Matt and Richard gave glasses to their wives.

"To us, Your Grace." He touched his glass to hers. "And a long and happy life."

"To us, Your Grace." She smiled again. "May we always be as happy as we are now."

Chapter Thirty-Four

Between Gideon's mother, Louisa's mother, and Grace Worthington, the entire *haut ton* had been invited and accepted the invitation. The ballroom was full and their guests spilled out onto the terrace.

It was gratifying, but he had been more than happy to be on their way north. Not only because of Sullivan, but Gideon truly did want to take Louisa home. Guilt ate at him that he had not been able to bring his own sisters to their wedding. Perhaps he could make it up to them by having some sort of entertainment at the abbey.

Gideon and Louisa arrived at the Swan three hours after they had almost sneaked out of Berkeley Square. The inn was large, four stories, and built of gray stone. Knowing his valet's exacting standards, Gideon was certain the inside would be as imposing as the outside was. The coach Worthington had lent them, which was much more luxurious than Gideon's and much better sprung, rolled under an arch to the yard beyond.

The door opened and the steps let down. Gideon jumped out first, offering Louisa his hand.

A short, spare man awaited them at the inn's entrance.

"Your Grace, Your Grace, welcome to the Swan. We have prepared our best chambers for you."

Louisa inclined her head regally. "Thank you. I am sure they will be perfect." To Gideon, she whispered, "I have only stayed in one other inn when we traveled to Town."

He could not stop his lips from tilting. "I will endeavor to make this stay unforgettable."

"I am sure you will, husband."

The landlord, who had neglected to give them his name, led them to their chambers and proceeded to recite what they were serving for dinner that evening. "We have a rack of lamb, salad . . ."

Gideon glanced at Louisa, who shrugged. "I shall send my valet down with our order. We shall dine in our rooms."

"Of course, Your Grace, Your Grace, I will wait to hear from Mr. Rollins. There is no rush, and may I congratulate you on your wedding."

Although the room was not huge, the bed was. At least four people would easily fit in it. Flowers in vases and bowls had been set on almost every flat surface, and a door on one wall was open to a second room with a table, chairs, and sofa.

The landlord handed Gideon the key, and Louisa began to laugh. "Oh, dear. I fear I am not yet up to snuff when it comes to staying at inns, but look at this room. I would never have expected it to be so welcoming."

"I have a feeling that was more due to my valet and your maid than the landlord." Gideon wrapped his arms around her. "Kiss me."

Raising her face to his, Louisa melted into him. "Gladly."

"Oh, Your Grace." Rollins, followed closely by a young woman Gideon supposed was Louisa's maid, stood at the open door. "Forgive us for the interruption. Miss Cottonwood and I were just now informed of your arrival. If you will give us a moment, we have some items." Rollins paused, for a moment. "Yes, items to set out."

Louisa giggled into Gideon's neckcloth, as their servants scurried around the room.

"The sheets are ours, Your Grace," her maid said before closing the door.

Gideon glanced around the chamber. "Well, they did have some items to leave."

"I am quite impressed." Actually, it was even better than Louisa thought it would be. Champagne, fruit, cheeses that could not have come from the inn, chicken, and small pastries that looked French, were artfully arranged. A vase of red and pink roses stood in the middle of the table. "I suggest you open the wine, husband."

"How did they know to do this?"

"Ah, well, it might have been a suggestion of mine." Louisa drifted toward the table. She had not been at all hungry during the wedding breakfast, but now she was ravenous.

"You?" Gideon prowled after her, a wicked twinkle in his eyes. "And how would you know to do this?"

Louisa gave him what she hoped was a sultry look. "I may have had some help."

He opened the champagne, and she arranged their plates. They fed each other morsels of food, kissing in between, and slowly, very slowly removing pieces of clothing until they were drinking champagne naked as the day they were born.

"What now, husband. Will you ravish me?"

"No," he drawled, his low voice making her shiver. "I am going to make love to you as slowly as is humanly possible."

She swallowed in anticipation. "That sounds nice."

"I'm glad you think so."

Gideon carried Louisa to the large bed. The sheets smelled

of lavender, and he grinned. She had arranged it well, and he had every intention of thanking her for it.

"Ah, love." He touched his lips to hers.

"I love you." She opened her mouth to him.

"No more than I love you." He kissed Louisa slowly, sweetly, showing her all the feelings he had for her, worshiping her body as he'd vowed to do. Later, when she shuddered, tightening around him, he swallowed her cries with a kiss. Soon they would be in their own chambers at the abbey and not have to worry about anyone hearing them. For now, he would protect her in any way he could.

He woke to the sun streaming through the windows. She was warm, and he held her closely to him. Either the curtains had not been closed last night, or someone had opened them this morning. For several minutes, he simply reveled in waking up next to his wife. Thanking fate for giving Louisa to him.

His member stirred, urging him to make love to her again. "Louisa?"

"Hmm?" Her lids fluttered, but remained closed.

Was she even awake? "I'll show you something different."

Her lush bottom wiggled against him as he slid into her.

Lord, to think he could enjoy this every morning. Her body tensed and she cried out her release. Holding her closer, he nuzzled her hair. "I hope you liked that as much as I did."

Louisa opened her eyes and smiled. "Enough to make it a morning tradition."

Later that day Gideon ordered the coach to stop. "We are on a rise where you can see the abbey."

Standing on a large flat rock he'd led her to, Louisa peered through an opening in the trees. The house was immense. Even larger than Worthington Place. Built of sandy colored stone, it seemed to reflect the sunlight. Most of the house appeared to have been rebuilt, but she could still see the parts that reflected a much older style. "Gideon, it's beautiful."

"I hoped you would like it." His arms snaked around her waist. "I believe you will find many of the modern conveniences you are used to. Most of the work is in the older part of the building. One of the carpenters found dry rot in some of the rafters. Since I returned, I have ordered the servants to report any sign of deterioration."

Louisa reviewed what she had been told of the Rothwell staff. A skeleton staff including Mrs. Boyle remained in London. Mrs. Grant, the abbey's housekeeper, Louisa would meet today. "Your mother told me that we have a household staff of forty. Twenty-five of which are maids. I shall have the housekeeper ensure that all the rooms are cleaned and aired at least weekly. That way, we will be able to keep up with any maintenance."

"An excellent plan." Lifting her down, he kissed her. "Shall we go home?"

It took another forty minutes before the coach drew up in front of the house. The servants were lined up, women on one side and men on the other in order of rank. The moment Louisa's feet had touched the ground, the introductions were made.

"My dear," Gideon said, "may I introduce you to Rothwell Abbey's butler, Fredericks Junior. He is the eldest son of—"

"Fredericks our London butler." Smiling, Louisa inclined her head as the butler bowed.

"Just so, Your Grace."

"And here is Mrs. Grant, our housekeeper at the abbey."

"Your Grace." The woman sank into a deep curtsey. "Welcome home."

"Thank you, Mrs. Grant. I am pleased to be here. If you can be ready, I would like to begin looking over the house tomorrow morning."

"Certainly, Your Grace."

Louisa was pleased to see that many of the servants from the London town house were here, including their chef. The old cook had already taken up residence in the dower house, where her mother-in-law had decided to immediately reside.

As she and Gideon made their way up one side of the grand staircase, he whispered, "I had hoped that we would have a few days to ourselves before the work started."

"Let's agree to limit work to half days, leaving the other half to play."

"That will have to do, I suppose." He sighed, making Louisa giggle.

"You are incorrigible."

"I am trying. Ah, here we are. I had almost forgotten how long a stroll this was."

They had reached the end of a corridor on the first floor of the east wing, which was where the family's rooms were located. A footman, standing at attention, opened a door.

"These are our apartments," Gideon said.

The door had opened to a smaller version of the hall below. It was as if they had entered a small house inside a larger one. The walls were lined with cream-colored silk decorated with a pattern of vines and birds. Even the corners were scrupulously clean. Dismissing the footman, Gideon led her through their bedchambers, dressing rooms, and parlors. They could live here for weeks and never need the rest of the house. Though she knew that would never happen.

"Here is our pièce de résistance," he said, opening another

door. “At least for me and the servants who had to trudge water up here.”

It was a bathing chamber, tiled, and with its own tile-covered stove. “My love, this is remarkable. Stanwood House has three, but none are so large.”

“My father had it added a few years ago.”

“It must have cost a great deal. If I am not mistaken, those tiles come from Holland.”

“Yes, well. We could afford it at the time.” He grimaced.

Her heart clinched at the look of pain in his face, and she renewed her vow to help him any way she could. “That is water under the bridge. We must deal with what we have, and you are right. It frees up servants for other tasks. Have you had to let many of them go?”

“No, I could not do that. The abbey is the life’s blood of this area. If we were to begin sacking servants, it would harm the economy.”

He was right. It was something she had not considered before. “Of course. When will I meet your brother and sisters?”

“In a few days. Mama wanted to give us some time alone. They are at the dower house with her for the nonce.”

For the next three weeks, they followed the pattern of spending the mornings on estate and household business, and the afternoons learning more about each other. Gideon was not surprised to find that Louisa excelled at whatever she put her hand to, whether it was running the abbey, swimming, or archery. She did not have the patience for fishing, which was just as well. He did need to shine at something.

However, that Tuesday he came in from visiting their tenants with Louisa to find a letter from Lord St. Eth. The missive was short and to the point. St. Eth was back in Town and ready to accompany Gideon to the Lords before leaving again for another niece's lying-in. The second was from his solicitor. Mrs. Petrie had been served notice to quit the Brick Street house. The letter stated that the Rothwell parure had been found in the woman's bank deposit box, and was now in Templeton's possession. No one had seen Sullivan.

"Louisa, sweetheart."

She glanced up from going through a stack of mail. "What is it?"

"I must go to Town." Praying she would say no, he asked, "Would you like to accompany me? It will only be for about a week or so."

"Normally, I would love to go with you"—a line formed in her wrinkling her forehead—"but I have some things I am working on here. Do you mind very much if I beg off?"

"No, of course not," he replied, trying not to show his relief. "I'll leave immediately."

Coming up to him, Louisa slid her arms around his neck and smiled. "So that you can return to me sooner."

"Yes." For all he wanted was to have her by his side forever. She was his heart and soul. He wasn't even gone yet and already he missed her. "It is not yet noon. Perhaps we can steal an hour before I must leave."

"I think that is an excellent idea, my love."

Louisa glanced around the morning room. Gideon had been gone for almost two weeks, but he was returning today. She was now positive that she was breeding and wished she had asked her mother what to expect. Perhaps she would be lucky and, like Grace, not suffer from morning sickness.

During that time, she had taken the opportunity to refurbish, from her very generous pin money, several of the main rooms as well as her parlor. The room had been furnished with only a sofa, chairs, and a few tables scattered around. Fortunately, the fabric store in Bedford her mother-in-law had told her about had proved to be every bit as good as what one might find in London.

She had also taken it upon herself to modernize the kitchen. That had come from her own funds, which Gideon would not like at all. Not that her husband would notice that kitchen. She had it on good authority that he had not visited it in years. She did hope that he would notice the morning room or perhaps her parlor, especially as she had added a daybed to that room.

Placing her hand on her still flat stomach, she said a prayer. It was early days, but, for the first time in her life, her courses were late, giving her hope that she would be holding their child in her arms before spring.

The clock chimed one, and she rang the bellpull. If Gideon held true to form, he would be arriving at any time.

"Your Grace?"

"I think we may expect His Grace to return soon. Please tell Cook to have luncheon ready when he arrives."

"Very good, Your Grace."

The menu she and her cook had put together consisted mostly of a cold collation of meats, cheeses, and fruit, but with the addition of the white soup Gideon enjoyed so much.

She sank onto one of her new French cane-backed chairs, placed her feet on the matching footstool, and picked up her book. All there was to do now was wait.

A tap sounded on the door, and Fredericks Junior entered. "Your Grace, the post has arrived."

"Thank you, Fredericks. I shall attend to it." He placed the silver salver on the small marble table next to her chair.

Louisa just hoped none of the correspondence was from Gideon. He had delayed his homecoming by almost a week as it was, and she was impatient to see him. In fact, if he did not arrive today, she would take a bolt to Town.

Sifting through the letters, she sorted them into two stacks: one for bills and the second for personal missives. There was a third note whose hand she did not recognize, and she was fairly sure she did not know anyone residing on Brick Street. Laying the other two stacks aside, she opened the garish pink seal on the letter.

My dear duchess,

Louisa did not consider herself at all high in the instep, but considering that the person was unknown to her, the address was so informal as to be encroaching. The note continued.

I write this letter to you woman to woman.

The hairs on Louisa's neck began to rise, along with a sense of foreboding.

When last I saw him, the duke was in good health. You might ask how I know this. The question is quite easily answered. I am his mistress.

For a moment Louisa couldn't breathe. It was as if someone had punched her in the stomach. Tears rose and stung her eyes, even as she tried to blink them back. She wanted to set light to the letter and throw it in the fireplace. Yet she kept reading.

I had thought he would give me up when he married, however, he insisted that it was not necessary. Yet, the more I considered the matter, the more I felt badly for you, a young wife who is probably in love with the duke. Therefore, I have resolved to give him up for the small sum of one thousand guineas.

Louisa's eyes dried, and the knot in her stomach released. One thousand guineas? The woman was mad!

I trust I will hear from you soon concerning my generous offer.

Mrs. R. Petrie

Louisa sucked in a breath, blew it out, and did it again. She must trust Gideon. He loved her. He had said the words. He had shown her how much she meant to him. When he returned, she would ask him about this Petrie woman. There would be a reasonable explanation. There had to be.

Chapter Thirty-Five

It was almost two o'clock. Gideon couldn't wait to be home. He felt as if he were a medieval warrior returning from battle. Maybe not the sort fought on a field but battle still the same. He had regained his property as well as much of the money, and soon he would be back in Louisa's arms where he belonged.

The old traveling coach pulled up to the steps leading to the front door. Frederick Junior had the massive doors open before Gideon jumped down from the carriage.

"Your Grace." The butler bowed. "We are glad to have you home. Her Grace bade you bathe before meeting with her in the morning room."

"Thank you." Gideon wanted to see Louisa immediately, but he did smell as if he'd been traveling hard for two days. "Has Rollins arrived?"

"Indeed, Your Grace. I believe he is in your chambers."

Good. That meant Gideon's bath would be ready by the time he climbed the stairs.

Sinking into the tub, he considered all the ways he would make love to his wife. If he never spent another hour away from her it would be too long.

Less than a half hour later he opened the door to the

morning room and was dumbstruck. How had she managed to do this in the time he had been gone? Before, the room had been decorated in hues of green and brown. Now yellows and whites predominated, making the parlor appear brighter than it had ever been before. It was welcoming and comfortable—but deuce take it—where had the money come from? Had she defied him and used her own funds? And where the hell was she?

Scanning the parlor, he finally saw her standing with her back to the door, gazing out one of the many windows. She was dressed in a bright yellow gown that seemed to complement the room, and he had not seen her at first. God, she was beautiful, and he really did not wish to fight with her about her redecoration. Not when all he wanted to do was lose himself in her arms. "Louisa, my love."

She turned slowly, as if she was reluctant to leave the view. "Gideon."

Her voice was low, but the warmth it usually held was missing. Was she expecting an argument? Well, she wasn't going to get one. At least not now. He started toward her.

"Remain there if you would." Though phrased as a request, the command was evident in her tone.

He halted, wondering what she could be about. Perhaps he should mention the room. "I like what you've done in here."

"Thank you." She inclined her head. "There is a matter we must discuss."

Damnation. He had just returned. Did she really want to talk about using her money to refurbish the house? "If you wish." If she was so intent on having this conversation now, they might as well settle it. "You defied my orders not to use your funds on the house or the estate without my permission."

Louisa raised one haughty dark brow, and his temper

rose along with it. "I do not recall an order. I recall you stating a preference. One, I might add, to which I did not agree. If you must know, I used my pin money, not my funds, but that is not the reason I wish to speak with you."

What the devil . . . Louisa had just dismissed him. "If you think you may—"

"Who is Mrs. Petrie?"

Bloody hell! After everything he'd done to make sure that woman's name never sullied Louisa's ears.

"How did you hear . . . No. I do not wish to know. She is none of your concern."

"Not my concern?" Louisa asked in a dangerously low tone. "I take it she is a"—she hesitated for a moment as if looking for the word—"high-flyer."

"I will not discuss her with you. This is a matter you will remain out of." Gideon never wanted to hear that whore's name on his wife's lips.

He had almost destroyed his father's former mistress, yet he had been generous as well. He had given her the option of being hanged or transported, or fleeing to the Continent. Naturally, she had chosen the latter. She should be on a ship making her way to France very shortly.

Louisa's mouth formed a thin line. "In that case, I have nothing more to say to you." She dipped a shallow curtsey. "Good day, Your Grace."

If that was what Louisa thought, she could think again. She was not leaving this room until—the door on the other side of the morning room that led to the garden shut with a snap.

Devil take her. He was tired and hungry. Gideon had wanted nothing more than to feel her arms around him and kiss her. But he'd be damned if he was going to chase her all around his estate. Sooner or later, she would calm down and come back to the house. Then he'd use all of his skill to seduce her out of her temper. In the meantime, he was going to eat.

Stepping out into the corridor he yelled for his butler. "How soon can you have nuncheon served?"

"It is already ready for you in the breakfast room, Your Grace."

"Fine." He'd almost growled the word.

Perdition. Taking his foul mood out on the servants, particularly his senior staff, was not a wonderful idea, but at this point, he just didn't care. He would have something to eat, calm down, and wait for his wife to return.

Louisa's worst fears had been confirmed. If the Petrie woman had meant nothing to Gideon, he would not have been so defensive. Once again Louisa found herself blinking back tears, the back of her throat so raw it was hard to swallow. As soon as she could, she would make arrangements to leave Rothwell Abbey. There was no way Louisa would share her husband with another woman.

Neither Grace nor Matt would expect her to put up with that type of behavior.

Skirting the rose garden, she reentered the house through the music room, located off the hall. Moments later she was sitting at her desk, an empty piece of pressed paper in front of her. Gritting her teeth together, she began to write.

Dear Grace,

I have discovered Rothwell is not the man I thought he was. He is keeping a mistress, and I have decided to leave him. Please tell me that you have no objection to me going to Worthington Place.

Your devoted sister,
Louisa

She considered using her proper signature, but decided not to. She did not wish to be either the Duchess of Rothwell or Louisa Rothwell any longer.

After sealing the letter, she called for her maid. "Take this into the town and post it. I wish to send it by special messenger if possible."

"Yes, Your Grace."

"When you return, begin packing. We are leaving the abbey. I shall sleep in here until we depart."

Cottonwood frowned but said not a word. "I'll make up your bed and have everything else ready to go in no time."

Once her maid left, Louisa took a key out of the desk drawer. If honor didn't keep Gideon out of her room, the locked door would. Her mother had been right. One cannot know everything one needs to know about a potential husband in just a few weeks. Louisa would never have suspected Gideon would have a mistress. She had not wanted to believe it. Yet it was true.

Later that evening as she lay on her daybed trying to force herself to sleep, the latch on the door between their bedchamber and her parlor jiggled.

"Louisa, I demand you open this door at once."

"I wish to be alone."

"There is no reason for you to be upset. I have done nothing that other men in my position would not have done."

Quite frankly, she did not care how many married men had mistresses. She would not stay with a husband who did. "Go away, Rothwell. I have no wish to speak with you."

"You have to come out at some point."

She refused to answer, and a moment later heard the sound of him leaving the door. Her throat tightened again.

I will not cry, I will not cry, I will not *cry.*

Yet she couldn't keep the tears from flowing down her cheeks.

Two very long days and nights later, her maid brought her a letter with a familiar seal.

My dearest Louisa,

I am distraught to hear that you wish to leave Rothwell. However, under the circumstances, I believe your judgment to be sound. I assume that you will not wish to be subject to the questions that would arise from returning to Worthington. Therefore, I offer you the use of Stanwood for as long as you wish to remain there.

I pray that Rothwell will come to his senses, but many men never do. I am sending one of our traveling coaches. Expect it in no more than two days.

With much love,
Your sister,
Grace

A drop landed on the letter, blurring some of the words. Louisa brushed her tears away, then blew her nose. She had hoped that her family would understand her reasons for leaving Gideon, yet one was never truly sure. Many families would have instructed her to remain with her husband. Thank God, hers was not one of them.

She rang for her maid and waited until the door opened. "We are leaving as soon as the Worthington coach has arrived."

"Yes, Your Grace. What should I tell everyone?"

"That I have gone home for a visit. Surely, that will not surprise anyone." Although none of the staff would have dared mention the argument she and Gideon had had, the servants knew relations between the duke and duchess were seriously strained.

"No, Your Grace, but what about the babe?"

Touching her stomach, Louisa sighed. "I will cross that bridge when I come to it."

She stood and shook out her skirts. It was time to tell her husband she was leaving him.

Gideon sat behind his desk in his study and rubbed his hands over his face, wondering how he had let his life, his marriage, get so out of control. If only he had trusted Louisa with the truth, he would not have hurt her. Somehow he must find a way to win her love again. Yet would she ever truly forgive him for his betrayal?

Worthington had been right when he'd counseled Gideon never to attempt to hide the truth from her. Remembering her reaction when he had told her that the Petrie woman was not Louisa's business and ordered her not to question his behavior made him cringe. That would have been the time to confess all. Tell her about his father, and the mistress, and the gambling debts. But he'd been so convinced he was right to protect her from the sordid business.

Yet even then, when she had announced that the conversation was at an end, he had not realized that she had meant *all* conversation, henceforward, was at an end.

Forever.

Since Louisa had walked out, Gideon had barely seen her, and then only from a distance. Even in a house of this size, that took some doing. Somehow he must find a way to make it up to her.

A light tap sounded on the door, and a moment later, Louisa swept in. Rising, he studied her countenance. But he could tell very little from her calm mien. Only her right hand smoothing the fabric of her skirts showed her distress.

He rose quickly to his feet. "Louisa, please have a seat."

"That will not be necessary, Your Grace."

Apparently, they were no longer using their first names. "What can I do for you?"

"I have come to tell you I am leaving in two days."

Leaving? No. She was his wife.

The ache in his chest spread and for a moment he thought he would fall to the floor. Staring at her, Gideon caught a brief moment when the pain and anger she felt seeped through the polite mask she'd donned. He had caused that anguish, and hurt, and he could not allow her to leave. If he did, he would never be able to save his marriage. "I shall not allow it."

Her lips twisted into a travesty of a smile. "Just how do you propose to stop me? Lock me in my chamber?"

"It is an idea." Even as he'd formed the words, and they had flown out of his mouth, he knew it had been the wrong thing to say.

Her chin rose, and she looked more like a princess than a duchess. "It may not be fashionable, but I refuse to share my husband with another woman. If you had wanted a wife who would look the other way, you should have married another." She turned toward the door, then glanced back. "If you attempt to stop me, you had better bar the windows as well, Your Grace."

Mistress? She actually believed he would take a mistress? How the devil could she have come up with that idea?

He started to go to her when the door closed with a loud snap, and he sank back into his chair. He had no doubt that she would make good on her threat, and the image of Louisa, his love, climbing out the window and breaking her beautiful neck was not one he could contemplate.

But what the deuce was he to do now? He had two days to come up with a plan to convince her to stay. Convince her that he would never take a mistress. That Louisa was the only woman he wanted or would ever want.

Had everyone else been right about telling her about his father's mistress? He'd only wanted to protect her. Was it too late for the truth? Would she even believe him?

Chapter Thirty-Six

"Your Grace?"

Louisa paused as she traversed the great hall. All her bags were packed and being loaded on the coach. Even her cat was ready for the journey, having settled in her traveling case a few moments ago. "Yes, Fredericks."

The butler held out a folded and sealed piece of paper. "His Grace asked me to give you this."

She took the missive gingerly from his hand, half expecting it to scald her fingers. She and Gideon had not spoken since she had told him she was leaving. She could only assume that he had decided to respect her decision. "Thank you."

Ducking into the small front parlor, she tore open the note.

Meet me in the rose garden next to the gate.
G. R.

She could not imagine what he wanted, but whatever it was they were unlikely to be overheard there. She debated fetching a bonnet or sending for it and decided she would rather get the conversation with her husband over.

Leaving the room, she made her way down the long

corridor to the back of the house then to the first garden. A few minutes later she approached the gate, but there was no sign of Gideon.

What the deuce is he playing at?

Suddenly, Potter, the head gardener, strode up to her. "Yer Grace. I'm to give you this."

As the butler had, he held out a sealed letter. "Thank you."

I have been delayed. Please go to the summer house.
G. R.

Her throat closed painfully. Why would he want to meet her at a place where they had spent hours making love in the first weeks of their marriage? A place that held such memories for him? For her? Or was it because he would find it easier to say good-bye to her there?

Straightening her spine, she walked rapidly down the path leading to the small cottage. About fifteen minutes later, she stared at the footbridge leading to the summer house. Bouquets of flowers adorned the bridge and Gideon appeared in the open door.

"I have come." Her voice sounded rusty as she shoved the words past the ache in her throat.

"I see." He stayed where he was for a moment, then his long strides ate up the distance between them. "Louisa." His hands hovered to the sides of her shoulders, then he touched her, wrapping his warm, strong fingers around her upper arms. "Have I lost you forever?"

Part of her wanted to shrug off his hands and the other part wanted to sink into him, but she stood quietly, searching his stormy gray eyes. "How can you lose something you threw away?"

His throat worked as he swallowed. "I was wrong. I have hurt you when all I wanted to do was to protect you and love you." He dragged his eyes away from hers. "If it wasn't for my wretched pride."

Unbidden tears sprung to her eyes, as anger at all they had lost surged through her veins. To her ears, her voice was a low, harsh roar. "You took a mistress almost as soon as we married. What, pray, does that have to do with your pride?"

"That is just it. She was *never* my mistress. She was my father's mistress." Louisa would have believed him if she had not received the letter. "I wanted to handle it all myself. I did not want you to know what my father had done. I convinced myself that you should play no part in it." He shook his head. "Come, please, I must show you."

She allowed herself to be led into the cottage. Lace curtains fluttered in the breeze. On the rough-hewn table lay a black cloth and a parure that was clearly ancient and must have cost a fortune.

"That has been in my family for 250 years. Queen Elizabeth gave them to the second Duke of Rothwell upon his marriage to one of her favorites. My father gave them to Mrs. Petrie." His voice became rough. "He had no right to do so, and I had to get them back. She stole so much from me, from us. It was due to his behavior and her greed that the estate was suffering."

Jewels! Granted, they were old and priceless jewels that the old duke had no right to give away. She completely understood that Gideon had to retrieve them, but that did not address the real problem. Louisa breathed slowly, trying to calm her thudding heart. He may never have bedded that woman, but the fact remained that he had not trusted her enough to tell her, or allow her to help him. That was as much of a betrayal as what she had thought he'd done. Refusing to look at him, she raised her chin to keep the tears that threatened to fall at bay.

"Please, say something."

Once Louisa had herself under control again, she looked at him square in the eyes. "You may not have betrayed the sanctity of our marriage bed, but the fact that you did not trust me, *could* not trust me, is almost worse. How can we have a marriage without trust?"

His arm circled her waist, as if he thought she would run away. Well, he might have a point. She had been on the verge of departing.

"My love." He tightened his hold on her again. "It wasn't that I didn't trust you." She tried to pull away, but he stopped her. He gave a rueful laugh. "I had put my scheme in place before I knew we would wed. It never occurred to me you would discover anything of what I was doing, and when you did, I reacted badly. I was wrong not to have told you in the first place, and I was an imbecile to have said you had no cause to question me."

Louisa was very still, too still. Gideon brought his other arm around her. If she made a run for it, he'd do everything possible to stop her.

Finally, she took a breath. "What exactly was your plan, and how, for the love of heaven, did you think I'd never find out about *her?*"

"Let me start at the beginning." Gideon closed his eyes as he thought about the best way to explain what had happened. He knew he had only this one chance to convince Louisa. "According to my mother, my father had dementia. It wasn't that noticeable at first. He'd forget things, and someone would always find them or remind him. Then he began to forget the people around him. At some point, he did not even recognize my mother. He left Rothwell and moved into the London town house. In a strange way, that makes perfect sense. He had spent much of his time after university there."

"That was when he took up with Mrs. Petrie."

It hadn't been a question, but he said, "Yes. Not only

that, but he had apparently lost any idea how to control his spending. He gambled as he had when he was young. Unfortunately, the parure was in Town to be cleaned."

When Louisa groaned softly, he knew she understood. He told her everything; the measures he'd taken to stop any further purchases and retrieve what had been bought, the first visit to Mrs. Petrie's house, and his suspicions she was hiding money and property in a safe-deposit box, the actions his solicitor had filed to recover the missing gems, and finally, at last the success in finding the jewels. And she told him about the letter. He could murder the whore for that alone.

"You should have discussed this with me." Louisa's tone was dispassionate, as if this were happening to someone else.

"I cannot argue that. I should have told you all of it before we married, but definitely afterward when I went back up to Town." He was tired, so very tired, and afraid of what she would do, terrified of what would happen to him if she left. "I did not expect her to write you, and when you confronted me . . . I should have explained all of it then. I am very sorry I did not."

"It would have saved us a great deal of trouble," she murmured dryly.

"I know that now. A pity I didn't see it then."

She turned in his arms, and her brows furrowed as she looked up at him. "You have taken most of her money, horses, carriages, and the house she was living in. In short, everything she cared about. Where is she now?"

"I don't know, and I don't care. She has caused enough trouble for my family." Suddenly, a shot rang out and one of the windowpanes shattered, spewing glass. He pulled Louisa down to the floor.

Instead of screaming or whimpering like most well-bred females, she scowled. "I think we found her. For goodness' sake, Gideon, didn't anyone tell you that wounded animals are dangerous?"

Her tone held such disgust, he wanted to laugh. "I seem to remember someone saying something to that effect." All he'd wanted to do was keep her safe from harm, and he had brought her into the middle of it. He glanced around the cottage. How the hell were they going to get out of here? "Wait here."

"Oh, no you don't." Grabbing his shoulders, she rolled on top of him. "I am a much smaller target, and I have a pistol. Do you?"

He gaped. He couldn't see himself, but he knew it all the same. "You have a pistol?"

"Of course I do. I was getting ready to depart."

And he, fool that he was, didn't even have a slingshot, much less his sword stick. "Very well, ma'am. You are in command."

"It's about time," Louisa muttered.

She scanned the room, paying particular attention to the broken window. When she removed her body from his, he wanted to grab her and pull her back, but he knew it would be a mistake.

"Did you plan to eat while we were here?"

How the devil could she be hungry now? "Of course, the servants . . ."—God, he was an idiot—"would have heard the shot."

She nodded. "Help should be on the way soon." Holding her skirts up, she crouched, making her way to the window. Once she could not be seen from the outside, she rose, her back against the wall. "Who is out there and what do you want with me?"

"It's not you I want, duchess," Mrs. Petrie called. "I want the parure. It was given to me, and it's mine."

Louisa nibbled her lips, and Gideon's desire to taste them once more, well, more than once more, surged.

"Very well. If they are in fact yours, please, come get them."

"As if I'd trust you."

"*I* have given you no reason to *distrust* me." Louisa's tone was as haughty as it was honest.

"You have me there. I have a friend with me."

"Was he the one who shot at me?"

"He didn't mean to hurt you."

Who would help the woman kill him? Oh God, Sullivan. And Gideon hadn't even had a chance to tell Louisa about him yet.

"Thankfully," Louisa said calmly, "he accomplished that, but I have a strong aversion to being shot at."

"Yes, Your Grace."

A few moments passed where nothing was said. Louisa cast a glance at the ceiling and made a *come on* motion with her free hand. Despite the mess they were in, he wanted to laugh. If any woman deserved a parure given to the family by Good Queen Bess, a female who'd ridden out to lead her army, it was his duchess.

Finally, Mrs. Petrie shouted, "Does the duke have a weapon?"

That encompassed a great deal. He looked around the room for anything that could be used as an armament and shrugged.

"No, he does not."

"Now that I think about it, why are you talking with me and not him?"

"In my considered opinion, His Grace has done more than enough."

"Well, I'd feel safer if my friend came," the woman said.

"By all means, let us make this a party. However, his gun must be left outside."

"Yes, Your Grace."

Gideon rose and took a position next to the door, back

flat against the wall. He glanced at Louisa, who nodded her assent as she pulled a small, elegant, and deadly dagger from her skirt, and handed it to him.

Truly, he had to stop underestimating his wife. "It is a good thing that no one expects a gently bred woman to carry a pistol"—he grinned—"or a dagger."

For the first time in days, Louisa smiled. "Matt said it would be to my advantage. I hope help is coming, though. I have never shot a person, and do not wish to do so now." Walking to the door, she opened it, creating a deceptively innocent appearance.

She kept the pistol hidden in her skirts. "I hope her friend will not look for you there."

Gideon really needed to tell her about Sullivan. Particularly if the cur was here. "If she does what anyone would, she will enter and greet you. The man will follow behind, and before he gets through the door, I will have punched him." She threw him a dubious look. "I have been practicing, not to mention the experience I gained in the less than gentlemanly art of fighting in Canada, and I have your dagger."

Louisa rolled her eyes. "If there is anything else I should know, now would be a good time to tell me."

"Sullivan—" Steps sounded on the wooden bridge, making Gideon cut off his sentence.

"Leave the weapon on the other side of the bridge," Louisa called out.

"It's done, Your Grace."

He didn't trust Sullivan at all. The rifle might have been left, but he'd have another weapon. Gideon waited. He would have only one chance to overpower the thug.

A few moments later, Mrs. Petrie entered the cottage, Sullivan close behind her. She dropped a low curtsey to Louisa, giving him the perfect opportunity to plant a flush hit on Sullivan's jaw. Gideon was prepared to follow up the punch with one to the dastard's stomach, but the devil dropped to the floor like a rock. Who would have guessed the fellow had a weak chin?

"What—" Mrs. Petrie's exclamation was cut short by Louisa's motioning with her pistol.

"Please move away from your friend and have a seat, Mrs. Petrie," Louisa said in an affable tone.

Louisa smiled and sat on a chair facing Mrs. Petrie. "Now, shall we discuss the reason you believe the parure is yours."

The other woman looked affronted. "He, the old duke, gave them to me. That's why."

"Ah, but there is a slight difficulty. He did not have the authority to give you the jewelry."

Mrs. Petrie appeared confused. "But he was the duke, and he had the gems. If the current duke doesn't give them back to me, I'll take him to court."

"Yes, but"—Louisa searched for an easy way to explain. However, it actually was a simple concept—"they were not his to give away. They belonged to the dukedom, not to him personally. He has the use of the property during his lifetime, but is not allowed to sell, mortgage, or give it away. It is called an entailment."

Mrs. Petrie was not a stupid woman, and Louisa could see her mind working. "In that case I deserve something of the same value."

From the corner of her eye, she saw Gideon's jaw clench. "Unfortunately, the late duke ruined the worth of the estate. He was not himself during the last couple of years. Indeed, he did not even recognize his wife, before he met you."

The other woman's shoulders dropped. "Then there is nothing I can do?"

"Mrs. Petrie," Louisa said gently, "His Grace has refused

to pay his father's gambling debts. It is all he can do to support his dependents at the moment."

"All for nothing." Mrs. Petrie slowly shook her head. "Two years wasted."

For a moment Louisa felt sorry for her, then she remembered the forged letters to Rundell and Bridge's, the modiste, and a few other shops, and the letter to herself, and held her tongue.

"If you let me go, I'll leave you alone."

Gideon pushed off the wall he'd been leaning against. "I would be willing to do as you bid. But I cannot allow you to simply depart. Indeed, you were supposed to have left our fair shores by now."

"I must say, I agree with my husband." The threat was over, and Louisa's temper began to rise. "Generally, I have a great amount of pity for women who are forced to sell their bodies to live. Yet you went far beyond what a normal courtesan would do. You forged letters with the sole intent of stealing not only from an old man, but from his family as well." She stabbed her finger at the prostitute. "You led me to believe you were my husband's whore." Even the woman's flinch did not soothe Louisa's ire. "You did not care whose lives you ruined. If I were allowed, I would place the noose round your neck myself." Mrs. Petrie's face drained of color. "Yet you did not, fortunately for you, kill anyone. Therefore, I will agree to a sentence of transportation for a period of time that ensures you never return to England. Gideon." Louisa reached out, and immediately he was with her. "Call the magistrate. I do not ever want to set eyes on these persons again."

"It will be as you wish, my love."

"Louisa?"

She heard her brother's voice. "In here, Matt. We are all right."

He entered, followed closely by Grace. "We came to help

you two straighten matters out. Yet am I correct that you have managed to do it yourselves?"

Shaking her head, Louisa finally summoned a grin. "You are. You knew all along that Rothwell wasn't having an affair, but you sent the carriage just the same."

Her brother shrugged. "It was not something I would trust to a letter. Not only that, but you needed to know you could depend on us, and Rothwell needed to know that you are never alone."

Gideon was in the process of slipping his arm around her waist when he shouted, "Worthington, behind you! Go for the jaw."

Her brother whirled around and drove his fist into the dastard's jaw. Once again, the man fell to the floor. "I take it that is Sullivan. Is there a reason you didn't tie the thug up?"

"I couldn't find anything to use," Gideon said ruefully. "Short of cutting up the sheets, that is."

From the corner of her eye, Louisa saw Mrs. Petrie rising from the chair. "You remain where you are."

The woman dropped back down with a huff.

"Gideon, I am very glad you did not sacrifice the sheets, but could you use your cravat to bind this woman? I do not want her to escape before the magistrate arrives."

The corner of his mouth lifted in a lopsided smile. "Certainly, my love."

Chapter Thirty-Seven

Once Gideon had secured the Petrie woman, Louisa looked from him to her brother and back to him again. "Who is Sullivan?"

"I did not get to that part before he shot at us." Gideon winced. He'd be lucky if she didn't leave him. "My father also frequented at least one gambling hell and lost quite a bit of money."

"I take it that he was one of the people to whom he was indebted?"

"Yes. I thought he was dead until a few weeks ago." Naturally, his statement prompted the confession that the thug had attacked him.

When he was finished, Louisa said, "I am not usually a bloodthirsty person, but I truly believe Sullivan must hang. He came much too close to murdering you. Even if he was transported, I would be afraid that he'd someday return to finish what he began."

"It goes against my inclinations as well, my love, but you are correct."

"I'm pleased to see all the loose ends are tied up," Worthington said.

"Thank God for that." Grace tugged at her husband. "I believe, Louisa, that we shall bother your housekeeper for a chamber and ensure the magistrate has been summoned." Grace glanced out the window. "Ah, help has arrived. As soon as these prisoners are taken away, you and Rothwell may get on with making up. We shall see you at dinner. Not before."

Three of his largest footmen, who had arrived with Fredericks Junior, took Sullivan and Mrs. Petrie out of the cottage.

"Where will you put them until the magistrate arrives?" Louisa asked.

The butler bowed. "We have some very fine cells that have not been used in some years, Your Grace. These blackguards will be secure there."

Several minutes later, after a substantial meal including two bottles of wine had been laid out on the table, now covered with snowy white linen, Gideon and Louisa were left alone.

"Forgive me, please," he said, prepared to get down on his knees and beg if he had to.

"Only if you promise me that you will never again shut me out."

"I promise." Thinking the problem was settled, he snoodled toward her.

"There is one other thing." She held up her hand, stopping his progress. "I shall use my funds as I see fit."

He should have known that would come up. "I suppose there is no way I am going to be able to change your mind even though we are not nearly as poor as we were."

"No way at all. I have a quarterly allowance I receive." She frowned for a moment. "Although you may have to make me a loan. I spent it on kitchen renovations. Anton was threatening to return to London if something was not done immediately."

Laughing, he pulled her into his arms. "Only you would spend your money on kitchens and furnishings instead of clothing and jewels. I love you."

"I love you, too."

The daybed beckoned as he walked her backward, removing pieces of clothing on his way. By the time he felt her legs hit the bed, she was standing in her chemise, and he had only his breeches to remove.

"Louisa, my heart, it has been much too long since I've made love to you."

"Now that I agree with."

The thin linen covering her floated to the floor along with his breeches. Moments later they tumbled onto the daybed.

"I've missed you. I've missed this." Gideon pressed kisses from her ear to the corner of her lips.

"I have as well. You do not know how much I ached for you, even when I thought you had betrayed us." Louisa reached down, taking hold of his already hard cock. "I want you now."

Several hours later Louisa snuggled against him. "We must return soon. It has got to be time to change for dinner."

A strange sound, almost like something being sick, sounded at the door.

"Chloe!" Louisa jumped up. "How did she get here?"

She opened the door and the kitten ran inside. "Goodness. With everything going on, she must have slipped out."

Gideon lay on his side watching his wife with the gray ball of fluff. "I wonder how she'll like having a playmate in . . . oh say . . . about three months. Your brother has promised us one of Daisy's pups."

"I think she'll be fine with it. Chartreux are supposed to be good with other pets." She gave him a sly look. "I wonder how you will like being a papa in about eight months."

"You're pregnant?" Gideon jumped off the bed.

Smiling shyly, she said, "Well, that is the only conclusion I can come to."

Hauling her and the kitten into his arms, he kissed her. "I shall love it. Just don't tell my mother."

"Why not?"

"I have another confession to make. . . ."

Author's Note

One of the reasons I adore the Regency is because of its rules that, combined with the leftover freewheeling behavior of the Georgian period, can create some very interesting customs.

Gambling became extremely popular during the Georgian era and continued on into the Regency with one major difference: Ladies were discouraged from the activity. That said, older ladies still gambled. The vast amounts of money lost and the families ruined by gambling were astounding. Members of the aristocracy would fail to pay their debts to tradesmen and women, putting many of them out of business. But heaven forefend they would not honor their gambling debts, which, by the way, were not enforceable by law. Why, you ask? It was a matter of honor. In fact, gambling debts were called debts of honor. That said, no one of honor would gamble with a minor (anyone under the age of twenty-one) or an adult who was mentally incompetent.

That brings me to dementia. The medical community at the time did seem to recognize it as a medical condition sometimes brought on by old age. I did find one reference to it being a disease. However, what we now know as Alzheimer's was yet to be named. Any mental problems an elderly person had were categorized as dementia.

A little bit about customs. Unlike the Victorian era, during the Regency once a couple was betrothed they were allowed to be alone together. This included being in a closed carriage alone, looking at a house, the lady visiting his house, you get the picture. There was plenty of time to be together. That was the reason a gentleman could not end an engagement. Doing so would ruin a lady's reputation as the assumption was that if he cried off she had not been a virgin. I'll leave it to your imagination how he might discover that bit of information and leave you with a few facts. Well over 50 percent of births took place well before nine months after the marriage. There was no requirement to report births; therefore, only the gentry, and possibly the wealthy merchant class, took care to keep a careful record of them. Early first births were so common that there was a saying: "The first babe is frequently early. The rest are all on time."